Once in a Blue Moon Guesthouse

CRESSIDA McLAUGHLIN

HarperCollins*Publishers*

HarperCollins*Publishers* Ltd
The News Building
1 London Bridge Street
London SE1 9GF

www.harpercollins.co.uk

This paperback edition published by HarperCollins*Publishers* 2017
1

First published in Great Britain as four seperate ebooks in 2016–17 by HarperCollins*Publishers*

Copyright © Cressida McLaughlin 2017

Cressida McLaughlin asserts the moral right to
be identified as the author of this work

A catalogue record for this book
is available from the British Library

ISBN: 978-0-00-821928-4

Set in Birka by Palimpsest Book Production Limited,
Falkirk, Stirlingshire

Printed and bound in Great Britain by
Clays Ltd, St Ives plc

MIX
Paper from
responsible sources
FSC www.fsc.org **FSC˙ C007454**

FSC™ is a non-profit international organisation established to promote
the responsible management of the world's forests. Products carrying the
FSC label are independently certified to assure consumers that they come
from forests that are managed to meet the social, economic and
ecological needs of present and future generations,
and other controlled sources.

Find out more about HarperCollins and the environment at
www.harpercollins.co.uk/green

To Katy Chilvers, the best romantic hero
research wing-woman a girl could hope for

Acknowledgements

I can't believe this is my third book! How did that happen? As always, you wouldn't be holding this paperback or ebook without the support, encouragement and hard work of all these wonderful people.

Kate Bradley, my inspiring, brilliant and reassuring editor and friend, who keeps me on course, and does everything to ensure my books are as good as they can be. Charlotte Brabbin, who has the patience of a saint, and makes everything seem easy when I know that it's not.

Everyone else at HarperCollins – Kim Young, Martha Ashby, Ann Bissell and Emma Pickard. They are the loveliest and most dedicated people, and I still can't quite believe I get to work with them. Alice Stevenson and Heike Schüssler, for creating the stunning covers for my book – all five of them! I want to dive into each scene and spend my holidays there.

Kati Nicholl, Anne O'Brien and Yvonne Holland, who

have tirelessly polished and tightened my book at the final stages, and got it release-ready.

Hannah Ferguson, who is the best agent, and gives me encouragement, confidence and words of wisdom, and of course takes on all the hard bits.

Many lovely author friends for cheerleading and reassurance, especially Alex Brown, Kirsty Greenwood, Katie Marsh, Isabelle Broom, Miranda Dickinson, Vicky Walters, Lisa Dickenson, Katey Lovell, Poppy Dolan and Rachel Burton.

Katy C, for the endless GIFs and dedication to the romantic hero cause, and for being an awesome friend. One day I will convince her about Mr. Nintendo.

My mum and dad, for inspiring my early love of books, for reading my first novels and giving me advice, and for being so encouraging and enthusiastic (and listening to me witter on for hours) now that the hard work has paid off. They deserve a lot of the credit for me being in a position to write these acknowledgements. LC, for being brave and brilliant, having an amazing understanding of language, and for not despairing when I ask about grammar.

David, who is my rock, my best friend, and my real life romantic hero. I simply wouldn't be doing this without him.

Lastly, the bloggers and readers, the people who take the time to read my books, and let me know that they've enjoyed them. Sometimes I imagine my characters sitting inside the pages of my books, swinging their legs or resting chins in hands, waiting for someone to open the cover and start their story. If you've done that, then you've helped my characters to come alive – and as a writer, that's all I really want. Thank you, and happy reading!

The Once in a Blue Moon Guesthouse

OPEN FOR BUSINESS

Chapter 1

Even with its cloak of December grey, Campion Bay was beautiful. Robin Brennan tucked her gloved hand through her mother's arm and slowed her pace. The sand was compact beneath their feet, and Robin wanted to take her boots off and feel it against her bare soles, despite the blistering cold.

She had been back here for three months; back in her childhood town, with its quaint teashops and Skull Island crazy golf course and the sea stretching out alongside them, never the same, today a dark, gunmetal grey with barely a hint of blue. It was the last day of the year, a time to think about starting afresh and promised resolutions, but Robin felt in some respects like she'd gone backwards.

'It's encouraging that we've got a full house for the New Year,' she said to her mum. 'We can celebrate properly tonight.'

'Yes, darling.' Sylvie Brennan patted her arm. She was trying to inject enthusiasm into her voice, but Robin could tell her mind was elsewhere. 'No empty rooms for the first time in

. . . well, months.' She gave Robin a quick, unconvincing smile.

'Maybe things will improve now.' Robin bent to pick up a pebble polished smooth by the sea, the thin sliver of quartz running through it glinting in the weak sun. 'I know there are going to be fireworks later, but it's not exactly an extravaganza. Most people like to spend New Year's Eve in big cities or at house parties, not the Dorset seaside, so the fact that people have booked to spend it here means that . . . that they *want* to come here.' It was a pathetically obvious statement, but Robin was finding positivity as hard to come by as her mum was.

The Campion Bay Guesthouse, Sylvie and Ian Brennan's pride and joy since the family had moved to the area when Robin was four, was in trouble. Robin had returned from London because of her own problems, feeling like she had nowhere else to turn, and had discovered that she wasn't the only one who was suffering. She'd thrown herself into helping out, managing the changeovers, baking fresh bread for the breakfasts, setting up Twitter, Instagram and Facebook accounts. She'd used her experience to try and give the guesthouse a boost, and it had taken her mind off her own struggles for a time, but then her parents' worries about the business – the worries they had obviously been trying to keep from her – had become her own. Now it was New Year's Eve, they were hosting a party for their guests and for a few friends in the bay, and if her mum and dad were feeling anything like she was, it would be hard to muster up enough celebratory spirit to pop a single champagne cork.

Sylvie steered her daughter left, angling them towards the water, and the icy December wind met them head on. Robin felt her dark, shoulder-length curls tugging out behind her,

her cheeks burning from the cold. She squinted against the assault, wondering why her mum had brought her out for an impromptu walk when the weather was so hostile, and whether she could encourage her back home, or perhaps to the Campion Bay Teashop. It was a few doors down from the guesthouse along Goldcrest Road, the seafront street of houses with an unimpeded view of the English Channel.

The seafront was colourful despite the December gloom. Most of the three- and four-storey buildings had, over the years, been converted to guesthouses, or businesses on the ground floor and accommodation above. As well as the Campion Bay Guesthouse and the teashop there was an Italian taverna, its façade in sunny greens and yellows, the candyfloss-pink door of Molly's beauty parlour, and the cornflower trim and net-curtained windows of the Seaview Hotel, run by Coral Harris.

A couple of the buildings had remained single dwellings, and Robin could just make out the gleam of blue glaze on the clay plaque next to number four's front door. Tabitha Thomas had lived there, observing everything that had happened on Goldcrest Road with a quiet watchfulness, until her death earlier that year. Robin felt the familiar twinge of regret when she thought of Tabitha, who she'd known so well growing up, but who had become a distant memory after Robin's move to London.

'Robin,' Sylvie said, raising her voice to compete with the whistle of the wind, 'I wanted to have a chat with you about something.'

'Righto,' Robin said warily, her shoulders tensing. 'Fire away.' Her mother was the more serious of her parents, but this tone was especially solemn, and Robin felt that whatever was coming was the reason Sylvie had brought her out here.

It wasn't likely to be about the fireworks. She tried to interpret the expression on Sylvie's face but found that it was unreadable, her features scrunched up against the wind. Her mum was a couple of inches shorter than she was, her frame more fragile. She'd always said that Robin was lucky to have been gifted her delicate features and her dad's long, lithe limbs in equal measure.

'Your dad and I have had a talk,' she said now. 'To be honest, we've had thousands, on a daily basis, and long before you came back to Campion Bay in September.'

'You *are* married,' Robin said. 'It would be strange if you didn't.' She smiled, but the joke remained unanswered. Robin bit her lip, dreading what was coming next.

'We can't run the guesthouse any more,' Sylvie said bluntly. 'Bookings are down too much, with no sign – despite your optimism about tonight – of picking up. Our advanced bookings for the spring are paltry, and by now we'd usually have a few full weeks in May and June. We're both getting on and the truth is, darling,' she turned towards Robin, grasping her hands and looking her square in the face, 'we've made an offer on a house in Montpellier, and it's been accepted.'

Robin stared at her mum, trying to let the words sink in as the winter gusts squeezed tears out of the corners of her eyes.

'What?' It came out as a hoarse whisper. 'I knew you'd been looking, thinking about retiring, but . . . but you're actually going? When? What will happen to – I mean, what about the guesthouse?' She released a hand and flung her arm in the direction of Goldcrest Road.

'That's what I wanted to talk to you about. Obviously we don't want to leave you here without . . .' She sighed, the sentence trailing off.

'Anything to do?' Robin gave her mum a quick, humourless smile, realizing how pathetic it was to depend on her parents to give her purpose.

'You can't spend the rest of your life helping us run our guesthouse,' Sylvie said, her tone softening. 'You're destined for greater things. I know this was – is – a stepping stone, that you needed to come back here after what happened in London, but you were always going to have to think about your future.'

'I know that,' Robin murmured, turning towards the water. She hadn't even started to think about what she wanted to do after London; she'd come back to Campion Bay to regroup and hadn't realized she was working to a deadline.

'We're buying the house in France with the money your gran left me,' Sylvie said, 'so it's not dependent on us selling the guesthouse. There's no rush for you to move out, though I imagine you won't want to stay in such a big place.' She resisted adding 'alone', but Robin heard the inference.

'But what about the business?' she asked, choosing to focus on less complicated things than her emotions or her own future. 'You can't just close it. It's been running for almost thirty years, it's nearly reached its pearl anniversary.'

Sylvie smiled at Robin's attempt to lighten the mood, but her tone was grim. 'Yes, but it's failing. It's had some wonderful years, we've been very successful, but it's not what people want any more. Sometimes you have to count your losses.'

'Everyone wants to come to the seaside,' Robin protested, flinging her arms wide. 'The seaside never goes out of fashion.'

'What we're offering is behind the times, then. It happens. Your dad and I are past trying to keep up with newer, more fashionable hotels.'

'Mrs Harris is still going,' Robin said, as they turned away from the sea and began walking back. 'She doesn't show any signs of closing down, and she doesn't even advertise it as a Bleak House hotel.'

'Robin,' her mother chided. 'She caters for a different market; she has a steady, loyal clientele who return each year – often more than once. The Campion Bay Guesthouse is slipping through the gaps. We're not traditional, but we're by no means trendy any more.'

'So renovate then,' Robin said, whirling to face her as the sand gave way to shingle. 'Give it a makeover. Don't let it go so easily. When I was running Once in a Blue Moon Days I saw hundreds of amazing hotels – boutique and modern and classic and themed and, sometimes, downright bizarre. I've got some ideas, we could work on it together.' The rug was about to be pulled out from under her feet, and she couldn't get her head around the thought of having to start all over again quite so soon.

'Robin, darling. If the guesthouse ran solely on your enthusiasm, then we wouldn't be struggling at all. Things have been so hard for you over the last year, and you haven't given up.'

'I gave up on Once in a Blue Moon Days,' Robin whispered, looking down at the pebbles.

'No.' Sylvie shook her head. 'You kept working at it until the bitter end, until there was nothing you could do. A luxury event company like that can't survive on one person's energy and determination to keep it going. You're a fighter, Robin, and we're so proud of you. But your dad and I, we don't have the energy, or the fight, left in *us*. We've spent a long time talking it over – we're not taking this decision lightly – but this is right. I know it's a shock, but we didn't want to tell you until it was definite.'

Robin's legs felt heavy as they made their way past Skull

Island Crazy Golf, closed down for the winter, and back to the Campion Bay Guesthouse.

Robin had returned to Campion Bay after her London life had fallen apart because it was safe, because she knew what to expect and she could slip back into a familiar, almost mindless, routine. But now that, too, was coming to an end. As the shock started to dissipate, Robin discovered that what was underneath was panic. What would she do if she had no guesthouse to help out with? How would she cope without her parents' gentle, unobtrusive comfort? She hadn't felt like partying before their walk, but now the thought of putting on a dress and eyeliner and spending the evening socializing seemed impossible.

She understood why her parents had made their decision. She knew, as soon as her mum had told her, that it was the right time for them to retire. But that still didn't answer the question thrumming through Robin's head as she took her coat and gloves off and went to put the kettle on: what would she be left with?

'Just open it,' Molly said, thrusting two glasses underneath Robin's nose and waggling them, her charm bracelet tinkling delicately in the quiet. They were standing in the Campion Bay Guesthouse's huge living-room-cum-dining-room, the French doors at the back leading out to a small patio garden, the windows at the front looking out on to the sea. It was close to six o'clock and it was dark outside, the lighting low, the textured, teal-green wallpaper making it seem slightly gloomy.

'The guests won't be coming down for at least half an hour,' Robin protested, trying to sidestep Molly and put the bottle of prosecco on the table.

'But you've organized this party,' Molly said, 'we're both here now, and you've had a shock. We've just got time to sink the bottle before anyone else turns up, and nobody'll be any the wiser.' She flashed Robin a grin, her teeth pearly white behind her bold pink lipstick.

Robin tried again, and was again blocked by her friend. She rolled her eyes and began to open the bottle.

'At least you didn't discover a secret talent for willpower while you were in London,' Molly said. 'That's a relief.'

Robin laughed and then, realizing she couldn't remember the last time she'd used those particular facial muscles, grinned at her friend.

She'd known Molly since she was eleven. The petite blonde had been two years above her in secondary school, but once they'd said hello in the short-lived school orchestra – Molly admitting she'd only started to learn the flute as a way to stay inside during the windswept winter lunchtimes – they'd become solid friends. When Robin had accepted a place at university in London, Molly's daughter Paige was two years old and she'd committed to settling in Campion Bay, but their friendship had lasted the distance. While Robin had been seeking the unconditional love of her parents when she'd decided to come back to Campion Bay, she'd also known Molly would be here. If she hadn't, the decision wouldn't have been so straightforward.

'I can be stubborn when I want to be,' Robin protested, filling the glasses with bubbling liquid. 'I just agree with your assessment of the situation.'

'Assessment of the situation?' Molly clinked her glass against Robin's. 'You mean I'm right, as usual. Let's make a toast – to new years and new beginnings.'

'Zero points for originality.' Robin leaned against the table, which held an array of nibbles and glasses, and her mum's crystal bowl full of homemade punch. She'd changed into a black, knee-length dress with a high neckline and swooping back, her curls loose – and slightly frizzy – around her shoulders. She looked a lot more prepared for a party than she felt, but she still wasn't anything to match Molly, whose perfectly made-up face couldn't hide the natural beauty underneath. Her friend was always immaculately turned out, but then, as the owner of Groom with a View, the beauty parlour two doors down from the guesthouse, she was bound to be. She was wearing a thigh-skimming plum-coloured dress and towering heels, her short blonde hair styled expertly into corkscrew curls.

'It's not meant to be original,' Molly said, after she'd taken a swig of prosecco, 'but it's true, isn't it? For you. You've been forced into a new start. You're beginning to make a habit of it.'

Robin sighed and dropped her head forward. 'What am I going to do? They're moving just before Easter, to beautiful, sunny southern France. It should seem a long way off, but it feels like it's hurtling towards me at a hundred miles an hour. Do you think they'd mind if I went with them? Robin Brennan, once a successful entrepreneur, now committed to life as a recluse, hanging on to her parents' coattails at the age of thirty-two.'

Molly leaned against the table alongside her, and she caught a whiff of her friend's heady, seductive perfume. 'That is not an option,' Molly said. 'Firstly, you've got too much spirit to live such a humdrum existence, you'd be bored in ten minutes, and secondly, you're *not* moving away again so soon. Not now I've just got you back.'

'I'm not moving, not really. Mum and Dad have left me

the house, when they could have legitimately booted me out and bought a chateau.' Robin chewed her lip. 'But it'll be weird rattling around in this place without a job or a purpose or my parents.'

'Right,' Molly said. 'So you need to do something. You don't want to start up Once in a Blue Moon Days again?' She asked it tentatively, shooting a glance in Robin's direction then looking quickly away.

Robin stared at the floor, her chest squeezing at the mention of the upmarket events company she had started with her friend Neve. They had planned exclusive days for their clients – weddings, anniversaries, extravagant birthday celebrations. No request was too big or difficult; Robin and Neve would track it down, make it happen. It wasn't cheap, but the experiences they organized were unforgettable – as rare as seeing a blue moon in the night sky.

'No,' she replied quietly. 'I gave it up because it didn't work without Neve. I couldn't do it. Not just because I missed her, although that was a part of it, but because she was the organized one. She did the planning, made everything run like clockwork, and I kept the clients happy. She said that I was the shiny exterior, putting everyone at ease, and she was the frenetic back office that nobody wanted to see.'

'You were the serene swan and she was the swan's legs pedalling frantically beneath the water.'

'Exactly. I tried to keep it going after she died, but without her to execute her meticulous plans, things went wrong. Sooo wrong.' Robin winced and tried to shrug away the memories. 'And London is so well-connected. You can get anything online these days, but lots of the bespoke orders we were placing needed to be negotiated face to face. I'd be starting with too many handicaps if I tried again down here.'

'All very fair and logical,' Molly said, waving her glass at her friend. 'No more Once in a Blue Moon Days, and no more Campion Bay Guesthouse.'

'Let's try and keep it positive, shall we?' Robin elbowed her gently in the ribs. 'Frame it as an opportunity, rather than the end of everything.'

'That's what I'm trying to do, if only you'd keep up. So,' she spun to face Robin, who jumped and spilled prosecco all over her wrist, 'you can't help your parents with the guesthouse any more, because they won't be here.'

'Right,' Robin said, narrowing her eyes. 'I'm still waiting for your positive spin?'

'But you'll be here, and so will the guesthouse.'

'They're closing it – it's going downhill, not getting the bookings any more, making a loss. I see it every day. My tomato and parmesan bread is going uneaten, except by me, and that can't go on for too much longer unless I take up triathlons.' She sighed and sipped her drink. 'And I don't want to take up triathlons – sometimes getting out of bed is hard enough.'

'Don't get off topic, Robin. Listen. You *see it every day*,' Molly repeated, raising her little finger. 'And you ran a successful luxury experience company.' She held up the ring finger. 'And you have your head around modern marketing and social media; Instagram, Periscope, Twitter.' Her middle finger came up, and she waggled them triumphantly.

Robin's stomach did a tiny somersault, competing with the prosecco bubbles. 'Yes,' she whispered. 'Three valid points, if you discount the total disaster Once in a Blue Moon Days became when I was on my own.'

'So take it over.'

'What?' She chewed her cheeks frantically as her friend's

13

eyes got wider, the seed of the idea planted firmly inside both their minds.

'Take it over – the guesthouse.' Molly put her glass on the table and clapped her hands together, her blonde curls bouncing. 'Do all the things you told your mum to do. Give the place an update, refurbish the rooms, launch the new and improved Campion Bay Guesthouse with a killer marketing campaign. They're not asking you to move, so why not just take over from them and bring the place up to scratch at the same time?'

Robin shook her head, more out of disbelief than refusal. It was a huge decision to make, but instantly she saw the possibility. She'd grown up in the guesthouse; she'd helped out all the time, slinking past strangers on her journey to or from her attic bedroom. She'd seen guests arguing with each other on the stairs, returning home in the dead of night giggling and covered in sand, complaining to her dad that their porridge was more like wallpaper paste. She'd seen it at its most popular and, more recently, at its most bereft. She drummed her fingers on the edge of the table.

'I see those fingers,' Molly said. 'You think it could work, don't you? I *know* you could do it. Luxury experiences, but all under the same roof – not to sound like Toys R Us or anything, don't use that tag line. But it would be . . .' Molly stopped, swallowed, held Robin's gaze.

'Carrying on Neve's baby,' Robin finished. 'Keeping the idea of Once in a Blue Moon Days alive, but here in Campion Bay.'

'Her dream, and your parents' dream. The guesthouse won't close, yours and Neve's brainchild won't be forgotten, and you'll be making a living, running your own business again.'

Robin stared at her hazy reflection in the window,

surrounded by the pre-party scene, the ideas buzzing inside her mind like fireflies. It was obvious when she thought about it. Her parents couldn't keep the guesthouse going – they didn't have the will to do it any more – but she did. It wouldn't be the same as the events company. The groundwork was in place, the booking software, the rules and routines her parents had lived by. She wouldn't be creating unique experiences from scratch on her own, and so was less likely to cause any disasters. She realized her glass was empty and turned towards the table to find Molly already holding the bottle.

'Now,' Molly said, her pink lips smiling, 'we really have something to celebrate. Let's get another glass down us before Mrs Harris arrives. I'm not sure I can face her sober, especially knowing that you're going to crucify her in the local guest-house scene.'

Robin laughed. 'I am not going to crucify her, Molly. That's not fair. But' – and now she couldn't help grinning as the idea, out in the real world for a few more minutes, began to take hold – 'there's nothing wrong with a bit of healthy competition, is there?'

'The Seaview Hotel won't know what's hit it,' Molly said, draining her second glass. 'Not now Robin Brennan and her quiet determination are in the game.'

'In what game?' Robin's dad asked, bustling genially into the room with a box of party poppers under his arm.

Robin exchanged a glance with Molly. 'Nothing,' she said quickly, deciding that pre-party was not the best time to spring this on her parents. She'd wait until the dust and the streamers had settled, and she'd had at least one night to sleep on the idea. 'It looks like it's going to be a great party, Dad.'

'And all the better for having you here to celebrate with us,' he said, reaching out to squeeze her hand. 'Especially now, with all that's behind us, and ahead of us.'

'Hey,' Molly said, 'don't start that. It's too early in the evening for deep and meaningfuls.'

Robin saluted her friend. For the first time in what felt like ages, and – as her dad had said – despite all that was behind her, she could see a glimmer of hope in what was to come. The idea had been planted, and Robin could tell that it was already beginning to grow in the background, working quietly away in her subconscious. By the time midnight struck and the New Year had dawned, the seed might even have generated a few solid roots.

Robin watched the party guests from her prime position on the top step of the guesthouse. She could feel the warmth of the hallway at her back, seeping out through the half-open door to meet the cold night air, and the solid heat of Molly sitting next to her on the step, wearing Robin's navy wool coat. She could see the backs of her parents, of Mrs Harris, of Ashley and Roxy from the Campion Bay Teashop, and the couples who had chosen their small corner of the south coast to celebrate the New Year. And then, as the bongs of Big Ben reached her from the radio in the kitchen, Robin watched the night sky light up with the first golden fireworks. She could just make out the boat they were being launched from, the smoke drifting through the air in the split seconds between one burst and the next. The pops and bangs were like a starting rifle in her mind. *On Your Marks, Robin*.

'Happy New Year,' Molly said, slurring slightly, holding her champagne flute up to the sky, the strobes and chrysanthemums and brocade bursts reflecting in the glass.

'Happy New Year, Molly.' Robin clinked her glass against her friend's.

'I'm envious,' Molly said. 'You've already got your resolution. I'm still deciding whether I want to learn how to windsurf or take that tattooist course I've been threatening to do for ages.'

'Why not both? They sound pretty challenging, but somehow still a lot less daunting than taking over the guest-house.'

'You're having second thoughts?' Molly sat up and turned towards her.

'No, not at all. I've thought of nothing else all evening – not even when Dad threatened to give us all a rendition of "Mack the Knife" after his fourth glass of punch. It made me wonder if I should have the dining room redecorated to look like a fifties American diner. You'll be happy to discover I quickly decided no, by the way.'

'You're thinking of having themed rooms?'

Robin gave a quick shake of her head. 'Not themed, exactly. Styled, definitely. I want each room to have a name and its own individual look, but maybe that's too ambitious.' She scrunched her nose up, cross with herself for letting the doubt circle closer and closer, like a shark.

'You know I can rope Paige in to help around her college course, don't you? She's tired of clearing up glasses at the Artichoke, and helping with refurbishments would play to her creative strengths.' Molly's daughter, Paige, was studying jewellery design at the local college, with ambitions of setting up her own studio. 'And I've got a couple of builder clients I can talk to,' Molly added, 'depending on the scale of work you're thinking of.'

Robin sipped her champagne and watched as a blue water-fall firework lit up the sky, shimmying down towards the water. 'I don't know. It depends how much money I can put into the refurbishment.'

'Ian and Sylvie?'

Robin nodded. 'I've not even mentioned it to them yet.'

'They'll be delighted. It's a much happier bombshell to drop on them than the one they landed you with.'

'It might be the bombshell I need. To get properly going again, after Neve.' It sounded like a new era: After Neve, and that was exactly how she felt about the death of her friend. She had to get going again, to live on in this strange new world where a big piece of her existence was missing.

Molly threaded her fingers between Robin's and squeezed. 'You're in the right place. Even when your mum and dad have gone, you're not starting it all on your own.'

Robin returned the gesture. 'I appreciate all of this – the encouragement, the not abandoning me when I first came back, when I was greasy-haired and in my pyjamas, getting through a box of tissues a day. I'm not sure I've told you how much.'

Molly dismissed her gratitude with a quick frown and headshake, carrying on as if Robin hadn't spoken. 'You've got me and Paige. Paige will rope in Adam, and if you want any expert advice, there's always Tim Lewis, junior partner at Campion Bay Property. I'm sure he'd be keen to offer you a free consultation about your renovations.' She raised her eyebrows suggestively.

Robin gave a shallow laugh, but her palms were suddenly slick. 'Oh God, don't.'

'Have you seen him, since you've been back?'

She shook her head. 'Sometimes I think I have, a head of blond curls in the supermarket or on the beach, but it always turns out to be someone else.'

'He must know you're here. The Campion Bay rumour mill would have spat that nugget of information in his direction. He's obviously picking his moment.'

'Or he's decided to stay away.'

'Oh, come on.' Molly laughed. 'That's not exactly his style, is it?'

'No,' Robin admitted, her stomach churning unpleasantly. 'No, it's not.'

The patter of the fireworks was replaced by a meagre smattering of applause from the crowd as the display came to an end. Robin found herself searching through the darkness for that head of blond curls, wondering if Tim Lewis, the ex love of her life, would miss the one New Year's Eve event that Campion Bay was putting on. Then she realized that he was more likely to be at an exclusive house party somewhere in the Dorset countryside, drinking Taittinger and fifty-year-old Macallan, if Molly's updates over the years were anything to go by. But if her friend was right and he was choosing his moment to reacquaint himself with her, then what was that moment; why was he waiting? Suddenly it wasn't just the thought of taking over the Campion Bay Guesthouse that was on her mind, and when she finally made it into bed, a sliver of pale moon glinting at her through the converted attic window, she slept fitfully.

Chapter 2

'This,' Robin said, rolling out a piece of A0 flipchart paper on the king-sized bed and putting a selection of coloured Sharpies on top of it, 'is going to be our project plan.'

Molly scooted up to the pillow end and grabbed a neon orange marker, cradling her coffee mug in the other hand. They were in one of the first-floor bedrooms, sadly unoccupied now that New Year had gone and the cold comedown of January had set in. The view through the window was of grey sky and greyer sea, the colours muted like a Lowry painting. Seagulls sat along the rail of the promenade, and Skull Island's artificial greens looked too bright in the washed-out tableau. Robin shivered and pulled her oatmeal knitted cardigan around her. She scrunched her toes into the thick, aquamarine carpet, finding a crumb that she must have dropped the day before when she'd been touring the rooms with a packet of cheese TUC biscuits and dreaming up her ideal guesthouse.

'No carpets,' she said. 'I want every room to have floorboards and rugs.' She turned to the bed, knelt on the duvet and wrote *Campion Bay Guesthouse* in dark blue in the middle of the sheet. Then she picked up a red pen, drew a line branching out from the centre and wrote *no carpets*.

'That's a big move to start us off,' Molly said. 'Do you know what the floors are like underneath?'

'Not really.' She sank further into the bed. 'We took my bedroom carpet up when I was sixteen, but that was half my lifetime ago and I can't remember what work was involved. But the dining room is polished boards and I think it looks classier, more contemporary.'

'OK,' Molly said. 'No carpets, and no American diner-style breakfast bar. What *do* you want? Who do you want coming to stay here? Who used Once in a Blue Moon Days?'

Robin took a grey pen and doodled an image of a crescent moon in the corner of the page. 'The days we offered were bespoke, so they weren't cheap. We sourced the best hotels, restaurants, private planes, speedboat trips, one-on-one wildlife experiences, day trips to Lapland, Northern Lights tours with added personal touches. Special occasions that were more than a weekend away or a hired-out village hall.'

'So wealthy people, then?'

'People who were looking for something unique, often that they'd been saving hard for. Campion Bay has the crazy golf, but it's also got some upmarket restaurants, and it has a classic feel with Ashley and Roxy's vintage teashop and the picture-postcard seafront. It could be the perfect weekend by the coast if there was a luxurious, unique guesthouse in pride of place. It needs to be contemporary, but with a natural feel. And I want to decorate it using local products if I can.'

'How local? Like beach scavenging, bits of driftwood into tables, that sort of thing?'

'Maybe.' Robin stared out of the window again. She

thought she could see a dot of red, a small fishing boat on the horizon, bobbing alarmingly on the waves. 'And I want my room – the attic room – to be themed around the night sky. It's the closest to the stars, it has the best view and the tiny balcony.'

'Suicide strip?' Molly's eyes widened innocently when Robin shot her a look. 'Come on, it's bloody terrifying up there!'

'I'm going to get a telescope,' Robin said, ignoring her. 'I've always wanted one, and just imagine what you'd be able to see, the constellations, planets, the Milky Way. It'll be breathtaking. But we'll do that room last – we'll have to wait until Mum and Dad have gone and I can move downstairs.'

'You're not keeping your bedroom?'

Robin shook her head. 'The attic room will take us up to five chargeable rooms, all doubles, all with an en suite. The rooms downstairs will be more than enough space for me, and the attic could be really special if we do it right.' If she closed her eyes, she could picture it. The telescope, the navy feature wall, pinprick lights dotting the ceiling and globe reading lamps set in snug recesses either side of the bed. She'd seen her fair share of luxury when scoping out Once in a Blue Moon Days projects, and she remembered Neve's favourite. It was a five-star penthouse suite in Switzerland, its glass ceiling inviting the night sky in, as if you were sleeping on the edge of the world. For Neve, who had believed wholeheartedly in astrology, in finding truth and love by reading the stars, it was perfect. Robin couldn't quite manage the penthouse-level of extraordinary, but she could capture the essence of what had made it so magical.

'So,' Molly said, leaning forward, speaking through a

mouthful of pen lid, 'let's do the rooms in turn. What's the attic room going to be called?'

Robin finished the doodle of the man sitting in the curve of her crescent moon, took her grey pen and wrote *Starcross* in large, swirling script. 'There,' she said. 'Room number five.'

'Starcross,' Molly read. 'Robin Brennan, you crazy romantic. Just don't call one of the rooms Elsinore, or you'll be tempting fate. What ideas have you got for the other bedrooms?'

They worked for hours, coming up with more and more ideas, words in minute writing squashed up to the edge of the sheet as the new and improved Campion Bay Guesthouse took shape, albeit just on paper.

'And I was in charge of social media at Blue Moon Days, so I can get that working to promote us,' Robin said, even after they'd declared their ideas banks empty. 'I can make bread, I've got a mean kedgeree recipe and I saw this incredible wall in a hotel that was actually a fish-tank. How amazing would that look in the sea-themed room?'

'It would look stunning,' Molly said slowly, 'as long as your parents have left you a million quid, which is about what we've spent already, judging by this.' She waggled the sheet of paper.

Robin stood and stretched her hands up to the ceiling, undoing all the knots in her back. The sea had taken on a deep, inky hue as the weak January sun had emerged, and it winked on Molly's Murano glass earrings. She thought that she could put stained-glass window panels in one of the rooms, taking advantage of the ever-changing Campion Bay light.

'It's not as bad as all that,' she said, pushing away a wave of unease. 'Mum and Dad have offered to invest a fair amount

– I think partly they feel guilty about going to France even though I'm resurrecting the guesthouse.' On New Year's Day she had made a maple and pecan loaf cake, sat her parents down with that and a pot of Ceylon tea, and introduced the idea of taking over the guesthouse. She had expected them to tell her that they didn't think she was ready, that it wasn't possible, but instead they had cautiously embraced the idea, offering as much support – moral and financial – as they could. 'Besides,' Robin continued, 'once we start investigating suppliers, putting the research in, we'll find affordable options. And with your friends, Jim and Kerry, agreeing to help with the decorating, we're going to make some savings. I can't believe Jim was sold by the offer of free haircuts for life.'

'It's for his beard. He's beyond proud of it, and nobody trims a beard better than at Groom with a View.' Molly grinned and then, catching Robin's eye, her expression became more serious. 'When I met them in the Artichoke the other night to discuss your plans and see what bartering could be done, I did also, uhm, happen to see Tim.'

Robin went very still, one hand pressed between her shoulder blades, her elbow sticking up towards the ceiling. 'You did?' Her mouth was suddenly dry.

Molly nodded. 'He was there with his boss, Malcolm. Tall, weaselly, gives me the creeps – you've probably not run into him yet. It looked like they were celebrating a deal.'

'Right,' Robin managed. 'You didn't speak to him – Tim, I mean?'

Molly shook her head. 'But he flashed me one of those what-a-man-I-am grins, as if maybe he knew I was going to relay the encounter to you.'

'That's how he smiles at everyone.'

'I had a feeling that this smug grin was *extra* special. I'm unnerved by the fact that he's not dropped by to see you yet. It makes me wonder what he's up to.'

'Maybe he heard about London, about what happened to Neve, and thought he'd give me some space.' Robin chewed her lip. 'Actually, no, if he'd heard about it, he would have offered me a shoulder to cry on.'

'His shoulder would be the best, obviously.'

'Oh, of course,' Robin said, smiling at her friend, 'none better in the whole of Campion Bay – or on the south coast, for that matter.' She turned away, thinking how wrong it felt to talk flippantly about her grief, even though she knew it was progress – returning to some semblance of normality, making fun of the darkness when you were relieved to be emerging into brighter days. There had been a time, not so long ago, when even smiling had seemed like too much of a stretch.

'Lunch?' she asked.

Molly rubbed her stomach. 'If you're offering, otherwise some of these Sharpies might mysteriously disappear.'

'Make yourself comfortable downstairs and I'll bring in some sandwiches.'

Robin boiled eggs, fried rashers of streaky bacon and brewed Lapsang Souchong in one of the ruby-red breakfast teapots. As she did, she found her thoughts turning unavoidably to Tim.

Tim Lewis had been her childhood sweetheart. The most irritating, prank-playing, arrogant little shit at school who, somewhere between the ages of twelve and fourteen, had become utterly desirable. He had still played the odd prank, but his ridiculous blond curls were tamed, and his arrogance had honed itself into a confidence and determination that he was going to do something with his life.

Robin had, like all the other girls, harboured a not-very secret crush on him, and was more surprised than anyone else in the school – though only by a small margin – when, on a balmy September day, aged fourteen, he had asked her out. She had never been a wallflower at school, but she hadn't reached the heights of popularity that put her automatically within his reach, either. He'd seemed over-confident when he'd asked, accidentally spilling the can of Coke he was holding nonchalantly in his hand, and Robin liked him all the more for that. They'd travelled on the bus to Bridport cinema and watched *There's Something About Mary*, nervous at having got in a year too young. Towards the end of the film, Tim had slipped his hand in hers.

They'd dated, declaring each other boyfriend and girl-friend, their relationship surviving against the odds right up until Robin went to London to study Sociology. They'd thought they could make it work; Robin had harboured ideas of Tim coming to join her in the capital – she was sure his ambition would outgrow their cosy Dorset town – but she had misjudged him. Tim was happy where he was, staying close to his family and being a big fish in a small pond, working for a local estate agent, graduating from first homes and small flats to manage country estate sales. Now, it seemed, he'd progressed even further.

Robin poured out the boiling water and ran the eggs under the cold tap, the smell of sizzling bacon filling the kitchen. Of course she'd thought about Tim when she'd made the decision to return to Campion Bay, but they hadn't spoken for over ten years. They were both in their early thirties now. Molly had kept her updated with significant news while she was in London, and so as far as she knew he wasn't married, but did he still leave his hair that bit too long, allowing those gorgeous blond curls to flourish? Robin bit her lip. It was only a matter of time before they bumped into each other.

There had been something magnetic about his confidence, something altogether irresistible. It was the thing that made her heart beat faster now, so many years later, and even after the way it had ended. The problem was that Tim knew how irresistible he was, and over time the kindness and warmth that he'd directed at her had begun to fade, especially once Robin had moved away and their relationship had become more like hard work. Maybe she hadn't been there often enough, telling him she loved him, keeping his ego inflated. Whatever it was, he'd eventually found comfort and adoration with someone else, and had admitted it to Robin during an argument weeks later, as if wanting her to know what she was missing out on.

And yet the thought of seeing him again left her feeling more than just unease. There was anticipation there too, which she was trying to put down to simple curiosity. Robin found she was bashing the eggs into submission, her chunky mayonnaise becoming more of a purée. She scooped the filling into two rolls, emptied packets of Kettle crisps on to the plates and took them through to where Molly was waiting on one of the sofas facing the sea view.

This room, she had already decided, would be called Sea Shanty. The upright piano, its keys remaining dusty for years, sat in one corner, and Robin had plans to distress the long wooden table that ran down the room's centre, buy a tea-chest coffee table and antique globe, and soften the room by replacing the teal wallpaper with ivory and adding navy and red rugs, curtains and sofa cushions.

She sat down, her breathing slowly returning to normal.

Thinking about the guesthouse was becoming a balm to other, more troubling imaginings, somewhere comforting she could turn to when thoughts of Tim, or memories of Neve, tried to take over. But, it seemed, Molly wasn't prepared to let the subject lie.

'Something else I should tell you about when I saw Tim,' she said slowly, scooping up some stray mayonnaise with her finger.

'What?' Robin asked, a little too sharply. 'Sorry, what else? Was he with someone we know?'

'Uh uh.' Molly shook her head. 'I didn't speak to them, but I might have scooted close to their table on a couple of occasions, and I heard them mention Goldcrest Road. Specifically number four.'

Robin swallowed too quickly and started coughing.

'Shit, Robin!' Molly slapped her vigorously on the back until the coughing had subsided and Robin's shoulder blades were throbbing. 'I should have waited until you'd finished eating.'

'They want to buy Tabitha's house?'

'I didn't hear enough of their conversation – I could only pretend to be interested in last year's New Year's Eve menu for so long. But they definitely mentioned next door.'

'Do they want to develop it?' Robin asked. 'What's it like inside, is it sellable?'

'No idea,' Molly mumbled through a mouthful of crisps. 'But Malcolm and Tim are moving on from straightforward sales these days – except for "high end" properties.' She accompanied the last words with quote-mark fingers. 'They're all about the developments. Replacing the old with the new, smartening up the area, as if Campion Bay needs to be turned into a sea of luxury high-rise apartment blocks. No beach finds in their properties, and I expect the word "guesthouse" would be laughed at for sounding too quaint.'

'Well,' Robin said, 'they can't do that with Tabitha's house. It's got special status.'

'The Jane Austen plaque?'

Robin narrowed her eyes. 'I will fight you to the ends of the earth on this point, Molly. Ends. Of. The. Earth.'

'Tabitha was eccentric,' Molly said, in a tone that reminded Robin she'd said it all before. 'She put it up there herself. I've *always* thought that, even though she denied it.'

'No,' Robin shook her head. 'Tabitha was just lonely; she lived on her own in that huge house, and she liked to know what was happening with the neighbours and sometimes, *sometimes*, she would embellish the stories she told us, but that doesn't mean she made this up. It's a good quality plaque!'

'Any sign-maker could copy it – you can probably buy them on gift websites and create your own slogan. And there's no evidence that Jane Austen wrote a book here.'

'A lot of *Persuasion* is set in Lyme Regis! It's a few miles down the road. It's so plausible and it's been there for years, since before online gift shops existed.'

Molly turned her gaze towards the window. 'Honestly, if that plaque being genuine meant the difference between number four staying as it is and Tim and Malcolm getting their hands on it, I'd swap sides. She was a laugh though, wasn't she, Tabitha?'

Robin grinned. 'She was amazing. I'm just sorry I lost touch with her when I went to London. I should have made more of an effort to visit her when I came back to see Mum and Dad. And now her house has been empty for nearly a year and, if what you heard is anything to go by, it's about to be gobbled up and turned into posh flats that are only lived in for two months out of twelve, just to fill Tim Lewis's pockets.'

'See if you can borrow an extra million off your folks and double the size of the guesthouse.'

Robin rolled her eyes and polished off her sandwich. That idea was obviously well beyond her means, but maybe there was some other way she could prevent next door from falling into the hands of the developers. It had been years since she'd been inside Tabitha's house, but as a child she'd spent hours there, playing Monopoly and Gin Rummy and being introduced to Tabitha's strange taste in tea. She'd been devastated when she'd heard the old woman had died, but it had been too close to Neve's death for her to fully absorb it.

It was only now that she was back in Campion Bay that she'd been reminded of the time she spent with her, wondering if the figurines she'd had, the sheep collection that, as an eight-year-old, Robin had adored, were still in the cabinet in the dining room, the glass front keeping out years of dust. She wondered what the house would look like to her adult eyes. Maybe if Tim did get his hands on the property – or the front door keys at least – and Robin plucked up the courage to see him again, he'd let her have one last look before he wiped out the original features in a fit of magnolia paint and stainless steel.

Campion Bay town centre, a twenty-minute walk from the guesthouse, was a mixture of chain stores, quaint seaside gift shops and independent cafés. Bunting was strung up along the brick weave, pedestrianized Seagull Street all year round, the pink, orange and blue fabric flapping enthusiastically in the January wind, and the warm glow of shop interiors beckoned Robin in out of the cold.

She pulled her large jute bag further up her shoulder and pushed open the door of Seagull Street Gallery, the bell giving an appealing 'ding' as she stepped inside. The gallery owner, a grey-haired man in his fifties with rimless glasses and a round, pleasant face, looked up from a desk in the corner and nodded her a greeting. She returned it and began a slow tour of the room. It had white walls and polished pine floorboards, each painting given its own space.

In London, when she and Neve had gone on fact-finding missions, or after an initial meeting with a client, Neve would often take Robin into the National Gallery, dragging her by the arm to look at the latest exhibition and always, without fail, the room that housed Turner's seascapes: *The Fighting Temeraire* and *The Evening Star*. Her friend could stand in front of them for hours, absorbing them, though she'd usually limit it to ten minutes in deference to Robin's waning interest.

Buying one of the Turners was about a hundred times less plausible than Robin being able to purchase Tabitha's house in an act of preservation, but she had the idea that one of the bedrooms in the new guesthouse would celebrate the work of local artists, with seascapes and portraits on the walls, the understated furniture giving it the feel of a mini gallery.

Her boots echoed on the floor and she stilled her movements, walking almost on tiptoe as she looked at the paintings; vibrant still-life acrylics in chunky frames; oil portraits with bold brush marks and, as she'd been hoping for, a wide array of seascapes. She stood in front of a large painting of the sea at dawn. The sky was burnished with golden streaks against the first, pale beginnings of blue, the water a dark turmoil beneath and a single smudge of colour on the horizon that, despite its lack of detail, was undoubtedly a boat. It was mesmerizing, an image to be stared at for hours. Robin felt her throat tighten, closed her eyes and willed Neve to be standing alongside her, to whisper to her all the reasons why she liked it.

When Robin opened them again, tears had squeezed themselves into the corners of her eyes and it was the gallery owner who was standing next to her. She hadn't heard him approach.

'Oh!' Robin jolted and wiped at her eyes. 'Sorry, I didn't see you there.'

'Spectacular, isn't it? A new artist, Arthur Durrant. This is the only one we have of his at the moment, though we've more on commission. It's a special introductory price.'

Robin nodded. It wasn't cheap, but if it was the centrepiece of the room, on the wall facing the bed, then she could make it work within budget. 'It's beautiful,' she managed, her voice croaky. 'If I pay for it now, can I bring my car down later to collect it? I'm not sure it'll fit in here.' She gestured at the jute bag and smiled.

'Of course. We'll package it up for you when you're ready to pick it up.' He remained quiet, his movements small, but she could see the gleam in his eye – whether at a large sale or someone else appreciating the art that he loved, she couldn't tell.

She stepped outside and took a deep breath, which turned into embarrassed laughter. She took the bag off her shoulder and swung it as she walked. Did she really think she could buy a few original paintings and pop them in a shopping bag? Shaking her head at her own ridiculousness, and distracted by an orb lamp glowing at her from its matt silver stand in a shop window, she wasn't looking where she was going.

'Whoa,' said a familiar voice, and Robin turned just in time to see an overcoat-clad man take a quick sideways step.

'Sorry, I—' she stopped as the breath left her in a single exhalation. Overcoat man had a crop of blond curls, very blue eyes and, as their gazes met, a winning smile. 'Tim?' He didn't belong in her reverie about Neve and paintings and the guesthouse. He belonged in a different part of her thoughts altogether – one that she was trying not to visit too often.

'Robin Brennan. I was wondering how long it would take for us to bump into each other, though I hadn't expected it to be quite so literal.'

His hand was on her arm, and he applied gentle pressure. For a horrifying moment she thought that he was going to hug her, but instead he leaned down and kissed her cheek. His skin was smooth, as always – he'd never sported even a hint of designer stubble in the time she'd known him – and she could tell that his overcoat, and what she could see of the suit beneath, was expensive. She had to admit that, despite the years that had passed without her seeing him, he looked as good as ever.

'You look well,' she managed. 'Things are – OK?'

'They're great. Really good.' He was appraising her unashamedly, his blue eyes taking her in, which she supposed was only fair as she was doing the same to him. 'It sounds like you're heading in a new direction, too. Back from London for good, and taking over your parents' guesthouse?'

She nodded, cursing the Campion Bay rumour mill, though Molly had reminded her it was still in full swing, and she shouldn't be surprised that Tim knew about her plans. 'It's a work in progress at the moment. I'm refurbishing the rooms. Bookings are always down in the winter, so we can concentrate on one room at a time, working around any guests we do have.'

'Your parents are still here?'

'They're moving to France in April.' She found she was stuck on a constant nod, the encounter having more of an effect than she had been prepared for. She'd spent a lot of time thinking about him but the reality was altogether different, somehow exhilarating and claustrophobic all at once. He'd cheated on her, had seemed almost proud of it at the time, and yet here he was without a hint of embarrassment or shame, acting as if it was only the distance that had ended their relationship.

'Robin, you look incredible. Let me buy you a coffee, I'd love to hear how you've been.'

'You don't have to get back to work?'

'Not for a while.' His gaze lingered on her, his smile hinting at some secret between them, his ability to make her seem like the most important person in the world returning in a flash. 'Half an hour, Robs. You can't deny me that.'

Robin looked away, watched a seagull strutting down the street as if on patrol, and realized that she couldn't say no. She wanted to hear about Tim as much as he seemed to want to know her news. 'Half an hour,' she agreed. 'But only if you take me somewhere they have Bakewell tart.'

Tim laughed; a loud, open laugh that Robin had always loved. 'It's a deal. You haven't changed, Robs. Not one bit.'

'I wouldn't be so sure about that,' she said, but she let him take her arm and lead her up Seagull Street towards an independent café called Cool Beans, and tried not think about how the closeness of him was making her feel.

Chapter 3

'I can't believe you've brought me to a café called Cool Beans,' she said after they'd sat in rounded, chocolate-brown leather armchairs, and the waiter had taken their order. Their table was low and very small, almost an afterthought, and Robin felt exposed without anything significant between them. She made a mental note that her guesthouse shouldn't lose sight of practicality for the sake of style. Not that this place was stylish, but it definitely thought it was.

'Hey,' Tim said, eyes wide with mock hurt. 'You set the parameters. This is the only place in town that's guaranteed to do you a slice of Bakewell tart, and it's good tart, too.'

'The Campion Bay Teashop does Bakewell tart. Roxy and Ashley were telling me that they make all their own cakes and pastries.'

'The place just along from you?' Tim wrinkled his nose and sat back in his chair, elbows on the armrests. Robin could see the shimmer of silver cufflinks as his shirt protruded from the expensive grey suit. 'We're in town, and I don't have time to head out to the seafront.'

'So you do have to go back to work? I heard that you were doing well, that you've moved up to junior partner in your property firm.'

He ran a hand over his jaw, but he couldn't hide the smile. 'Things couldn't be better, if I'm honest. I'm working on my own portfolio of sites, looking to develop them, bring Campion Bay a bit more up to date.'

'You're not a fan of the quaint seaside feel any more?'

'Quaint is fine, but there are too many buildings – domestic and commercial – that are unlived in, unloved, and it has an effect on the whole area. Malcolm's firm is working hard to eradicate those, to turn them back into desirable accommodation. I'm proud to be a part of that.'

'Not least because it's lucrative, I'll bet.' She gave him a quick smile, but Tim wasn't offended. He never was. He was entirely sure of himself and of his place in the world, and wasn't afraid to let people know it.

He spread his arms wide. 'I'm not going to apologize for being successful. And isn't that what you're doing, just on a smaller scale? Taking your parents' fading guesthouse, renovating it, smartening it up and looking to make a profit?'

'Yes, but without me doing all that the guesthouse would close.'

'And these buildings would become dilapidated if we did nothing, having an effect on adjoining properties. It's no different.'

Robin narrowed her eyes, but she knew he was right. 'Is that what you're planning with number four Goldcrest Road?'

He gave her an amused, almost admiring look. 'Nothing's been confirmed about that site yet.'

'But it's on your radar?'

'We're looking into who owns it, seeing what options we

have. And, if I'm honest, the thought of working on the building next to yours has moved it near the top of my wish list. But no decisions have been made, as yet.'

He was as charming and confident as ever, and despite the alarming admission that he wanted to get his claws into Tabitha's house, Robin felt a tug of the old emotions, the headiness of first love that, a long time ago, had been strong enough to knock her sideways. As their coffee and cakes arrived – Tim had opted for a slice of brownie that looked about as impressive as the table – she noticed that the initials *TL* were inscribed on his cufflinks, and also, confirming what Molly had told her, that he had no ring on the fourth finger of his left hand. Tim thanked the waiter and turned just in time to see her looking. His gaze was penetrating, a hint of a smile on his lips.

'Tell me about London,' he said. 'What made you come back here after all this time? Your plan was always to stay in the big smoke. Unless of course you couldn't resist your feelings for me any longer?'

Robin stuck her fork in the Bakewell tart and tried to organize her thoughts. Someone cycled past, ringing their bell to scatter the seagulls. He was being flippant, she knew, but she felt the flush of her cheeks all the same. 'We didn't exactly end on the best of terms, did we?' She met his gaze with her own. She wasn't going to let him overwhelm her. She waited for a flicker of unease, but none came.

'And if we hadn't,' he said, leaning forwards, 'we'd still be together today, nearly fifteen years later.'

'You sound like you actually regret what you did.' She sipped her coffee, eyeing him over the rim.

'I do. Seeing you again, Robs, here in Campion Bay, it . . .' He shook his head. 'I'd heard you were back, and I'd be lying if I said I hadn't been looking forward to us meeting again, to seeing you in the flesh.'

Robin's stomach fluttered unhelpfully. She'd been lost in Tim's blue-eyed gaze and his carefully crafted compliments for five years. At the time it had been the most real thing in her life, but after what he'd done to her, it had all seemed like an act. He was gorgeous and charismatic and successful; he had many good things going for him, but she had to remind herself of the negatives. She had to remind her senses that feeling betrayed and heartbroken made the rest worthless.

'It's good to see you too,' she said, keeping the emotion out of her voice. 'Are you still surfing?'

He grimaced. 'I haven't for a while, but I'm hoping to get back into it. I broke my coccyx a few months ago, landed badly on a submerged rock. It was a real pain in the ass.'

Robin rolled her eyes, resisting the laugh. 'It sounds awful. But at least you didn't do it slipping on a banana skin or falling drunkenly out of a taxi.'

'What's your point?'

'I don't think you can lose any cool points for a surfing injury.'

'Pretty sure your dignity is affected when you can't sit down for three weeks.'

'Oh, come off it, Tim, you're—' She stopped, caught herself. She would not feed his already overinflated ego. 'You're lucky it wasn't a worse injury,' she said instead, and then wished she hadn't, her thoughts drawing the inevitable, unhelpful comparisons. She cut off a slice of Bakewell tart with her fork, but before she could bring it to her mouth Tim's hand was over hers. The contact was warm and familiar, and unsettling in the unspoken comfort it provided.

'Did something happen in London, Robs?' He was suddenly sincere, his bravado hidden behind concern, and she felt herself being drawn towards it.

'My friend died,' she said, not shrugging his touch off. 'Neve.'

Tim's eyes widened, and for the first time since she'd seen him he looked less than composed. 'Neve, who you met in your first year? The – your business partner?'

She nodded, her throat closing as Tim's features clouded with shock. He'd met Neve on a couple of occasions while he and Robin were still going out, and he'd travelled up to London to see her in her first-year halls of residence.

She and Neve had hit it off instantly, and Robin had often wondered what would have happened if their rooms hadn't been next door in halls, if they would still have found each other and come up with the idea of Once in a Blue Moon Days. She'd thought a lot about fate and destiny, and not only since Neve's death. Her friend had been a big believer in those intangible things, in finding meaning in the cosmos, divining who you were meant to end up with from a horoscope. It was part of the reason Starcross was so special, with its focus on stars, on looking beyond the immediate.

'Are you OK?' she asked softly, wondering if she'd been callous in firing this bombshell at him, for using it, somehow, as a shield against his charm.

'God, I'm so sorry, Robin.' He moved his chair closer to hers, squeezed her hand. 'I had no idea.'

'Why should you have?' She thought of the rumour mill, which had clearly kept him informed of some, but not all, of her news. She waited a few beats, grateful that he didn't try to fill the silence, allowing her composure to return and her heart rate to settle. 'I hadn't planned to come back here, but then, afterwards, it was where I needed to be. And when Mum and Dad said they were moving away . . .' She shrugged. 'Molly's helping out. She's roped Paige and Adam in, and offered some builder friends haircuts for life if they'll help with the redecorating. It's a long way off being finished, but I'm excited. I've just bought a painting.'

'A painting?' Tim raised his eyebrows, matching her new enthusiasm, the solemn moment gone. It felt good, talking about the guesthouse again. It had become her safe place. Of course it would be hard work, it would be challenging, but she was ready for that. After all, Once in a Blue Moon Days hadn't always been easy. The clients had been demanding, wanting – understandably – sheer perfection. As she told Tim some of her ideas, her mood lifted. The coffee and the sugar gave her a boost of energy, and she felt suddenly, overwhelmingly excited about the future. She was embracing the guesthouse as if it was her salvation. In lots of ways, it probably was.

'When can I come and see it?' Tim asked once Robin had finally run out of steam.

'Not yet, it's not ready.'

'I don't get a sneak peek?' He pouted, looking so ridiculously crestfallen that she laughed.

'No. What made you think you would?'

'Our history.'

'Not all good history,' she reminded him, but she felt a flutter of unexpected longing. She risked looking at him. He was sitting perfectly still, his blue eyes trained on her.

'The course of true love never did run smooth,' he said quietly.

She shook her head, incredulous, but her heart was racing. She stood, catching her fork with her knee and knocking it to the floor. She bent to pick it up, but Tim was already there. They rose to standing together, so close that she could feel his breath against her cheek.

'I have to get back,' she said quickly.

'Repurposing some furniture?'

'Endlessly, for about the next four months.'

'It's been great catching up.'

Tim refused to let her pay the bill and walked her to the door. The cold was bracing, and Robin welcomed it; she needed to clear her head.

'When can I come and see the rooms?' he asked.

'When they're finished, not before.'

'Robin Brennan, ever the perfectionist.'

'Takes one to know one.'

'I wouldn't have it any other way.' He smiled, their eyes catching hold of each other's. Tim was first to look away.

'I'd best get on,' Robin said. 'Thanks for coffee.'

'Next time let's make it a glass of something celebratory to toast your new business.' Before she had a chance to protest, Tim's arm was around her and he was kissing her cheek, smelling of spicy, no doubt expensive, aftershave and filling Robin's senses with heady nostalgia.

She watched him stride away and thought again about fate. She'd known that seeing Tim was inevitable once she moved back to Campion Bay, and she'd also known that their five-year, first-love relationship would always hold a special place in her heart, but she hadn't been prepared for her heart to be quite so keen to see him again. Was this what was destined for her, what was written in the stars? Could she forgive his indiscretion, aged nineteen and with her too far away for their relationship to flourish? They were both so much older now, both with their own histories and heartaches behind them, but still with an undeniable chemistry. Could it be rekindled? As she started to walk back to Goldcrest Road, Robin chided herself for even entertaining the thought.

'Where is she?' Robin heard her dad's voice, always on the right side of amiable, drifting up the stairs.

'Up here!' Paige called, and then glared at her mother as Molly made a loud shushing sound. Robin tried not to laugh. Paige was sixteen, Molly thirty-four, and they often acted more like sisters than mother and daughter. Paige's hair was the same, expertly applied blonde, only three times longer than Molly's.

'This is a delicate operation,' Molly hissed at her daughter.

'Why?' Paige asked. 'Will the fish get scared?'

'Not sure we'll know if they do,' Jim said, his back towards them, intent on securing the large fish-tank into the newly cut hole in the wall of Robin's Rockpool room. Molly had been right, the wiry but – as Robin had discovered over the last few months – ridiculously strong builder and glazier had a very neat, impressive beard, and in her head he'd instantly become Beardy Jim. She was worried she'd say it out loud, but on voicing her fears to Molly had been led to understand he'd probably be quite pleased with the nickname. He'd worked solidly and cheerfully alongside his partner Kerry, and Robin knew that free haircuts for life would not be enough for all they'd done. But she'd held back some budget for labour costs, and was confident that she could pay them for their time.

Right now, they were making Robin's vision of a fish-tank wall come true. Between the main bedroom and en suite bathroom of Rockpool, instead of plasterboard there would soon be a beautiful aquarium, reflecting the light from the window opposite, filled with colourful discus, rainbow fish and fantail guppies. It was a risk, she knew, but she couldn't imagine a better feature for this room that, along with its bleached floorboards and hints of turquoise, held the essence of the sea.

Her mum and dad appeared in the doorway and the room, now full of bodies, seemed suddenly too small. Ian Brennan glanced at the large polythene bags on the floor, the assortment of fish waiting for their new home, and looked anxiously at his wife.

'Ah.'

'What's wrong, Dad?' Robin asked. 'Has something happened with your ferry?'

It was the first week in April and her parents were about to leave for France. Robin had been working harder than ever, while also trying to ward off the encroaching panic that she would soon be in sole charge of the guesthouse. Not to mention that her mum and dad, who had been such a comfort to her after Neve's death, would be hundreds of miles away, for good.

Sylvie approached her daughter, her narrow face pinched. She was holding a red, fleecy blanket. On closer inspection, Robin could see that the blanket was wriggling.

'Mum, Dad?' She looked from one to the other, then back at the blanket, and then at Molly who shrugged her shoulders. 'What's going on?'

'Maybe this isn't the best room,' her dad said.

'For what?'

Without answering, Sylvie thrust the blanket into her hands and Robin looked down at it. A tiny black paw emerged from the fleecy material, claws finding and holding on to the cotton of Robin's paint-splattered jumper. She pushed back the blanket and found the fuzzy head of a kitten. It let out a huge yawn, exposing a tiny pink tongue.

'A *kitten?*' Paige yelped. 'Oh my God, it's adorable.'

Through her confusion, Robin felt a surge of love for the helpless creature. She looked at her mum. Sylvie Brennan had her hands clasped together, the look in her dark eyes both defiant and tentative, ready to accept either congratulations or rebuke for the decision she and Ian had made.

'Mum,' Robin started, 'what is this – he, she – for?'

'*He's* for *you*,' Sylvie said. 'For when we've gone.'

'A perfect replacement, I'd say,' her dad chuckled and put his hand on Sylvie's shoulder, giving it a squeeze.

'I don't need a kitten,' Robin said softly, though already she knew that she wanted him, that he was hers, and she would struggle even to release him from his temporary bed in her arms.

'We don't want you to be lonely,' Sylvie said, shooting a nervous glance at her husband, the two of them sharing tight smiles. 'Now that you're taking this on all by yourself.'

'Does this look lonely to you?' Robin asked, giving them a warm smile. 'I've got Molly and Paige, Jim and Kerry, and—'

'About a hundred fish,' Kerry added.

'Which I'm sure Mr Kitten here is going to absolutely adore, aren't you, Mr Kitten?' Molly stroked a small black paw, her voice taking on a soppy tone.

'I promise, Mum,' Robin said, ignoring her friend, 'you don't need to worry about me.'

Sylvie nodded but her hands wrung together, the knuckles white, and Robin could see the gleam of tears in her eyes.

'Oh, Mum, don't cry.' Robin stepped forward, carefully

removing one arm from the kitten, holding him tightly against her with the other hand, and gave her mum an awkward, one-sided embrace.

They looked at the small, black bundle to avoid seeing the emotion on each other's faces.

'We'll look after her, Mrs B,' Molly said, patting Sylvie on the shoulder.

'I know you will,' Sylvie said.

'What if the guests don't like cats?' Paige asked, stroking the kitten between the ears. His purr increased as if she'd found the volume button. 'Some of them might be allergic,' she added, though her gaze was adoring.

Robin grinned. The kitten was magic. Anything small and soft and vulnerable had a powerful effect on people. 'I'll make sure I put it on the website – the guesthouse comes with a cat – and a couple of the rooms are going to be dog friendly anyway.'

'I'm still not sure that's the best idea.' Sylvie's voice was sharp through her sniffs. 'It'll mean an awful lot of extra work.'

'I don't think it will,' Robin countered. 'Why would people with dogs have less respect for the guesthouse than those without? And as long as we clean the rooms thoroughly in between, I can't see how it'll be a problem.'

'There's always the possibility of accidents,' Sylvie said.

'Accidents happen in every walk of life,' Molly added sagely. 'You just have to be as prepared as possible.'

'Exactly.' Robin took a deep breath and turned away. 'Now, where am I going to put him? I can't leave him in here.'

'We've set up a basket in the kitchen,' her dad said. 'We'll take him back down now, love. Just packing the last bits into the car.'

Robin nodded and went to pass the kitten back, then realized she wasn't ready to give up either the furry bundle or her parents quite yet. She followed them to the doorway, then turned.

Jim waved her away. 'Go on, we'll be fine with the fish.'

'All under control,' Molly said, smiling. 'Bye, Mr and Mrs B, have a great trip. Don't do anything I wouldn't!'

The three of them stood on the front step of the Campion Bay Guesthouse. The April day was crisp but clear, the wind buffeting Robin's curls around her face, the chill snapping at her fingers and cheeks.

'So you can start on the attic room now, then?' her dad asked wistfully. 'What's that one going to be called?'

'Starcross,' Robin said. 'I'm going to get a telescope for the balcony.'

'You've worked wonders,' her mum said. 'It looks like a new place before it's even finished. I can't imagine . . .' She shook her head. 'We just didn't have the fight any more, but with all that you've done, I wonder if we should be staying, helping you. It's a huge task, running this place on your own, my darling.'

'You've already helped me so much, though,' Robin said, a lump forming in her throat, 'with the renovations over the last few months. And you know I wouldn't have been able to do any of it without some of Grandma's inheritance.'

'You're keeping the Campion Bay Guesthouse going, love,' her dad said. 'You have no idea how proud we are that you're taking it over, what it means to us to see you here – to think of you running it – and to see how far you've come since you lost Neve.' He embraced her, his hug solid and comforting. For a moment, Robin wondered how she'd ever be able to survive without it, but then she steeled herself. Now was not the time to fall apart.

'I'm doing it for you,' Robin said, 'and for her. For all of you. And I'm sure I'll enjoy it.'

'You've got The Bible?' her mum asked. 'It's got all you need to know, all our tips and tricks. Though of course you have your own ideas, and you'll probably end up adding to it more than you refer to it.'

'It's got pride of place,' Robin said. 'I'll use it all the time.'

'And Skype us, won't you?'

'You too,' Robin said. 'Call me once you've arrived.' Their goodbyes seemed far too short for such a permanent departure, but once she'd watched the maroon Volvo estate disappear down Goldcrest Road and turn the corner, her cheeks streaked with tears, she couldn't feel her feet for the cold. She turned to see Molly standing on the top step, the kitten in her arms.

'No time for tears,' Molly said gently. 'We've got the last room to transform. You, me, and this bundle of fun. Any idea what you're going to call him?' Robin joined her friend in the hallway, accepting the kitten from her and bringing his warm, purring body close to her face. There was a tiny half-moon of white beneath his chin, but other than that he was a perfect, silky black. She thought of her inspiration for Starcross, thought of Neve and how much she would have loved a cat – a mascot for Once in a Blue Moon Days.

'Eclipse,' she said, kissing the kitten's nose. 'I'm going to call him Eclipse.'

It was the last day of the old Campion Bay Guesthouse, the last day before Robin opened up her doors and invited in her guests. The website was up, with images of all the new rooms. On the first floor was Rockpool, with its aquarium feature, and Wilderness, the reclaimed wood furniture offset by subtle, outdoor hues in sage green and powder blue, injections of colour coming in the form of stained-glass murals on the walls. On the second floor was Canvas, her gallery-inspired room with Arthur Durrant's *Campion Bay at Dawn* as the feature painting, set against a white and pine background, and Andalusia, which was in the style of Neve's favourite region in Spain, her home country. For this room, Robin had concentrated on textures to create the effect she wanted. There were fabrics in warm reds and golds, a terracotta feature wall stood out from the clean white of the other three, and the furniture was polished walnut save for the black wrought-iron bed frame.

Starcross had had to wait until last, when her parents had gone and she could move into their old rooms downstairs. They had worked solidly, finishing it in less than a month. It was the room she was most proud of, and most apprehensive about. While the other rooms were influenced by either her or Neve's passions – Wilderness and Rockpool signifying her return to Campion Bay, the beach and the exposed wild land along the top of the cliffs; Canvas and Andalusia representing Neve's love of art and of her home country – Starcross belonged to them both. It was about her fascination with the stars and Neve's compulsion to find meaning in them. It had been Robin's childhood bedroom and was modelled on the luxury suite Neve had fallen for. It held more meaning than she would ever reveal to anybody else, because it held pieces of both their hearts.

The new, pealing doorbell resounded through the guesthouse and Robin stopped grappling with the GuestSmart software to go and answer it. On the doorstep she found

Molly, Paige, Paige's boyfriend Adam, Mrs Harris from the Seaview Hotel and Tim, wearing an expertly crumpled white linen shirt, a pair of sunglasses wedged in the open collar. A black gleaming Audi was parked against the kerb.

'Surprise!' Paige shouted.

'What's going on?' Robin glanced behind her to check that Eclipse, three months old and adventurous despite his tiny legs, hadn't followed her to the doorway.

'Your social media campaign must have worked,' Molly said, 'because everyone seems to be aware that you're relaunching tomorrow. Paige, Adam and I wanted to have a shufty at the finished rooms, and we picked up these stragglers on the way.'

'Tim's brought champagne, so Mum said we'd best let him in.' Paige grinned and Tim caught Robin's eye, nodding her a greeting. Robin returned it with a nervous smile.

'Well then,' she said, 'you'd better come in.' She let them file into the wide hall and showed them into Sea Shanty, which ran the whole length of the house, the sea view at the front, French doors to the patio at the back. The garden could be reached through Sea Shanty or through the kitchen, and similarly Sea Shanty had two doors – one straight into the kitchen, and one into the hall. When she was much younger, Robin and her school friends had made a game out of running in a loop through the kitchen, living room and hallway, until one of her friends, too giddy from going round and round, had broken her toe by running into the doorframe instead of through the gap.

The room was split into two areas, the fireplace acting as a divider, and the long table was towards the back of the house, nearest the patio garden. It had wooden benches rather than seats, and Robin had decorated it with flowers in vases, lighthouse-shaped salt and pepper shakers, and a ceramic bowl filled with interesting shells and pebbles she had picked up on the beach.

Towards the front of the house the room became a cosy living area, with navy sofas looking out on the sea, blue-and-white striped cushions and a patterned rug over the floorboards. Hints of postbox red added brightness; the shade of a reading lamp, a print on the wall of a rainy city scene, monochrome apart from red umbrellas. Against the near wall was Mum and Dad's ancient upright piano, freshly tuned for whenever Robin found the time – and courage – to play it again.

'Can I give Mrs Harris a tour?' Paige asked.

Robin looked at the older woman, wondering what her motive was. She had always been friendly with Robin's mum and dad, and had never shown signs of being outwardly competitive. Now she looked somewhat disgruntled, her beady eyes trained on Robin, her arms folded over a green flowery apron.

'Let me come with you,' Robin said slowly. 'I'd like to show Mrs Harris myself.'

'And I *have* to show Adam Starcross,' Paige said. 'It's my favourite room, and we've not seen it finished yet. We're going to stay in it when—' She stopped abruptly as she caught Molly's eye, and Robin saw the look that passed between them.

'Come on then,' Robin said, hoping to defuse the tension, 'let's all go together.'

'Tim and I will sort out the champagne.' Molly took the bottle from him, and while Tim showed no signs of being upset, Robin imagined he hadn't expected to share it with quite so many people. He gave Molly an amused smile and followed her into the kitchen.

Robin let Paige lead the tour, her and Adam's enthusiasm at the rooms they'd worked on together giving it the kind of positive sales pitch that Robin had dreamed about, but Mrs Harris remained resolutely silent. She peered closely at everything – the spotlights and sound-systems built into the walls, a stained-glass mural in Wilderness, the freestanding bathtub in the rustic en suite of Andalusia – the only bathroom big enough for more than a drench shower. As the tour continued and Mrs Harris didn't utter a single word of delight or approval, Robin's nerves took hold. Was this how everyone was going to react to the new bedrooms? After a fortnight without bookings to make sure she had time to get everything finished, she had four out of the five rooms occupied from lunchtime tomorrow. The thought that they might not like what she'd done was too traumatic to contemplate.

Paige pushed open the door of Canvas and Mrs Harris stepped inside, her attention immediately turning to *Campion Bay at Dawn*. Robin held her breath, and a quick glance in Paige and Adam's direction elicited uneasy shrugs from them both.

'Where did this come from?' the older woman asked, failing to turn round.

'Uhm, well, it was painted by a local artist. Most of these were, actually,' Robin said, gesturing at the other paintings. 'Some Mum and Dad had dotted throughout the guesthouse, and others I've been buying in the run-up to today.'

'It's very modern,' Mrs Harris said, turning. Her hands were squeezed into tight fists on her hips, and her iron-grey hair was piled up on her head, accentuating the sharpness of her features. 'What's the point of having so many paintings in here?'

'Because they're beautiful,' Paige rushed, and Robin was

touched by her loyalty. 'The whole room is. *All* the rooms are. Whether you want the calm and quiet of a gallery, or to be transported to rural Spain, or get to sleep under the stars or on the beach without the cold or sand in your pyjamas. You get all the experience but with comfort to match. Don't you see, Mrs Harris? I would pay all I had to sleep in one of these rooms, to have an unforgettable experience.'

Robin inhaled, a lump forming in her throat at Paige's explanation, at the way she had understood her vision for the guesthouse so completely. 'Paige—' she started, her voice a whisper.

'Why change it?' Mrs Harris asked, cutting her off. 'Sylvie and Ian had these rooms lovely and simple. Why all the fancy-pants arty stuff?'

'I wanted to refresh the guesthouse, to try something a bit different.'

'Change is unnecessary,' Mrs Harris said. 'And mark my words, the grass isn't always greener; the sky could be just as grey, the tea just as weak on the other side.'

'Right,' Robin said, wondering if Mrs Harris was about to launch into a cliché-ridden song. 'But it *can* be positive. And everything moves forward, whether we want it to or not. Why not be in control of it?'

Mrs Harris gave her such a long, piercing look that Robin felt her skin prickle.

'Do you want to come and have a glass of champagne?' she asked, an edge of desperation in her voice.

'At eleven in the morning? Good Lord, no. This is what I mean. You with your crazy rooms and your drinking in the morning and your fancy bathtubs. Why is that man here? That developer? You're conspiring with him, aren't you? I know what he wants to do, and you're a part of it. If he had his way, Goldcrest Road would be razed to the ground and replaced with a huge, seaside shopping complex. This,' she said, jabbing her finger at Robin, 'is the first step.'

'No, not at all. How could—' But the older woman walked straight past her. 'Mrs Harris?' Robin hurried after her.

'I'm going home now,' Mrs Harris called up. 'I'm going to see to my own guests. They know what to expect, they know they can trust me.'

Mrs Harris swept down the stairs and out of the front door, leaving a trail of sweetly floral perfume in her wake. Molly appeared in the doorway of Sea Shanty, a glass of champagne in her hand, and Tim peered out over her shoulder.

'Mrs Harris didn't like the rooms, then?' Molly asked. 'Don't pay any attention to her, she's just jealous because her hotel's stuck several centuries back.'

Robin stopped on the bottom step and leaned her arms on the banisters. 'She accused me of being involved in some huge, destructive plot to demolish Goldcrest Road and replace it with a shopping complex.'

'What?' Molly's eyes widened. 'What planet is she on?'

'Planet suspicion,' Robin said, her gaze going to Tim, who looked as relaxed as ever, no suggestion that Mrs Harris had touched a nerve. 'She thinks I'm in cahoots with you.'

'Me?' Tim's eyebrows shot up.

'You. You're responsible for this plan, apparently, and me taking over the guesthouse is the first step.'

'Because launching a brand new seaside B&B is definitely the right course of action when the building's about to be demolished.' Molly rolled her eyes and tapped her toes against the floorboards.

Robin sighed. 'She's nervous. She feels threatened – not by

this place, specifically, but by any kind of change. Apparently things should just carry on, exactly the same as they always were.' She caught Tim's gaze and he flashed her a knowing smile. Robin swallowed. 'I'll go and talk to her later,' she rushed. 'See if I can reassure her that Goldcrest Road isn't about to disappear in a cloud of fancy restaurants and TK Maxx stores.'

'God, I'd love a TK Maxx in Campion Bay. This playsuit came from the Bridport store.' Molly did a slow twirl in the hallway, and Robin nodded approvingly. The playsuit was hot orange, Molly's lipstick matching, the overall effect with her blonde hair and smooth skin was tanned, summery and utterly gorgeous. From Tim's expression, she could see he was also a fan.

'Don't give him any ideas,' Robin said and then, realizing how that might sound, tried to clarify. 'About building a TK Maxx, not about . . .' She gestured lamely at Molly's outfit. 'Though of course it's up to you what you . . . It isn't any of my . . .' She stalled, mortification presenting itself as a red flush across her cheeks, her friend and her ex staring at her with confusion. 'Is there a glass of champagne for me?'

'Of course!' Molly thrust one into her hands. 'Where are Adam and Paige?'

'Still upstairs.' Robin clinked her glass with Tim's, and then Molly's, her toast lodged in her throat as she saw Molly's expression.

'You left Paige and Adam alone in one of the bedrooms? It wasn't Starcross, was it?'

'What's Starcross?' Tim asked. 'When do I get a tour?'

'They're in Canvas,' Robin said. 'And I don't see why you're worried. It's daylight, and it's not like they've booked the room, is it?'

Molly shook her head, pityingly. 'They're sixteen, Robin. I find it hard to trust them alone together in any room with a soft surface – or a wall, for that matter.' Molly hurried up the stairs, her low heels tap-tapping on the wood. 'We need to watch those two, it's worse than when she was a toddler. I thought her getting into the biscuit cupboard was bad enough, but now when I compare it to Adam getting in – well, you get the picture.'

'I heard that, Mum!' Paige screeched. 'Oh my God, could you be *any more* embarrassing? We're just Snapchatting!'

When they were alone, Tim took a step towards Robin. 'She's worried about her daughter losing her virginity in one of the guesthouse rooms? Wouldn't that be a turn-up.' Robin focused on his chin, on how close his shave was, rather than meeting his gaze. But she couldn't help smiling, the memory distant but still there – the excitement, nerves, the clumsiness, the fear of being discovered by her parents as they snuck into the bedroom – now Wilderness – when it was unoccupied. At the time her attic bedroom hadn't seemed exciting enough for what they were planning, and there was more chance of them being discovered there, despite it being at the top of the house.

'You brought your dad's homemade wine,' she said, the smile becoming a grin as she finally caught his eye. 'It was awful. And those Superman boxer shorts.'

'Hey,' Tim said, but he was smiling too. 'I seem to remember you had made an effort as well. Lilac matching underwear.'

'From Debenhams,' Robin said. 'I loved that underwear. I felt so grown up.'

'I was fond of it too. God, it was awkward, wasn't it?'

'It was,' Robin admitted. 'But somehow perfect.'

'You'd better not let Molly know that you're an advocate of losing your L-plates at sixteen, or she'll never let Paige round here again.'

'I'm not an advocate, you're the one who brought it up.'

'It was hard not to,' Tim said. 'This house is full of memories.' He glanced around the hall, as if picturing how it had looked all those years ago. 'I seem to remember we had lots of opportunities to get better.'

Robin swallowed. 'We did.' While the memory of their first time together was sweet and nostalgic, and held no lingering feelings of passion for her, there were plenty of memories that did. She was finding that, though she'd spent less than an hour with him since she'd been back, those feelings were being brought to the surface, like a stick churning the mud up from the bottom of a lake. They were swirling through her, clouding her thoughts, not entirely welcome.

'Robin,' Tim murmured, his face close to hers.

'I need to get on, I need to check everything's ready for the guests.'

'You've not shown me the rooms yet.'

'Another time,' she said quickly. 'I'm sorry, I know you've come here specially, that you've brought champagne.'

'I can bring more,' he said easily. 'Just tell me when.'

She nodded. 'I appreciate you coming round today.'

'I wouldn't miss it. Now that we're reacquainted, I feel like I want to know more about the last fourteen years. I want us to get to know each other again.'

'I do too,' Robin whispered, his eyes on her suddenly uncomfortable. She forced herself to look at him, at the linen shirt, his blond curls and his open, easy expression. She wanted to move forward with her life, to start a new chapter, but Robin was in danger of being dragged backwards by her ex-boyfriend, whether deliberately or not. As he said goodbye, giving her another warm, lingering kiss on the cheek, and Robin was left standing alone in the hall, she wondered how much danger she was actually in.

Robin had never been able to resist Tim. Only the pain of him being unfaithful while they were trying to make long-distance love work had been devastating enough to sever her attachment to him all those years ago. Now, despite the growing up she'd done, and all that she'd been through, she felt herself weakening in his presence. But she wasn't convinced the feelings were real, as opposed to simply the cosy nostalgia of happy memories. She felt all at once like the grown-up, thirty-three-year-old Tim was a complete stranger, and equally, that she knew every inch of him.

But she had to push thoughts of Tim aside. In twenty-four hours' time her first guests would be arriving at the new and improved Campion Bay Guesthouse, landlady Ms Robin Brennan, ably supported on breakfasts and changeovers by Paige Westwood, with Eclipse the kitten adding the cute factor. Suddenly worried that the kitten had strayed somewhere he shouldn't have, Robin left Molly and Paige quietly bickering upstairs and went to seek out the newest member of the Brennan household.

Chapter 4

'Mr and Mrs Barker.' Robin smiled up at the couple as she stood in front of the computer and clicked through to their reservation. 'So lovely to see you.' Her palms were sweaty, as they had been all day, and she felt like she'd had a whole pot of coffee to herself, despite having stuck to a single cup when she'd woken at six o'clock after a restless night. This was it, her guests were checking in; there was no time to turn back.

'Sea's looking pretty choppy today,' Mrs Barker said in response. 'Bracing.'

'It is,' Robin agreed. 'The wind's up a bit.' She clicked that her guests had arrived, and a confirmation sheet printed out on the sleek black printer behind her. 'Are you planning on swimming?' She placed the paper in front of them. 'If you could check the details and give me a signature, I can show you to your room.'

'Love to swim in the sea,' Mrs Barker confirmed, while her husband leaned his wide frame over the paper, squinting slightly. 'It's always biting where we live in Wales, so the south coast should be a welcome change.'

'You have lovely beaches in Wales, though.'

'Oh yes,' Mrs Barker said. 'Some of the best.'

Robin filed the completed confirmation sheet, and took the keys to Andalusia out of the drawer of the wooden desk The hall had never been wide enough to house a proper reception area, so she'd continued her parents' tradition of having a desk and computer station in the living room – now Sea Shanty – where the keys and paperwork were kept. Mr and Mrs Barker stepped back, allowing her to lead the way.

'We have got a tiny lift,' she said, 'or we can take the stairs up to the second floor.'

'Stairs are fine,' Mr Barker confirmed, hefting his Barbour bag on to his shoulder.

'Can I take anything?' Robin asked.

'Oh no, we're fine, aren't we, love?'

'That we are.'

They both had tanned, weatherworn faces, and their clothes were smart but practical, their jackets and boots indicating that they worked outside, riding or gardening or managing country estates. Robin wondered if they owned a huge, secluded mansion in North Wales, with meticulous rose gardens, acres of grassland and a river running through a woody copse. 'Good-oh,' she said quickly, snapping herself back to reality. 'If you'd like to follow me, then.'

When she opened the bedroom door, allowing Mr and Mrs Barker to go in first, she couldn't help but grin. Mr Barker's reaction was subtle, his eyebrows shooting skywards, but his wife clapped her hands together in glee.

'It's even better than the photo,' she said, turning in a slow circle.

'I'm so glad you approve,' Robin rushed, her heartbeat beginning to return to normal.

Andalusia was the boldest of her bedrooms, with its rustic styling, red and burnished orange fabrics and dark wood furniture. The sun was streaming through the window, adding to the impression of being in another country, and Robin thought she couldn't have picked a more perfect moment to invite her guests in.

'This is incredible,' Mrs Barker said, running her hands over the red-and-gold runner at the end of the bed. 'You'd hardly believe you were in Dorset if it wasn't for the view outside. Have you spent lots of time in Andalusia?'

'I've never been there,' Robin admitted, 'but I've heard a lot about it.' Neve had promised to take her there, to show her the narrow streets and old churches of the Pueblos Blancos, but with Once in a Blue Moon Days getting off the ground, it had never happened. 'A friend of mine was born in the area, and she made it sound so magical. I know you don't have the amazing Spanish hills outside the window, but Campion Bay beach is beautiful in its own right, and this way you get a sense of the exotic alongside the English seaside.'

'I don't suppose it comes with a Spanish breakfast as well?' Mr Barker sat in the nook in the window and peered out at the sea. Robin had made sure that the window seats, a feature of every room except Starcross, were as snug as possible, but she thought Mr Barker was perhaps too big to make full use of this one. She couldn't imagine him leaning back against the cushions, his feet up on the padding, reading glasses perched, owl-like, on the end of his nose.

'I've got tostadas on the menu, with tomato and olive oil,'

Robin said. 'Or you can have your scrambled eggs with avocados, chorizo and a dash of Tabasco sauce. All the information is in the folder on the chest of drawers: fire procedures, breakfast times – as well as the menu – and ideas for things to do in the area. If you need anything at all, or have any questions, then please ask. I'm usually around, but my mobile number is in the folder if you can't find me. I hope you enjoy your stay.'

'Thank you,' Mrs Barker said. 'I'm sure we will.' Mr Barker nodded from the window seat.

Robin stepped out of the room and pulled the door closed behind her, then did a little dance on the landing. This was the fourth positive reaction she'd had to the rooms, from people who were actually staying in them. A couple who looked almost as young as Paige and Adam had checked into Rockpool, and had been instantly mesmerized by the wall of fish; and the middle-aged couple in Wilderness, Ray and Andrea, had seemed very taciturn, but as Robin had closed the door behind them, she'd heard Ray say: 'Well, this is pretty bloody nice.'

Dorothy, who had checked into Canvas for the week, had stared at the painting of *Campion Bay at Dawn* for so long that Robin had simply closed the door behind her, without giving her prepared spiel about breakfast times and mobile numbers. She'd noticed that, along with her suitcase, she had a fold-up easel and an A3 portfolio case.

Now Robin glanced up at the narrower staircase, the one that led to Starcross. It was the most personal room, the one that was most precious to her, and part of her was glad she hadn't booked it out immediately. She had been nervous enough as it was, but now the hurdle of having happy guests – at least on first impression – was out of the way.

She had many more challenges ahead; cooking successful breakfasts, coming up with new ways to promote the guest-house and keeping on top of the finances. Actually making a profit would be preferable, and balancing everything with only Paige to help with the breakfasts and changeovers was going to keep them both busy, but she was prepared to expand if it got too much. At least that would mean the bookings were continuing.

She made herself a cup of tea and checked that she'd booked everyone in properly on the GuestSmart software. The sea beyond the window was choppy, though not quite enough to release the white horses, and the sun scattered rays on the water, creating a patchwork of light and shade.

Robin realized she had dipped her pen – instead of her digestive biscuit – in her tea, and was holding the biscuit absent-mindedly aloft, scattering crumbs all over the keyboard. She didn't need to be here now the guests were all safely booked in. They had keys to the front door as well as their rooms, and could come and go as they pleased, but part of her felt like she should just sit there, waiting to see if they needed anything.

She wiped her pen down her trousers, locked the door of Sea Shanty and wrote on the hanging whiteboard she'd placed below the name sign: *Popped out for half an hour, call my mobile if you need anything.*

The wind buffeted Robin's loose hair around her face as she walked along the pebbly sand with her ballet pumps in her hand. Campion Bay beach was a mixture of sand and pebbles below Goldcrest Road, good for barefoot walking if you didn't mind the odd, sharp wake-up call, and a treasure-trove of shells and stone peppered with quartz. But stroll for ten minutes in an easterly direction, to the beach below the cliffs, and you had thick, pebble-free sand that you could bury friends in up to their necks, and forget that civilization existed save for ships passing as grey shadows on the horizon. Robin loved that there was a tame beach, close to the crazy golf and ice cream hut and parking spaces, and a wild beach that was narrower, more prone to disappearing underneath a high tide. A beach that felt exciting because it was never entirely safe, cliffs that harboured small, intriguing caves, a place where the sea was vast and all consuming.

For now, Robin walked along the tame beach, listening to cries of triumph from Skull Island, imagining the owner, Maggie Steeple, sitting in her hut, passing out clubs and balls, score cards and miniature pencils, all the while with a cryptic crossword book open on the desk.

Spray buffeted Robin's face as she walked closer to the water, digging a pale pink pebble out of its sandy surround with her big toe. London had been fun – energetic and wild and breathless – but it didn't have the beach.

She remembered one of the 'Once in a Blue Moon' days she had organized with Neve, for a woman called Janine whose passion was being close to the sea. It was a fiftieth birthday present from her husband Artem, and it turned out to be more of a challenge than they had first thought. She and Neve had sat at the round table in the tiny London flat they shared, Robin's back pressed against the wall, and tried to work out how to do it. Because beaches are easy, but making a beach visit truly memorable, truly Once in a Blue Moon, was trickier.

She had called up a hotel that owned a stunning, private beach in West Cornwall while Neve arranged for a top-class chef to cook them a Michelin-starred meal and serve it on a table close to the waves. They arrived by speedboat, had a day's uninterrupted access to the perfect sand and magnificent Atlantic Ocean, and then a night in the luxury hotel with a bay-view suite and a hot tub on the balcony. Artem had been ecstatic when they'd shared their plans with him, and they'd received a thank you card and box of chocolates from Janine, alongside a photo of the two of them on the beach – a snapshot of pure, undiluted happiness.

'This,' Neve had said, thrusting the photograph up towards the ceiling, her dark eyes wide with the joys of success, 'is why we do this. To create moments and memories like this. Look at their faces.' They'd hugged it out, as they always did, and then celebrated by sharing a bottle of prosecco and watching six episodes of *Don't Tell the Bride* back to back, Neve always saying it was research for how *not* to surprise people.

Robin had seen that look on several faces already today. Maybe a uniquely designed bedroom wasn't quite as special as having a private beach and a Michelin-starred chef to yourself for the day, but in her own small way she was carrying on the Once in a Blue Moon Days legacy. She turned the pink pebble over in her hands, and then thrust it forward into the water. It made a loud 'plop' before the ripples were swallowed up by a wave, crashing forward and, in all likelihood, depositing the pebble back on the beach. 'Everything goes in circles,' she muttered to herself and then, unhappy with how that soundbite could relate to her own life, turned away from the sea.

'Coming for a round, Bobbin?' Maggie called as Robin climbed the steps and walked around the edge of the golf course.

She narrowed her eyes, giving the older woman a practised

glare. Maggie had called her Bobbin since Robin, aged five or six, had bounced her way round the golf course with her parents, swinging wildly and gasping at the pirates and skeletons that decorated Skull Island. Maggie had been in her thirties then – close to Robin's age now – and was as much a part of Campion Bay's fabric as the sea and the promenade.

'I'm on my own,' Robin said. 'Competing against myself would be sad.'

'So bring Molly with you, but tell her not to wear heels or it'll ruin the course.'

'That's not a rule, is it?' Robin asked, peering at the *How to avoid walking the plank* sign pinned to Maggie's hut.

'It should be,' Maggie said. 'And I have asked a couple of women to do it barefoot in the past, though the majority realize before they come that skyscraper heels are not the best footwear for a game of golf.'

'And I'm sure Molly will too; she wears flats at work.'

'So you'll bring her? You've not been on the course since you've been back, and I've installed a great new water feature.'

Robin folded her arms. 'Which hole?' A water feature in this case meant that all who walked in the path of the new installation would get a soaking.

'You think I'm going to tell you? Where's the fun?'

'I'll remember to wear my cagoule, then. Bye, Mags.'

'Catch you later, Bobbin.' She waved a fond farewell as Robin turned away, back towards the Campion Bay Guesthouse and, she smiled at the thought, her guests.

'So congratulations,' Molly said, pouring a generous amount of Pinot Grigio into Robin's glass. 'You're going to smash this place – no offence to Ian and Sylvie. I'm sure they could have stepped up to the challenge if they'd wanted to, but you deserve this.'

Robin frowned, wondering what her mum and dad 'smashing it' would look like. 'No disasters so far,' she agreed. 'No mishaps with any of the rooms, people running out in horror at the décor, leaking aquariums or cats on the bed. Though I think Catriona in Rockpool would quite like Eclipse warming her feet from the way she was looking at him when they checked in.'

'You're doing great,' Molly said, clinking her glass against Robin's, 'even if your nails are appalling. Don't think I haven't noticed.'

'It wouldn't have been worth it while I was decorating.'

'But now? That side's all done with, isn't it? And if you've got *other things* on the horizon . . .' Molly let the sentence trail off and gave Robin a firm look.

It was after eight and they were sitting on the navy sofas in Sea Shanty. The sea was a dark mass with a hint of late-sunset glow, mostly hidden behind the reflection of their interior, the fairy lights that Robin had strung up like constellations on the glass.

Guests were able to use the room when Robin was at home. She had a small living room at the back of the private area of the house, behind her bedroom, but it wasn't anywhere near as cosy as Sea Shanty, and she wanted her guests to feel comfortable in the house, rather than hide away and leave the downstairs feeling deserted.

'Other things?' Robin asked lightly.

'Don't think I didn't notice the chemistry between you and Tim yesterday. I know you were apprehensive about seeing him, but it didn't look like you were having a totally horrible time. If I lit my cigarette between the two of you . . .'

'You don't smoke.'

'Just don't wear hairspray around him.'

'I'm not going to go back there.' Robin tried to look out of the window, but was faced with a faded, blurred version of herself. 'It would be the least sensible decision ever, even if I wanted to – which I don't.'

'Not even a little bit?' Molly asked, holding up finger and thumb close together.

Robin knew her friend was testing her. 'I can't forget what he did to me. I know I was in London by then and you didn't get the full force of the fallout, but you know how much it hurt. You've been through it yourself – and you had a baby on the way when Simon left you.'

'It just proves that teenage guys are unfaithful bastards, and we should never commit to anything until the men involved are at least thirty.'

Robin laughed. 'The sad thing is, I don't know if that would help in Tim's case. He's so similar to how I remember him. I think anything I *am* feeling towards him—'

'Lust, you mean?'

Robin gave her friend her best scowl. 'It's just nostalgia. I loved Tim with that wide-eyed, first-love enthusiasm. And he's still so confident about everything, reminding me of our relationship – the good parts – without any hint of embarrassment or regret. It's a bit overwhelming.'

'You'll get past it. It's strange seeing him again, I get that, but when you've bumped into him a couple more times you won't feel a thing. He'll go back to being ex-boyfriend, love rat, arrogant try-hard.' Molly finished her wine and refilled their glasses.

Robin sighed. 'I hope so. Tim is in the past. We may manage to be friends in future, but revisiting what we had would be a bad idea.' She shook her head vigorously, trying not to think about the way he had placed his hand over hers in the coffee shop.

'So we turn our attention to the rich male pickings of Campion Bay?' Molly held her glass up.

'You're being ironic, right?' Robin grinned, happy to stop talking about her ex-boyfriend. 'Or did Campion Bay become a hotbed of male loveliness while I was away?'

'Oh, you just wait, Robin Brennan. Though,' Molly added, 'you might be waiting a long time. I'm going to get another bottle of wine.'

'No,' Robin said as Molly stood up, 'I've got to cook breakfast for seven guests in the morning. I can't be hungover.'

'You'll cook a better fry-up with a hangover than without one, because you'll be more invested in it. It's the perfect cure. Besides, Paige will be there to help if you need a break.'

'Molly,' Robin said, a warning in her voice as her friend, shoes discarded next to the sofa, danced lightly to the door.

'What? We don't have to drink the whole bottle, do we?'

'You're a bad influence on me.'

Molly waved her away with a hand and disappeared into the hall. Robin sat back on the sofa and closed her eyes, grateful that Molly was there to talk things over with, to make her laugh, and to make light of the worries that she was storing up inside.

A loud bang from outside startled her eyes open, and she sprung up and turned the lamp off in a single movement, pressing her face to the glass. A blue car pulled up between Robin's Fiat 500 and the Barkers' Land Rover. Robin squinted. It was an Alfa Romeo; it looked old and rather battered, and not just because of the exhaust fumes puffing out into the night-time air. She watched as the driver's door opened and a man unfolded himself, then stood and peered up at the house fronts. He was tall and broad-shouldered and probably around her age, though Robin couldn't see his features clearly. He walked round to open the passenger door and a small curly-haired, caramel-coloured dog hopped on to the pavement. The man wrapped the lead around his wrist, pulled a holdall out of the boot and then, to Robin's astonishment, walked up the stairs of Tabitha's house.

Robin's nose was completely squashed against the glass as she tried to keep her eyes on him, but the angle was too acute and he disappeared from view as soon as he'd reached the top step. She saw the dog's tail for a few more seconds, and then they were both gone.

'What on earth are you doing?' Molly asked, returning with a fresh bottle of wine, a lurid pink rosé that had been on offer in the supermarket but Robin hadn't yet plucked up the courage to open.

Robin rubbed her nose, listened for the sound of Tabitha's front door closing, and then flopped on to the sofa. 'Someone just went inside next door. Someone who arrived in a battered old Alfa.'

'Who?' Molly asked, sounding as shocked as Robin felt. 'Squatters? *More* property developers?'

'It's after nine,' Robin shook her head. 'He had a holdall and a fluffy dog and . . . and I don't know what else. But he's gone inside, or at least he disappeared up the stairs and I heard the door close.'

Molly made a 'come on' motion with her hand and Robin finished her wine, then allowed her friend to refill her glass. 'Borrow some sugar.'

'What?'

'Let's go round and ask to borrow some sugar.'

'No. No way.'

'Why not? I bet Mrs Harris would.'

'Don't lump me in with her,' Robin warned. 'How would it look? Someone goes into a house that's been empty for a year, and then someone else who lives in an open, functioning guesthouse asks the new person for a cup of sugar. It's completely back to front. I may as well scrawl *nosy neighbour* on my forehead.'

'So go and say hello. Introduce yourself.'

'Why me?'

'Because you're next door.'

'You're on the other side,' Robin protested. 'You're a neighbour too.'

'But I'm not at home right now.' Molly clutched her wine to her chest and pulled her legs up on to the sofa.

Robin sighed. 'I am *not* going to go and knock on the door. Not until at least tomorrow, otherwise he'll know I noticed him arriving.'

Molly whooped and let out a loud peal of laughter. 'I knew I could rely on you.'

'Shush. Now, how's this wine? Is it as toxic as it looks?'

It was after midnight, and the doorbell was ringing. Robin looked up from the sink and glanced down the hallway as if that would give her clarity. All her guests were safely tucked up in their rooms. She knew this because as they'd come in throughout the evening she had invited them to have a glass of wine with her and Molly. Catriona and Neil had accepted, and the four of them had spent an hour in Sea Shanty, Robin and Molly extolling the virtues of Campion Bay to the young couple, who turned out to be on their first holiday together

– paid for with Neil's work bonus – and had travelled from just outside Birmingham.

But now it was officially tomorrow, and the doorbell was definitely ringing. Robin had had it replaced, having spent far too long listening to sound-snippets on a website before picking the perfect chime, so there could be no mistaking it. She padded down the hallway, wondering whether Molly had, in her slightly tipsy state, left her phone behind, but as she got closer to the door and turned the outside light on, the figure behind the coloured glass became clearer, and it wasn't Molly-shaped.

Robin pulled the door open and tried not to gasp. 'H-hello,' she stuttered, 'how can I help?'

It was the man who'd gone into Tabitha's house. He had the same tall frame and broad shoulders, and the same small dog at his feet. A closer look confirmed he was her age, or perhaps a couple of years older. He was blinking at her under the outside light, and he was soaked. Robin peered behind him to check there hadn't been a sudden, silent downpour, and when she was satisfied, turned her attention back to him and the dog who, she realized, looked equally bedraggled. It was adorable, the kind of breed that could be mistaken for a cuddly toy, and she had to resist scooping it into her arms.

'There's been a leak,' he said. 'I mean, there *is* a leak, next door.' His voice was deep and slightly breathless, his expression was apologetic, and his eyes, Robin couldn't help noticing, were very green. He had a spread of freckles across a straight nose and tanned cheeks, and his short hair, which was plastered to his forehead, gave a suggestion of being chestnut brown when it wasn't wet. The dark stain on his grey jumper looked like he'd been dumped

71

under a bucket of water rather than an impromptu rain shower.

'Oh,' she said. 'I'm sorry, I – have I caused the leak?'

He frowned. 'What? No, I don't think so. I think the roof needs repairing.'

'*My* roof?' Robin stepped outside and peered up at the front of the guesthouse, her heart hammering with alarm. She was very close to him now. She caught a whiff of mildewed water and something else, something much more pleasant that brought back a childhood memory: full paper bags from the traditional sweet shop in town.

'No,' the man said, his voice now with a hint of frustration. 'Next door. Look, I'm not accusing you of anything, and I'm sorry to knock so late, but you are still a guesthouse, aren't you? The sign says so.' He pointed upwards. Robin resisted the urge to look up at her own name sign, and instead stepped back inside, facing him.

'Sorry.' She rubbed her forehead. Damn Molly and that second bottle of wine. 'Sorry, yes I am. You're staying next door?' she asked tentatively.

'Well,' he said, giving her a wry smile. 'I was trying to, but it seems the house has other ideas. I can't . . . I mean, I *could* stay there. It would probably be the manly thing to do, style it out on the floor in another of the rooms, do the whole Bear Grylls thing, but the place needs a complete overhaul. Then I remembered that, as luck would have it, my aunt lived next to a guesthouse.'

'Your *aunt?*' Robin had been about to tell him that she was pretty sure Bear Grylls grappled with terrains a bit more hard-core than seafront houses, but now she was distracted. 'Tabitha was your aunt?'

The man's eyes widened, and then his smile registered

something that was either genuine happiness, or possibly relief now that he was finally getting some sense out of her. 'Yes, yes she was. Hi.' He held out his hand. 'Will Nightingale.'

Robin took it. It was warm and firm and – unsurprisingly, given the rest of him – slightly damp. 'Robin Brennan,' she replied, trying to find similarities with the woman she had lived next door to for most of her childhood. Tabitha's eyes had been hazel rather than startling green, but, along with a growing spread of grey, she'd had the woody, mid-brown hair that Robin suspected Will's would be once it dried. And Robin remembered her neighbour once telling her that her maiden name was Nightingale, and that the only sadness she'd had in getting married to the love of her life was losing such a beautiful surname for the mundanity of becoming Mrs Thomas.

'Hi, Robin.' Will dropped his hand. 'I don't suppose, by any chance, you've got any rooms going? Just so I can be a wuss in comfort and deal with the leak tomorrow, in the daylight. And I know it's a lot to ask, but could you also accept my dog? I don't want Darcy to be left in a strange, empty house on her own.'

'Yes,' Robin said, 'of course. Please come in.' Will grinned, his shoulders dropping in relief. He picked up his bag from the porch and stepped into the hallway. 'Darcy?' she asked tentatively.

'Long story.' He was standing close to her, looking around him, failing to meet her eye all of a sudden. 'This place is great,' he said. 'A far cry from what Tabitha's left me with. Look,' he turned towards her, 'I do appreciate this. I know it's after midnight, and you're probably not in the habit of accepting guests – and dogs – so late. So if you just tell me where my room is, I'll dry Darcy off, get out of your hair and we can regroup in the morning.'

'Sure, sure. No problem,' Robin managed, her head so full of questions about Tabitha, and how come he'd appeared now, and why had Robin never met him while she was growing up, and did he know about the plans that Malcolm and Tim had for the house, and had they found his number and got in touch with him, that for a moment she forgot the reality of the situation. 'Your room. Yes, of course – let me show you.'

'Please don't put yourself out. I'm sure I can find my way. I've got navigational skills like Bear Grylls, even if I don't have his stamina.' His face fell as he caught Robin's eye and she didn't return the smile. It had just dawned on her, through the shock of the unexpected situation, which room she was going to have to put Will in for the night.

'I'd like to show you if that's OK?' She hurried into Sea Shanty and took the key from the top drawer, the icon of GuestSmart winking accusingly at her from the desktop. She would check him in later. 'My rooms are a bit . . . unique,' she managed, taking a towel out of the bottom drawer and handing it to him.

'Oh?' Will raised his eyebrows, suddenly looking slightly nervous. They stood in the hallway, facing each other, as the rest of the guesthouse settled into darkness around them. 'Unique in what way?' He crouched and rubbed Darcy with the towel. She stood perfectly still while she was dried into a caramel puffball.

'You'll see,' Robin said. 'Come with me.' Without asking, and with her heart pounding in her chest, she picked up Will's holdall and started climbing the stairs towards their destination at the top of the house.

She was going to have to put Will Nightingale, Tabitha's nephew, and his little dog Darcy, in Starcross.

Chapter 5

'Here we are,' Robin said, her chest tightening as she stopped on the tiny landing outside Starcross. Will stopped on the top step behind her. There wasn't enough room for both of them on the landing, and she could feel his breath on her ear, but for some reason she couldn't open the door. She had a mental block. She looked at the name-plate, pearly white with Starcross written in swirling blue, as with all the other name signs, and wondered if she could do this. Put this tall, imposing, though so far very nice-seeming man in this special room. A room full of dreams and hopes and finding meaning in the stars.

'Uhm, is everything all right?' Will asked.

'Yes, of course.' She put her hand on the door handle. Pushed it down. And he had a dog. A very cute dog, some kind of poodle-cross, though she wasn't sure exactly what. She had only ever intended for dogs to go in the rooms on the first floor. Not up here.

'Robin,' Will prompted, 'if this isn't convenient or . . . or if the room is *really* specialist, then I can always—'

'No no,' she said, not wanting to encourage his mind to wander. If she hadn't wanted guests here, then why had she designed it in this way? Angry with herself, she pushed the door open quickly, forcefully, almost falling into the room. She turned on the light and took another two steps, allowing Will to follow her. Darcy ran ahead and put her paws up on the duvet.

'No, Darcy.' Will covered the room in a couple of strides and gently lifted her paws off the fabric, stroking her fuzzy coat. He stood up straight, his eyebrows rising as he noticed her looking. 'Are you sure this is OK? You're not bending your rules for me, are you?'

Robin shook her head, enamoured by how softly he spoke to his dog. 'Not much,' she admitted. Will's attention turned to the room, to the telescope in front of the balcony doors, a framed map of the constellations next to the glass, the modern, slate-grey furniture with subtle silver accents. She chewed the inside of her cheek. She'd put solar-powered sun and moon jars on the chest of drawers alongside the mini Kilner jars containing teabags and sugar sachets, but realized that unless she turned the LEDs on, guests wouldn't know what they were.

'The bathroom's in there.' She pointed to the only other door in the room. 'And details about breakfast, and all the other information about the guesthouse, is in the pack on the dressing table.'

'It's a beautiful room,' he said, as she put his holdall on the floor. 'Are you a bit of a stargazer, then?'

'Not at much as I'd like to be,' she admitted. 'I have good intentions, but never seem to take enough time to learn what everything is. But I do love the stars, and this room has a perfect view of them on a clear night.'

'No light pollution over the sea.' Will was moving slowly around the room, looking at everything. He stopped at the balcony doors, the curtains still open, and flipped the light switch that Robin had put there for that very purpose. The room was plunged into darkness, and she held her breath as Will peered out. After a moment, he turned. 'It's too cloudy tonight, so – oh!'

The pinprick lights that Robin had installed in the ceiling began glowing softly, casting the room, and Will, in an eerie bluish hue, like moonlight.

'Nice touch,' he said quietly. 'So you get stars, even if they're hiding behind cloud cover.'

'They fade after a while. You can set the time they stay on, so you don't have to sleep with it like this.' She pointed to a small timer on the wall behind the headboard, then hugged her arms tightly around herself. It was close to one in the morning, but she felt as tight and fidgety as a wind-up toy desperate to be released. She hadn't quite prepared herself for a guest staying in Starcross, and had definitely not been ready for Tabitha's nephew to turn up and be so imposing. *Was* he imposing? He was certainly making his presence felt, but then Starcross was the smallest room, and there were three of them in it – if you counted Darcy.

'Does she need some water? I've got a bowl downstairs.'

'I've got that covered, at least.' Will pulled a metal bowl out of an end-pocket of his holdall. 'I didn't know what I'd be faced with when I arrived. Clearly, I didn't account for all eventualities.' He indicated his sodden shirt.

'I'd better leave you to it,' Robin said, backing towards the door. 'Let you get some sleep.' She realized she hadn't given him his keys. 'Here you go. One key for this room, and one for the front door.'

'Thank you,' he said, his voice weighted with sincerity. 'This room is perfect. Unique, granted, but not in the way I was imagining.'

'What were you imagining?'

His green eyes fixed on hers for a moment, the smile there rather than on his lips. 'Maybe I'll tell you when we know each other a bit better. I'm not sure you'd appreciate it, and the last thing I want to do is get kicked out now I've found a great place to stay.'

Robin gave a nervous laugh. 'OK, sleep well, then. I'm on the ground floor if you need anything. You or Darcy.'

'Thank you, Robin. For coming to my rescue.'

'You're very welcome.' She backed up to the door, slid through it and closed it. No dancing on the landing this time; she fled down the stairs as quietly as she could, scooped Eclipse into a hug as he pattered into the hall, and then went to bed herself, pulling the cover up to her chin, her kitten buzzing gently, his soft fur warming her feet.

Most of her guests appeared for breakfast at the same time. Officially, Robin ran it from seven thirty to nine thirty, though she was prepared to deal with requests that deviated from her plan. On her first morning everyone picked eight thirty to appear, and so she led them, en masse, out to Honeysuckle, the patio garden where she would serve breakfast on days the weather allowed it.

Robin was prepared for this. She had learnt much of it by osmosis, by just being there during her teenage years, and now she had her mum and dad's bible. *Running the guest-house*, Sylvie and Ian assured her at the top of the first page, was *completely different* to being on the periphery.

Robin kept her focus, staying in the kitchen while Paige

served and cleared the tables. Molly's daughter was the perfect balance of polite and cheerful with the guests, and Robin could hear chatting and laughter through the open door. She had baked sourdough and parmesan bread, and had found a recipe for shredded hash browns. Outside, each room had its own table, so Robin could keep track of any food requirements or allergies included on booking forms. Mr and Mrs Barker both went for full fried breakfasts with extra hash browns, Neil had the vegetarian version and Catriona picked scrambled eggs and smoked salmon on toast. Ray and Andrea, the guests in Wilderness, opted for croissants, and Dorothy seemed happy with muesli and toast.

The only empty places were at the Starcross table, but Robin thought Will was probably having a lie-in after his late arrival.

Robin could have done with a lie-in too. She was usually a morning person, and had pictured herself rising at five thirty during the summer to walk on the beach before breakfast, but after dealing with Will she had lain in bed and stared at the ceiling, wondering how long he had set the timer and watched the gently glowing lights above him. She had known that her first guest in Starcross would feel strange; she would care what anyone thought of it, regardless of who that person was. If it had been an old married couple, instead of Tabitha's nephew, with the broad shoulders and green eyes and that way of being completely present, even in the long, high-ceilinged hall, she would have felt equally anxious. That's what she told herself as, the cooking finished, she took a pot of Marmite out to Dorothy.

'Thank you,' Dorothy said, squinting as she turned her face up to the sun. 'The weather seems to have welcomed our arrival.'

'This is the first properly warm start we've had in a while,' Robin said. 'It feels like summer is almost here.'

'It always feels closer by the sea, somehow,' Dorothy said. 'Probably because summer memories are beaches, sandcastles and ice creams. Down here you get a bigger summer quota than in big cities.'

'I don't know,' Robin said, picking up an empty juice glass, 'there's something lovely about sitting outside a city pub and soaking in the atmosphere and the heat from the tarmac after a long day at work.' As she said the words, she contemplated whether she still felt that way. She'd loved doing that with Neve and other friends in London, but had it ever come close to being by the sea?

Dorothy was looking at her closely, her pale eyes unblinking. 'It's not the same though, is it?'

Robin shook her head. 'No, you're right, it's not. I should be promoting Campion Bay, not sending everyone scurrying back home.'

'Nobody wants to leave once they come here,' Paige said, wiping down the Barkers' table. 'Campion Bay ticks all the boxes.' Robin stared at her for a moment, searching for signs of sarcasm, but couldn't find any. She'd wanted nothing more than to escape when she was Paige's age, not because she hated the seaside town, but because she felt there was so much more to explore. Maybe Paige was made from the same mould as Tim, finding everything she wanted in the quaint Dorset town, seeing no need to look further afield for her future.

'Birmingham has its moments,' Neil chipped in as Robin wove through the tables, 'but it doesn't have the views.'

'A sea view is pretty unbeatable,' Robin admitted. 'It's never the same, from one day to the next. Can I get either of you anything else?'

Neil shook his head. 'I'm going to have to think hard about lunch at this rate. I couldn't eat another mouthful. It was delicious, thank you.'

'It'll keep our energy up round the wildlife park,' Catriona added.

'Oh, you'll love it.' Robin's thoughts drifted back to the times she'd been there growing up, with her parents and then friends. 'It's got a great petting zoo.'

'And monkeys,' Paige added. 'Though don't take your car through that bit, or you'll lose a wing mirror.'

'I'm heading straight for the penguins,' Catriona said.

'Too smelly for me, even if they are cute.' Neil wrinkled his nose and Catriona gave him a playful slap on the arm.

Robin left them to their excitement, and was stacking plates in the dishwasher as she heard the front door close. She peered down the corridor and saw Will walking towards her, wearing knee-length black shorts and a faded blue T-shirt. He had a red towel looped around his shoulders and Darcy at his feet, which were only half in a pair of battered trainers, his heels pushing them out of shape at the back. 'Hi,' he said, giving her a quick smile. 'Am I too late for breakfast?'

'Not at all.' Robin saw that his hair was, again, damp. 'Been for a swim?'

He nodded. 'The water's freezing, but it's the best way to wake up. And Darcy loves it.'

Robin laughed. 'You take your dog swimming with you?'

Will shrugged. 'I couldn't go without her. There aren't any restrictions, are there? I didn't see any.'

Robin shook her head. 'No, not yet. Campion Bay is dog friendly, but you won't be able to take her on the main beach from June. You've still got a month, though.'

'That's good to know, thank you.' Will looked down at Darcy, who was standing obediently beside him. Robin couldn't help but smile. They seemed so out of place next to each other, as if Darcy had adopted Will without him having any say in the matter. She could imagine the little dog following him around until he got bored with trying to shoo her away. 'So, I'll just . . .' He pointed upwards and Robin nodded, trying not to laugh. She heard him tread lightly up the stairs, the patter of Darcy's paws following closely behind.

As Robin went back to her work, she wondered if she'd ever get the chance to see Will with dry hair. Then she wondered why she was even thinking about it.

By the time Will and Darcy came down to breakfast, the other guests had left to start their days, exploring Campion Bay and beyond. Robin had let Paige go home, and was tidying up the last of the crockery.

'Where do I go?' Will asked, peering into the kitchen. 'Can Darcy come into the breakfast room, or should I take her back upstairs?'

'Out here.' Robin dried her hands on a tea towel and led him into the garden. 'And of course Darcy can come – it's just me now. Take your pick of the tables and see what you fancy off the menu. Tea or coffee to start?'

'Coffee, please.' Will sat at the table closest to the kitchen door. He was still wearing the faded blue T-shirt, but the shorts had been replaced by dark jeans that emphasized his long legs, and the trainers exchanged for tan Wrangler boots.

'Does Darcy have dry or wet food?'

He looked slightly surprised. 'Dry. But I've fed her already, upstairs. I didn't realize you actually catered for dogs, I thought you just agreed to have her because I didn't give you a choice.'

'I could easily have said no to both of you.' Robin said it with a smile, and Will narrowed his eyes as she disappeared inside.

'Coffee coming right up!'

She cooked her last breakfast for the day: scrambled eggs, Cumberland sausages, grilled tomatoes, local smoked bacon and homemade hash browns, and took a photo of it for the guesthouse Instagram feed before she gave it to Will. She left him to eat and cleaned and wiped down the kitchen, then went outside to offer him more coffee. His plate was clean and he was intent on his phone, Darcy lying a few feet away in a wide patch of sun, her head resting on her paws. Robin noticed with amusement that Eclipse was sitting beyond the French doors looking out at the dog, and that Darcy's large brown eyes were trained on the kitten, her tail wagging gently.

'More coffee would be great.' Will put his iPhone in his pocket. 'I've got a long day ahead of me.'

'What are you doing down here? If you don't mind me asking,' Robin added hastily.

'I've come to clear out Tabitha's house,' he said with a sigh, glancing up at the building next door and squinting slightly. His hair had dried in the suntrap of Honeysuckle and Robin saw she had been right; it was a toffee-brown colour with a few natural blond highlights.

'You've got to clear out the whole place on your own?' She took a step closer to the table.

He shrugged and turned to look at her. 'There's nobody else to do it.'

'What will you do with it once you're done?'

'Sell it, I suppose. I haven't thought that far ahead.'

83

Robin's stomach clenched as she thought of Mrs Harris's scorn at the prospect of a modern development on Goldcrest Road. Even if her assumptions of a shopping centre were way off, this was likely to be the easiest negotiation Tim had ever done.

'You'll sell it?' She hadn't meant to sound so stunned, but Will looked at her closely.

'I'm going into this blind,' he said. 'I know nothing about Campion Bay, about what's in my aunt's house and really, I have no clue what I'm going to do. I only know it falls to me, and the longer I leave it the worse things will get. Hence the impressive leak.'

'I'll get your coffee,' Robin said quickly. 'I'm sorry, I shouldn't have asked. It's none of my business.'

'Hey' – he reached his hand out towards her, palm up – 'why not make enough coffee for both of us? You can give me a crash course in Campion Bay – if you've got time.'

Robin smiled, relieved that he hadn't taken offence at her intrusiveness. 'Give me five minutes.'

When she sat down, Robin's knees, clad in orange skinny jeans, briefly pressed against his before he moved them.

'You don't seem too happy that I might sell the house,' he said, after Robin had added milk to both mugs.

Robin kept her eyes focused on the table. 'It's not up to me,' she said. 'It surprised me, that's all. Tabitha has owned the house as far back as I can remember, and then, after she died, it stayed empty.' She glanced at him but his gaze was steady, no flicker of emotion at the mention of his aunt's death. 'I hadn't thought about what happens next,' she added, pushing her coffee shop discussion with Tim from her mind.

'You and me both.' Will rested his elbows on the table.

'I've known about the house – that it would fall to me – ever since her will was read, but this is the first chance I've had to come down here and take a look at it.'

'What do you do, if you don't mind me asking?'

He pressed his lips together, seeming to weigh something up before he answered. 'I work – worked – at a historic house, in Kent.'

'Doing what? It – you don't own it, do you?'

Will shook his head, giving her a rueful smile. 'No, nothing like that. I do a bit of everything – help to manage the estate, odd jobs, pitching in as a tour guide. It's not a large house, not English Heritage or National Trust, but it's open to the public so there's always work to keep on top of.'

Robin tried to imagine him wearing a Barbour jacket and Hunter wellies, striding across a manicured lawn with a lurcher at his feet. She couldn't do it, and not least because when she tried to picture it, the lurcher was immediately replaced with Darcy, scurrying to try and keep up with Will's long strides, unprepared to let him out of her sight. 'But you said *worked*. You've quit?'

Will sighed, his chin dropping to his chest. 'It's obviously not something I can do freelance. I've known for a while that I'd need to come and sort out Tabitha's house and it – it was suddenly the right time.'

'Did you enjoy it?'

'I did. No two days were the same, always a new challenge, always meeting new people. Being a guide is fun, as long as the guests are vaguely interested. You can measure your success by how many of them are still maintaining eye-contact at the end of the tour.'

'Did you make things up?' Robin took a sip of her coffee but it was too hot, and she spluttered, spilling some over her hand. She put her mug on the table and sucked at the scald.

'Here,' Will said, pressing a paper napkin into her free hand. 'Are you OK?'

Robin nodded, stopped sucking the injury like a small child and wiped at it with the napkin.

'Make things up?' he asked. 'You mean on the tours?'

'You know, embellish the stories, add a few more juicy details.'

Will shook his head slowly. 'I can't believe you'd even ask that. Of course not. People come to find out about the history of the house, not hear some sensation-filled fabrication.'

Robin felt a flush of shame, but she could see that he was amused by the suggestion. She took another, tentative sip of her coffee. 'At least your love of old buildings will help you today,' she said softly.

Will winced, lines forming at the edges of his eyes. 'Clearing out an empty house isn't quite the same thing.'

'So do you know how long you'll be down here? Will you have to find another job, or can you focus on next door?' Robin knew that she was firing too many questions at him, that it was none of her business, but she had such a strong desire to know. Now he was sitting at her table, he could give her more insight into Tabitha and into her house, which suddenly seemed the object of so many people's attention.

Will leaned down to stroke the top of Darcy's head. 'I have no idea how long it'll take, but if it stretches into months, if I'm making slow progress, then I'll have to start looking for something round here. I knew I'd need space away from everything to make a proper start. I didn't want the pressure of employers waiting for me, however reasonable they were about it.'

'I can understand that,' she said quietly. She watched him sip his coffee, drawn to his forearms, tanned and with a dusting of pale brown hair. It looked like he spent a lot of time outside, and Robin could picture him leading a group of awed tourists across a beautiful garden, an impressive stately home behind them – it fitted much better than the Barbour and the wellies, though Darcy was still in place, trotting loyally alongside. He had the presence to be a tour guide. She could see him commanding everyone, holding their attention with his green eyes. Especially, she thought wryly, the females of the party.

'Have you run the guesthouse for long?' Will asked, startling her out of her reverie.

'Nearly twenty-four hours,' Robin said, laughing at Will's confused expression. 'It reopened officially yesterday, with me at the helm. My mum and dad ran it for years, but they've moved to France and . . . well, now it's my turn.'

'Wow.' Will's eyebrows went skywards. 'So this morning was your first time cooking everyone breakfast? You look like you've barely broken a sweat.'

'I helped Mum and Dad out over the years, so I was more prepared than someone starting from scratch, and I've got my friend's daughter working with me. Your breakfast is actually an Instagram star.' She took out her phone and showed him.

'That's an accolade I never thought I'd get – devourer of a famous breakfast.'

'You'd better remember this moment,' she grinned.

'Pretty sure I will,' he said quietly, and her smile faltered under the weight of his stare. 'Unflappable even when I turned up at midnight on your first day. But it must have been much more of a disruption than I imagined. I'm sorry.'

'Stop apologizing. I had a room, I was still awake, and you didn't put me out at all. Though I can't claim to have been *entirely* unflappable.'

Now it was Will's turn to grin. 'Maybe not. The room is great. Very calming. The pinprick lights especially. Did you know that if you stare at them for too long it looks like they're twinkling?'

'I didn't,' she said. 'But maybe that suggests it's not a good idea? I don't want you suing me for eye damage. I haven't actually spent much time in there, it was the last one we finished and it went right up to the wire. What did you think it was going to be like – when I told you my rooms were unique? You didn't want to say last night.'

Will held her gaze, his fingers drumming on the glass tabletop. 'Honestly?'

Robin nodded.

'I was imagining, y'know, red satin sheets and a heart-shaped bed, maybe some fluffy handcuffs.'

Robin gasped. '*Handcuffs?*' she squealed, and then, remembering how small the garden was, lowered her voice. 'Is that the impression I gave, answering the door to you last night?'

'No, of course not,' Will said, a gleam of amusement in his eyes. 'But you looked so panicked when I asked about a room, and then you said they were "unique" in this mysterious voice and then stood outside the door for so long, as if you didn't want me to go in. What was I supposed to think?'

'Well, now I know which direction your mind wanders, I'll be more careful.' She shook her head scornfully, but a smile was threatening. She could see how she had come across as over-concerned, perhaps even a little bit unhinged.

'Hey,' Will laughed. 'Come on. I was glad to be proved

wrong. It would have been too much, on top of the late drive down, Tabitha's house and the leak, to then be offered a different kind of service when you let me in. I slept like a baby, and I'm looking forward to using that telescope to check out the real stars later, if you're happy for me to stay another night?'

'Of course,' Robin said. 'I have no bookings in that room immediately, so stay as long as you need to. Though, I should remind you that Bear Grylls would have any leak fixed within twenty-four hours.'

'Yeah,' Will said, leaning back in his chair and putting his hands behind his head, 'but I'm not under as much pressure as he usually is. And now I've got this cosy guesthouse bedroom to stay in, with fantastic cooked breakfasts every morning, I'm wondering if maybe the leak will turn out to be really difficult to repair.'

His face lit up with a lazy, easy grin, his eyes catching hers and holding on, and Robin felt her cheeks bunch into a smile. She wondered if, maybe, she wanted the leak to take a long time to fix as well.

'So what happens now, Bear?'

Will dropped his arms, running a hand through his short hair and leaving it tufty like an unruly hedgehog. 'Now I have to stop sitting in the sunshine chatting to you, and go and see what Tabitha's house looks like in daylight. I can't say it's the most appealing prospect.'

'Well.' Robin stood and picked up the empty mugs and the milk jug. 'This is not a service I was planning to offer, but I'm not going anywhere today, so if you need a refreshment break I'll do you tea or coffee, maybe even lunch if you'd like it.'

'You will?' He stood too, bending briefly and holding his

hand out towards Darcy, who got slowly up and padded after him, obedient as ever. 'That would be beyond generous.'

'It's only until you get a kettle set up in the house.'

'Of course. You've just made today a lot brighter.' He followed her inside. She could sense him behind her, could hear the patter of Darcy's paws on the linoleum.

'It's just a sandwich and a cup of tea,' Robin said, leaning against the kitchen counter.

Will stopped in the doorway, almost filling it. 'Believe me, when you're faced with clearing out your dead aunt's four-storey house that's been empty for over a year and has accumulated a leak and at least fifty thousand cobwebs, a cup of tea isn't "just" anything.'

Robin began to dry the mugs, soaking up his gratitude and, if she was honest, the pleasing sight of him standing in her doorway. 'If you'd gone down to Mrs Harris at the Seaview Hotel you wouldn't be getting this treatment.'

'I picked the right place then,' he said. 'Thank you, Robin. Is it OK if I come begging for my first cup of tea in about twenty-five minutes?'

'Don't push it,' she warned, but as she listened to her unexpected guest climb the stairs, followed by his curly-haired and completely adorable companion, she realized she would be happy to make him as many cups of tea as he wanted. Not only because she'd enjoyed the brief amount of time she'd spent in his company, but also because she hadn't been inside Tabitha's house for years, and she still felt bad about not making more of an effort to see her on her fleeting return visits from London.

She wanted to see the task that Will was faced with. She wanted to see if the house brought back any childhood memories, to find out how her loving and eccentric neighbour had lived the last years of her life, and whether there were any clues, any proof as to the origin of the plaque on the wall. Despite the promise of fifty thousand cobwebs, she was desperate to see inside number four Goldcrest Road.

Chapter 6

Robin pressed her hand against the blue plaque next to the tall, black front door with the brass knocker and remembered, when she'd been much smaller, standing up on tiptoes to try and touch the cool, smooth surface. Now it was level with her shoulder. She read the familiar words: *Jane Austen, 1775–1817, Noted Novelist, stayed here during the summer of 1804.*

Why would it be here if it wasn't true? Why was everyone so sceptical about it? It wasn't just Molly who laughed it off whenever she mentioned it; her mum and dad had never entirely believed it, and Tim had always rolled his eyes. She'd read *Persuasion*, and lots of it was set in Dorset. Lyme Regis with its Cobb wasn't far away, so surely it was plausible. And what reason could Tabitha have had to fabricate it? Maybe, now that Will was here, with his knowledge of historical houses, they would be able to get to the bottom of it. Maybe he knew the truth already.

She lifted the brass knocker to announce her arrival, but the heavy door moved forward a fraction and Robin realized it wasn't closed. She pushed it slowly inwards, peering into the gloom.

The first thing that she noticed was the dust. The air was thick with it, dancing in the shaft of sunlight she'd let in, and there was a pervading smell of damp.

'Hello?' she called. 'Door-to-door tea service?' She stood in the hallway, listening, her eyes drawn to the telephone table below a gold-framed mirror hanging over thick green wallpaper, a white, rotary-dial telephone almost glowing in the sunlight. She had a vivid memory of lifting the heavy receiver, dragging the dial round with her finger, calling random numbers purely because it was so much more exotic than her parents' push-button telephone.

'Hello?' she tried again, and this time she heard a series of clunks and bashes from upstairs, and then Darcy appeared, padding slowly down the stairs as if she wasn't used to such a steep descent.

Robin crouched and put the cup of tea on the floor, already rehearsing her counter-argument for when Will finally made an appearance and discovered his drink was no longer hot. 'Darcy,' she whispered, holding out her arms as the small dog came towards her, and gathering her into an embrace. 'You're so cute,' she whispered. The dog licked her chin and, putting a paw up on her shoulder, let out a sound that was halfway between a bark and a whine. Robin laughed, kissing her on the head, her fur impossibly soft.

'Where's Will?' she asked. 'Where's your master?'

'Master? I like the sound of that.' She heard him before she saw him, his boots heavy on the stairs, and when he appeared in the dim light of the hall he was drying his hands on a piece of old sheet. Robin could see that he was soaked again, and also filthy, with dark streaks on his T-shirt and black smudges across his forehead and cheeks.

'I brought you tea,' she said, pointing at the mug but

refusing to release her grip on Darcy. 'What happened? Did you find the leak, or have you been investigating the chimney?'

He ignored her last remark. 'I've found one of them. The roof is in serious need of repair, but I think the plumbing's shot too. I doubt if Tabitha had any maintenance work done here in the last five, or even ten years. This place is a mess.'

Robin nodded slowly, glancing around. 'How do you know that?'

Will frowned, crouched in front of her and picked up his tea, nodding his gratitude as he sipped it. 'Thank you for this. What do you mean?'

'I mean,' she said, 'how do you know it's a mess when everywhere's so dark? It's like a classic haunted house.' She winced when she realized what she'd said. 'Sorry, that was insensitive.'

Will shook his head. 'I get your point, but I blew the fuses when I tried to turn on the light last night, and one of them needs replacing before I can get the electricity working.'

'So why not use that most exciting and recent of inventions?' Robin let go of Darcy, stood and moved towards the room on the right of the hallway, but tripped on something she couldn't see and bashed her shoulder against the wall.

'What's that?' Will asked, following her. He touched her arm gently, whether to get her attention or steady her, Robin wasn't sure.

Undeterred, Robin found the edge of the curtain and pulled it dramatically backwards. 'Sunlight,' she announced, the word becoming a splutter as the movement released at least a year's worth of dust into the air. She turned away, coughing into her hands.

'Great reveal,' Will said, deadpan. 'Go as well as you'd planned?' His cough was deep but efficient, and Robin

94

thought he was probably used to clearing his throat in rooms full of dust.

She tried to give him a withering look, but her eyes were streaming. She blinked just in time to see Will's jaw tighten, his expression unreadable as he surveyed the room.

Robin did the same.

It was Tabitha's living room. The solid, green, William Morris-patterned sofas facing each other, the lace runners along the backs discoloured an unappealing yellow, the cherry wood coffee table matching the dresser on which were a number of small china sheep. The rest of the collection, she knew, were in glass cabinets in the dining room on the opposite side of the hall. Robin had played cards in here, eating Tabitha's homemade scones thick with unsalted butter. Gin Rummy, Snap, sometimes dominoes. Even Tim, she remembered, liked coming round to see Tabitha, and they'd often stayed until they were called back next door for dinner.

Why hadn't she kept in touch with her properly? Robin felt a surge of anger at herself. The older woman had been so much a part of her childhood, but had quickly become out of sight and out of mind once she'd moved to London, rarely seeing her on her return visits to Campion Bay. Either she'd been too caught up with Tim, or – after they'd broken up – the fledgling business she was starting with Neve. Planning, researching locations and luxuries, her head in London even if, physically, she was spending a weekend in her parents' company. Time had passed almost without her noticing, a part of her thinking that Tabitha would always be here. But of course that wasn't true, and now it was too late.

She pushed the anger aside. Tabitha hadn't been her relative; this must be so much harder for Will, and he hadn't moved a muscle.

'Are you OK?' she asked.

'Yeah.' He cleared his throat again. 'Yeah, of course. It's just strange, seeing it now, like this.'

'When was the last time you saw her?' Robin asked, running her fingers along the back of a sofa.

'About six months before she died. And I didn't even know she was ill. I couldn't get down as often as I wanted to – I didn't come as often as I *could* have. And I should have . . .' He shook his head, hands on his waist as he looked around the room. The bedraggled sheet was sticking out of the back pocket of his jeans, looking like a ridiculous tail.

'Should have what?'

'I should have come here before now. It wouldn't have seemed so . . .'

'Intimidating? Difficult? Monumental?'

He flashed her a look that could have been irritation, but it disappeared in a smile of resignation. 'Impossible. It's going to take months to get anywhere.'

'So you *will* have to look for work round here?'

He nodded. 'I've got some money set aside, but it looks like I'll need to supplement it. I can turn my hand to whatever's needed – odd jobs, estate management – and tourist season on the south coast should throw up some possibilities. Once I get the electricity sorted out, clear a small patch of calm in amongst all this, I can start looking at job sites.'

'You can do that next door,' Robin said. 'You've got Starcross, or Sea Shanty, the room downstairs. Guests will come and go, and I'll be there a lot of the time, but it shouldn't be too distracting. I can see you wouldn't want to spend every day working on this – it'll be draining.'

Will nodded, his eyes narrowed as he looked over his aunt's belongings. 'Thank you.'

Robin bit her lip. 'And I could . . . I could help you, here. Sometimes.'

Was she really offering this? She'd just opened up a new guesthouse, and should be spending all her time and energy getting comfortable with the routine. But, perhaps because she didn't have the same weight of responsibility as Will had, because Tabitha had been a neighbour and not a relative, a happy part of her childhood, she saw the task as intriguing, a treasure-trove of the past to investigate. Something Will might relish in his usual line of work, but which he was too close to see without feelings crowding in on top of him. There were bound to be spiders and grime and mess, but Robin wasn't bothered by any of that. Molly would probably be more upset because Robin would have to delay her manicure.

Will turned to face her, his arms dropping to his sides. 'I can't ask you to help me.'

'You're not asking, I'm offering.'

He took a step towards her. 'I could just sell it, leave it to whoever buys it to sort out. If a developer was interested, then none of this would matter.'

Robin pictured Tim rubbing his hands with glee, his blue eyes alight at the prospect. 'But would that be doing justice to your aunt? Leaving everything like this, not going through it? It's not going to be easy, but maybe if it's not just you and Darcy, then it will seem more manageable.'

They both watched as the dog explored the room, her short tail sticking up excitedly, wagging as she delved into the darkest corners.

'Where did Darcy come from?' Robin asked. 'I know I'm being judgmental, but I wouldn't have put the two of you together. What is she, a cockapoo?'

'Cavapoo,' Will said, giving her a quick glance. 'And no offence taken. I had a neighbour, when I lived in Beckenham. Selina. We exchanged pleasantries, but nothing more than that. She was going to Seville for three weeks.' He ran his hand back and forward through his hair, absent-mindedly. 'She couldn't take Darcy with her, and asked if I'd be happy to look after her while she was gone. She told me Darcy'd had a bad reaction to a previous kennel visit, that she couldn't bear the thought of her being locked away. I didn't have much experience with dogs, my family were never pet people, but she'd always seemed well-behaved. As you can see, she's not much trouble.'

As he said this, Darcy tried to back out from underneath a table and knocked a vase off the top of it.

'Perfect timing,' Will said, smiling gently. The vase seemed to have survived its fall to the thick carpet, but neither Will nor Robin moved forward to be certain.

'What happened to Selina?' Robin asked, her voice almost a whisper. 'Why didn't she come back for Darcy?' A catalogue of horrendous things fired through her head, culminating in a memory rather than a fantasy; a night that still replayed itself to Robin in flashbacks and nightmares. The ambulance, blue lights in the darkness, screams and shouts and running feet.

'She met someone,' Will said, shrugging. 'She said he was her soul mate, and that she wasn't coming back to London. She'd organize her belongings, but could I take Darcy to a rescue centre?' He shook his head, sucking air in through his lips at the memory, and Robin tried to hear him past the pounding in her ears. 'I'd spent nearly a month with Darcy by this point, and it . . . well, there was no way I could see her going into a cage, however temporary it might be. So'

– he flung his arms wide – 'me and Darcy, BFFs forever. She came with me when I moved into Downe Hall. She thinks she's in charge of the gardens.' He turned to her, his smile dropping as he saw her expression. 'Are you OK? You look pale.'

'I – I'm fine,' Robin managed. Her heart was thumping, her mind swirling with unwelcome emotions. It had been a long time since she'd been overcome so unexpectedly with the horror of that night. She thought she had reached a place of control, able to access the memory and the grief when she chose to, then put them neatly back in their box. She stared down at her shoulder, realizing the weight she felt was Will's hand. She thought about blaming the dust, but he didn't seem like the kind of person who could be easily fobbed off.

'Do you want to get some fresh air?' he asked. 'You don't have to help me. It was an offer over and above the remit of guesthouse owner, or friend, even.'

Robin peered out of the window, but it was so smeared she could only see a hazy approximation of the promenade and the sea beyond. 'Fresh air would be good. But that doesn't mean I'm bailing on you so soon after offering. What time do you want your next break?'

Will glanced at his watch, but before he'd had a chance to reply Darcy started barking, her yelps short and high-pitched. She raced across the room, weaving between table legs, and sat behind Will, her tongue sticking out.

'What was all that about?' Will's tone was more curious than anxious.

'Ah.' Robin pointed to the far corner of the room, giggling with relief as her composure began to return. 'Not a great hunter, then?'

Will looked in the direction of her finger, then raised his eyebrows and shook his head slowly. 'It's not even a rat, Darcy. It's just a mouse. A tiny, helpless little mouse.' The dog whimpered in response. 'Come on then, let's get some fresh air as well.'

Robin stepped into the sunshine and waited for Will and Darcy to join her on the top step. 'When shall I bring you more tea?'

'You don't have to, Robin. You've helped me enough already.'

'I'm only next door, and I've got full access to a kettle and electricity.'

Will looked down at her, his eyes searching her face. 'Let me sort out my own lunch. I'll take Darcy along the prom and see what I can find, but maybe later this afternoon?'

'Done,' she said, pleased with the compromise. 'I have a feeling that it's easy to get lost in that house if you spend too long inside.'

'I might risk opening a few more curtains when I get back.'

'Brave move, Mr Nightingale.'

'No less than Bear Grylls would attempt.' He flashed her a quick grin and then jogged down the stairs, leaving Robin standing on Tabitha's top step with only the plaque for company, wondering why she was being quite so helpful to a man she'd only just met.

'Tabitha's nephew?' Molly asked, leaning over the white desk in her airy reception area and pouring another sugar sachet into her tea. 'Where did he come from? I didn't know about any of Tabitha's family. Mind you, she wasn't the chattiest to me, always bright and breezy but never that forthcoming.'

Robin screwed her nose up, thinking back. 'I'm not sure she was ever like that with me, though I guess it's different when you're young. I never looked for moods or motives, just took advantage of her friendliness. But I'm almost certain she never mentioned a nephew to me either.'

'And you didn't even have to offer him a cup of sugar,' Molly said, grinning. 'He played right into your hands. And what did he think of Starcross? Think its magic will work on him?'

'Magic? What do you mean?'

'All that astrology stuff. It's not just a room for stargazers, is it?'

'It's a room for whoever wants to stay in it,' Robin replied sniffily. Neve's influence on the room had collided with her thoughts about Will even though she'd known him for less than twelve hours, and that was after thinking that Tim's return to her life was significant. She was going to wish she'd never picked cosmic destiny as part of the room's inspiration – or at the very least she would have to do some research into how it worked, instead of believing every encounter with a person of the opposite sex had a special meaning.

'Get you, Robin!' Molly laughed. 'You've already thought about it, haven't you? I want *all* the details. What's he like? What's he going to do with the house, and on a scale of one to ten, how sexy is he?'

Robin sank back into Molly's white leather sofa, wondering briefly if any of the grime from Tabitha's house was still clinging to her and was about to upset the pristine simplicity of Groom with a View.

'He's nice,' she started, noncommittally, 'and his dog is adorable. I think he's a bit overwhelmed by having to deal with Tabitha's house on his own – I have no idea where the rest of her family is. If he's her nephew, then she's at least got a brother – or a sister who kept her own surname – somewhere.'

'Unless they're dead, and it's all been left to Will.'

Robin tipped her head on one side, considering. 'Possibly. Anyway, he's not sure what to do with the house. He's made noises about selling it, but I think he's a long way off making that decision.'

'So you have time, then.' Molly made a few swift clicks with the mouse, and then joined Robin on the sofa.

'Time for what?'

'To get him to change his mind, to convince him not to sell.'

'Why would I want to do that?' Robin asked, although she knew what Molly was going to say, and she had a couple of reasons of her own that had nothing to do with Tim or Malcolm.

'To protect Goldcrest Road, of course. God, Robin, haven't you been paying attention to anyone? To Mrs Harris's mad tirade, to Tim's blue-eyed, weasely charisma.'

'That's not how you described him last night!'

'Oh come on, he's gorgeous, but we both know he has his sights fixed firmly on number four. If Will's there dealing with his aunt's stuff, all vulnerable and confused, Tim's going to pick him off like a duck at a fairground. We need to launch a campaign, and you need to be at the heart of it, because you've already wormed your way in. He's in your guesthouse, under your roof, drinking your tea.'

Robin pressed her fingers to her lips. 'I offered to help him with Tabitha's house,' she murmured. 'Why did I do that? I don't have the time.'

'There you go, then,' Molly said triumphantly. 'You're

already doing it. You're in the perfect place to prove to Mr Nightingale just how great Campion Bay is, and that Tabitha's house, once it's been put right, is an ideal second home for him – or first home – whatever.' She sipped her tea and beamed at Robin.

'Why do you care so much?'

'Because I'm here too, silly. I don't want Tim turning this place into some swanky seafront apartment building, or a bloody Costa Coffee.'

'Even if you end up with lots more rich clients on your doorstep?'

Molly shrugged, not quite meeting Robin's gaze. 'I'm not selfish, and I know that, as much as it's tempting, it's not going to suit everyone. If this Will bloke is decent, then much better that he keeps the house intact, or sells it privately. So, what shall we call our campaign? It has to have a catchy name – or a code name, so he doesn't find out what we're doing. The *Campion Bay Crusade*, or *Will he, Won't he*. How about *Where there's a Will there's a Way?* What would that acronym be? WTAWTAW. That's almost catchy – how about "Tawtaw" for short?'

Robin shifted on the sofa, uneasy with the idea of launching a campaign to keep Will here, as much as she agreed with the outcome. 'It doesn't have to be an *official* campaign,' she said. 'Let's just show him how lovely Campion Bay is. We'd welcome any new neighbour like that.'

'Don't be such a wuss, Robin. What's wrong with Campaign Tawtaw?'

'It's too close to *twat* for my liking.'

Molly rolled her eyes. 'If you don't go into this with any oomph then you won't get the right result. Anyway, you didn't answer my other question. Is this Will guy attractive? Does he up the totty-factor in Campion Bay? Oh,' she said, inhaling sharply, 'don't tell me, I can see it all over your face. It's like a bloody map of your heart.'

'What's wrong with my face?' Robin asked aghast, feeling heat creep across her neck. 'I haven't formed any meaningful opinions about him, other than that he seems fairly nice and he's got a cute dog.'

'Cute *dog*? Is that what you're going with? You've already picked out chair coverings for your wedding. Oh, Robin, what a turn up for the books this is, huh?' She stood as the door-bell went, signalling the arrival of her next client. 'So much landing on your doorstep, and so soon after opening, too. You'd better book yourself in for that manicure – and a facial while you're at it. Hello, Mrs Wilkinson, make your way through and I'll be along in a moment.'

Molly led Mrs Wilkinson into the treatment room and then turned round to give Robin a direct stare. 'Campaign Tawtaw,' she said in a loud whisper. 'I can see you're already invested in it. Get the hottie and his dog to stay, and the residents of Goldcrest Road will be indebted to you forever.' She closed the door behind her, leaving Robin alone in the airy reception room, the purple orchid on the windowsill dancing gently in the breeze.

'Campaign Tawtaw,' she murmured. 'Ridiculous idea.' She left her friend to it, closing the front door and hurrying down the steps, turning not towards the guesthouse but crossing the road towards the promenade and the beach. The best place to clear her head and sort through her thoughts was beneath the cliffs on Campion Bay's wild beach.

The waves crashed beside her as she walked, a constant and steady rhythm that Robin found comforting. Molly was right

– a lot had happened in the last few days, and that was if she put aside the opening of her new business, welcoming holidaymakers through her doors, seeing the new, improved Campion Bay Guesthouse become a reality.

She'd known it would only be a matter of time before she saw Tim, but for him to be so attentive and keen to see the rooms, to seem to want to slot himself back into her life, was unexpected. Had she encouraged him? She couldn't believe that a man like him, with charm and ambition and those golden curls, would be single for very long. But maybe old habits died hard, and she wasn't the only one he was being attentive to.

Then there was Tabitha's house. It was, in essence, an empty house. But now it was at the centre of a tug-of-war that Robin didn't think she had fully grasped the extent of. What was it Molly had said? *The residents of Goldcrest Road will be indebted to you forever.* Were they all as passionate as Mrs Harris – Ashley and Roxy, Stefano and Nicolas at the taverna? Robin didn't want the beautiful seafront houses being developed – they had history, and looked out to sea with a grandeur Robin had always loved. But was there a strong underlying current that Robin had missed since she'd been back?

She jumped as a loud wave crashed alongside her, and realized she had unconsciously steered towards the water. Was it Tim and Malcolm's influence that had led to Will turning up? Had they tracked him down and called him, told him not to mention their involvement to anyone else he met in Campion Bay?

She had offered to help him clear out Tabitha's house, but didn't feel like she'd been fully in control as she'd spoken the words, as if there were stronger forces at work. It made her think of Neve's belief in destiny. Robin couldn't fully agree with her friend's convictions, not least because of the unfairness of what had happened to her, but there were certain things about the last few days that were making her wonder. They had started to distract her from thoughts of the guesthouse, of future check-ins and the shopping she needed to do over the next few days.

She'd had no choice but to put Will in Starcross and then, when she'd been with him in Tabitha's house, her last memory of Neve had returned as powerfully as a blow to the stomach. Robin hadn't felt that way for months; since focusing on the guesthouse she'd started to see her grief as a permanent, but manageable, part of her life, and had been completely unprepared to be taken back to that night.

Eventually Robin began to make her way back to Goldcrest Road. The sun was sparkling on the water, and the breeze was gentle with a promise of summer warmth. Skull Island was full of people taking advantage of the good weather and the last day of the weekend, and the smell of fish and chips wafted through the air, making her stomach rumble.

She looked up at the seafront houses as she passed them; the teashop that Roxy and Ashley ran, Mrs Harris's net-curtained guesthouse, the pink front door of Groom with a View. Will's Alfa Romeo was parked outside number four, and while the downstairs curtains were open, Robin couldn't see any movement inside. She was worried that she'd unnerved him with her offer of help, and that he was planning on waiting until after dark to sneak back into Starcross so he could avoid seeing her.

As Robin crossed the road she saw the taillights of a black Audi, braking hard and turning up a side street towards the centre of Campion Bay. She thought of Tim's assurance that no plans had yet been made about Tabitha's house, and Molly's insistence that Robin could play a role in convincing Will not to sell. As she stood in front of her guesthouse, Robin took a deep breath.

She had been worried when she'd made the decision to move back to Campion Bay that she'd be bored; that the sleepy seaside town wouldn't come close to the excitement she'd had in London. Her new business had been open for twenty-four hours and, while the guests themselves were no trouble at all, she didn't think boredom would be on her list of problems. If anything, she would struggle to fit everything in, but already the thought of taking back her offer to Will, of not helping him go through Tabitha's things or spending time getting to know him, left her with a dull ache in her chest.

Robin opened the front door and took a second to listen, to see if any of the guests were home and in need of a mid-afternoon cuppa. When she was met with silence, she went into Sea Shanty to check Will in on GuestSmart. She found that she was grinning as she typed his name. She hit enter, and a blue box in the top of the screen flashed: *Fully Booked*.

It was her first weekend, and she was fully booked. Being back in Campion Bay was starting to feel like coming home, but a fresh, sparkling home with a new coat of paint and more intrigue and opportunities than she had ever imagined. Reopening the guesthouse, Robin realized, was just the beginning.

The Once in a Blue Moon Guesthouse

FULLY BOOKED

Chapter 7

'Maybe if we back off a bit, he'll decide to come out of his own accord?'

The voice was coming from the top of the stairs and Robin paused at the bottom of them, frowning. It sounded like Mrs Barker, one of the guests who had checked in the day before.

'But we tried that for ages,' said a younger voice. 'I think he's in for the long haul, unless we can actually get to him.' Robin thought that was Catriona, who was staying in Rockpool with her boyfriend, Neil. He was the one who spoke next.

'I don't see how we're going to do that, unless anyone happens to have any chicken or prawns on them? Shit, what are we going to say to Robin?'

'I'm sure by the time she returns it will all be resolved,' Mrs Barker said, though her tone wasn't very convincing.

Unable to restrain her curiosity any longer, Robin dumped her shopping bags on the floor, hung her coat on the hook in the hall and climbed the stairs to the first floor. She knocked on the door, which was already wide open, her movements slowing as she took in the scene in front of her.

All three of her guests were crouched on the floor around the bed; Catriona looked like she was in the process of crawling underneath it, and the top of the chest of drawers and floor surrounding it was a mess of sugar, teabags and make-up. It looked like there had been a mini explosion in the room, and the occupants were trying to retrieve something vital from where it had landed, just out of reach.

'Hello?' she asked. 'Is everything OK? I heard voices and I wondered if I could be of any help?'

Neil turned towards her, his eyes widening in alarm. 'We've got a bit of an issue.'

'Easily solvable, I'm sure,' Mrs Barker quickly added, putting her weight on the duvet cover and pulling herself up to standing.

'It's my fault,' Catriona said, her voice muffled. 'I left the door open and when I came out of the bathroom, Eclipse was climbing up there.' She gestured forlornly at the huge tropical fish-tank set in the wall, and Robin could just make out scratches in the turquoise paintwork alongside it.

'Ah,' she said, pressing her lips together.

'And then when Catriona tried to get him off,' Neil said, 'he jumped out of her arms, bounced across the chest of drawers and lodged himself under the bed. Now none of us can reach him.'

'I promise we'll pay for any damages,' Catriona rushed. 'Nothing looks broken, I think it's just the paint.'

Robin crouched next to Catriona and put a hand on her shoulder. 'He didn't scratch you, did he?'

Catriona shook her head sheepishly.

'Then no damage done,' Robin said softly. 'Eclipse is my responsibility. He's curious and he's not going to ignore a huge tank of fish when he discovers it. It's not up to you to keep the door closed. As long as you're OK, and none of your things have been broken, then that's the main thing.'

Catriona visibly relaxed, and Neil sighed behind her.

'So all that remains,' Mrs Barker said, 'is to work out how to get your kitten out from under the bed.'

'I'm pretty sure I can solve that one. Give me a moment.' Robin squeezed Neil's arm reassuringly as she left the room and set off down the stairs, silently berating herself for letting her guests get in that situation. She didn't know how she could stop Eclipse exploring when the bedroom doors were open; she'd have to be stricter about where he could go when she was out of the house, when she wouldn't be available to deal with any issues that arose. She collected the pot of cat treats from the kitchen cupboard and hurried back to Rockpool, shaking it as she crouched on the floor.

Within two seconds the kitten appeared, his front paws clawing into the rug to pull himself out from his hiding space. He purred loudly, his eyes shut in contentment as he wound himself around her, as if to prove that he was the loveliest and most well-behaved cat in the world.

'You little terror,' she said, and then to her guests: 'I'm sorry to have caused you so much upset.'

Catriona knelt next to her and stroked Eclipse. 'You haven't, honestly. I was just worried he'd be stuck under there for ever, and I'm so sorry about the wall.'

'Please don't be,' Robin urged. 'I can have that patched up in no time. Don't feel bad about my cat's terrible behaviour. I'll take him downstairs before he can cause any more damage.' She lifted Eclipse into her arms and he went limp, looking up at her adoringly. 'What a suck-up. Let me fix you afternoon tea to make up for this, I've bought some fresh cream cakes that I shouldn't eat all by myself.'

113

Mrs Barker sighed. 'It sounds lovely, but I've got to go and retrieve my husband. I left him talking to a local fisherman on the beach an hour ago, and we're meant to be walking into town this evening.'

'I'll have a cake,' Catriona said. 'I must have used up a few hundred calories wiggling backwards and forwards under the bed.'

Robin took Eclipse downstairs and was arranging the cakes on a plate when her phone buzzed with a message from Molly:

Will is going to love it here. Debrief soon. Xx

Robin's stomach flipped over. From her text Robin thought her friend must have already started to put her ridiculous Campaign Tawtaw into action.

She'd known Will for less than a day, but – if she was being perfectly honest with herself – she had spent rather a lot of that time thinking about the man with the toffee-coloured hair and startlingly green eyes.

Because of this, she was uncomfortable that Molly wanted to go behind his back to try to convince him not to sell. Robin would prefer him to stay, but felt that it made sense to tell him outright what was going on.

And if she was a part of her friend's plan, didn't that mean that she was also going behind Tim's back?

She tapped out a reply to her friend.

What are you doing? Don't be too obvious.

She shouldn't be encouraging Molly at all – she should tell her that she wasn't going to have any part of it. But Molly was her closest friend, and she didn't want to risk upsetting their friendship. She was concerned, too, that if she told Will about Tim's plans for his aunt's house, he might be encouraged to take him up on whatever he was offering, especially after seeing the state of the house for herself earlier. Shoving her phone back in her trouser pocket she took a tray of cakes and tea to Neil and Catriona.

Once her guests had all returned in a flurry of activity and then left again for their various evening entertainments, Robin put her dinner in the oven and sat on the stool in front of the old upright piano in Sea Shanty. She'd had it tuned, the dust on the keys removed, the wood polished until it gleamed. She had hardly played since she'd been back in Campion Bay, and not at all when she'd lived in London, so to say she was rusty was an understatement.

She pressed middle C, let the sound echo out in the quiet room, and then pressed D. At least with a piano the individual notes sounded good even if you didn't know what you were doing. With a wind instrument, the hesitation came out with each breath. She thought back to the tunes she had once known off by heart: 'Chopsticks', 'The Entertainer', and the *Beverly Hills Cop* theme she'd learnt from a boy at primary school.

The memories seemed to have stayed in her fingers, if not her head, and while she was far from note-perfect, she found that the sound she was making wasn't awful. Eclipse didn't move from his position on the sofa, which she took as a good sign, and it was only when the smoke alarm went off that she realized she'd played through the timer.

'Shit!' She ran into the kitchen, which was now impersonating a horror film set, the smoke thick and acrid. Shoving on the oven glove, she took out what was left of her chicken Kiev and put it on the thermo-mat. It was a shrivelled, sizzling black lump, the potatoes boiled dry and foul-smelling in their saucepan. She flapped at the smoke alarm to shut it up, left the ruined food to cool down and began grating some cheddar.

'Bonfires usually take place outside, you know.'

Robin jumped and turned to see Will standing in the doorway. He had looked messy this morning, but now he was a complete wreck. His T-shirt's original colour was unguessable, his face was a mixture of grime and sweat, and his hair was flattened and dusty. But his green eyes shone out at her, despite his obvious weariness.

'How many rounds did you go with the house?' she asked. 'Not that it matters, you clearly lost.'

Will gave her a triumphant smile. 'I won, actually. The plumbing is fixed for now, though at some point I'll need to get a professional to take a look at it. And I've cleared one of the rooms to an acceptable level. Six bin bags and a year's worth of dirt later, my first day's work is done. And it wouldn't have gone nearly so smoothly without refreshment breaks, so thank you.'

'You're welcome,' she said. 'It sounds like you've made lots of progress. Though I, uhm . . .' she gestured towards him '. . . not sure about the new look.' She didn't want to be rude, but she'd spent a lot of time getting her guesthouse up to a luxurious standard, and she didn't know how much of the grime on his clothes was indelible grease.

He glanced down and then looked at her, aghast. 'God, I'm so sorry. How about I leave these clothes next door? I haven't tried the shower yet, though, so if I could . . .' He pointed in the vague direction of Starcross.

'Of course,' Robin said hurriedly. 'And you don't have to leave your clothes next door. But if you could maybe get changed in here?' She gestured to the kitchen. 'I can find you a robe, I'm sure.'

'Oh. No problem.' He moved carefully into the kitchen, passing her, and Robin set off down the hall, abandoning

her half-grated cheese. The door to her bedroom was opposite the door into Sea Shanty. She stood inside and looked
frantically around for the robe she'd promised him, her eyes
falling on the short, silk summer dressing gown, navy with
silvery stars covering it, hanging on the wardrobe door.

'Shit.'

There were towelling robes in all of the bedrooms, but
that would mean going up to Starcross. She hurried back
into the hall, trying to remember if there was a spare in Sea
Shanty that she could give to Will, and almost ran straight
into him. He was heading towards the stairs, carrying his
clothes in a bundle, and she found herself very close to his
broad chest. Her eyes followed it down, to his toned stomach
and then a hint of red boxers behind the clothes and boots
in his arms.

'Sorry!' she squeaked, dragging her gaze up to meet his.

'You disappeared.' He gave her a lopsided smile. 'I thought
I could sneak away unnoticed. That's failed, clearly.'

'Yes, well, you wouldn't have wanted my robe anyway. It
wouldn't have covered much more . . .' Her voice trailed off
and she felt her cheeks turn as red as his boxer shorts.

He cleared his throat. 'Do you want any help with your
bonfire when I come down?'

She shook her head. 'It's beyond rescuing. I'm going for
cheese on toast, if you want any? I wasn't sure if you had
plans for tonight.' *Apart from standing half-naked in my
hallway.* He didn't seem that embarrassed, certainly nowhere
near as flustered as she was, and she was the one who'd asked
him to strip in the first place.

'No plans,' he said. 'I've not got enough energy to hit the
nightspots of Campion Bay, whatever those might be. I didn't
realize you offered a restaurant service.'

'Only cheese on toast,' she blurted, and then added weakly: 'It's my speciality.'

'I'd love some. Give me ten minutes?' He glanced down apologetically and Robin nodded, dropping her gaze to the floor. Darcy was sitting quietly between them, her brown eyes wide with curiosity, and Robin's blush went deeper.

'Take as long as you need.' She heard him climb the stairs and then, despite the strong urge to see what the boxers looked like from behind, when she was sure he'd turned the corner to the second flight, raised her head and exhaled. She would have to tell him about Molly's plan to charm him into staying. She couldn't bear the thought of lying to him; there was something about Will Nightingale – a man who was comfortable talking to her in only his boxer shorts – that demanded honesty.

The sun had picked that Sunday evening to set spectacularly, bold streaks of peach and fuchsia lighting up the sky, highlighting the dark waves with a golden edge. Robin and Will stood side by side in Sea Shanty watching it, with the window open and the sound of the waves filling their awed, slightly uncomfortable, silence.

'Sunsets never look this impressive in London,' Will said eventually, 'mainly because there just isn't as much sky. The buildings dilute the effect.'

'It is a hazard, living down here,' Robin admitted. 'Being in sight of the sea the whole time means there's always something interesting to watch. I could spend entire days standing here, watching boats pass or the different cloud formations, or just people walking by on their way to the beach or town.'

'Ah, people watching.' Will nodded knowingly. 'One of the greatest pastimes.'

'I expect you got to do a lot of that, working at a stately home?'

'I did,' Will said. 'Meeting new people was one of the best parts of the job. You're ideally placed for human observation too – inviting guests into what is essentially your home.'

'I am,' Robin said, surprised. 'I hadn't thought of it like that. But, let's face it, only a day in and I've already had a few interesting things happen.'

She felt Will shift slightly beside her. 'I take it you're referring to the imbecile who turned up on your doorstep at midnight looking like he'd just gone for a swim.'

'Well, there's that,' Robin said, smiling.

'And, Robin, about before. I really did think I had time to get upstairs.'

She shook her head. 'It's forgotten. Well, not forgotten, but I had a cat saga this afternoon. I'm going to have to get used to eventful days.'

'Cat saga?' Will turned to her, his brows lowered. His hair was fluffy after his shower and, she assumed, some extensive towel drying, and she realized that the frown didn't sit well on his face. Maybe it was because it obscured his eyes, but she got the general impression that he didn't do bad-humoured very often.

'I'll tell you all about it, but I'd better rescue the cheese on toast or it'll go the same way as dinner number one.'

They sat opposite each other at the long table, the golden cheese still fizzing on top of the toast, with pots of Robin's homemade garlic mayonnaise on the side and large mugs of steaming tea.

'It doesn't work with anything else,' Robin said. 'Cheese on toast can't be improved with wine or beer – or even coffee. It has to be tea.'

Will narrowed his eyes, cut a soldier off his toast and dipped it in the mayonnaise. 'Did you say you made this mayonnaise? It's delicious.'

Robin sat back, enjoying the compliment before she gave the game away. 'It's Hellmann's mayo. I just added some crushed garlic cloves.'

Will nodded, a smile tugging at the edges of his mouth. 'Classy move. Why go to the effort of making it from scratch when a couple of well-placed modifications will do?'

'I am running a guesthouse, after all,' Robin said. 'I have to strike the right balance between quality and efficiency.'

'It sounds like you're already a pro.' Will sipped his tea and glanced towards the sofas, where Darcy had chosen to snooze.

'My parents ran the guesthouse before me,' Robin said. 'So I grew up in the environment, absorbing it all without ever considering that I would end up making my living this way.'

'This wasn't your plan all along, then?'

Robin shook her head. 'I lived in London for a long time and only moved back here last year. My parents wanted to move to France, and it seemed like the logical thing to do, taking over from them. I've restyled it completely, though. My parents didn't go in for room names or themes.'

'It's a great idea. I saw the other rooms in your welcome pack, and I think I should be staying in Wilderness.' He smiled at her, and Robin took a moment to get the joke.

'Ah,' she said, 'Bear Grylls. Of course.' Remembering how Will had compared himself to the celebrity adventurer when they'd first met. 'Well, Starcross is my favourite room, so in my opinion you've got the best deal.' She glanced at the table, suddenly embarrassed that she'd admitted this to him.

'I'm honoured. And a little bemused, if I'm honest.' Will

mopped the last of the mayonnaise up with his final piece of toast and rested his elbows on the table. He was wearing a navy jumper speckled with threads of different colours, the sleeves rolled up, exposing his forearms and reminding Robin – as if she was likely to forget – that she'd seen a lot more of him than that.

'Why?' Robin asked, wrapping her hands around her large mug and letting the steam hit her face.

'Because – and don't take this the wrong way – I hadn't expected everyone to be so friendly.'

Robin felt a wave of discomfort. 'You've come from near London to the seaside. Everyone's bound to be friendlier down here – we're not all trying to live our lives at a hundred miles an hour.'

'Yeah, but this is extreme. The guy from the teashop a few doors down – Ashley – brought me a box of cupcakes as a welcome present. And then he stayed and helped me bag up loads of rubbish. How did he know I was here? And does everyone go out of their way to help here – I mean, all the time? How do you live your own lives?'

Robin closed her eyes. *Will is going to* love *it here.* Molly must have asked Ashley to take those cakes round to him.

'It . . . uh, Will?'

'Yes?' He looked directly at her, his face open and expectant, clearly pleased by the acts of kindness, and Robin found she couldn't tell him. She *should*, but already, the thought that he might see her behaviour towards him – offering to help with Tabitha's house, the cheese on toast – as something other than genuine, was too horrible. And if she told him about Tim's plan for his aunt's house, and of Molly and Mrs Harris's concerns about the possible development, then that's what he would think. It was inevitable that her kindness would

121

be seen as part of Molly's charm offensive, with the sole aim of stopping him from selling the house to Tim.

He gave her a questioning smile when she didn't answer. 'Are you OK?'

'Yes, sure. Of course. What flavour cakes are they?'

'Sorry?'

'The cakes Ashley brought you? What flavour? They do an amazing lemon and poppy seed muffin down there, and their scones are the best I've tasted.'

'I haven't even looked, to be honest,' Will said. 'I was so busy sorting things out that I just took the box and put it down . . .' His words faded away and his eyes widened. 'Shit, I've left them at Tabitha's house.'

'Well, that's OK, I don't think the grime will be able to get *inside* the box.'

'But what about the furry friend Darcy was so terrified of?' Will was already standing. 'After having to hunt out scraps in an abandoned house for the last six months, mice will home straight in on cake. I'll be back in a few minutes, and if they've survived, we can have them for pudding – the cakes, not the mice.' He grinned at her.

'You don't need to—'

'You provided the first course, it's only fair. Darcy, stay.' He pointed at the little dog who, from what Robin could see, had no intention of leaving her cosy spot on the sofa, and hurried out of the room.

Robin couldn't resist.

As soon as Will had gone she went over to the sofa and sat next to Darcy, putting her hands in the Cavapoo's soft, springy fur. Darcy sniffed and moved her head forwards, licking Robin's hand with her rough tongue. Robin bent and buried her nose in the dog's coat, and then felt the lightest weight land on her lap. She sat up to find Eclipse looking at her, his kitten eyes too big for his face. He gave a squeak of a meow and then put a paw out and tentatively tapped Darcy's leg.

Robin held her breath, waiting for Darcy to spring to her feet and bark, but Eclipse kept pawing gently and Darcy just looked at the small cat, her eyes barely visible beneath curly eyebrows, and after a moment started whining, so quietly that Robin could only just hear.

'Oh, Darcy,' she said, stroking the dog with one hand and Eclipse with the other, 'it's OK. Eclipse won't hurt you, he's about a fifth of your size. You won't, will you?' She smiled at her cat and he blinked at her. 'You could be great friends. It would be like *Homeward Bound*, only without the horrendous journey.'

The doorbell pealed and, thinking Will had forgotten his key, Robin put Eclipse in her space next to Darcy and went to answer it. When she opened the door, it wasn't Will and some cupcakes smiling down at her.

'Tim,' she said, startled. 'Hello.'

'Robin. How are you?' He stepped into the hallway before she had invited him. He was still wearing his suit, dark grey with a white shirt beneath. The tie had gone, the top button open, and he looked like a model doing post-work dishevelled for a magazine shoot. 'How was your first night with a house full of holidaymakers?'

'Good,' she said, and then remembered she hadn't told Will about the incident with Eclipse in Rockpool, just as she realized she didn't want to give Tim this anecdote. Even though it was harmless, revealing any signs of imperfection to Tim didn't sit right with her. 'I've actually got a full house. Someone booked into my last empty room yesterday evening, so it couldn't have gone better.'

She gave him a bright smile and he nodded distractedly, surveying the hallway as if talking to her was bottom of his to-do list.

'Can I help you with anything? Did you come round for a drink, or . . .?'

'No,' Tim said. 'I came by with a question. You see, I've heard that—'

His words were cut off by a loud commotion coming from Sea Shanty, which Robin recognized as unhappy animals.

'Oh no.' She rushed into the room to find Eclipse standing on the arm of the sofa, his tail fluffed, squeaking down at Darcy, who had managed to fit herself under the piano stool. Anyone else would have found her kitten's attempt at dominance hilarious, but she already knew that Darcy was lacking in the bravery department.

'Eclipse,' she said, pulling him into her arms. 'What happened? What did she do to you? I'm sorry Darcy's here; I shouldn't have left you alone together so soon. I promise she's lovely, and if you just give it time . . .' She stroked him and eventually his body stopped shaking, his purrs much louder than his attempts at meowing. She kissed him on the forehead and put him gently on the sofa. He eyed Darcy warily.

Tim appeared in the doorway. 'That's a lot of commotion for such a small cat.'

'It's my fault,' Robin said. 'I should have prepared him for dogs.' She crouched next to the piano stool, turning her back on Tim. 'Come on, Darcy, you can come out now. I'm sorry about Eclipse. He's just protecting his territory.' She stroked her paw and the dog padded forward, whimpering, and allowed Robin to gather her on to her lap. 'You're a soft thing. You and Will are like chalk and cheese.'

'Who's Will?' Tim asked. 'And more to the point, who's this? Are you opening a home for stray animals as well as a guesthouse? I'm not sure they're the most harmonious businesses.'

'This is Darcy,' Robin said. 'She belongs to a guest. And I shouldn't have left her alone with Eclipse – not so soon.' The dog was still whimpering, but Eclipse had calmed down and was curled into a ball, almost lost against the navy fabric of the sofa.

'Right,' Tim said, his pale brows knitting together, his voice laced with irritation. 'Look, Robs, I just came round to ask about next door. Malcolm hasn't had a chance to get in touch with Tabitha's family yet – there's a nephew he's tracked down – but I heard that someone's moved in. And the curtains were open as I passed.'

Robin focused on Darcy, rubbing the thick fur on her nose. 'You've been driving past?' She knew she sounded cross, but if she ended up being the reason Tim and Will met, and then Tim used his salesman tactics to secure a sale while Will was off guard and undecided, then she'd have let everyone on Goldcrest Road down, not to mention lost Will before she'd even got to know him properly. It was so hard to think with Tim standing over her.

'I drove past just now,' he said. 'There's a light on, too. If you don't know anything, then that's fine.' Robin didn't answer. He shrugged and turned towards the door, and Robin breathed a sigh of relief. But then his whole body stiffened and he rotated slowly, staring down at her. 'Hang on. You mentioned someone called Will?'

'Did I?' Her voice was falsely light.

'You said to the dog that it and Will were like chalk and cheese. Will is the name of Tabitha's nephew.'

'It *is*? What a coincidence.'

'Robin, come on. You've always been a terrible liar. Is it Will next door? Is Tabitha's nephew in Campion Bay?'

'Tim.' His name came out as a sigh as her brain scrambled madly for a way to get out of this, just for tonight. She needed more time with Will before Tim got his claws in, so that he was more resilient against the expert sales patter. She stood slowly, placing Darcy on the floor and facing him at full height. 'Today has been so busy. Is there any chance we could have this conversation tomorrow?'

'Why?' Tim asked, folding his arms over his chest. 'I'm pretty sure I know the answer to my question. What I'm not so clear on is why you would want to hide it from me.'

Because I don't want Will to sell to you, she thought, unable to meet his gaze. *I want him to stay here, to become my neighbour. Nobody wants you to do this.* Saying the words in her head made her feel better, but it didn't give her a reply that she could actually use.

The front door banged and she closed her eyes, knowing she was out of time. Darcy barked and raced into the hall.

'The mouse didn't get them,' Will called. 'And I'm not sure what the flavours are, but they might be lemon and chocolate. Hey, Darcy, I wasn't that long, come on.'

Will appeared in the doorway of Sea Shanty and came to a sudden stop. 'Oh, hello.'

'Will,' Robin said, swallowing down her panic, 'this is—'

'Tim Lewis.' Tim was advancing on Will with his hand out, a grin planted firmly on his face, beaming smile switched on like Christmas lights. 'Great to meet you. Robin's been telling me a lot about you. It's so nice to see a new face in Campion Bay – these seaside towns need a new injection of life from time to time, don't you think?'

Robin watched as Will gave Tim a wary smile and held his free hand out. Tim had, in only a few seconds, already made her complicit in his plans by suggesting she'd been talking to him about Will. She wanted to kick his ankles, to push him out of the front door and tell him never to come back. Instead, she offered the two men cups of tea and hurried to the kitchen, thinking her only chance now was to act as mediator, to temper Tim's advances.

She didn't want to leave them alone for too long. Knowing Tim, she thought it might only be minutes before the damage he did was irreparable.

Chapter 8

Robin carried the tray with teapot, mugs and plates down the hallway, the crockery jingling. She heard the two men laughing before she had reached Sea Shanty, and swore under her breath. Planting a smile firmly on her face, she put the tray on the coffee table and sat on the sofa next to Tim, as if by being close to him she could somehow control what came out of his mouth.

'I was just telling Will about Campion Bay property,' Tim said, taking over the role of mother, handing out the plates and opening Will's box of cupcakes. 'It's not as heartless a job as people think it is. We encounter a lot of sadness, houses that have fallen into disrepair because of a death in the family, businesses that have run out of capital and have had to close. Tabitha was loved by everyone she knew – I used to visit her, along with Robin, when I was a teenager. I was very sorry to hear about her death, Will.'

Will waved a dismissive hand, but Robin thought she could see a tension in his shoulders that hadn't been there before. 'If I'm honest, I didn't know her as well as I should have done. She was estranged from her brother, my dad, and mentioning her name in our house was forbidden. My mum finally put me in touch with her, against my dad's will, when I was old enough to make my own decisions. I only started to get to know her in my twenties.'

Robin felt a squeeze of sadness alongside the flurry of questions Will's words had opened up. Why had Tabitha and her brother been estranged? Had Will's dad cast him out when he found out he'd been in touch with her? What did Tabitha think about the whole situation? But she didn't want to ask him while Tim was there. She could see that Will wasn't entirely comfortable, but already, in a couple of swift moves, Tim had made him open up more than he had to her. She didn't want to break down his defences any further or he wouldn't survive the evening, and would have signed the house away to Tim – maybe his soul too – before his tea was cold.

'I'm so sorry,' she said instead. 'I didn't realize any of that had happened, though it explains why I didn't meet you when I was growing up. Tabitha never mentioned it.'

'She wouldn't discuss it with me either,' Will said. 'The subject of my father was strictly off limits whenever I visited.'

Tim whistled through his teeth. 'That sounds tough. It must be hard, having to face it all now. I know what it's like having to work through a property of someone who's sadly passed on, and if there's a family rift, that must make it all the more difficult.'

Robin could see Will's jaw muscles work as Tim played the sincerity card a bit too strongly.

'I don't think any situation like Will's is easy,' she said carefully. 'But Tabitha was his aunt, so even though it's hard, I think it's worthwhile to go through her belongings, to find out more about her.' She risked glancing at Will, and he gave her a quick smile. 'You know I'll help you as much as I can.'

'You?' Tim laughed gently. 'Aren't you supposed to be running a guesthouse, Robs? You don't want to spread yourself too thinly. I can always give Will a hand. I've offered to pop in tomorrow and take a look at the place, and we've got professional house-clearers if it comes to it. As I said, I'm familiar with this kind of situation. Besides, Will, if you're a friend of Robin's, then you're a friend of mine. I'm sure we can sort something out.'

Robin rolled her eyes.

'More kindness.' Will shook his head.

'What do you mean?' Tim asked.

'I've been wondering if Campion Bay is the friendliest place in the world. The cupcakes came from Ashley, down the road. Robin's already offered to spend time at Tabitha's house when she can, and now you. Though I'm sure your services come at a price.'

Robin looked into her tea mug and held her breath. Was Will suspicious, or was it just Tim's overbearing nature putting him on edge?

'A very fair price,' Tim said, offering Will his winning smile. 'I agree that Campion Bay is great, and you've fallen on your feet with Robs here, but the house clearly doesn't have very happy memories for you.'

Robin sensed that his assault was moving to the next level. Tim wasn't stupid; he would be aware that the residents of Goldcrest Road would be against any kind of change to the seafront houses, and now he knew that not only was Will dealing with some difficult family business, but he was being treated as a Very Important Visitor – and Robin was doing some of the treating.

Will ran his finger round the edge of the plate, scooping up the butter icing that had tried to escape. 'The house always had happy memories. It's the situation around it that doesn't. My time at Campion Bay certainly hasn't been all bad, so far.'

Robin's insides flipped as he trained his green eyes on her, the smile not quite reaching his lips. 'And just having one more person to sift through things will make it easier,' she added, encouraged. 'I often get some free time in the middle of the day, and I'm perfectly placed to help Will out.'

'I don't think living next door trumps being an industry professional, Robs.' Tim patted her knee.

Robin opened her mouth to speak as irritation coursed through her, but she didn't want to raise her voice. If she did, Tim would win. He needed to leave. He had already had a cupcake that wasn't meant for him, and he was circling closer and closer to Will, like a charming vulture. Robin remembered Molly describing Tim's boss, Malcolm, as weaselly, and wondered how she could suddenly be feeling the same way about Tim when only two days before she'd been entertaining the possibility that their romantic reunion was in the stars.

It was Will, she realized. His appearance in her life – his presence, his eyes, his warmth – affected everything, as if he'd tilted her world on its axis and given her a different perspective.

'Right then,' she said, injecting forcefulness into her voice.

Tim cut her off. 'Of course, Robin's not been back here very long, have you, Robs?' This time his hand stayed on her knee, rubbing it.

Robin stared down at the white shirt cuff with another expensive cufflink, this one with a dark red stone. She was too shocked to move his hand, and instead looked up at Will, who turned away just as she caught his eye.

'September,' she said. She moved her knee, forcing Tim to release his hand. 'But it was the right decision. Leaving one life behind and starting a new one – even if it's returning to a place you know well – is always difficult. It's hard to be absolutely certain you're making the best choice, but I have no regrets about moving back here.'

'Some things are worth coming back to, aren't they?' Tim gazed at her adoringly.

Robin inhaled, trying to work out whether Tim was being genuinely territorial over her, or if it was a ploy to show Will that he was out of luck if he was harbouring those particular ideas. The thought that he might be gave her a surge of adrenaline, but it was swiftly replaced by anger at her ex-boyfriend. Whatever his motives, she wasn't going to be a part of it.

'I have to do a few things before bed. Nice to see you, Tim.' She stood and hovered, waiting until he got reluctantly to his feet. 'I'll just show Tim out.' She gestured for Will to stay where he was.

She walked towards the door, shepherding Tim in front of her, and then opened it.

'Sorry if I'm intruding on anything.' He gave her a wolfish grin. She sensed that he didn't feel threatened by Will, more that he was amused by the situation. His arrogance was unwavering.

'It's late,' Robin said, 'and I'm still getting used to the routine of running the guesthouse.'

'Well done for finding Tabitha's nephew.' He whispered it, leaning in close and moving one of her curls off her face.

Robin flinched. 'I didn't *find* him. God, Tim. You're so—'

She stopped as Tim stood up straight and raised his hand, and Robin realized Will was standing behind her.

'I'll pop round tomorrow,' Tim said to Will, 'and you can give me the grand tour.'

'Not so much of the grand,' Will said. 'It's a bit of a wild-life park at the moment. Spiders, mice – there might be a family of jackdaws nesting in the roof.'

'Can't wait! Catch you later, Robs. Nice to meet you, Will.' He kissed Robin on the cheek and then was gone – hurrying down the steps and jumping into the polished black Audi, screeching away from the kerb.

Robin shut the door slowly and rested her forehead against the wood. She sighed, mustered up a smile and turned to face Will.

'I should head up,' he said.

'You don't have to, I just wanted to get rid of Tim.'

Will frowned. 'You don't get on? I got the impression you were close.'

'We used to be, but that was a long time ago. Sometimes he can be . . . full-on.'

'I noticed.' He gave her a wry smile and followed her back into Sea Shanty. Darcy had taken advantage of their absence to stretch out full length along one of the sofas, her paws twitching as she tried to be more courageous in her dreams than she was in real life.

'You don't have to show him round Tabitha's if you don't want to.' Robin risked looking at him.

His smile was gentle but amused. 'He's a property developer. He's spent a lot of time in rundown houses and said he could give me a few pointers, show me what I need to concentrate my time on. Are you OK? You seem on edge.' He stepped closer to her. He smelt of mint shampoo and buttercream,

133

and the image of him standing in the hall, his torso bare, popped into her head.

'I'm fine.' She bent to stroke Darcy's tummy. The more time she was spending with the dog, the more she could feel herself falling for her; her gentleness and her cowardice. 'Tim and I have a history. It – things are . . . complicated, after such a long time apart.'

'Oh. Oh, right.'

'Sorry, that came out wrong. I don't mean that there's anything between us, now. I – it's been a long day.'

The doorbell chimed, and Darcy flipped on to her stomach, her ears alert.

'And it's not over yet,' Robin said with a sigh. For a horrifying moment she thought Tim had returned for a second assault, but their second visitor was much more welcome. 'Molly, what can possibly have brought you round here?'

Molly stepped past her and walked purposefully up the hall towards Sea Shanty. 'I've brought back the nail varnish I borrowed from you,' she said distractedly, and then smiled and disappeared inside the room. 'Hi, you must be Will. I'm Molly, I'm your neighbour – on the other side. Robin and I are mates.'

Robin rolled her eyes and, grinning, followed her friend. She was surprised that Molly had left it almost a full day before coming to meet Tabitha's nephew for herself.

'Molly, nice to meet you,' Will said.

Molly smiled unashamedly up at him. She was holding a bottle of nail varnish in a neon yellow that Robin recognized as one of her professional manicure gels. It was possibly the lamest excuse she could have given to come round, especially as Robin wouldn't be seen dead wearing that shade.

'Ashley brought Will some cupcakes,' Robin said. 'Wasn't that kind of him?'

Molly's lips formed a perfect 'o' of surprise. 'Wow, very kind. Are there any left?'

Robin shook her head. 'Tim popped round a while ago to offer Will some professional advice about the house, and we ended up eating them all.'

'Tim?' Molly said sharply. 'The sneaky bugger.'

'It seems I'm destined to meet the whole of Campion Bay while I'm here. Possibly tonight.' Will grinned. 'Do you want me to leave you to it?'

'You're more than welcome to stay,' Robin said. 'I'm sorry that it's a bit of a parade here sometimes. I'm beginning to realize that running a guesthouse means my front door is always open.'

'Or it could be that you're just very popular,' Will said softly, meeting her gaze. 'Which is perfectly understandable.'

'Please don't go on my account. I only popped by to drop this off.' Molly waved the nail varnish and then, in one of the worst acting performances Robin had ever seen, gave a horrified gasp. 'This isn't yours. I've picked up the wrong one! So sorry, Robin.'

Robin closed her eyes in despair.

'Bye, Will.' Molly stood on her tiptoes to peck him on the cheek, and ruffled his short hair. 'If you need a trim while you're here, a pedicure, a facial – I have a great range of *for him* treatments that are to die for. I can see you look after yourself, so why not take it to the next level? I'll do you a deal, as you're Robin's guest.'

'That's very kind of you,' Will said. 'I'll bear it in mind.'

Robin followed Molly into the hall. '*What was that?*' she asked, her voice an angry whisper. 'Will's going to think we're a pair of lunatics!'

'Oh, I guarantee he doesn't think *you're* a lunatic. I can

see why you want him to stay, but trust Tim to turn up so soon. Did he get his claws in?'

Robin glanced behind her to check that Will hadn't followed them. 'He tried to, but I don't think Will was buying it. Not a hundred per cent, anyway.'

'Good. Keep it up. Between us, we'll make Will Nightingale a permanent fixture in Campion Bay. I'd better get Lethal Limoncello back to its friends.' She held up the nail varnish. 'Can't say it played the role of accomplice to perfection, but who cares. Have fun!' She kissed Robin on the cheek and let herself out.

'I'd lock the door now, if I were you.' Will stopped at the bottom of the stairs. He was carrying a sleeping Darcy in his arms.

Robin laughed. 'Molly's lovely, but she's not exactly a shrinking violet. I don't know what I would have done without her when I first moved back to Campion Bay.'

'Oh? Why's that?'

Robin focused her attention on Darcy, the way her paws twitched slightly while she dozed. 'It was hard, returning, after so long in London. I was – I wasn't running away, exactly. But I needed a friend, and Molly was there for me. You'll see how warm she is as you get to know her, but I'm sorry about her whirlwind visit. And Tim. I bet you're wishing you were bunking down at Tabitha's, despite the wildlife.'

'Trade in the luxury of Starcross and those delicious breakfasts, not to mention your company, for a saggy mattress surrounded by dust and creepy-crawlies? I don't think so.'

'You're not beginning to feel like a circus attraction?'

'I'm incidental. They came to see you, not me. I just happened to be taking advantage of your hospitality at the time.'

Robin nodded, but couldn't bring herself to reply.

'You look tired,' he said. 'And I should get some sleep so that I'm bright-eyed and bushy-tailed for another dust-filled trip down memory lane tomorrow.'

'I'll make sure you get one of those delicious, fortifying breakfasts,' she said.

'Oh, I'm counting on it. Goodnight, Robin.'

'Night, Will.'

She watched him climb the stairs, Darcy sleeping in his arms like a fur baby. When she took the mugs into the kitchen, Eclipse was staring at her from beside his food bowl. Robin knew that it wasn't the lack of a treat that her kitten was annoyed about, but she was sure the two animals could learn to love each other – it would just take time. And the more she was getting to know Will, the more she hoped that time was on their side.

The first week of May in Campion Bay was one of bright, hazy mornings and late-afternoon downpours, as if summer was trying to squeeze out too early and the April weather was reining it back in. Robin quickly found that running a guesthouse was both fun and exhausting, a constant flurry of breakfasts and cups of tea, of being welcoming and cheerful and not visibly irritated when someone told her they'd spilt coffee all over the cream cushions in their room. She was worried about the dishwasher and the washing machine, about how hard she was working them, even though her mother had assured her they were more than up to the task.

Sometimes, when she thought she'd have a quiet half-hour to herself, to update the accounts or plan a new promotion for June, a guest or two would pop their head around the door and ask for information, some more biscuits or directions to a particular restaurant. Robin had known all this would happen, and yet she found that her feet were barely touching the ground.

After her first guests – Mr and Mrs Barker, Neil and Catriona, Ray and Andrea, and Dorothy – had checked out, Robin felt like she'd passed the second test. The first night had gone without a hitch – unless she counted Will as a hitch, and she wasn't sure he deserved that less-than-appealing label – and now she could say that her debut as a seaside landlady had been a success. Her guests had all left happy; she had given them an enjoyable, memorable stay in the Campion Bay Guesthouse.

Her current guests included a couple in their thirties from Edinburgh, visiting friends who'd recently moved to the area but didn't have room in their tiny cottage to put them up. Felix and Olivia had soft Scottish accents and the kind of expensive, subtle dress sense that reminded Robin of some of her Once in a Blue Moon Days clients.

'Portland Bay Marina,' Felix said, waggling his phone screen at Olivia. 'Finally, they tell us! But have they given us any directions? Have they heck!'

Olivia gave Robin an apologetic smile. 'Our friends have bought a boat and we're supposed to be going out on it today, but they're not the most organized people.'

'I don't know how they expect us to spend the day on it with them, if they won't tell us where it is!' Felix threw his hands up in exasperation.

'I'll get a map, hang on.' Robin turned away, hiding her smile, and took the map out of the drawer. 'Which marina? Portland Bay? It's not too far from here, look.' They leaned over the map, Robin taking an envious peek at Olivia's long straight russet hair as she pointed out their destination and told them which roads to take.

'Thanks, Robin,' Felix said, rolling his eyes. 'I'm glad someone round here's got some common sense!'

'Don't listen to him,' Olivia said. 'He's just het up because he's desperate to see the boat.'

'What kind is it?' Robin asked.

'Luxury cruiser, apparently.'

'About three times as big as their cottage,' Felix added. 'I don't know why they don't just live on that, instead of trying to cram all their fishing gear into a house with five-foot-high ceilings.'

'Come *on*, Felix, stop gassing at Robin.' Olivia pulled him by the sleeve of his Ralph Lauren jumper.

'It's no problem,' Robin said, laughing and waving them goodbye.

She was trying to fold the map back up without being suffocated by it when Will appeared in the hall.

He'd been in Campion Bay just over a week and Robin couldn't deny that she liked having him around. She could recognize the tread of his boot-clad feet on the stairs and his turn of the key in the lock in the evenings.

'What joys have you got on today?' Robin called, smoothing down the creases of the map.

'Today Darcy and I are working on the cupboards at the back of Tabitha's living room. At a glance, they look like a paper-recycling facility, so I think it's going to take a while.' He gave her a look of mock delight, and Robin laughed.

'I need to pop round and see Molly,' she said. 'Let me come out with you.' The walk would take less than thirty seconds, and yet Robin found she was craving his company, however limited. She'd managed a couple of hours at Tabitha's house three times the previous week, for which Will had been grateful, even though Robin felt she wasn't being much practical help.

'How are the new guests?' Will asked. 'They seem nice from the brief conversations we've had at breakfast. Felix invited me to go and see this spectacular boat his friends have bought. A day skipping across the waves sounds pretty appealing.'

'A *luxury cruiser*. Oh, how the other half live.'

Will laughed. 'They're staying in *your* guesthouse. You're facilitating their lifestyle; you're a part of that.'

Robin thought of the levels of extravagance involved in Once in a Blue Moon Days. 'It's not quite the same thing, though, is it?'

'Isn't it? I've never stayed in a hotel room as beautiful or upmarket as Starcross.' Will watched as Darcy bounded to the top step of Tabitha's house and stared up at the front door.

'Someone's keen,' Robin said.

'Keener than I am. If only she could help me decide what to do with it all.'

'I can try and pop round a bit later today.'

'Robin, you don't—'

'So *this* is the famous Will Nightingale,' said a familiar, accented voice. Robin turned to see Nicolas, one half of the father-and-son team that ran Taverna on the Bay, approaching them. His walk was more of a saunter, and his dark eyes were as sparkling as his smile.

Will frowned as he shook Nicolas's hand. 'Hi,' he said. 'Famous?'

'The new, mysterious neighbour,' Nicolas clarified. 'Any intrigue on Goldcrest Road, news spreads like wildfire. You are Tabitha's nephew, yes? My father and I, we loved Tabitha

140

– she came for lunch with us every Thursday. I am sorry for your loss.'

'Thank you,' Will said. 'I remember her mentioning it, but I never got round to going with her.' He ran a hand through his hair.

'Ah!' Nicolas threw his arms up into the air. They were very well-defined arms, the biceps trying to escape a T-shirt that was a size too small. 'Then we will make up for it. You two will come to dinner, Wednesday night. We will reserve you the best table, serve only the best food, do you an exclusive deal.'

'Oh no, Nicolas,' Robin started, 'we don't—'

'Sure,' Will said at the same time, glancing at Robin. 'I mean, why not? It's a very kind offer.'

Robin swallowed. Dinner, for the two of them? The thought was thrilling and terrifying; a lot more serious than cheese on toast in Sea Shanty. 'I, uhm, OK. It sounds lovely. Thank you, Nicolas.'

'My pleasure.' He gave her a double-handed handshake, and slapped Will firmly on the shoulder. 'Wednesday,' he called, as he strode in the direction of town.

Will grinned at Robin. 'That was random. But then, I'm beginning to understand that random is perfectly normal in Campion Bay.'

'Nicolas is – they're both – very kind. And the food at the taverna is amazing.'

'I hope I didn't overstep the mark, accepting their offer?' He touched her arm. 'If you'd rather not go with me . . .'

'No, no, I'd love to,' she said hurriedly. 'I was caught off guard as much as you, that's all. It'll be good to get out of the guesthouse for an evening. I'll try to come by later, see if we can get through the mountains of paper together.'

'Thanks, Robin. Say hi to Molly for me.' She didn't watch him go inside, but raced next door to Groom with a View, where her friend was waiting. She had the distinct impression that Nicolas's invitation hadn't come purely out of the goodness of his heart.

'You know why you're so tired, don't you?' Molly said, patting Robin's knee.

Robin thought she knew what was coming, but she feigned ignorance. 'No, why?'

They were sitting on a bench on the promenade, the guesthouse, beauty parlour and other Goldcrest Road houses behind them, the charcoal sea in front. After Robin had turned up at Groom with a View, Molly had forced her straight back outside again, and now they both had ice creams in their hands and were grabbing hold of the thirty minutes in between guest breakfasts and the first facials of the day.

'Because you're helping Will. All the spare time that you say you don't have is because you're using it to go round to number four.'

'He can't do it all by himself,' Robin said defensively.

'No, not a big, strong man in the prime of his life, with all the time in the world. God forbid he should have to deal with a *whole house* full of grime and clutter. Maybe it's the doilies he's finding particularly hard to tackle?'

Robin turned sideways on the bench, pushing hair out of her face as the wind whipped it in, holding her ice cream out of the way. 'Isn't this what you wanted? Trying everything we can to get Will to fall in love with the place and not sell Tabitha's house? It's not like I'm the only one who's been doing it, either. What exactly have you offered Nicolas?'

'I have no idea what you're talking about,' Molly said,

crossing one leg over the other. 'You're a one-woman publicity campaign. Though I'm not sure if it's the wonders of *Campion Bay* you're advertising, as opposed to the delights of Robin Brennan.'

'Molly! You—'

'How's it going in there, anyway?'

'Slowly.' Robin sighed. Even with the curtains open, Tabitha's house was dark and dingy, as if the dust had worked its way into the fabric of the building and tainted the air. After spending a couple of hours going solidly through the rooms with Will, boxing up things for the recycling centre or, occasionally, charity shops, Robin found herself having to spend longer than usual in the shower before she felt clean. She had been keen to help Will, to find out more about Tabitha and her house, to recall her childhood memories, but so far – other than getting to know Tabitha's nephew and Darcy – it had been an adventure in dirt.

'You're not enjoying it?' Molly asked. 'I didn't think you were afraid of mucking in?' She tapped Robin's nails, still chewed to the ends and distinctly manicure-free.

'I'm not! It just feels a bit . . . morose. Tabitha was estranged from her brother, Will's father, and I think after her husband died she must have been lonely. I've asked Will what happened, why there was a rift between them, but he doesn't know. His dad refuses to talk about it, and even Tabitha closed up whenever he tried to find out the story behind it. It must have been so hard for her, being cut off from her family like that.' She thought back to all the times she'd gone over there, playing cards and board games, occasionally baking with the older woman. 'It's funny, I can't remember ever seeing her outside that house – not on the beach or in the shops, or at crazy golf.'

'She was older, though, wasn't she?'

'Not that old. She was only in her sixties when she died. Maybe there's a sadness in the house.' She chewed her cone thoughtfully.

'And being with Will doesn't make up for that?' Molly glared at Robin over the top of her Mr Whippy.

Robin swallowed and dropped her gaze.

'I know I've only met him briefly,' Molly continued, 'but I'm not stupid. He's not exactly a punishment on the peepers, is he? And I got the impression he was enjoying staying in your guesthouse a bit more than most people.'

'He's . . . very nice,' Robin said, not taking the bait. 'And I'm in love with his dog. Darcy. She is the sweetest, kindest, gentlest thing. Her fur is so soft, and she has the most expressive eyes.'

'You're deflecting. And that's not a good enough answer. Did Will tell you what happened when Tim went to see the house?'

Robin shrugged. 'He said that Tim had looked round, confirmed the house had lots of potential, that it was a beautiful building with original features, and has apparently invited him out for a drink to "discuss things further". No doubt it'll be a very manly drink, with lots of backslapping and pints, and all the opportunity in the world for Tim to make his pitch. Ugh.'

'And what does Will think, about Tim?'

'I'm not sure he's entirely convinced,' Robin admitted. 'He called him my "smooth friend". I don't think Will's about to have the wool pulled over his eyes. My only concern is, because going through Tabitha's things is such a mammoth task, I can see how selling up would seem like the easiest option.'

'But he's still staying in Starcross and eating your breakfasts, and spending time with you?'

'Yes, Molly. All those things.'

'There you go then. Nothing to worry about.'

'What's that supposed to mean?' Robin asked as a seagull swooped low over them, squawking in an attempt to scare Molly's cone out of her hand. Molly shoved the whole thing in her mouth in defiance and the seagull drifted off, its cry plaintive.

'Nothing,' Molly said, standing up and giving her a butter-wouldn't-melt smile. 'Best be getting back – I'm doing a pedicure at ten thirty.'

Robin walked with her friend across the road. They stopped in front of number four, the grey-fronted house between their cream buildings, Robin's with blue accents to match her guesthouse sign, Molly's Groom with a View adorned with clean white and bold pink.

'Lights are on,' Molly said.

'Will's in there,' Robin confirmed.

'Have him on *find your friends* yet?' Molly waggled her eyebrows.

Robin's smile was involuntary. 'I'm going inside. I've got new guests coming today.' They said their goodbyes and Robin went back to the guesthouse, wondering what Molly had offered Nicolas to get him to make his move on Will.

She felt unsettled that her friend wasn't keeping her in the loop, that she could be organizing all kinds of charms and tricks to convince Will to stay that she didn't know about. Molly was nothing if not enthusiastic, and Robin was worried that she'd take it too far, that Will would discover the truth behind the kindness he'd been experiencing – that he was nothing more than a welcome barrier between Tim and number four Goldcrest Road becoming soulless apartments. To Robin, he was already far more than that, but if Molly's plan was discovered, he was bound to think she was part of it. That, Robin thought, as she picked up the post from the mat, was the last thing she wanted.

'Mr and Mrs Hannigan,' Robin said to the couple on the doorstep, a battered leather holdall on the porch between them, 'welcome to the Campion Bay Guesthouse. It's lovely to have you here.'

They were a striking couple. Both in their mid-forties, Robin guessed, though Mr Hannigan was already a silver fox, his hair and neatly trimmed beard a mix of steel and white, his eyebrows still dark. His wife was several inches taller than Robin and quite willowy, with long golden hair on the frizzy side of curled. Her eyes were very pale blue, almost grey. The resounding impression that Robin got, regardless of their looks, was that they were happy.

'Jonathan, please,' he said, as she stood back to let them inside.

'And I'm Emily.'

'Nice to meet you, Jonathan and Emily. I'll get you booked in and then show you to your room.'

They were booked into Canvas, and while Jonathan seemed in awe of the room, walking slowly round it and examining the paintings, Emily went straight to the window. It was on the second floor, so the view over the sea was spectacular, and Robin smiled as Emily knelt on the window seat and put her hands on the frame. The sun was trying to break out through the clouds, and shards of light cut into the dark grey of the water.

'We live in Shropshire,' Jonathan explained. 'Coming to

146

the coast is always a real treat, and it's our wedding anniversary so we wanted somewhere special.'

Robin's heart skipped a beat at the admission they'd picked her guesthouse because it was special. Unless, she thought, they just loved Campion Bay. 'Congratulations on your anniversary,' she said, annoyed with herself for not finding it out when they had booked. She would have to put a bottle of sparkling wine in their room retrospectively. 'How many years?'

'Three,' Emily said, turning round. 'This time.' She gave her husband a wide smile.

'We're a bit peculiar, you see,' he admitted. 'We've been married twice.'

Robin nodded slowly, wondering when the punchline would come. But then her cogs worked harder, and the significance of Emily's words made sense. 'To each *other*?' She hadn't meant to sound so surprised, but the couple laughed.

'Turns out we were soul mates after all,' Emily said. 'We were just too young the first time round.'

'Oh, really? So you – you got back together again, after time apart?'

'I discovered that, after seeing a lot of the world, there was nobody else for me.' Jonathan shrugged. 'There was no possibility of fighting it. We were meant to be together; it was fate. So, there you go.'

Robin nodded, her mind whirring. She thought of Starcross, and Neve's belief in exactly those things. 'So,' she said, trying to focus on her guests, 'you just count the years this time round? How many years would it be if you included the time before?'

'Seven,' Emily said. 'Nobody's ever asked us that before. What would seven be, in terms of material?'

147

'Copper or wool,' Robin said without hesitation. 'I used to run an events company,' she explained, when Emily gave her a questioning look, 'organizing special days for people. Lots of them were anniversaries, so I got to know those traditions very well.'

'That sounds like an amazing job. Very creative.'

'Quite like this place.' Jonathan gestured at the painting-adorned walls.

'I loved it,' Robin said. 'There was always a new challenge, fun and unusual things to investigate. But then, it's pretty varied running a guesthouse, too.'

'Not just endless rounds of washing and cleaning?'

'Well, there's that. But no, there's a bit of time for other things.' Robin wondered how Will was getting on next door, and thought she would have time to pop in on her way back from buying Jonathan and Emily a bottle of wine. 'I'll leave you to it,' she added, 'but if you need anything, you know where I am.'

As she hurried down the stairs, she considered whether it was possible to go back to an old flame after a less than happy parting and years of living separate lives. If there were still feelings, the residue of love or even fresh lust, could it work? Emily and Jonathan were making it look like it could, but Robin couldn't imagine that things wouldn't be strained, that they wouldn't have both moved too far in different directions.

'You didn't have to,' Will said, as Robin walked into Tabitha's front room and found him on one of the green sofas with a large photo album on his lap.

'What?' she asked, sitting next to him.

He pointed at the gold foil bottle-top sticking out of her

carrier bag. 'I've not made much progress today, so I'm not sure we should be celebrating.'

'It's for some guests,' she said, her eyes fixing on the album. 'It's their wedding anniversary. What's this?'

'I found it in the bureau over there.' Will pointed to a tall, dark-wood writing bureau in the corner of the room. Robin thought it gave the impression of being backed up against the wall, as tall and thin as possible, as if using the shadows to hide from someone.

'Pictures of your aunt?' she asked softly, sensing that the photographs mattered; that he was affected by them. It hadn't been many days since he'd appeared at her front door, but already she knew that when he was trying to keep emotions in check he went very still, as if by doing that he could prevent anything escaping.

'And Dad,' he said. 'Seeing both of them together is . . . unusual.'

Not upsetting or depressing or even wonderful – just unusual. She resisted the urge to squeeze his arm. 'Are you OK?' she asked instead. It was the blandest of questions, warranting an answer of 'Fine', but she didn't feel she could go too deep unless he instigated it.

He turned to face her, and she could see his jaw working. The sweet smell was there again, the one she'd noticed on first meeting him, and she'd since discovered that he had a seemingly endless supply of rhubarb-and-custard sweets. Perhaps they were a stress reliever – she hadn't yet found the courage to ask.

'I'm all right,' he said, smiling at her.

'But . . .?' She tried to hold his gaze but found that she couldn't, so worried at a nonexistent mark on her black trousers instead.

'I don't know, I guess I hadn't expected to find all this stuff. I don't know why I hadn't – obviously, it was going to be here – but I approached it as a task to work through, like clearing out one of the storerooms at Downe Hall. I thought I'd find some vaguely interesting things, but I hadn't counted on being dragged back into the family history. Maybe it would be different if it had been happy, between . . . y'know.' He rubbed his cheeks.

Robin could see that the emotions were trying to escape. He seemed frustrated, angry, even, though she wasn't sure who with. 'Your dad and Tabitha? You wish they hadn't been estranged?'

He looked directly at her, his green eyes piercing. 'I wish someone had told me why. I still wish they would. Dad refuses to talk about it, and whenever I broached the subject with Tabitha she'd always say it was up to my father to tell me. Mum just shakes her head, even though she was the one who put me in touch with my aunt when I was old enough. She doesn't like it, but she doesn't want to appear disloyal. I think she must have sent Tabitha this – let me show you.' He began flipping through the album and Robin held her breath, wondering what he was about to show her.

'Hello? Anyone here?' Molly's voice broke through the quiet, and Robin jumped. When she caught Molly's eye, her friend gave her a quick, gleeful grin. 'Don't you look cosy?'

Will slipped the album behind him on the sofa. Robin's heart sank.

'Hi, Molly,' Will said. 'How are you?'

'Good, thanks, Will. This looks like hard work.'

'We're getting there.'

'Well then, this is bound to perk you up.' She gave them a beauty-technician grade-A smile, and waggled a piece of paper, the print green and yellow like the décor of Taverna on the Bay. 'I bumped into Stefano on your doorstep. He was on his way to give you this. Dinner for two, eh? And with twenty per cent off, too. It sounds like just the thing.' She handed Robin the voucher, gave her a distinctly unsubtle wink and then left, the dust dancing behind her like a ticker-tape parade.

Chapter 9

'Dinner with Will, just the two of us. What's that about?' Robin asked Eclipse as she rifled through her wardrobe, rejecting dresses and tops, pulling out a maxi dress in navy and orange oriental patterns and then sliding it back on the rack. 'It was so out of the blue, Nicolas accosting Will on the doorstep, so how did Molly do it, huh? Offer *them* both free haircuts for life?'

Eclipse was sitting in the middle of the bed, licking his paw with an intent focus. Robin left her wardrobe and sat next to the kitten, stroking his still-fluffy fur. She couldn't deny that she had fallen hard for Darcy, but she had to remind herself that she had an impossibly cute pet of her own, and couldn't ignore him. 'I'm sorry about the other day,' she said, as the kitten jumped on to her lap and burrowed his face into her jumper, 'but I do think you could be friends. That is, if tonight isn't a disaster. It feels too much like a date. I don't know why Molly thought this was a good idea.'

Robin was sure that Molly was behind the latest act of kindness, the unexpected invite from Stefano and Nicolas to have a discounted dinner at Taverna on the Bay, the Greek restaurant at number one Goldcrest Road. Had she thought that leaving her and Will to it was a good idea, because Robin – in her position as guesthouse owner and next-door neighbour – knew Will better than anyone else in Campion Bay? Or did Molly have a caveat to her plan that involved a bit of matchmaking?

Robin's stomach churned, and she reminded herself that, on a basic level, it would give them a break from running a guesthouse and sorting through a dead relative's house. Robin knew from experience that it was almost impossible to have a bad night at the taverna, where Nicolas and his father, Stefano, welcomed all their guests with laid-back charm and simple, mouth-watering food. And it would give her another opportunity to find out more about her unexpected guest without anything getting in the way.

She finally selected a short grey dress with a keyhole neckline, and accompanied it with a plum cardigan and low, patent heels, hoping the outfit struck the right note for dinner out two doors away from her house. As she was applying mascara, she heard the familiar footsteps descending the stairs. She grabbed her handbag and opened the door into the hall, waiting for Eclipse to jump off the bed and follow her out. Will was standing on the bottom step wearing a shirt in a dark, inky blue, the colour of the deepest sea on a sunny day. He gave her a wide smile, his eyes even more intense than usual, as if given an extra depth by the sea-like fabric.

'Hi.' Robin returned the smile, her stomach flipping in appreciation.

He rested his elbow on the newel post. 'You look great.'

'You too,' she said, lamely.

'You mean I look clean? It makes a change. Your drench shower has been a lifesaver. The plumbing at Downe Hall hadn't exactly reached twenty-first century standards; I'm sure some of the dust set up home in my hair.'

'I aim to please,' Robin said, picturing Will standing under the shower in Starcross's en suite, water running off him in rivulets. 'Right,' she said shrilly, 'shall we get going? Let me just . . .' She scribbled a note on the miniature whiteboard pinned on the door into Sea Shanty, telling her guests she was out for the evening but to call if any of them needed her.

They stepped out into the spring dusk. It was warm, but with a lingering crispness that reminded Robin summer hadn't yet arrived.

'Is Darcy going to be OK without you?' she asked, as they made their way past Maggie's house at number two.

'She'll be fine. I expect she'll sleep for the whole evening. Are we here already?'

'The most convenient – and delicious – restaurant in Campion Bay.'

Taverna on the Bay had a warm, sunny feel to it even on the grimmest of days, its signage and trim bright yellow and grass green, and this evening it called out to them with its lit, bustling interior. Robin felt her taste buds awaken in anticipation. She pushed open the door, and Stefano, wearing a white T-shirt and faded jeans, held his arms out towards them, his dark eyes twinkling.

'Robin, Robin, always a pleasure. Come for our special night, huh? And Will Nightingale, our newest friend. Do you sing as sweetly? Come inside, please.' He pumped their hands up and down and kissed Robin's cheek, before steering them to a cosy table next to the window. It had a white linen tablecloth and blue serviettes, a lit tea light in a blue glass holder. Stefano disappeared and returned a moment later with a jug of water and menus.

Robin sat opposite Will and pulled her chair in, her foot nudging his ankle. She flashed him a quick smile and looked away. Nicolas was at another table, taking down orders, a second pen sticking out from behind his ear. He was taller than his father, with a toned physique that entirely lacked Stefano's paunch, but he too was in a white T-shirt and jeans; their unofficial uniform.

Will poured water into their glasses and rolled the sleeves of his shirt up to the elbows. 'It's busy for a Wednesday night.'

'It's very popular. They serve traditional Greek food. Stefano and Nicolas were born here, but they have tons of family in Greece and go back there often. They lay it on a bit thick, but that's what makes this place special.'

'It was kind of Nicolas to invite us,' Will said. 'Me, especially. It's strange how many people know I'm here, though.'

Robin laughed. 'Campion Bay's not the biggest place, so gossip travels at quite a pace. Besides, lots of people loved Tabitha, so it stands to reason they'd be interested in her nephew turning up.'

'I've not surfaced much beyond Tabitha's house, so far. This already feels like a breath of fresh air, though I wouldn't have minded a longer walk – I could do with stretching my legs.'

'Did you discover much more today?' Robin asked.

It had been two days since he'd been interrupted while showing her the photo album, and she'd been dying for an opportunity to work their conversation back to it, and what he'd been about to show her.

'I did. Do you want to know what it was?' he said, grinning

155

and resting his forearms on the table. 'A whole new cupboard of porcelain sheep.'

'*More* sheep? Oh, I loved Tabitha's sheep. When I was little, I'd go round giving them all names. By the time I got to the last one, I'd have forgotten the names I'd given to the first ones, so I would start all over again. I must have driven her mad.'

'She would have loved it. I think after Nigel died she must have been lonely, despite living on such a neighbourly street. Whenever I went to see her, I got the impression she was quite reclusive, didn't like to go and talk to people in case she was unwelcome. But if they came to her, she'd invite them in with open arms. It . . .' He ran a hand over his hair. '. . . It makes the whole business with my dad even more unforgivable. He cut her off completely. If it hadn't been for Mum going against him to put me in touch with Tabitha, she would have died estranged from her whole family.'

Robin felt a fresh stab of guilt that she hadn't seen Tabitha more on visits down from London. 'You still don't know why? You haven't found anything that might explain it?'

Will shook his head. 'I'm sorry. I didn't mean to bring the mood down so early on. You won't let me come out again at this rate. Tell me what's good on the menu.'

She wanted to ask more, but Will had closed the conversation down, and Robin realized he probably didn't want to talk about the house, having managed to escape it for the evening. They ordered a couple of starters to share, a Greek salad and calamari, and then let Stefano choose their mains for them. He brought a carafe of red wine over to the table, pouring it into the glasses with an exaggerated twist. When he'd retreated, they clinked glasses. The wine was thick and syrupy, sliding like velvet down her throat.

'Great calamari,' Will said, spearing one with his fork. 'A slice of the Mediterranean in Dorset.'

'Better than cheese on toast?' Robin asked.

'Never. Though I won't admit that to Stefano or he'll start to worry about the competition.'

'I get the impression that Stefano doesn't worry about much when it comes to his restaurant. I'm prepared to admit it's better than my cheese on toast, and a *hundred* times better than my chicken Kiev.'

'Your indoor barbecue?' Will asked, raising his eyebrows.

'That's the one. Wasn't that just before Tim turned up? Did he ever invite you for that drink?'

'He said he was hoping to meet up one evening next week. By then he'll have something concrete to discuss with me, whatever that means.'

'Oh,' Robin said, popping an olive in her mouth, trying to swallow it past the lump in her throat. 'He didn't say what?'

Will shook his head. 'Nope. But it must be to do with the house – maybe some information about the original features, or those professional house-clearers he mentioned. I'm not in a position to discuss any of that yet; there's still too much to do.'

'You're going to keep going with the clear-out?' Robin hoped her relief wasn't too evident.

'I realized you were right: I owe it to Tabitha to look through everything properly. Besides, I'm enjoying staying at the Campion Bay Guesthouse too much – there's never a dull moment.'

'Says the man who turned up looking like a shipwreck victim on my doorstep one day, and then proceeded to take all his clothes off and wander round my hallway the next.'

'Hey,' Will said, laughing. 'You were the one who asked me to get undressed.'

'I was finding you a robe!'

'Your hands were conspicuously empty, I seem to remember. I'm starting to think my original suspicions about fluffy handcuffs weren't far off, but that you spring it on your guests after you've lulled them into a false sense of security with the hospitality, the breakfasts . . .' He shook his head, his expression incredulous.

Robin gasped, feigning horror. 'I seem to remember you telling me that you never embellished your tours at Downe Hall. Do you expect me to believe that after such a ridiculous leap of the imagination?'

'I never make anything up,' Will said solemnly.

'OK, then.' Robin pushed her empty plate away and folded her arms. 'What's the worst tour you've ever led?'

'Do you mean in terms of the guests?'

'Did any of them ever flip out, or walk off, or – I don't know, heckle you?'

Will laughed. 'I love how much faith you have in my ability as a tour guide.'

'There's no question you're a brilliant tour guide,' Robin said, a bit too vehemently.

Will gave her a curious look.

'I mean, I can see you captivating people, holding their attention . . .' She could almost picture the hole she was digging herself into, and cleared her throat as Will's gaze stayed fixed on her. 'I know better than anyone that people can be unpredictable, so I just wondered what funny things had happened to you.'

'Well rescued, Robin Brennan.' He nodded solemnly at her and drummed his fingers on the tablecloth. 'Right, worst tour. Oh, yes – how could I forget?' He smiled, his green eyes crinkled at the edges, clearly lost for a moment in the memory.

Robin felt a flutter of attraction low down in her stomach. 'Don't keep me in suspense.'

He folded his arms on the table and leant forward, so that she caught a hint of apple aftershave. 'I once had one of the visitors contradict everything I said. Every single fact about the hall. He was walking round with a book on historic houses in Kent, and to each bit of information he would say, "I think you'll find . . ." Or, "Actually, it says here . . ."' He put on an adenoidal voice as he spoke, and Robin giggled into her wine glass.

'What did you do?'

Will sighed loudly. 'I'm not proud of it, I just – it wound me up so much.'

'What did you do?' she asked again, her eyes widening.

'I took his book off him. Snatched it out of his hands and told him to lead the rest of the tour because he obviously knew it all so much better than I did. I thought he'd be cross, but he was mortified – he genuinely thought he was being helpful, correcting me. I bought him and his wife afternoon tea in the restaurant afterwards to apologize.' Will winced. 'It wasn't my finest moment.'

'Sounds like he was just keen,' Robin said. 'And surely the keen ones are better than the bored ones who trail around looking like they'd rather be anywhere else on the planet? Speaking of historical facts and how trustworthy they are . . .' She traced a pattern on the tablecloth with her finger.

'I don't make them up, Robin, I've already told you.'

'That's not what I was going to ask! I was – I wanted to know about Tabitha's plaque. The Jane Austen one.'

'What about it? It's been there ever since I got reacquainted with her. She was very proud of it.'

'Not everyone thinks it's genuine,' Robin said. 'Some people have suggested that she had it made as a joke, or a talking point for when people knocked on the door.'

'Really?' Will frowned. 'Why would she go to the trouble? It was up there before the days of Internet shopping, and I don't think Tabitha even had a computer – we never exchanged emails, and I haven't found one in the house. I can't imagine something like that would have been easy to do.'

'Exactly,' Robin said, feeling a rush of triumph. 'What would be the point? Molly thinks Tabitha did it as a joke, that there'd be some mention of it elsewhere – in books and on websites – if it was true.'

'What is it with people in this place and making stuff up? I agree my aunt was good fun, but I can't see her fabricating something like a blue plaque. I knew her for less time than you did, but I'm sure it's genuine.'

Robin grinned at Will, feeling a moment of solidarity between them. It was a small matter in the scheme of things, but to find out that he felt the same as she did about something she'd believed in all her life was somehow important. He parted his lips, about to continue, when their main courses arrived.

'Kleftiko for the handsome gentleman,' Stefano announced, 'and keftedakia for the prettiest landlady in Campion Bay.' He placed the steaming dishes on the table, his voice raised to carry above all the other sounds in the restaurant.

'Thank you, Stefano,' Robin said. 'This looks delicious, as always.'

'Ah, no problem. You are my *favourite* guests. Anyone who lives on Goldcrest Road can only be sheer perfection, no?'

'More wine for our favourite guests,' Nicolas said, coming up behind his father with another carafe. Robin could see he was enjoying himself – whatever instructions Molly had given them being followed with an enthusiasm only Stefano and Nicolas could manage.

She was sure Will would realize something strange was going on, but she couldn't bring her gaze up to meet his. Instead, she topped up their wine glasses.

'Later,' Stefano said, almost bowing at the table, 'free ouzo and maybe, if you're lucky, music! I want to hear Will sing like a Nightingale!' He turned away from the table in a spin and Robin felt her cheeks burning.

'Wow,' Will said, once the owners had left them to their meals. 'They really major on the hospitality, don't they?'

'It takes a bit of getting used to,' Robin said, swallowing. 'But it's worth it for the food.'

'And, for the record,' he said, 'you really don't want to hear me sing. It's a sure-fire way to ruin a great evening, and I don't think Stefano and Nicolas would appreciate my ability to clear their restaurant in minutes.'

Robin shook her head sadly at Will. 'You can try any excuse you like, but if they've set their mind on something, it's pretty much inevitable.'

The food went down as easily as the second carafe of wine and by the time they'd finished Robin's cheeks were burning from the delicious meal and the alcohol. Will was sitting back in his chair, his green eyes slowly taking in the buzz and chatter of the restaurant. He seemed at ease, looking ridiculously handsome in his blue shirt with his freckled, flushed cheeks, and Robin couldn't understand why not everyone in the restaurant was staring at him.

Will insisted on paying the bill, and Nicolas brought his card back with two glasses of ouzo and a third carafe of wine.

'Oh no,' Will said, holding his hand up. 'We couldn't.' He glanced at Robin and she nodded.

'Not for now,' Nicolas said. 'For later.' He indicated the glass stopper in the carafe. 'You take our wine, you drink the wine, and then you return the carafe. This way, we know we will see you again soon. And when you do, you will sing for us, Mr Nightingale.'

He gave Will his widest grin, and Will seemed genuinely taken aback at the gesture. Their goodbye was long, with lots of hugs, back-slapping, and promises to see each other again soon. Robin even offered to cook Stefano and Nicolas cheese on toast, a suggestion which, she noticed, Will tried very hard not to laugh at.

As they stepped out into a clear, crisp night, the burn of the complimentary ouzo working its way down inside her, Robin knew she would have to concede to Molly that, whatever she'd said to Stefano and Nicolas, the evening had been a success. She didn't feel entirely steady on her feet, though she wasn't sure if that was the wine or the company. Will might like Campion Bay a little more than he had done before they left, but Robin's feelings for *him* had reached an entirely new level.

As they turned in the direction of the guesthouse, Will put his arm through hers. Neither of them had brought a coat, and the late-evening chill slipped easily through her cardigan. Despite that, when they reached Robin's front door, she turned in the opposite direction, crossing the road and leading Will towards the promenade. Skull Island was closed, low floodlights highlighting the sculptures of pirates and skeletons. Will didn't speak as she led him around the edge of the golf course and stopped inches short of the sand.

Robin shuddered involuntarily, and Will squeezed her arm.

'I'm not cold,' she said. 'There's just something so mesmerizing about the beach at night.'

The rhythmic back and forth of the waves was loud, no sounds of daytime chatter or seagulls to compete with it, the traffic on Goldcrest Road almost nonexistent.

'It's stunning,' Will said.

'That's the flower moon.' She pointed up at the glowing orb of the moon, which cast the beach in a strange, bluish light.

'*Flower* moon?'

'The full moons have different names every month,' she explained. 'Today, the tenth of May, is the flower moon, because it's the time of year when flowers bloom.'

'Where did you find that out?'

'One of Neve's astrology books,' she said softly.

'Who's Neve? Did she help you with Starcross if she's into astrology?'

'A friend,' Robin said, a lump forming in her throat. She wasn't sure if it was Will's presence, his warmth at her side, too much syrupy wine, or just the way the knowledge had popped into her head that had made the emotions come to the surface. 'And she did help with Starcross, in a way. In lots of ways.'

'The light reminds me of Starcross. The glow of the ceiling spotlights is like this.'

'Do you go to sleep with them on?' Robin asked, wondering if it was too personal a question, imagining him as he went to bed.

She felt rather than saw Will nod. 'It's funny. I never considered myself as someone who needed a night light, but now

– I can't imagine falling asleep without them. Does your friend Neve live around here?'

Robin shook her head. She wanted to tell him about her, but didn't trust herself to speak without the emotions overwhelming her. 'She is, was— I knew her in London. It's getting cold, shall we go back?'

'Sure. This view will still be here tomorrow night.'

'It won't ever be quite the same though,' Robin said as they turned and strolled back towards the Campion Bay Guesthouse. 'That's what makes it so magical.'

Robin unlocked the door, let Will in, and then shut out the moon and the sound of the sea. Everything was still and quiet, as it had been the night Will had arrived. It was less than two weeks ago, and yet it already felt like she'd been here, in charge of the guesthouse, for much longer. She paused, listening for sounds above them. She had no way of knowing if her guests were in their rooms, but at this precise moment her mind kept returning to the one unquestionable fact that she was alone in the hall with Will. His green eyes were trained on her, his presence seeming to overwhelm her even more than it had done on that first night, when he was an unknown quantity; a ripple in her perfectly planned opening day. A ripple that kept on rippling.

Suddenly, even the most straightforward sentence seemed impossible to say. Robin was convinced that whatever came out of her mouth would reveal her thoughts to him. After all the wine she'd had, it might well *be* her thoughts that tripped disloyally off her tongue. It seemed that Will, too, was stumped for words.

'I'm sorry if—'

'Why does it—'

They spoke at the same time.

'You go,' she said, pulling off her heels.

'Sure?'

She nodded.

'I was just going to say, why does drinking red wine feel like one of those heavy velvet theatre curtains, slowly being pulled down over your brain? I never feel this sluggish when I drink beer.' He put the carafe of wine on the stairs and leaned against the banister, shoving his hands in his jeans pockets.

'Stefano's wine is particularly thick, though. And fresh air always makes alcohol go to my head, rather than clearing it like it's supposed to.'

'The golf course looks pretty sinister in the darkness. All those grinning skulls – is that the impression it's trying to give?'

Robin laughed. 'Not at all. Maggie's owned it for as long as I can remember, and it's very popular with children. As far as I'm aware, they don't get terrified by it.' She sighed dramatically. 'I don't know, Will. Needing a night light, and now scared of a few plastic skulls? I'm beginning to see a different side to you.'

'I'm not maintaining my fearless Bear Grylls exterior?'

'Not one hundred per cent,' Robin admitted. 'Why don't you let me take you to Skull Island when it's open, lay the ghost to rest? I could give you a tour of Campion Bay at the same time.'

'Will you hold my hand if I get scared?' He grinned at her.

'That depends on whether you've perfected your one-armed golf-swing.'

'I could give it a go.'

'So it's a date? I mean, it's – we'll – you'll let me . . .' She stopped under the weight of his gaze.

'Yes, Robin,' he said softly, his smile faltering. 'I'd love you to show me round, although dare I say you've done so much for me already, I'm not sure I deserve a personal tour as well.'

'See how it feels, being on the receiving end of all the information for a change?'

'And you've obviously got a lot of it. I didn't know about the moon names. They're different every month?'

Robin nodded. 'There's the wolf moon and the sturgeon moon and the snow moon and the hunter's moon and harvest moon. There's flower moon and strawberry moon . . . and some others. They come from a tribe I'm not even going to try and pronounce the name of right now, who used them to track the seasons. So they all fit with what's happening at that time of year.'

'I had no idea.'

'It's a good night for it,' she said. 'Moon-gazing, at least. I'm not sure how many stars we'd see, being as it's so bright.'

'I haven't used the telescope yet – I've not even thought to. I've been falling straight into bed every night, drifting off under the glowing canopy. Obviously, that's your fault for providing such a comfortable room. But maybe, one night soon, you could come up and show me what I'm missing out on?'

'Sorry?' Robin stood up straight, her mouth suddenly dry.

'The stars,' he clarified. 'You clearly know more than you're letting on.'

She shook her head. 'I don't.'

He was standing so close, looking down at her. Robin thought that he'd taken a step towards her, but he was still leaning against the banister, and she realized she must have closed the gap between them. It would be so easy to stretch

166

up and press her lips against his. Her body was alive with the anticipation of how it would feel, how *she* would feel inside those strong arms.

'What about the books that belong to your friend Neve?'

Robin took a step back, his mention of Neve's name shocking her out of her daze. She shook her head, unsure what to say.

She had been imagining getting so close to him, and yet she couldn't bring herself to tell him one of the most important things about her. They knew nothing about each other, and there was so much going on. He was one of her guests, a customer, and she was already going above and beyond by helping him with the clear-out. If something happened between them and it went wrong, would Molly and the residents of Goldcrest Road forgive her for putting her personal feelings ahead of the wider aim of keeping Tim away from number four? Things were far, *far* too complicated for anything to happen between her and Will.

He shifted uncomfortably, his brows lowering in confusion. 'Sorry, did I say something wrong?'

'No, not at all. It − it's late, isn't it? We've both had a lot to drink and I have to get up in the morning, to make breakfasts, yours included.' She picked up her shoes and pushed her elbow against her bedroom door, forgetting she'd locked it before they'd gone out.

'Robin, are you OK?'

'Of course. I just need to get to bed.' She tried to select the right key and slot it into the lock without relinquishing her hold on her shoes or handbag.

'Here, let me.' Will took the key ring from her and opened the door, being careful not to push it too quickly so Robin fell inside with it.

'Thank you.' She stepped into her room and dropped her shoes on the bed. When she turned back he was closing the door slowly, shutting himself out and her in.

'Great room,' he whispered, nodding his head at the fairy lights that were wound around her silver, wrought-iron headboard. She hadn't put pinprick lights in her room – it had seemed like an extravagance she couldn't afford – but she had created the effect in her own, unsubtle way.

She'd switched the fairy lights on earlier that evening, and the glow-in-the-dark stars on her ceiling had absorbed their light and were giving off their greenish hue. She tried to picture what he was seeing; her standing there in the half-darkness, probably with wine-stained lips, in a bedroom that looked like it belonged to a teenager.

She wanted to explain that she needed the stars; that they weren't just for effect. She wanted to tell him that after Neve's death she hadn't been able to sleep in the dark, the blue flashing lights and the sounds of the screams returning stronger than ever whenever she'd closed her eyes. Will's comments had been flippant, but she *had* needed a night light. She wanted to tell him everything, but by the time she'd realized that she was willing to trust him with it, he'd whispered her a good night and was gone.

Chapter 10

The next morning Robin worked determinedly through her headache, refusing to give in to something that was self-inflicted. Felix and Olivia had asked for kedgeree, and she'd prepared a champagne breakfast for Emily and Jonathan and taken it to their room, looking as cheerful and perky as possible. Paige was in a particularly chirpy mood, humming what sounded like a very monotonous dance track – or else just one line of a song, over and over – and Robin felt, for the first time since she'd opened the guesthouse, that she was getting to the end of her tether.

'I can't believe he's been in Starcross for so long,' Paige said, alerting Robin to the fact that they were in the middle of a conversation about Will that she hadn't been paying attention to. 'How does he afford it? Isn't it nearly a fortnight?'

'Nearly,' Robin confirmed. 'But he's given up work to come down here and sort through his aunt's house, so it makes sense that he'd have some money for expenses.'

'Not if he had planned to stay in the house all along.' Paige waved a spatula around to emphasize her point. 'And he brought his dog, so – well, I dunno. Is it fair that he's hogging the room?' She spun to face Robin, her pretty face doing a perfect teenager pout.

Robin laughed and then winced as the red-wine anvil sliced through her head. Sixteen-year-old Paige had inherited her curiosity from Molly, and Robin was often reminded how similar mother and daughter were. 'Nobody else has booked it, so he's not stopping anyone from staying in there.'

'So what does it say on the website? If I were to go to the online booking system, when could I book Starcross from? Theoretically.'

Robin turned away as the toast popped out of the toaster, knowing that whatever she said Paige could check for herself anyway. 'I've held it until the end of the month, just until I know what Will's doing.'

'That's another three weeks! And there's only one of him. Isn't it the most romantic room you have? *I* think it is. Shouldn't it be reserved for couples?'

'No, Paige.' Robin shook her head. 'It's for whoever books it. And you never know, Will might decide Tabitha's house is habitable after another few days, and then I can free it up. Why are you so interested, anyway?'

'I just want to be involved,' Paige said sullenly. 'I do work here, after all.'

'And I couldn't be more grateful for that than I am today.' She gave the young woman a warm smile. 'Here, leftover hash browns. Nobody wanted extras this morning.'

'Don't you still have to feed Will? He hasn't appeared yet.'

'No, but he might be feeling a bit fragile, like I am. By the time he comes down, this will be cold – go on, save it going to waste.'

'Ta.' Paige nibbled it delicately and then poured a splurge

of tomato ketchup over the rest and shovelled it into her mouth.

There was a knock on the door, and Emily and Jonathan Hannigan stood in the doorway of the patio garden. Robin was struck again by how smartly dressed they were. Emily's long turquoise skirt glittered with silver thread detail, and the brown shirt Jonathan was wearing had cream stitching running round the seams.

'Hello, can we come in for a moment?' Emily asked. 'Is it allowed?'

'Of course. Please excuse the mess, though.'

They stepped into the kitchen and hovered awkwardly, as if waiting for Robin to start the conversation.

'How can I help?' she asked. 'Was there a problem with breakfast?'

'Not at all. The champagne breakfast was *perfect*. It's our anniversary today, which is why we chose it, and now we were wondering – I know you said if you could help in any way . . .' Emily glanced at her husband and he took up the mantle.

'Would you be happy to take some photos of us, on the beach? Just a few quick snaps that we can remember the day by? We didn't want to go over the top and hire a photographer, but we're after something a bit better than a few selfies. If it's too much of an imposition, though, please say.'

'I'd be more than happy to,' Robin said, her mind flashing back to the photo of the happy Once in a Blue Moon Days couple, Artem and Janine, on the private beach in Cornwall. 'Except, I might not be the best person for the job. Paige, would you like to do it?'

Paige shook her head. 'I'll stay here and finish the breakfasts. You look like you could do with the fresh air.'

Robin smiled gratefully, knowing Paige was only trying

to be helpful, but after the way she'd left it with Will the night before, she wanted to clear the air before he disappeared to Tabitha's house. 'It's fine, Paige. I feel fine.'

'Please, Robin,' Emily said, clasping her hands together. 'I'd love to hear more about the guesthouse, and where you got the inspiration for our room. Some of the paintings are local, aren't they?'

'Most of them are. Paige, if you're *sure* you don't mind holding the fort? We won't be gone long.'

'Half an hour, tops,' Jonathan added.

'You go. I'll be perfectly fine here.' Paige waved them away and turned to the kitchen counter, her humming starting up again.

Robin smiled. Paige had shown herself to be more than competent when it came to refurbishments, as well as breakfasts and changeovers, and would probably relish the opportunity to be in sole charge of Will's breakfast.

'I'll nip up and get the camera.' Jonathan headed up the stairs.

'Are you enjoying it so far?' Robin asked Emily. 'At least the weather's decided to be kind this week. Campion Bay always looks at its best in the sunshine.'

'We love it,' Emily admitted. 'The town centre is so full of interesting shops, and somehow has this lazy, chilled-out feel about it even when it's busy. And I could stroll up the promenade with fish and chips every day.'

'Have you seen—' Robin started, just as the doorbell rang. 'Hold that thought.'

She opened the door to find Will standing in front of her, a huge bouquet of lilies and roses obscuring most of his face. Robin was dumbstruck, her mind unable to juggle the scene into making any kind of sense.

172

'These just got delivered for you,' he said breathlessly. 'I was coming up the path, and a van pulled up. He asked if a Robin Brennan lived here, and when I confirmed it, seemed happy for me to give them to you.'

She could see his eyes above the pink blooms, and when she didn't respond, his brows knitted together. 'Sorry, did you think—'

'Who on earth are they from?' Robin cut in, hoping her confusion would mask the disappointment she felt that they weren't from him. Although, she reasoned, wouldn't that have been weird anyway?

Darcy skittered ahead of Will into the hall, barking repeatedly.

'Calm down, Darcy.' Will passed the bouquet to Robin. The bunch was heavy, the flowers beautiful and scented, the sort of thing she and Neve had often ordered for their Once in a Blue Moon Days. 'Darcy has never liked lilies,' Will explained, as the Cavapoo continued to yelp.

'Probably because they're associated with funerals,' Emily said.

'Who's got a secret admirer?' Jonathan asked, hurrying down the stairs and kissing his wife on the cheek.

'They're Robin's,' Emily said. 'How exciting! Shall we leave you alone to read the card? We can always do the photos later.'

'No, that's fine, I'll only be a moment.' Robin took the bouquet into Sea Shanty and placed it on the table. It took her a few seconds to find the card in amongst the sea of petals. There were white lilies, pale pink and vibrant yellow roses, some still perfect buds, some flowers fully open and filling the room with their perfume.

Glancing behind her, she could see that Will had his towel

173

round his shoulders, his trodden-down trainers half on his feet. He had been for his morning swim despite their wine-soaked evening. Now he was standing between Emily and Jonathan, and she thought she saw a flicker of annoyance pass across his face before he replaced it with a smile and pointed at the stairs.

She nodded and watched him disappear from view, Darcy, her barking halted, loping up behind him. Robin forced herself to turn back to the small white envelope in her hands and pulled the card out, reading the note inside without even looking at the image on the front.

I'm sorry for the other night. You're much more important to me than any sale. Can we get to know each other again? TL x

A strange feeling lodged itself in Robin's chest, mingling with her foolishness. She should have known. It was a classically expensive and over-the-top statement, one that screamed *Tim Lewis*. He was apologizing for his behaviour the night she'd introduced him to Will, but was he being genuine, or was this just another way of marking territory he wrongly thought was his? Would he have laughed at the perfect timing that had led to Will accepting the flowers from the delivery driver, or was she being overly cynical?

She put the card on the table and returned to her guests. 'A good surprise?' Emily asked.

Robin shoved her purse and phone in the pockets of her jeans. 'I don't know. It's complicated.'

'Oh no,' Emily said, sounding genuinely concerned. 'I'm sorry.'

'It'll work itself out, one way or another,' Robin said with a flippancy she didn't feel. 'Shall we?'

She opened the front door for them and then stepped out into a balmy spring morning that instantly soothed her head and made her feel brighter. The heaviness seemed to lift the closer they got to the beach, and she slipped her ballet pumps off and left them next to the wall as the three of them made their way to a clear spot near to the water.

The sand was damp and cool beneath her feet and, still relatively early, the beach was quiet, the sound of the waves filling her head.

'What about here?' she asked. 'I can take a few with the sea in the background, and then get some with the seafront behind, so you have a variety.'

'Thank you so much for doing this,' Jonathan said.

'It's my pleasure. I'm always happy to play even a small part in memorable occasions.'

'You used to do it for a living, didn't you? Before this?'

Robin nodded, closing her eyes briefly and letting the wind catch her hair. She started taking photos, concentrating her efforts on framing the shots, Emily and Jonathan turning out to be as photogenic as they were friendly. She took some with the sea and beach behind, and then moved round so that they had their backs to the houses and businesses on Goldcrest Road. Robin walked backwards, hoping to get in a few colourful long shots.

'Wait!' Emily shouted at her.

'What's wrong?' She found out a millisecond later as a low wave crashed across her ankles, soaking the bottom of her jeans. Her guests looked horrified, but Robin grinned. 'Hazard of the job. Have a look through these and see what you think. We can always take some more.' She handed the camera to them and they peered at the screen together, nodding and making approving noises.

'These are great,' Jonathan said. 'Exactly what we'd hoped for.'

'Thank you so much, Robin. This week is special for us, and we wanted to remember it.'

'Your seventh anniversary,' Robin said, remembering the conversation they'd had when they first arrived.

Emily nodded. 'If you count both times.'

'And it's really worked, despite all that time apart in between? I mean, you seem so happy – happier than most people – so I guess it has.'

'I understand your scepticism,' Jonathan said. 'Lots of our friends and relatives were incredulous, a few tried to talk us out of going through with it, saying there was no way it would last when it had failed the first time.'

'But that was the point,' Emily added. 'It hadn't worked the first time. We were too young, we didn't know ourselves well enough, let alone know each other. It went wrong, and we thought that was it. Of course, you do in your early twenties – the whole world is ahead of you once you come out of the other side of a break-up.'

'But you found each other again,' Robin said.

Jonathan nodded, wrapping his arm around his wife.

'I can't imagine it.' Robin picked up her shoes and walked alongside them. 'Even if there's some residual feelings, an echo of the attraction that had first drawn you together, how can you get past all that's happened since, or however it ended the first time round?'

Emily stopped walking and looked closely at Robin. 'It sounds like you're speaking from experience.'

Robin stared at her feet, and then the sea, and then made herself meet Emily's gaze. 'I grew up in Campion Bay, but I lived in London for over a decade. I've only been back a few months, and there's someone here . . . An ex.'

'Ah, the flowers.'

'That obvious?'

'That fits the definition of complicated,' she said. 'Especially if you're having feelings you don't know what to do with.'

'We didn't fall into each other's arms immediately the second time round,' Jonathan said, approaching the ice cream kiosk next to Skull Island. 'Coffee?'

Robin waved him away, and he went to order. 'It took you a while?'

'The trust wasn't there at first,' Emily said. 'We were both wary of each other, of how we felt. We may come across as dreamers, but we were practical about it, too. We understood that trying for a second time wouldn't be easy, that it would be hard to move past old recriminations or problems. But I couldn't ignore the way I felt about him, the love that was still there. Now we know we've been given a second chance, and that makes it even more worthwhile.'

'It sounds like a fairy tale,' Robin said.

Emily shrugged, the happiness radiating off her like an extra sun. 'We were lucky. It can't happen very often, finding love with the same person a second time round.'

'I bet it's once in a blue moon,' Robin said, tucking her hair behind her ear and gazing out to sea.

The guesthouse was silent when Robin got back, having left Emily and Jonathan to spend their anniversary at Corfe Castle, blissfully happy in their rekindled relationship. She threw her keys on the table in Sea Shanty, glared accusingly at the bouquet of flowers that was filling the whole of downstairs with its heady scent, then went to get a vase of water. Eclipse met her in the kitchen, meowing up at her until she abandoned what she was doing and pulled him into her arms for a hug. She let his buzzing warmth calm her down, and then tried to arrange the flowers while he lay across her shoulders like a mink stole, his tail tickling her cheek.

Her hangover had dulled after the sea air, and she made herself a cup of peppermint tea and took a notepad to the sofa, with the pretence of working on her next marketing campaign. Her bookings over the next few months were solid, if not sold out, and she wanted to take advantage of the hot weather and maximize her profits with as many fully booked days as possible. She had several ideas for promotions; there was a wine company she wanted to link with, and a couple of events coming up in Campion Bay – the summer fireworks and a vintage fair she thought she could use as selling points for last-minute breaks.

She started to make a list, willing herself not to get distracted by the enticing view beyond the glass as a group of friends in their twenties jostled and laughed their way to Maggie's crazy golf course, one of them eating from a huge ball of candyfloss while the others tried to push his face into the pink swirl of sugar.

She wanted to take Will to Skull Island. After the previous night, when she'd discovered that he agreed with her about Tabitha's plaque, and that standing close to him and looking into those green eyes felt like fireworks were going off inside her, she wanted to spend more time with him. And she wanted to do it away from his project and her guesthouse, where she felt they were both being at their most professional and subdued.

Molly's idea had been a great one, *if* the plan had been to make Robin fall for Will. Sadly, they were trying to make Will fall for Campion Bay, and after her sudden cold feet at the mention of Neve's name, and then revealing her princess-style bedroom to him, she wouldn't be surprised if he was itching to get away from his crazy landlady and the seaside town altogether.

Eclipse slipped off her shoulders and started pawing at her pen, which was moving across the paper. Robin realized that instead of doodling stars and flowers, she had written two names. *Will* and *Tim*.

'I'm hopeless, kitten, you know that, right? Your mum is a walking, mooning disaster. *Mooning* because I like moons, and because that's all I seem to do these days.' Eclipse let out a tiny squeak. 'No need to agree quite so readily.' She stared at the paper for a moment, then sat up straight. 'Moons. That's it!'

Ten minutes later she was back on the sofa with her notepad and Neve's astrology book on her knees. She turned to the section titled 'Love Matches', and flipped through to the pages detailing how compatible each of the star signs were with each other. Robin's birthday was the twenty-first of February, just inside Pisces, and Tim – of course – was a Leo. A summer baby, with blond, sunny curls and the confidence to match. She scanned through until she found *Love compatibility between Pisces and Leo*, and then read what it said, making notes.

Leo is assertive – no shit – *while Pisces chooses a softer path, and is the more reserved partner in any relationship. Leo will be in charge, while over-emotional Pisces can dampen the flames of Leo's enthusiasm.*

'Sounds great,' Robin said, rolling her eyes, thinking how perfectly it fitted with Tim. She skipped ahead to the summation:

Leo and Pisces are receptive to each other's teachings. They enjoy the new perspective the other brings to life, and to their love, making it a wholesome and worthwhile relationship. 'That doesn't sound like the greatest love story of all time,' she murmured. 'Who wants their love to be wholesome, apart from the Brady Bunch?'

With a flash of annoyance, she realized she had no idea when Will's birthday was; her great idea had fallen at the second hurdle. Then she remembered that the booking form on the overly thorough GuestSmart software asked guests to include their date of birth. Will had completed it the day after he'd arrived. Feeling a tug of guilt at looking at his record for unprofessional purposes, she hurried to the computer.

There it was – 2 November 1981. She worked it out quickly in her head – he was thirty-five, nearly three years older than she was, and a Scorpio. Returning to Neve's book, she found the right page. How would she, as an emotional Pisces, fare with a fearless, serious Scorpio? This time she read the last line first.

A union between Pisces and Scorpio is one of mutual respect and true, profound commitment. Their love will, above all things, endure.

This was much stronger. Enduring love, profound commitment. It was a love you could hold on to, one made to last. Robin smiled, but then, reading back over the rest of the page, her triumph faded. *For a Scorpio, everything is black and white, tarnished or golden. They will not tolerate deception.*

Suddenly this felt like one of the worst ideas she'd had for a long time, almost as bad as not shutting down Molly's stupid 'Saving Goldcrest Road' plan the moment she'd mentioned it. She shut the book and was carrying it across to her room when the doorbell rang. 'Hang on a sec!'

'It's open, can I come in?' Molly stepped into the hall wearing a pure white hoody over her jeans, her hair pulled back from her subtly made-up face.

'Molly!' Robin clutched the book to her chest.

'I came to see how last night went, but it looks like I've turned up just in time. What have you been doing with Neve's book – not showing it to Will, I hope?'

Robin's laugh was pure nerves. 'No, of course not. I was just—'

'What's that smell? Have you taken up floristry as well as everything else?' She peered into Sea Shanty, her eyes widening at the sight of Tim's bouquet centrepiece. She raised a perfectly groomed eyebrow. 'What the hell happened last night? Don't tell me, you seduced Will into your bed – or his bed, or one of the beds in this place – and it was so amazing he declared his undying love for you and bought out the whole of Bertie's Blooms to prove it?'

'Not quite,' Robin managed. 'These are from Tim.'

'Oh.' Molly's voice was flat. 'Or are you pleased? Honestly, Robin, how can your love life be so complicated when nothing's actually happening?'

'Don't you think I've asked myself that a hundred times? I've been trying to find the answers.'

'In *Neve's book*? This is a particularly sorry state of affairs.'

'She believed in it.' Robin leaned against the wall, too tired to be affronted.

'I know she did,' Molly said gently, squeezing her friend's arm. 'And I completely get that. But how can you believe in it when you don't even understand it? Aren't you going to just tie yourself in knots?'

'I've managed that perfectly well without the help of Neve's astrology tomes, thank you very much. Want a cuppa?'

181

'Yes,' Molly said. 'And a complete rundown of your date with Will Nightingale, from start to finish. Leave no detail out. We're all counting on you to convince Will to stay in Campion Bay.'

For the rest of that day and the next, Will and Robin skirted around each other. They were polite, on the edge of friendly, but without the warmth and easiness there'd been before their evening at the restaurant had ended so awkwardly. She felt uncomfortable about running away from their moment of closeness, about the flowers she'd fleetingly thought had been from him, and she had no idea how he saw the whole situation. He returned to the guesthouse late every evening, giving her a quick wave goodnight, and appeared for breakfast each morning after his swim.

He was immersing himself in the house, in Tabitha's past and in the dust and gloom, and not giving himself any space to breathe. Robin knew what that felt like. She'd focused so hard on Once in a Blue Moon Days after Neve's death, trying to blot out her grief and carry on their dream together, and it hadn't gone well for her or for the business.

She wondered if Will had gone for that drink with Tim, and what else he'd discovered in the house. She wanted him to have a day off, and she wanted to start helping him again, to relieve some of the burden he must be feeling. She hadn't been round to Tabitha's house since the day before their meal.

She knew that all she had to do was speak to him – to rip the plaster off, to clear the air between them. She was sure everything would be OK once she had got over that initial hurdle.

She resolved to do it by the weekend, so they could take advantage of the sunny weather forecast that was ideally suited to crazy golf and ice creams. But on Saturday morning, after she and Paige had completed changeovers for the new guests, she found herself doing paperwork in Sea Shanty and watching other people enjoying the balmy day through the window. Seagulls were strolling unabashed on top of a red Mercedes parked outside the guesthouse, leaving signs of their presence all over the glossy paintwork. The phone rang and she answered it to a young woman who was so quiet Robin could barely hear her, enquiring whether Rockpool was free for a week at the end of May.

She clicked through the screens on GuestSmart, asking the woman, whose name was Lorna, to hold on while she double-checked, and so she didn't notice Will come in.

'Yes,' she said, 'that's fine. Would you like me to reserve it for you? Do you have any special requirements – is it for a special occasion?' She took down the woman's details, jumping as something brushed against her leg. Darcy was looking up at her, her brown eyes huge, her tongue lolling out. Robin stared at the dog for a moment, and then allowed her gaze to take in the rest of the room.

Will was standing in front of the window with his back to her. She could see the definition of his shoulder blades through his thin white T-shirt. He was standing very still; an unnerving statue. Robin forced herself to focus on Lorna, on completing her booking and sounding as welcoming as possible. Finally, she put the receiver gently back in place. Will still hadn't moved, and Darcy had settled at Robin's feet, as if she, too, was waiting for her.

'Will?' she asked tentatively. 'Can I help with anything? Are you OK?'

He turned slowly, his eyes finding hers. Robin was shocked by the raw emotion in his expression; she hadn't seen him like this before, as if she would be able to knock him to the floor with a single finger. He'd always seemed so solid, so certain about everything.

'What's happened?' she asked, drinking in the sight of him. His white T-shirt was still pristine, unmarked with dirt or grime, and he was holding something. It looked like a bundle of letters, the envelopes small and creased at the edges.

She saw his Adam's apple bob as he swallowed, the words seeming to take an age to form before he spoke them into the silence. 'I found something,' he said. 'In my aunt's house. I found out why he did it.'

Chapter 11

The sun was shining down on them through the window and the sea, a glimmering deep aquamarine, was beautifully still. The room had a stillness of a different kind, and even Darcy and Eclipse were sitting close to each other on the rug, as if realizing now was not the time for petty squabbles. Robin had sat Will down and made a pot of coffee, and had then spent too long arranging biscuits on a plate because she knew that when she went back into Sea Shanty he was going to tell her something momentous about Tabitha; about his whole family. Whatever it was, he seemed completely stunned by it, as if he'd been encased in a block of ice and was thawing bit by bit.

She was sitting next to him on the sofa, and she could smell the sweetness of rhubarb and custard, even though he didn't seem to be sucking a sweet. He held the letters in his hand, and Robin didn't know whether to take them from him or click her fingers, startling him out of whatever unhappiness his mind had forced him towards.

'Will,' she said quietly, 'what did you find out? What are these letters?'

'They're from Tabitha to Dad.'

Robin frowned, wondering if he'd said it right. 'So why are they in your aunt's house?'

'Because he returned them all. Look.' He took the first envelope from the pile and handed it to her, his movements cautious, as if the paper might suddenly crumble into dust. There was an address in South London written in beautiful, fluid handwriting, but this had been scribbled out, and Tabitha's Campion Bay address, written in capitals in the top corner, had been circled next to writing that said *RETURN TO SENDER*. 'That's my dad's handwriting. Capitals all the time, which makes him seem angry. At this point, I'm sure he was.'

'Have they been opened?'

Will shrugged. 'They have, but I can't tell if it was by Dad, or by Tabitha when he returned them, wondering if he'd put a letter of his own in the envelope. They were tied with a ribbon in the bottom of Tabitha's wardrobe. I thought they were love letters from Nigel at first, from when they got together. Then I saw my dad's writing.'

Robin turned the envelope over carefully. It was undoubtedly old, a treasure of the past, and she would have been thrilled at this secret discovery if it wasn't for the obvious pain it had caused Will. The seal had been broken, but gently, as if with a penknife or letter opener.

'Have you read them all?' she asked.

'Yes.' He cleared his throat, and she put the letter on her knee while she poured him a cup of coffee. He took it gratefully, holding it with both hands while the pile of letters sat unassumingly in his lap.

'May I?' she asked, picking up the letter again.

Will nodded and sipped his coffee. She couldn't help but notice how the tan he'd arrived with had paled, and how his bottom lip was cracked. He had a line of red along his jaw, as thin as a paper cut, and she wondered whether he'd done it shaving or delving into dark corners in Tabitha's house.

She turned her attention back to the envelope. She lifted the flap and slowly pulled out the piece of paper – thick, good-quality writing paper with a watermark of the stationery company in the top centre. The writing was the same elegant script as on the envelope, and it was evenly spaced, giving the impression of being written calmly, perhaps drafted elsewhere before it had been finalized and sent.

Dear Rod, my brother,
Aren't you still my brother? Does this one decision, born out of love, mean that we can no longer be family? Is the principle that important that we can't put this behind us? We're living on the coast now, a place called Campion Bay, and I'd love you to see it, the blue sky and sea, the fresh air and space so different from London. He chose my love over his work and we moved here to put some distance between us. But now, can't we start to talk it over, to reconcile? It is the one piece of my happiness that's missing, and maybe it's selfish of me, but I believe it's possible to have both.
  Please write back,
  Your sister, always,
  Tabby xxx

Robin swallowed, rereading the words. 'What was the decision? Was it her decision, or his?'

187

'Hers,' Will said, handing her the pile of envelopes. 'She fell in love with his business rival. My dad built his own building firm from scratch when he was in his twenties. It's successful; he's close to retirement age but won't consider giving up, although now he only oversees the sites. He's a proud man, and while building firms are ten a penny these days, back then he had his patch of South London. He always told me he was unrivalled in the area. It seems that wasn't strictly true.'

'He kept that from you?' she asked, unfolding the next letter.

'I suppose it was tied up with Tabitha, and he refused to mention her name. I only knew about her through Mum, and she only talked about her when Dad was out of the house. Even then, she never went into detail.' He rested his elbow on his knee, his forehead in his hand. His coffee mug was leaning precariously, half-forgotten, and Robin resisted the urge to take it from him. 'My dad has a temper, so going against his wishes – especially on this – is too hard for her.'

Robin was torn between reading the letters for herself, and hearing it from Will. 'So there was another building firm, and it was run by Nigel, and your aunt fell in love with him?'

'That's what the letters say. When she told him, my dad gave her an ultimatum. There's mention of the wedding, and while my grandparents were there he refused to go, refused to see her at all, to even talk it over.' He looked at her, his brows lowered. 'I could *maybe* understand a grudge if Nigel had done something underhand, had harmed my dad's business in some way, and I can't know for sure, but . . . Tabitha always talked about him with such warmth. And would she have ended up marrying him if he'd tried to sabotage my dad's business?'

'I don't remember Nigel very well,' Robin said. 'I was only young when he died. Mum said he had a heart attack.'

'He wasn't even fifty,' Will said. 'I never met him, but I know Tabitha loved him, that was clear from the way she talked about him. I don't think she ever got over losing him. It makes me even angrier with Dad. How can falling in love with someone be worthy of being shunned by your family?' He sighed and sat back on the sofa, clutching his coffee mug to his chest.

'I don't know,' Robin whispered. She opened the next letter. 'And Tabitha never told you the truth, once you'd started coming to see her?'

'She said it wasn't her place. I suppose she didn't want to turn me against Dad, to reveal how cruel he'd been.'

'What will you do now you know? What will you say to him?'

'I honestly haven't got a clue.'

Robin read the second letter, and then the third and the fourth, her coffee going cold as she absorbed Tabitha's entreaties to her brother, reminding him of how close they'd been before Nigel had come between them, pleading with him to let her visit, or for him to come to Campion Bay, to start rebuilding bridges. Robin could see so much of her next-door neighbour in the letters, anecdotes about their childhood – perhaps hoping to make her brother laugh, appealing to his better nature. What was clear in all of them, though, was that Tabitha wasn't prepared to apologize for loving Nigel, or for choosing him. Rather, she wanted her brother to see sense. *I love Nigel, and if only you were prepared to see what kind of person he is, I'm certain that you'd love him too.*

This stubbornness, which Robin silently applauded Tabitha for, was the reason they had never reconciled. She wouldn't give up, or say sorry, for the husband she had chosen, and Rod would never see it as anything but betrayal.

She could see why Will was shocked by the revelation, and while the letters couldn't reveal exactly why his dad felt the way he did about Nigel, she had known Tabitha and, like Will, she couldn't imagine her loving someone who was inherently cruel or underhand. Will seemed to put the blame wholeheartedly at his father's door, as if it wasn't entirely out of character. Rod Nightingale seemed, from the little she understood, a proud, fiery man, and one who wasn't prepared to see things from other people's perspectives.

While she read, she kept glancing at Will. He was perfectly still on the sofa, his eyes closed, and she thought of the way he tried to hold his emotions inside, controlling every nerve right down to his little finger. She couldn't imagine what a blow it would be to find out her own dad had done something so devastating, and had never softened or taken the first, tentative steps towards a reunion. How did Rod feel now, Robin wondered, knowing Tabitha was dead and he'd never be able to make it up to her? She couldn't imagine that he didn't care.

She got to the last letter in the pile, noticing the difference immediately. The address on the front was Tabitha's, the writing the capital scrawl of Will's dad. Robin held her breath. This was a letter from him to her, a change in direction after all those returned letters. She glanced at Will but he still had his eyes closed, and she wondered if this was the letter of reconciliation, if Will had missed it and there'd been some huge miscommunication he didn't know about.

She turned it over and saw it had been ripped open without hesitation. She could picture a younger Tabitha seeing this letter on the mat, her face lighting up with happiness and relief, thinking that after years of being shunned, this was finally the moment when she would be forgiven. Her hand trembled slightly as she opened the piece of paper. There were too few words, she realized, her heart swooping like a rollercoaster as she took only seconds to read them.

Mrs Thomas,
It cannot have escaped your attention that I have nothing
to say to you. My views are unchanged. Please stop writing
to me.
Rodney Nightingale

Robin pressed her lips together, feeling a jolt of shock at the coldness of the letter. Eclipse gave a gentle meow from the rug, where he and Darcy were sitting close together, Darcy's tail wagging in a scene that was straight out of an old Real Fires advert, their initial altercation forgotten. Robin turned back to the letter. It was devoid of passion or personality, as if he was writing to a woman he'd just met who had shown him unrequited affections. It was the most loveless thing she'd seen, and it made her heart break to think of Tabitha reading it over and over, her hopes dashed in a few short lines.

Closing the piece of paper, she slipped it back in its envelope and placed the pile of letters on the sofa next to her. She sipped her cold coffee and stared out of the window. When Eclipse got up, stretched on his short legs and walked out of the room, Robin sank on to the rug and pulled Darcy against her. The dog came willingly, glancing in the direction of her master.

'I think he's exhausted,' she whispered to Darcy. 'He's been working so hard, and then to find this out – to find out what his dad did to Tabitha . . . Let's leave him to sleep, shall we?' She kissed the impossibly soft fur on the top of Darcy's head, and then got quietly up and left the room.

After giving Eclipse and Darcy some lunch, she had gone upstairs to carry out a final inspection of Wilderness and Andalusia before the new guests, booked in later that day, arrived.

Emily and Jonathan Hannigan were staying for a week, their check-out scheduled for Monday morning, and they were already professing their regret that their holiday was coming to an end. As she put together a shopping list for her trip into Bridport later that afternoon, Robin wondered if she should get them a parting gift, something that would remind them of their anniversary. She had begun to see some of the guests as friends, and had to remind herself that the bonds that were formed were purely between landlady and guest, and nothing more.

Even with Will, she realized, she couldn't be sure that his feelings went any deeper. She wanted them to; she had been shocked by the letters while also being touched that he'd come straight to her, but had quickly realized that she was simply the only person he knew well enough in Campion Bay. It made her realize that, despite the start of a few tentative friendships, while he was here, Will was essentially alone.

She'd left him sleeping on the sofa, and when she'd checked on him half an hour ago he'd still been there, his breathing even and gentle, Darcy lying with her head on his lap.

At least, she thought as she burrowed through the

freezer, he had felt able to show her. Despite having few options, he had trusted her enough to come to her with the letters, when he could have kept the revelation to himself, worrying it over until he made a decision about how to approach his dad. She closed her eyes, not envying him that conversation.

She'd been replaying it over and over, what she'd found out about his family, how Will had seemed defeated by it. His dad had a temper, but did that mean Will did too? From what little she'd seen, she couldn't imagine him enraged about anything. Was he more like his mum, who had clearly tried to keep the peace, feeding him titbits of information that she felt he deserved while trying not to anger her husband?

Her shopping list written, Robin started work on the hob, scrubbing it with force, her jumper rolled up to the elbows. Eclipse dug his claws into her ankles, requesting a hug. She spun quickly, then jumped and dropped her cloth at the sight of Will standing in the doorway.

'Sorry, I didn't mean to startle you.' He was blinking and rubbing his jaw.

'No, you're fine.' She took an edge of the cloth, which Eclipse had pounced on, and spent a few moments wrestling it from the kitten before picking him up. 'Are you OK?'

He nodded. 'I think so. You shouldn't have let me fall asleep.'

'You clearly needed it.'

'Your sofas are too comfy.'

'Seems to be a common complaint from you.' She met his gaze and offered a smile, which he returned.

'You know it's only because this place is showing me up to be a sleep-loving softy.'

'I never believed the Bear Grylls thing anyway.'

'You didn't?'

'Not for a second.'

His smile widened, reaching his eyes, and Robin's tummy shimmied in response.

'I'd better get back,' he said. 'It's already the afternoon and I've achieved nothing.'

'No.' She stepped forwards, shaking her head. 'Not today.'

'What?'

'You're not going back there today, or tomorrow.'

His face creased into a frown and she grabbed his hand. Eclipse leapt up to her shoulder to watch the unfolding scene from the best vantage point.

'You've had a shock, Will. I read all the letters, I read the last one, from your dad . . .' He turned away from her, but she held on, squeezing his hand. 'It's awful, the whole situation, and I think . . . you need to take time out. Don't go back there this afternoon, go into town or something, get some fresh air, and then tomorrow I'm giving you a tour of Campion Bay.'

'There's too much to do. You've been in there, and you know how little impact we've made, despite the long hours. It's a huge house, she was there for so many years, storing things up . . .'

'Exactly. So a day and a half away from it isn't going to set you back too much, is it?'

'Are you sure about that?' His green eyes flashed with irritation, but she held her ground.

'Yes, I am. On this occasion. Look, Will, you've shown me these and I – I don't know how to help, or what I can do about it, and I know you have to work it out on your own.

But what I *can* do – because, let's face it, it's my job – is provide some TLC, which you could really do with right now.'

'You're a guesthouse owner, not a counsellor.'

'Exactly. My expertise is in having a good time, and that's what I'm offering. Just think about it, please. Don't go back to that house for the next couple of days.'

He stared at her, his chest rising and falling. She waited, biting her lip. Her hand still held his, and she focused on how warm it was, despite the sudden coldness of his expression. She knew he wasn't angry with her, but she was prepared to take it if it would help him feel better. She didn't look away.

Eventually, he hung his head, his breath coming out in a long exhalation. 'I'll think about it,' he said, and then released his hand, turned and walked away from her.

She sagged back against the counter, listening as he trudged towards Sea Shanty – picking up the letters? She waited to hear his tread on the stairs as he made his way up to Starcross, but instead she heard him call sharply to Darcy, and then the front door banged. She closed her eyes and swore under her breath, trying to believe that he was heading into town and not back to Tabitha's house. Had she overstepped the mark? She didn't think so – for once she wasn't regretting what she'd said to him. But he was hurting, and he had to deal with it in his own way.

Trying to push thoughts of Will out of her mind, reminding herself that he wasn't her only guest, Robin turned back to the hob and polished it until it gleamed.

She checked a couple in their mid-twenties, Katy and Dean, into Wilderness, and a retired couple from Orkney into

Andalusia. Elisabeth and Charles were travelling the whole of the south coast, finishing with a trip to Paris on the Eurostar. Robin was impressed, and a little bit envious, when they told her they'd spent several nights in Cornwall glamping close to the beach. She offered them all afternoon tea, and when Emily and Jonathan returned from a trip on a mackerel boat, she ended up setting teapots and cake along the table for them all in Sea Shanty. Tim's flowers were still impressively radiant and Katy commented on them.

'They're from a friend,' Robin said, giving her what she hoped was a relaxed smile.

'Friend, eh?' Charles cut off a chunk of coffee cake with his fork. 'It's a good friend that buys flowers like that. They speak of deeper feelings than friendship.'

'Oh, Charles, don't be so impertinent,' Elisabeth said. 'Honestly. Do ignore my husband, Robin. He feels he has to comment on *everything*.'

'That's fine,' Robin said, 'comment away. Unless you're going to tell me you hate the rooms. That would be hard to take.'

'Oh shush.' Elisabeth gave her a disapproving look. 'You're only saying that because you know we couldn't possibly hate them. Your guesthouse is beautiful, you should be very proud. And cake, too!'

'I didn't make these,' Robin confessed. 'They come from the teashop up the road. Ashley and Roxy bake them all. They have a great afternoon tea offer on a Sunday as well.'

'We might go tomorrow,' Emily said, 'for one final hurrah. I don't want this week to end.'

'We'll come back, love.' Jonathan put his hand over hers.

'I've got special deals for returning customers,' Robin said. 'I'll show them to you when you check out and you

196

can have a think.' She grinned as Emily's eyes widened in delight, and realized how good it felt to be talking about normal, guesthouse things, about her rooms and Campion Bay, to visitors who were here on joyous, uncomplicated holidays.

The events of earlier that day had been preying on her mind – she hated the way Will had looked at her. She had his best interests at heart, and yet there was this niggling voice that reminded her about Molly's plan, the random acts of kindness designed to make Will feel part of Campion Bay, and her own role in going along with Molly's deception. She hadn't told him about her – and others' – fears that Tim would buy Tabitha's house and ruin the seafront. And she hadn't told him about Neve, that the friend she missed so much was the inspiration behind her guesthouse. Why hadn't she just been honest with him from the start?

She made fresh pots of tea and sat alongside Elisabeth, cutting herself a slice of lemon drizzle cake. Charles began telling a story about how their tent in Cornwall – during their attempt at straightforward camping – had been invaded by a large, docile cow, nearly giving him a heart attack and making them rethink their accommodation.

'That's when we decided to give glamping a go,' he said, his eyes twinkling. 'They promised no cows.'

'They couldn't guarantee entirely bug-free nights,' added Elisabeth. 'But the odd spider or bumble bee is fine.'

'Even I can't promise that,' Robin said. 'I found a peacock butterfly in here yesterday.'

'That's not surprising with those flowers making it smell like Kew Gardens!' Charles sniffed exaggeratedly.

Robin chuckled, but her laughter died out quickly when she heard the front door clicking softly closed, as if someone was trying to come in unnoticed. She heard the unmistakable patter of Darcy's paws on the floorboards and then saw Will walk past the doorway.

'Give me a second,' she said to her guests. She went into the hallway and pulled the door of Sea Shanty closed behind her. 'Will?'

He stopped on the second stair and turned slowly to face her, his arms hanging limply at his sides. His face had a sheen of sweat on it and his white T-shirt was covered in telltale smudges.

'Robin.' She looked for signs of anger but couldn't find any, his expression open and contrite. He took a step towards her and she noticed he was sucking on one of his rhubarb-and-custard sweets. 'I'm sorry,' he mumbled, then crunched the sweet and swallowed it. 'I'm sorry about earlier. I was rude to you, it was unforgivable.'

'No, it wasn't. I forgave you as soon as you left. Being angry is understandable—'

'But not with you.' He shook his head. 'You've been so kind and generous, so patient with me. You've gone out of your way to make me feel welcome.'

Robin swallowed. 'Will, about that.' She had to tell him what Molly had done. She reached out and took his hand but he snatched it away, pain flashing across his face. She stared at him, stared down at his arms. Darcy was sitting next to the stairs, and now she pawed at Will's leg, whimpering softly.

'What have you done?' Robin asked.

Will huffed angrily. 'It was stupid.'

'What was?' Very gently, she took his arm, and saw that the skin around his left wrist was bluish and puffy round the bone. 'What did you do?'

'You were right about not going back there.' He winced as she pressed his skin. 'I was angry, and when a cupboard door got stuck, I got impatient and pulled it, and it fell on my wrist.'

'The cupboard?'

'I'm sure it's just bruised.'

'I'd love to say it serves you right, but that would be cruel. I'm sorry you're hurt. How bad does it feel? Do you want me to drive you to the walk-in centre?'

'Some frozen peas will be fine, if you can spare any? And I do deserve it. You were right.'

'I was bossy.'

'You were *right*, Robin.' He pushed her chin up gently with his finger. 'I'm so sorry for the way I behaved. I dumped all my problems on you, and then when you tried to be kind I couldn't hack it. And here I am again, needing your help.'

Relief mingled with the fireworks his touch was sending through her. 'You tried to sneak past,' she said, grinning. 'You weren't going to ask for my help.'

'I would have done, once I'd cooled down. The cupboard got the rest of my anger, after it had the cheek to fall on top of me. It does seem that, for the moment at least, I can't get very far without you.'

Robin let the words sink in, unsure what to say as pleasure washed over her. She was vaguely aware of laughter coming from Sea Shanty, and the fact that Darcy was now pawing at her leg as well, unhappy at being left out. 'Your wrist isn't going to stop you playing crazy golf, is it? I'll be heartbroken if I don't get the chance to beat you.'

Will's green eyes met hers with the warmth she'd come to expect. 'Maybe my one-handed swing will be needed after all. Even with a bruised wrist, I'm going to be pretty unstoppable. You'll be licking your wounds before the end of the day.'

She laughed and turned away. 'Not sure I should help, if that's your attitude. Let you suffer.'

'Thank you, Robin. For this, for earlier – for tomorrow.'

'Tomorrow hasn't happened yet,' she said, her heart thrumming as she went into the kitchen to wrap some frozen peas in a tea towel. Already, she couldn't wait for it to start.

Chapter 12

The weather the next day was as glorious as the forecast had predicted and they walked along Campion Bay's wild beach carrying their shoes. Darcy raced ahead, bounding in and out of the water, yipping and running back to Will before racing off again, dancing with the waves.

'It's the most animated I've ever seen her,' Robin said, laughing.

'She loves the beach,' Will admitted. 'I feel guilty every time we finish our walk or our swim and she goes back to being a perfect, well-behaved dog. She should be having fun, you know? I wouldn't mind the odd chewed shoe or jacket if it meant she was really happy, but I think Selina drummed obedience into her.'

'The beach is where she feels free,' Robin said. 'I can identify with that. There are no restrictions on this part, so even in the summer months you can bring her here.'

'I've never been this far down,' Will said. 'The current looks wilder here – I'm not sure it's safe for swimming.'

'No, it's treacherous, and the waves come right into the

cliffs. Also, look.' She pointed at a dark hollow of a cave, a ledge inside it at roughly shoulder height. 'People go fossil hunting in there, though there can't be any left now, and I've heard teenagers use it for . . . other activities. But when the tide's high, it's so dangerous. I love walking here, knowing that you're moments away from being at nature's mercy.'

'Are you a secret thrill-seeker, then? I hadn't imagined that about you.'

'I'm not one for rollercoasters or jumping out of planes, I just like the wildness of this beach, how it still feels prehistoric. It's away from Campion Bay — away from everything. It's the perfect place to think.'

'I can see that.' Will crouched in the sand and ruffled Darcy's fur as she raced up to him, barking elatedly. 'We're converts.'

'That was easy,' Robin laughed, watching while Will played tug-of-war with Darcy and a stick, water splashing on to his faded navy shorts and black T-shirt. He seemed so much more relaxed today, the colour returning to his cheeks after only a short time in the sun. After icing his wrist the evening before, she'd got her first-aid kit out and inexpertly wrapped it in a bandage, despite his protestations. Now the bandage was damp and the end had come undone, flapping gently in the breeze. She didn't think it would last the rest of the day, but she was glad. She hated to think of him as injured or in pain, though the revelation of the day before and its impact on him wouldn't disappear as easily as a bruise.

'Come on.' She held out her arm towards his good hand and waited for him to grab it, before pulling him to his feet. 'I've got lots more to show you.'

'Why do you eat those sweets?' she asked as they walked along the promenade towards the centre of town. 'Rhubarb and custard. I used to get them from the sweet shop on my way home from school. You must have bought up all their stock by now.'

'It's a bad habit,' Will admitted. 'I used – years ago – to work for my dad's building firm. He always wanted me to go into the business with him; I think he saw me taking it over one day, so I started as a labourer.'

'Hence your ability to fix the leak,' Robin said.

'That's a patch-up job; I need to get a plumber in to take a proper look at it. But I'm generally handy with DIY – except when it comes to stubborn cupboards.'

'How's your wrist feeling?'

'Much better, thanks.' He held his arm out, and they both inspected the soaked, sandy bandage. 'Shit. Sorry, Robin.'

She waved him away. 'I'm glad you don't need it any more. Anyway, carry on. Why did working for your dad turn you to candy?'

'Most of the builders smoked on site. It wouldn't be allowed these days – health and safety regulations – but this was before the ban and so . . . I wanted to fit in. I smoked for five years and then, when I changed jobs, I tried to give up. Nothing worked, my willpower wasn't great, and then someone recommended boiled sweets.'

'It helped?' Robin stopped to take off her ballet pump and dispose of a pebble that had lodged itself in the toe.

'Yup. So now I'm going to die from diabetes instead of lung cancer. I need a new, healthier habit to get me over the sweets.'

'Peas?' Robin asked lamely. 'Apples, bananas?'

Will gave her a horrified look.

'OK, fair point. Bridget Jones replaces smoking and calories with sex,' she said, shocked by her own brazenness. 'But if you've got a twenty-a-day habit then maybe that's not practical.'

'It's a nice thought, though,' Will said, squinting up at the sun, 'and burns calories as well as replacing the sugar, so I can see the merits. Maybe I should be more creative.'

'Not sure I want to know what that means,' Robin said, catching his gaze.

He laughed and looked away from her.

Robin waited until her pulse had settled before she asked her next question. 'What did your dad say when you decided not to follow in his footsteps? He doesn't sound like the most forgiving person.'

Will sighed. 'He's not. He's – very strong-minded. We don't always see eye to eye, and my decision not to go into the family business was just one in a series of things I got wrong, in his opinion. Now I know about Tabitha, it makes a horrible kind of sense. Dad's prouder of his company than anything else, and he would have seen what she did as going against that, so . . .' He shook his head. 'We don't see each other very often, though I try and meet up with Mum when I can.'

'Are you going to talk to him about what you've discovered?' she asked gently.

'I don't know. I haven't got my head around it all yet.'

'Sorry, I shouldn't have asked. Today is supposed to be about fun, and I'm not following my own rules. I've got Paige covering for me at the guesthouse, and she won't do it often at the weekends so I want to make the most of it. I'm going to show you this beautiful gallery I've found, and then we can get some lunch.'

'What time does the tournament begin?' he asked, steering Darcy out of the path of a woman with a buggy who was coming the other way.

'After we've eaten. But I have to warn you, I've got my game face on.'

She showed him round Seagull Street Gallery and talked herself out of buying the new Arthur Durrant painting, even though Will was as mesmerized by the night-time landscape as she was, and then took him for lunch in the Artichoke. Over sandwiches and pints of local ale, he told her about working at Downe Hall, about how varied his days were, and how he'd begun to feel a part of the small team who owned and ran it.

'So you were sad to leave, then? To come here and have to start again?'

He nodded. 'I was, but also, it was the right time. One of my relationships there had become . . .' He searched for the word. 'Frayed.'

'A romantic one?'

'Why do you say that?'

'Oh, come on, Will. Relationships don't get "frayed" because you disagree with someone about which order to run the tours in, or you've hung a painting slightly wonky.'

He folded his arms on the table. 'How do you know? The staff at Downe Hall take their décor – and ancestral paintings, especially – very seriously.'

'Why else would you think it was best to leave, then?'

He narrowed his eyes at her and then nodded, conceding the point. 'People always tell you not to mix business and pleasure, especially when you live in the same place. Annie is the daughter of the couple who own Downe Hall. It was perhaps not the best decision to get involved with her.'

'Yikes,' Robin said softly, trying not to feel envious of a woman she'd only just found out about. 'It sounds like *Downton Abbey*. Do you mind me asking what happened?'

'She found someone else.'

'What a cow!'

He laughed. 'It happens; people move on. But it did make things at the hall strained. I tried to get on with it; I like to think I wasn't petty or jealous, but it certainly helped me to finally bite the bullet and come down here. Though that's been a bit "out of the frying pan".'

Robin's heart skipped a beat. 'What do you mean?'

'Going from one difficult situation to the next. Dealing with my aunt's stuff, her past, this never-ending treadmill of boxes and cupboards and shelves to sort through.'

'Oh yes, of course.' She gave him a quick smile. 'Shall I get the bill?'

Will insisted on paying for lunch, then they took Darcy back to the guesthouse and arrived at Skull Island just before two. Cumulus clouds had begun to roll in over the sea, obliterating the blue, and the wind was picking up speed. Robin wrapped her teal cardigan around her as they queued to pay their entrance fee and pick up their clubs.

'Bobbin, you came!' Maggie gave them a warm smile. 'And wow, Molly, you've changed since the last time I saw you.'

Robin laughed at Will's bemused expression. 'This is Will. He's Tabitha's nephew. He's staying here for a while, to sort through the house.'

'For my sins,' Will said, holding out his hand.

Maggie shook it. 'Ah. Will. Lovely to meet you.' She gave Robin a knowing smile and Robin's insides shrivelled a little bit. Had Molly roped Maggie into her charm offensive too?

She had to tell him this afternoon. She was sure it would be OK if she could just explain it all calmly: Tim's development plans, how the acts of kindness had started, and how she had always wanted to help him, to make him feel welcome, regardless of the fate of the house.

Maggie peered out of her cubicle at Will's wrist. 'Are you going to be all right? I don't want to be sued because you've damaged yourself further by choosing to play on my course.'

'I'm fine, honestly.' Will unwrapped Robin's bandage and, shooting her an apologetic look, shoved it in his pocket. Robin noticed that his wrist was purple, with a smudge of mottled brown bruising running up his thumb.

'You brave warrior,' Maggie said in a syrupy voice, and then gave them both a wicked grin and handed them their clubs and balls.

'What hole is the water feature on?' Robin whispered when Will had turned away.

Maggie leaned in towards her, handing her scorecards and a tiny wooden pencil. 'You'll have to wait and see.'

'So much for loyalty to your friend,' Robin shot back.

Maggie spread her arms wide. 'I'm all about the fun, Bobbin. You should know that by now.'

They'd reached the halfway hole and Will was three points ahead, despite his injured wrist and the fact that Robin had played this course on countless occasions, albeit a long time ago. She was frustrated by his standard male prowess and his ability not to jump at the various shouts and cackles echoing out of the statues dotted throughout the course. Although, she had to concede, it made him even more attractive.

She considered, as she tried to get a birdie on the ninth hole, that she wouldn't have found him any *less* attractive if he'd been hopeless at golf, but she might have felt a wavering of doubt if he'd screamed like a girl. But as it was, she realized as she putted the ball and lifted her arms into the air in triumph, she was very close to being completely spellbound by Will Nightingale. She was teetering on the edge.

'Two behind,' she reminded him as they moved on to the next hole. 'I'm creeping up behind you, and soon' – she pushed her arm out in front of her – 'whoosh. I'll go flying past.'

Will nodded. She noticed that he was looking at her with a new intensity, as if he was seeing her for the first time. 'Uh huh. I've been bracing myself for this moment since you finished four behind me on the first hole. Let's see if we can crown a winner before the heavens open.' He pointed up, and Robin saw that the white clouds had made way for grey, and that rain was threatening.

'So much for a balmy Sunday,' she muttered. 'Right then, your go. Let's see what you've got, Nightingale.'

The thirteenth hole involved putting the ball up a pyramid structure, so that it went over the top and shot down the other side, hopefully straight into the final hole at the far end of the green.

'You know the owner well?' Will asked as Robin updated the scorecard. They were neck and neck. 'Bobbin's a cute nickname.'

'That's because it's from when I was six. I'm not sure it's relevant now.'

'Oh, I don't know,' Will said, swinging his club back and forth absent-mindedly. 'Bobbin Brennan has a nice ring to it. I could call you Bob.'

'Not if you want breakfast tomorrow, you couldn't.'

Will grinned. 'Does anyone call you Rob?'

She shook her head. 'Tim calls me Robs. Not sure how I

feel about that, to be honest. It used to be endearing, but . . .'
She shrugged.

'You've moved on?'

Robin met his gaze. 'I've moved on. Not Bobbin, not Robs.'

'Just Robin,' he said softly.

She nodded, tugging her hair out of her face as a particularly strong gust took hold of it.

Will put his ball on the marker, and stepped on the red cross that signalled the hole's starting point. A jet of water whooshed out of an innocuous-looking pirate model standing at the side of the hole and hit him in the chest. He took a step back, swearing, and dropped his club. Robin was frozen for a moment, and then burst out laughing.

He looked at her, the water dripping off him as if he'd just emerged from the sea. He wiped his face with a hand, blinking his surprise.

Robin tried, and failed, to stop laughing, doubling over at the waist.

'Did you know about this?' he managed. He was breathing quickly, and Robin thought pityingly that the water must be freezing.

She shook her head. 'No, I didn't. I mean, I – I—'

'You knew it was coming?'

'I didn't! I didn't know where it was, I swear.'

'Robin Brennan,' he said, 'I can't believe you would lure me here . . .'

'I didn't!'

She squealed as he grabbed her hand and pulled her towards him, against his sodden T-shirt, the water dripping off his face and landing on hers. There were droplets on his eyelashes. He blinked them off and more ran on to them from his hair, making them glisten.

He put his arm around her waist, gently bringing her closer. She could feel the cold dampness seep from his T-shirt into her cardigan, but it couldn't compete with the warmth rushing through her body as he wiped a drop of water from her cheek. She held her breath, unable to unlock her eyes from his, and felt everything slow down as he brought his face to hers and kissed her, softly at first, then with more passion, his hand pressed between her shoulder blades.

She dropped her club and wrapped her arms around his neck, giving herself over to the kiss, letting herself fall over the edge, discarding her last bit of reserve. A rumble above tried to break into her consciousness but she barely noticed it; she could only focus on his arms around her, as strong and safe as she'd imagined, and the way the sugar-sweetness of his kiss sent shockwaves of desire through her.

Then the rain came. Fat thunderstorm drops that landed like pebbles on her head and arms. They ignored it at first, and it was only when people began shrieking and running from the course that Will finally released his hold on her and looked up, squinting against the assault.

Wordlessly they picked up their clubs and balls and raced back to Maggie's shed, arriving breathless and laughing. They handed them in and turned to go, but Maggie caught hold of Robin's hand, her dark eyes in shadow. Robin saw her mouth the words 'Be careful' before she let go, and Will was pulling her along the promenade and across Goldcrest Road, the rain heavier than ever, the thunder rumbling in off the sea.

They fell into the hall of the Campion Bay Guesthouse, dripping puddles on to the floorboards.

'At least we're on an even footing now,' she said, pulling off her sodden ballet pumps, emptying her soaked handbag on to the shelf by the door and checking her phone had survived.

'That doesn't excuse the fact that you tricked me,' Will said, kicking off his trainers. 'I had no idea about that bloody water hydrant.'

'Neither did I,' Robin said, laughing. 'I knew there *was* one, but Maggie wouldn't tell me where.'

'I'm supposed to believe that?'

Eclipse padded into the hallway, sniffed at the nearest puddle of water then edged round it warily.

'Shit,' Robin said, looking at the floor, 'slip hazard. Hang on.' She unlocked her bedroom door and grabbed two towels from her tiny bathroom, passing one to Will, using the other one to mop the floor. She stood and Will held his towel out to her. She took it, passing it over the ends of her hair, anticipation fizzing through her.

'What happens now?' he asked softly.

'Uhm, let me . . .' She picked the sodden towel off the floor and took them through to her en suite, lifting discarded clothes off her bed as she passed, shoving them in a drawer and dumping the towels in her bathtub. She stepped back into her bedroom, surveying it quickly for dirty underwear or stray doodles mentioning Will.

Her phoned pinged from the shelf by the door.

'Robin, your phone,' Will called.

'Can you check it, see if one of the guests needs anything?' She plumped up her pillows, her hands shaking slightly.

'It's a text from Molly.'

'What does it say?' she asked, and then Maggie's face, her mouthed words of warning flashed in Robin's mind. She froze. 'Actually . . .' she said, but Will had started reading.

'*A little birdie just told me what happened at Skull Island,*' he read. Robin gripped on to the duvet, then raced around the bed. As she did, Will pushed the door open and stepped inside, his eyes still on the phone, his voice taking on a tone of incredulity as he read Molly's message aloud. '*Robin Brennan, one-woman publicity campaign. If you've made Will fall for you then he's not going to sell, is he? Goldcrest Road thanks you for keeping number four out of Tim's evil clutches.*'

'No no no,' Robin whispered, but Will shot her a look and kept reading.

'*You've saved the day R, and nabbed the cute guy too. I need to know all the details – hotness out of ten? Debrief later. Kiss kiss.*' He said the last words with heavy sarcasm, his confusion turning towards anger as Molly's text laid the truth bare. Will dropped his hand to his side, still holding the phone, and looked at her. 'Publicity campaign?'

'That's not – that's just a joke; Molly's joke.'

'And how about keeping number four out of Tim's *evil clutches?*'

Robin closed her eyes. She couldn't bear seeing the disappointment on his face. 'Tim has plans to buy Tabitha's house and probably convert it into flats.' It came out as a scratch, and he took a step closer to her, only a few feet separating them. She swallowed. 'I mean, you would have to agree to the sale, of course, but – but none of us wanted that.'

'So?'

'So Molly came up with this idea – she thought that . . . that if she showed you how great Campion Bay is, tried to convince you to stay on as our neighbour, then you wouldn't sell to Tim. But I liked you from the beginning Will, none of this – none of . . . of what's happened is because of Tim, or the house.'

Will stared at her for such a long time that she thought

212

he hadn't heard. She was still in her sodden clothes, and she began to tremble. She wrapped her arms tightly around herself, trying to stop the shivering.

'So all the people going out of their way to be friendly to me, that was to stop me from selling Tabitha's house?' He rubbed his forehead.

Robin nodded. 'But it doesn't mean they wouldn't have been friendly anyway – you have to believe that. We like you, Will. Me and Molly, Ashley, Stefano and Nicolas – you fit in here.'

'Oh yes,' Will said, 'the restaurant. The bottle of wine, the offer of mate's rates at Molly's beauty parlour. And the cupcakes from Ashley? Your personal tour of the area today? All so I wouldn't relinquish the house to your pal Tim and leave you in the middle of a building site?'

His expression was accusing, making her feel even colder. 'No,' she said forcefully. 'Not today – none of that, or offering to help you with the clear-out, or the . . . the cheese on toast, or . . . Will, please.' She moved closer to him, but he took a step back towards the door.

'You must think I'm really gullible,' he said, his voice quiet but edged with anger, this time directed solely at her. 'You must take me for a complete idiot. And do you know what? Maybe I am, because I believed all of it – I believed in Molly's charm and in Stefano's over-the-top hospitality, but above all I believed in *you*, Robin. I believed that what we had – what we almost had – was real.'

'It was,' she said, clasping her hands in front of her. 'What happened at the golf course, what I feel – what I've felt all along, *is* real. Do you really think I'd make that up? Didn't it feel like I was wholly there with you? Because I was, Will.'

'*If you've made Will fall for you,*' he said, repeating Molly's damning words. 'Well, congratulations, Robin. I *was* falling for you, I trusted you, and I was beginning to think about what my future might look like in Campion Bay. But that was the whole plan, wasn't it? You couldn't leave me to make up my own mind about Tabitha's house; you had to force my hand. It turns out I don't know you at all. It turns out I *am* the idiot you hoped I was.'

'Will, no – please, that was never part of it.' She stepped towards him but he threw her phone on to the bed and walked out of the room, closing the door behind him.

Robin leaned against the bed and then slid down it, sinking to the floor, her bare feet finding a puddle she'd made when she'd rushed in for her towel moments before, before everything had come crashing down around her.

It couldn't have been any worse. Molly's cheeky message, complete with in-jokes, had reduced her feelings for Will to a box-ticking exercise: get the guy, save the seafront. *Well done, Robin Brennan, fist-bump!* And Will reading it to her, his tone changing as he'd realized he was the subject of the message, the subject of a calculated charm offensive, the Campion Bay spies updating everyone on the tender moment they'd shared in an instant.

She could see how it looked; she couldn't blame Will for being angry. She wouldn't blame him if he never wanted to see or speak to her again. But, as she sat in a puddle on her bedroom floor, she also knew she wouldn't give up on him.

She had known Will Nightingale only a short while, but already he was someone she would fight to hold on to. Even before today, when he'd kissed her and made her feel whole again for the first time since she'd lost Neve, she'd been prepared to give in to him, to tell him everything and see where it took them.

She knew she could trust him. That was the most important thing and the most bittersweet, because he couldn't say the same about her.

She picked up her phone and reread the message, torturing herself with the reality of the situation. She wasn't sure if she could come back from that, if she could make Will see that she had never meant to hurt him, that Molly's scheming had been irrelevant because as soon as she'd met him she had wanted him to stay in Campion Bay anyway.

Loud footsteps sounded on the stairs, followed by the skitter of paws on the floorboards and the front door closing. She pulled herself up on heavy arms and looked out of her bedroom window. She watched Will walk past quickly, angrily, his mouth set in a hard line. He hurried up the stairs to Tabitha's house and went inside, the door slamming and making her windows rattle.

Robin was facing another huge challenge. She didn't know if it would be as big as refurbishing and opening the guesthouse, or as difficult as trying to wade through her grief and the darkness of Neve's death and come out, blinking, on the other side. But she had done both of those; she had survived and, in the case of the guesthouse, triumphed. She pushed herself up to standing, dusted down her jeans, and switched on the fairy lights around her headboard.

It was going to be almost impossible to get Will to trust her again, to return to where they had been in the moments before Molly's text message came through. It might test her to the limits and it might all be in vain, but the one thing that Robin was certain of, the thing that forced her out of her slump by the bed and into a long, hot shower to clear her head, was that Will Nightingale was already too important to her not to try.

The Once in a Blue Moon Guesthouse

DO NOT DISTURB

Chapter 13

Robin opened the oven door and, waiting for a waft of steam to disperse, took a second batch of moon-shaped chocolate-chip cookies out and slid them on to the cooling rack. She stared at them, her hands on her hips. The cookies, once they were cold, would go in the heavily stoppered glass jars she had bought at a gift shop in the centre of Campion Bay, and would sit on the landing next to a sign that said *Midnight cookies; please help yourself.*

Running a successful guesthouse, her mum Sylvie had written in The Bible, *is all about attention to detail. That's what guests will notice, that's what will complete their stay and make them want to come back again and again.*

Robin hoped the cookies would be popular with her guests, but wasn't convinced they would complete anyone's stay. She had thought that making them, mixing the dough and chunking chocolate up into irregular chips, using the cutter to create moon shapes, would take her mind off what had happened the day before. So far, however, it had failed.

She had been running the Campion Bay Guesthouse for

just two weeks. It was her third Monday, and she was confident that, for most of her guests, the experience of staying had been a good one. But there was one guest – and Robin wasn't sure he was a guest any more – with whom she'd managed to get it spectacularly wrong. She started tidying up the kitchen, putting the cooking implements in the dishwasher while her kitten, Eclipse, watched her from the doorway.

Once she had cleaned the counters, Robin poured herself a glass of water and sank into a chair at the kitchen table. Eclipse jumped immediately on to her lap, his tail tickling her nose as he circled and circled on her thighs, trying to find the most comfortable position. Robin scrolled to the messages in her phone, rereading the text Molly had sent her that she'd stupidly asked Will to read aloud. It was like picking a scab, it was painful and the result was inevitable, but she couldn't help it.

She heard the front door open and laughter drift down the hallway. Lifting Eclipse into her arms, she went to greet her guests.

Dean and Katy were staying in her Wilderness room for a few days. They both worked in London, but Dean's granddad lived in Weymouth, a little further down the Dorset coast.

'Good morning?' Robin asked.

Katy nodded. 'We've been on the beach and booked a boat tour for tomorrow. It's going to take us along the coast, spotting wildlife and exploring the cliffs, with a fish-and-chip lunch included.'

'A bit different from the Thames Clipper,' Dean said, chuckling.

'It sounds wonderful. And the weather's supposed to pick up, according to the forecast.'

It had been raining on and off since the previous afternoon, and Robin felt that it suited her mood perfectly. But, if the sun was set to make an appearance, then maybe things would start looking up for her too.

'I quite like the thought of a wild and windy trip, though,' Katy said. 'The boat's got indoor seating if it gets too rough.'

'I can lend you waterproofs, just in case?'

Dean shook his head. 'We're fine, thanks. We're kitted out if it's wet. But fingers crossed for sun.'

'Can I get you anything now?' Robin asked. 'I could do some sandwiches.'

'We're going to visit Dean's granddad once we've changed,' Katy said, pointing at trousers that looked as if they'd seen too much sea spray. 'Though the smell coming from your kitchen is mouthwatering.'

'Ah,' Robin said, smiling. 'That's something for later. Keep your eyes peeled when you get back.'

Katy's eyes widened. 'Ooh. OK, we will. Thank you.'

'Oh – I almost forgot,' Dean said, stopping on the bottom step. 'We bumped into the guy next door as we were coming in. He asked me to give you this.' He reached into his pocket, and Robin held her breath. He could only mean Will. She hadn't spoken to him since he'd left yesterday afternoon, though she'd knocked on Tabitha's front door and tried calling his number, listening to his voicemail message, *Hi, you've reached Will's phone, but unfortunately not Will* . . . more times than she could count.

Dean handed her an envelope. There was more in it than paper and, her heart sinking, she felt the familiar oval shape of the key ring attached to the room keys she gave guests.

'Is everything OK?' Katy asked. 'He was staying here, wasn't he?'

Robin nodded. 'Only until his aunt's house was in a better condition,' she said, thinking as she said the words that it wasn't, that there was no way he could be comfortable staying next door. 'Thanks for this.'

'No worries,' Dean said.

'He didn't . . . say anything? Give you a message?' She hoped she didn't sound too desperate.

'No, he just asked us to give this to you,' Katy said apologetically. 'There might be a note in the envelope.'

'Of course there will be. That makes sense.' She gave them what she hoped was a warm smile, and waited until they'd gone to their room, the envelope feeling unnaturally heavy in her hand.

Robin made herself a cup of tea and, Eclipse taking up one of his favourite places – lying across her shoulders – she walked through to Sea Shanty and settled on one of the sofas. The sea view was spectacular. Grey clouds bubbled on the horizon, dark streaks of rain far out over the water, while the May sun broke through closer to land, making the sea glitter. Robin spent a moment looking for a rainbow and then, when she couldn't find one, turned her attention to the envelope.

She took a deep breath and opened it, put the keys to one side and pulled out the single sheet of paper. The words were written neatly in Biro.

Robin, take what I owe you from my account. I won't be staying in Starcross any more.

It was followed by a Visa credit-card number, expiry date and his name as it appeared on the card: *Mr W. D. Nightingale.* She sighed, his anger evident in the formality of his words. He hadn't included his card security number, so even if he wasn't prepared to let her explain, she still needed to have what was bound to be an extremely awkward conversation with him. She put the note aside and picked up her tea, staring unseeingly out of the window.

She would have to go and clean Starcross, get it ready for new guests. The thought that Will was no longer staying there, sleeping beneath the pinprick lights, was so disheartening that Robin almost couldn't bring herself to do it. It was a toss-up between wiping all signs of Will from her guesthouse and going to see the one person who, other than her, was partly responsible for the rift.

Molly had been out with her daughter Paige when Robin had tried to speak to her yesterday, but she had a gap in her bookings this afternoon. Robin hadn't yet told her what had happened, so Molly didn't know that Will had seen her text message. Now she would have to explain that, while this was the least of her concerns, Will was no longer seeing Campion Bay – or any of them – in a favourable light. He might well have decided that selling his aunt's house to Tim Lewis was the only option he had left.

'God, Robin, you look awful,' Molly said when she opened her pink front door to her friend. 'What the hell's happened?'

'Are you up for making coffee?' Robin asked, her heart pounding at the thought of explaining everything to her. Not because she thought Molly would blame her for Will finding out about the charm offensive, but because her emotions were already dangerously close to the surface, and she'd never been able to hold them back from the woman she had been friends with since secondary school.

'Of course,' Molly said, shooting her a concerned look and leading her through to her pristine white kitchen. Neither of them spoke until they were sitting opposite each other at the central island. Robin clutched her mug, staring down at the chocolate shavings on her latte froth.

'I would have thought you'd be on cloud nine after yesterday,' Molly said cautiously. 'After what happened with Will. Paige couldn't wait to tell me. She was delirious with such a prime bit of gossip.'

'Paige?' Robin asked, incredulous. She had been convinced it was Maggie, the owner of the crazy golf course, who had seen them kissing and passed it on. 'She was the one who told you about us?'

Molly nodded. 'Who else would have let me in on something like that? She'd just finished cleaning at yours and was on her way back here when she spotted you. She said you were oblivious to the rain, that it was like *The Notebook* – whatever that is. You don't seem particularly happy about it. What's happened?'

'I bet you were so pleased that the plan was working, that Will looked like he was happy here.' She tried to keep the bitterness out of her voice, but wasn't entirely sure she'd managed it.

Molly sat back, taking a pink wafer biscuit from the plate between them. 'What do you mean?'

'Your plan,' Robin said, 'to get Will to stay in Campion Bay, and not sell number four to Tim. The cupcakes from Ashley, the night you organized at the taverna – all your scheming to get everyone to show him how welcome he was.'

Molly was shaking her head. 'I didn't get anyone to do any of those things.'

Robin frowned. 'But your campaign, the one you cooked up on Will's first day – the charm offensive. All that kindness people were showing him. You were behind it.'

'I bloody wasn't,' Molly said, sitting up straight. 'That campaign stuff wasn't *serious*. Of course I want Will to stay, but all I did was tell Ashley and Roxy, Stefano and Nicolas, that Tabitha's nephew was here for a while, and that he seemed like a great guy, a chip off the old Tabitha block.' Molly looked at her in disbelief. 'You thought I'd organized all those things? That I got Ashley to take him cakes and asked Nicolas to invite you for a discount night at the taverna?'

'You didn't?' Robin's voice was dry, her words a whisper.

'No way! I was being flippant, that's all. Besides, even before I'd thought of it, you were charming the socks off him. As I said in my text, you're a publicity campaign all by your-self. Robin, what's wrong? Please, tell me.'

Robin rubbed her eyes. 'So what Ashley did, and Nicolas, they were being genuinely friendly, welcoming Will to Campion Bay?'

'*Yes*, Robin.'

'But you called it a *campaign*! You said we needed to get him to stay.'

Molly leaned her elbows on the island and put her hand over Robin's. Her blue eyes were soft. 'How long have you known me? You seriously thought I'd be capable of orches-trating some kind of military-precision scheme to convince Will that he belonged in Campion Bay? Obviously we'd all much rather have a friendly, sexy neighbour like him than see the house and its blue plaque ripped apart for the sake of Tim Lewis's profit margins, but that's up to Will, isn't it? He has to make his own decisions. The odd show of gener-osity isn't going to sway him one way or the other. But falling in love with a beautiful, intelligent woman who runs her own luxury business – now *that* could be a game changer.'

As Molly explained, the sickening realization dawned on Robin. She'd mistaken Molly's enthusiasm and excitement at Will appearing, her suggestions of ways to make him a permanent neighbour, as something more calculating. It had all seemed to fit: the way the other residents of Goldcrest Road had been treating Will. That's what came of having lived in London for over a decade: she'd got out of the Campion Bay community mindset. She'd taken Molly's suggestion of a campaign and the displays of kindness, put two and two together, and come up with five.

'You thought I'd planned it all?' Molly asked.

Robin nodded and swallowed. 'And when Will commented on it, I thought you'd put your plan into action. To put him off the scent, I told him that people who live by the seaside are friendlier than people in London and that was how we treated all our new neighbours. But that was actually the truth.'

'Too right it was. We were the same with you when you came back here. But maybe you didn't see it because of Neve. You were grieving, oblivious, a lot of the time.'

'I remember your kindness,' Robin said softly. 'I'll never forget that. But . . . Oh, God, Molly. I've got it so wrong.'

'What do you mean? Will you *please* tell me why you've turned up on my doorstep looking like a ghost, instead of someone who's spent the last twenty-four hours snogging the most gorgeous guy in the vicinity?'

Robin looked up at her friend, and tried to keep her dismay at bay. 'Will saw your text.'

Molly's eyes widened.

'In fact, he read it out to me. All that stuff about me being a one-woman publicity campaign, that I'd saved the day and got the guy; *Goldcrest Road thanks you for keeping number four out of Tim's evil clutches.*' She'd read it so many times that she knew it off by heart, and now she watched Molly's curious expression transform into one of horror, which confirmed that the situation was as bad as she thought it was.

'Robin, what the hell? None of that— I was joking, you know that, right? I mean, great if Will doesn't sell to Tim but . . . I was being silly. I was just so happy that you and he— I could tell that you liked him, and that the feeling was mutual, the first time I met him. *That's* what I was hoping would happen. I mentioned the house and Tim as a joke, because we'd talked about it when Will arrived, because it would be the last thing on your mind. But he *read it out*? Shit, Robin. What happened?'

Robin sighed, her insides shrivelling. 'That kiss at the golf course, it felt so *right*, Molly. It was amazing and over-whelming. We came back to the guesthouse, and I . . .' She blushed as she remembered the anticipation, the recklessness of taking him to bed. 'I was tidying up my room, and your text came through. I asked him to read it, thinking it was probably from one of the guests, and he . . . he did.'

Molly closed her eyes. 'And you didn't explain that I was only being cheeky?'

'But I thought your campaign was *real*, Molly! I thought that you were genuinely thanking me for getting Will to stay, and so I – I told him all the generosity, from Ashley, Stefano and Nicolas, was so that he'd fall for Campion Bay and Tim wouldn't be able to buy the house. I didn't want to lie to him any more.'

'So he thinks we've been playing him since day one?'

'He thinks that's what I was doing, too. Offering to help him clear out Tabitha's house, being so . . . so . . .'

227

'Obliging? Warm towards him?'

Robin pulled at her hair. 'When Tim turned up that night, sniffing around Will like a hyena, I encouraged him to keep going with the sort-out, saying that he owed it to Tabitha to go through all her things properly. I meant it, but I was also angry with Tim for being so blatant and I wanted to put Will off him. But now he's going to think that all I cared about was the house.'

'No, Robin. That makes no sense. It's unfortunate – it's bloody crap – that he thinks we were only being kind to him to protect the seafront, but that's my fault for not being clearer with you.'

'I should have known,' Robin said. 'Or at least asked you if you were really behind it.'

'I shouldn't have assumed you'd get that I was joking. But Will has to realize that you care about him, that you weren't being the hostess with the mostest for the sake of some bricks and mortar. You *kissed*, for God's sake, and – I assume – were planning on taking it further until my ill-timed text messed it up.'

Robin nodded and picked up a wafer biscuit. 'I like him a lot, Molly. I can't remember the last time I felt like this about someone. I can't remember feeling so hopeful, so exhilarated since – since Neve died.' She inhaled, trying to calm her nerves. It was harder than she'd thought, admitting to her friend how important Will was to her. She'd known him for two weeks; was she just hanging on to him because he had seemed to like her as much as she liked him? She didn't think that was it; her feelings for Will went deeper, settling into the fabric of her. She was even more aware of them now that he was out of reach, now that she might have ruined their relationship irreversibly.

228

Molly squeezed her hand, her expression solemn. 'Then we have to make it right. What happened after he saw the text, and you told him we'd all been charming to him for our own gain?'

Robin chewed the inside of her cheek. This was the hardest part to recount. 'He was angry. He walked out, after . . . after he told me that I must have thought he was an idiot, treating him like that, making him believe that we all liked him. I tried to tell him that my feelings were real, but he left. He didn't stay in Starcross last night and then, this morning, he got one of the other guests to return his key and his credit-card details, so I can take payment for his stay.'

'Ouch!' Molly whispered. 'He's hurting; that's understandable. But once we explain to him that you got it wrong, that there never was a campaign, that we were only trying to make him feel welcome, then it will be fine.' Molly's voice was bright, but Robin could tell that her friend didn't believe it would be that easy.

'He was so upset. He said he had begun to fall for me, that he had started to think about his future here.'

'He's upset because he cares. As hard as it is to hear, that's a good sign. If he wasn't bothered about your friendship, about what was happening, then he would have shrugged, said we were all bastards, and moved on. He cares about you, so there's hope that we can rescue the situation.'

Robin ate a second pink wafer biscuit, thinking how typical it was of Molly to have biscuits that matched the decoration of her beauty parlour. Was it possible that Molly was right, and Will's feelings for her meant there was still a chance for them, or had her assumed betrayal gone too deep?

'Let me talk to him,' Molly said, patting her hand.

'But he thinks you were behind the charm offensive.'

'So I'll tell him the truth. And if he's a stubborn bugger, I'll tell him again and again until he believes it. He'll listen to me because he isn't falling for me. He's probably not feeling very rational about you at the moment.'

'You think that'll work?'

Molly nodded. 'I do. Will's a nice guy – you wouldn't be head over heels for him if he wasn't – so he'll listen to reason eventually.'

Robin stared at the tabletop, wondering if she could let her friend try to fix things. It wasn't that she didn't trust Molly – she had more fire and determination in her petite frame than Robin did – but would she say everything that Robin wanted to convey? Could she give her this task, which, while daunting, would potentially be the difference between Will forgiving her and never talking to her again?

'Thank you for offering,' she said. 'But I have to do this. What will he think of me if I can't even face up to what I've done?'

Molly appraised her, her blue eyes serious. 'I totally get it. Of course you need to speak to him. But that doesn't stop me feeling partly responsible.' She pressed her hand against her chest.

Robin shook her head. 'You didn't get the wrong end of the stick, and you didn't let Will read your text messages.'

'What this boils down to, Robin, is a simple misunderstanding. We haven't been using Will as a weapon against Tim's designs on the house, we've been kind to him, but he – with some inadvertent help from you – thinks that our friendship is fake. Doesn't it sound straightforward when I say it like that?'

'It does,' Robin agreed, exhaling. 'I'll go and see him later, and that's what I'll tell him. Thank you, Molly. I bet you thought you were done picking pieces of me off the floor.'

'I'm your friend,' Molly said. 'I'll put you back together again as often as you need it. But this one, I'm sure, is an easy fix. Let me know as soon as you've spoken to him.' She gave Robin such a reassuring grin that she allowed herself to feel a glimmer of hope.

Maybe it was that simple. Maybe, once she had explained it to Will, he would see that she had been confused, and realize that nobody's kindness had been engineered to get him to hold on to the house, least of all hers. Molly sent her back to the guesthouse in a sharp, sunny breeze that suggested the bad weather had been a temporary blip.

Robin found the tasks she needed to do around the guesthouse, cleaning and polishing, replenishing tea, coffee and biscuits and turning down the sheets, cathartic. She went into Starcross, but decided she wouldn't do the full change-over clean just yet, not until she had spoken to Will. All the sheets got changed on a Saturday anyway, so longer-term guests had fresh bedding too, and she didn't want to assume he was gone for good – she'd rather believe the opposite.

She wanted to wait until evening, when Will was more likely to have finished work on Tabitha's house for the day, and she wouldn't have to talk while he was sorting through drawers full of paperwork or wedged half under the kitchen sink. She fiddled with the timer in Starcross, making the pinprick lights dim in and out, and tried to convince herself she wasn't putting it off, taking time to summon up the courage to see him. If she waited until she felt completely ready, then it would never happen.

As dusk began to slip gently over the sea, muting the pinks and peaches of sunset into silky blue, the guesthouse was gleaming. Some of the guests were in their rooms, and Charles and Elisabeth, the old couple from Orkney, were enjoying a night at Taverna on the Bay on Robin's recommendation. Outside, the promenade lamps glowed softly, competing against the growing gloom.

Robin felt a sudden determination. She would explain everything to Will and he'd forgive her, and then she would make it up to the rest of the street. They had no inkling that she'd done anything wrong, but she felt guilty for believing they'd all be so underhand, tricking Will with fake generosity. She had to make it up to them somehow, even if they never knew her motivation. She would do something that showed she was part of the community, that she could enter into the spirit as they had done, and that she appreciated the kindness they'd shown her when she returned to Campion Bay, even if Molly had had to remind her of it.

With a positive sequence of events lodged firmly in her head, and her palms only a little bit sweaty, Robin slipped on her ballet pumps and quietly left the house.

Chapter 14

The curtains of number four were drawn, but there was a slender line of golden light at one side of the window, where one had been pulled too far over. Robin took a deep breath, climbed the stairs and lifted the knocker, banging it down twice. She rolled her shoulders, trying to ease her anxiety, wanting to appear calm in front of him.

After a few moments she heard footsteps approaching from inside. The latch clicked and the door swung inwards, Will's tall frame appearing in shadow, silhouetted against the hall light. He immediately turned away from her and started to close the door.

'Will, wait—'

'I have nothing to say to you.'

'Please.' She took a step forward, placing her foot over the threshold.

She could just make out his glance towards her foot, his face creasing in irritation as he yanked the door back open.

'Please, Will,' Robin tried again. 'Let me explain.'

'Molly's text did that perfectly well, thanks. I have to get on.' He looked at her foot again, but Robin stood her ground. He took a step towards her, his sigh loud, his face suddenly bathed in the glow from the streetlight.

Robin stared at him. She couldn't help it. Only the day before, he had seemed relaxed, happy, laughing with her as they ran back to the guesthouse, the press of his lips so tender as he'd kissed her.

Now, his hair was, again, damp, as if he'd not long emerged from the shower, but he hadn't shaved, and the dark smudges under his eyes told of a sleepless night. His expression was dark, closed off, and his hands, which had so recently caressed her face, were bunched into fists.

Robin swallowed. 'Molly's text didn't tell the truth,' she said. 'She's my friend, we have jokes and we— It seemed awful, I know that. It seemed like there was this whole, organized plan—'

'You admitted it.' Will gave a sharp, humourless laugh. 'You told me that's what happened, that you'd all been in on it together, so that you could stop your boyfriend from buying my aunt's house and messing up your seafront. Or don't you remember confessing all that to me?'

Robin winced at the anger in his voice, unsure which thing to refute first. She wanted to move her foot, to get comfortable – her thigh was beginning to ache – but she didn't want to give him the opportunity to close the door before she'd said all she needed to.

'I was wrong about so many things,' she said. 'I've spoken to Molly and there *was* no campaign. I thought she'd organized one – I thought she'd asked Ashley and Stefano to make you feel welcome, but she didn't. You were a new face on the road, Tabitha's nephew, and they were just being neighbourly. They did those things of their own accord.'

A flicker of confusion passed across his features. He looked so weary, and Robin couldn't imagine that, even if he hadn't been cross with her, he would have had a comfortable night in Tabitha's house. From what she could see of the hall it was still so disorganized, so full of dust.

'So it turns out you *were* a one-woman publicity campaign? Doing it all by yourself, thinking you were part of something the whole street was involved in?'

'No!' she said. 'That's not it at all! I didn't like Molly's idea. I wouldn't have been involved even if it *had* been real. I wanted to help you, to get to know you. What happened yesterday, I had wanted . . . that, I had wanted to spend time with you. I've loved your company, being with you, from the beginning. It wasn't anything to do with Tim or the house.'

He shook his head quickly and ran a hand over his stubble. She heard the familiar sound of paws on floorboards and Darcy appeared, her head peering round Will's legs. The Cavapoo yelped at Robin and bounded forward, her body vibrating with happiness. Robin stroked the dog, feeling instantly soothed by her unconditional affection. She wondered if Will would object, but he barely seemed to notice.

'How am I meant to believe that, after what you told me yesterday?' he asked.

'I got it wrong, Will. I thought there was a campaign, I thought that was really happening, and I didn't like it but I – I didn't want to tell you; I didn't want you to feel that you weren't welcome, that the friendship offered to you was cynical, calculating.'

She glanced behind her as footsteps and voices echoed into the dusk, people passing on their way to the town centre. Will looked over her shoulder and Robin wondered for a second if he was going to invite her in, but he didn't.

235

'So,' he said, his eyes creasing at the edges. 'You thought there was a campaign, but there wasn't? But you didn't tell me what you *thought* was going on, or that your childhood sweetheart had designs on my aunt's house, and had been sniffing around it even before I arrived? You knew all this, and you kept it from me while I confided in you about my dad, about Tabitha's past. You reeled me in, making me trust you, while all the time you were hiding things from me, being loyal to your ex, who – let's face it – doesn't seem to be fully out of the picture. Is that about right?'

'*No*, Will! Tim and I—'

'Have you been playing us off against each other while you try to decide who you want next door?'

'That couldn't be further from the truth!' She felt panic well up inside her, tried to remember Molly's words, the ones she had used to explain the simple misunderstanding. 'Nothing I've done has been false. I care about you. Tim and I – it's over! It has been for well over a decade.'

He stared at her, his green eyes narrowed and, somehow, duller, while Darcy sat silently next to him. Robin was struck all over again by how much she cared about them both, despite their short acquaintance. She couldn't lose them.

'You lied to me, Robin,' he said. His voice was quieter, defeated rather than angry. 'You kept Tim's plans from me, and you believed that your friends were tricking me into staying. It doesn't matter that they weren't – you didn't tell me about it. You've been keeping me in the dark about everything, and I—' His voice cracked, and he cleared his throat. 'I can't trust you. Please.' He gestured towards her foot, and Robin, her hope fading at his last words, stepped back. Her leg had gone dead, the pins and needles catching her off balance, and she put a hand on the wall to steady herself.

'I didn't mean for any of this to happen,' she said, as he started to close the door. 'At least come back to Starcross – you can't be getting any sleep staying here. Will, I—' But it was too late, and she found herself speaking to the black paint of Tabitha's front door. She listened to the footsteps receding inside and then, with a stomach that felt like it was full of iced water, turned away from number four and went back to the guesthouse.

Molly appeared ten minutes after Robin had texted her, a bottle in her hand. Robin poured two glasses of wine and handed one to her friend. Eclipse bounded on to her lap with springlike dexterity and an adorable chirrup, and Robin buried her face in his fur, breathing in his clean, kittenish smell.

'So what did he say?' Molly asked, slipping off her pumps and tucking her feet beneath her.

Robin wrapped her hands round the bowl of her glass. 'I tried to explain, to make it clear that it was a misunderstanding – just like you'd said. It sounded so innocuous the way you put it.'

'And?'

'He says he can't trust me any more. I don't blame him. I wouldn't trust me either.'

Molly leaned forward. 'What exactly did he say? Tell me from the beginning.'

Robin recounted their conversation, the fact that Will hadn't invited her inside, so it had played out on the doorstep, the way he had seemed at first angry and then defeated, and how even the admission that there had been no campaign, that the acts of kindness had been genuine, hadn't lifted his spirits. When she'd finished, she looked up at Molly, waiting for the verdict. She hoped her friend could find some glimmer of hope, because Robin was struggling to.

Molly drummed her fingers against her lips. 'Do you know what I think it is?' she said. 'I think it's more that you didn't tell him about Tim. You'd worked on Tabitha's house with him, and hadn't explained what Tim was up to, even after Tim had been round to see you both. It's Will's house now, and he felt that you should have been honest about what Campion Bay Property was planning – even if you didn't know the details. Plus, it's Tim, isn't it?'

'What's that supposed to mean?' Robin sipped her wine, but it tasted too acidic. She didn't want alcohol: she wanted a mug of hot chocolate with squirty cream and some of her home-baked midnight cookies.

'I don't think it helps that Tim is your ex. Whatever Will's feeling about what's happened, it's a lot more complicated because he *cares* about you, Robin. As I said before, he wouldn't be so bothered if you were just another resident of Goldcrest Road. It's only been a couple of weeks. He could wipe the slate clean. But he can't do that with you, because so much has already happened.

'He's developed feelings, and then suddenly he finds out that you've been holding things back from him, the biggest of which is to do with your handsome, successful ex-boyfriend. I'm guessing,' Molly said, leaning forward and rubbing Eclipse's paws, 'he's a big bundle of confusion, hurt, attraction and jealousy, and he needs to wait for it all to settle so he can figure out which of those emotions rises to the top. I'm confident it will be attraction.'

Robin thought of the way Will had suggested Tim wasn't fully out of the picture, the bitterness in his voice as he'd accused her of playing them off against each other. What Molly said made a lot of sense. 'You think so?'

Molly nodded determinedly. 'I do.'

Robin sat back on the sofa, her nerves settling slightly. 'He looked so tired, Molly. It can't be comfortable staying at Tabitha's house with the dirt and the cobwebs. I don't even know if there's a bed in a good enough state for him to sleep in.'

'He's cut off his nose to spite his face, moving back next door,' Molly agreed. 'Even if he decides to chance it at the Seaview Hotel, he's not exactly on to a winner, is he? I bet that's adding to the disgruntlement. Chances are, he'll realize how much he's missing out on by being cross with you, and he'll come back with his tail between his legs.'

Robin gave her a grateful smile. 'Thanks, Molly. Thanks for talking it all through with me, for stopping me from going mad.'

'Hey. It was my ridiculousness, my text, that created this situation in the first place. It's my duty as your friend to help you clear it up. But for now, let out Starcross. Did you get his security number for the payment?'

Robin stared at her for a moment, then shook her head. 'I didn't get a chance. I'll have to text him.' The thought of asking him such a perfunctory question via text made her slightly nauseous, but she didn't have a choice.

'Try not to worry about it,' Molly said. 'He's angry, but he's a decent guy. He'll pay up, and then you can get on with running the guesthouse while he cools off. At least he's still in Campion Bay, and if the house is still a tip then I doubt he's going anywhere any time soon.'

'I've got time,' Robin murmured. Molly's words about Will

cutting off his nose to spite his face had started her thinking. Maybe he wasn't prepared to talk to her now, to accept her apology, but would he turn down a package from the guesthouse; a few creature comforts to make sleeping and eating at Tabitha's house more bearable? Could she appeal to him in that way?

Molly nodded. 'I'll go round in the next couple of days, explain about the campaign misunderstanding, add my weight to your cause – if you think that would help? In the meantime, you'd best get on with things here and let it all play out in his head. He'll soon realize that what you've done isn't all that bad, and that you deserve his forgiveness.'

Robin looked down at her phone, thinking it would be better to text Will now and get it out of the way, and tried to imagine Starcross with a new guest staying in it. 'Do you want a hot chocolate?' she asked. 'I've got marshmallows, and cookies.'

'Why didn't you say so earlier?' Molly laughed. 'Bring on the comfort food.'

The next day Robin took her friend's advice and threw herself into running the guesthouse. The May day was blustery, but it wasn't raining any more, and the damp pavements were drying, the sand at the top of the beach fading to pale, soft gold that Robin could imagine beneath her feet.

Katy and Dean were off on their wildlife boat tour, and over breakfast were making a list of all the things they were hoping to see.

'I'd love to see puffins. Do you get them down here?' Katy looked up expectantly.

Robin screwed her nose up. 'I'm not sure. Maybe. If

there's one thing I'm not very good on, it's the wildlife around here.'

'I want to see an osprey,' said Dean.

Katy rolled her eyes. 'Trust you! And a shark, no doubt. How about a whale?'

Dean pursed his lips, considering this. 'They must pass along this way sometimes, when they get lost.'

'Oh my God. Talk about high expectations! When we see a couple of seagulls and a bit of driftwood, you're going to want your money back.'

'Trust me. This trip is going to be awesome.' He gave his girlfriend such a confident look that Robin almost believed he would be able to conjure up giant sea creatures. She felt a stab of envy, longing for the wind in her hair and sea spray on her face.

'You know,' Paige said, as they tidied up the kitchen after breakfast, 'I've lived here all my life and I've never been on a boat trip around the coast.'

Robin stared at her. 'Never? Not even when there was that dodgy little charter that moored up next to the crazy golf and puttered up to the cliffs and back?'

'When was that?' Paige frowned, pulling her ponytail tighter.

'Ah. It was when I was a teenager. Sorry, I always forget that—'

'That I'm sixteen?' Paige asked. She smiled, shaking her head slowly. 'Yeah, I wasn't out of nappies when you went off to university. Maybe you're starting to get me confused with Mum. Can you get dementia in your thirties?'

'Haha.' Robin threw a tea towel in Paige's direction. She could see so much of Molly's cheekiness in her daughter, and knew that she would be able to achieve whatever she wanted to. Luckily for Robin, at the moment that meant working for her at the guesthouse when she didn't need to be in college.

'Adam and his friends hired a boat to investigate the caves once,' Paige said. 'The ones you can't get to from the beach even at low tide, a lot further round the cliffs. I didn't fancy it. It sounded like a recipe for disaster.'

'You're wise beyond your years. I assume they all came back safely?'

'They did, but I'm not sure how far they actually got. Adam says they saw loads, and that it was really interesting, but I reckon they chickened out pretty early. You'd have to be skilled to get boats inside some of those caves without smashing against the rock.'

'Ugh!' Robin shuddered, thinking of the wild beach and its dark, snug recesses in the cliffs. That inevitably reminded her that she'd taken Will there, only two days before, and that she'd started to open up to him. She wanted him to know that she'd already told him more than she'd told most people, and that of course he could trust her, but she'd got things spectacularly wrong.

'I'm off now then,' Paige said, waving her hand in Robin's face.

Robin blinked her daydreams away. 'Thanks so much, Paige. See you tomorrow.'

Once Paige had left and the guesthouse settled into quiet, Robin took a deep breath and climbed up to the third floor. It was time to get Starcross ready for new guests. She'd been putting it off, but she had to accept that Will was gone and right now it looked as though he wasn't coming back.

The room was sparkling by the time she'd finished, the

telescope gleaming, all signs that Will and Darcy had ever been there gone. Bundling the linen and towels into the washing machine, Robin turned to the small wicker hamper on the kitchen table.

It was empty at the moment, but she set about filling it with luxury teabags, a few packets of biscuits and a bag of chocolate coffee beans that she'd meant to put in Sea Shanty for the guests to help themselves to. She added mini bottles of the toiletries she put in every bathroom and then, smiling to herself, popped in a packet of the mature cheddar she loved so much, a small jar of Hellmann's mayonnaise and a fat, silky garlic bulb.

It was a slightly odd hamper, but she hoped Will would appreciate it, would understand what she was trying to do and at least be able to accept this small token of apology from her. Before she had time to think whether or not it was a sensible idea, Robin raced outside, put it on his front door-step and ran back to the guesthouse, feeling like a schoolgirl who had almost been caught playing Knock Down Ginger.

Throughout the week Robin made the guesthouse gleam, using all the energy that she had begun to spend on being with Will, helping Will, thinking about Will. Now, she treated the Campion Bay Guesthouse as her most prized possession, and gave it all her attention. She made more midnight cookies, perfected a Canadian stack recipe of thin crepes, streaky bacon, blueberries and maple syrup that she would serve as a special on Sundays, and burned a vanilla lime Yankee candle in Sea Shanty while she drew up plans for marketing campaigns and special offers.

The weather was getting warmer, and she started opening the windows, filling the guesthouse with the crisp, seaside air and the sound of the waves that she found so irresistible. She revisited Seagull Street Gallery and spent a full ten minutes standing in front of Arthur Durrant's new nightscape, drinking in the textures, the sensation of night drawing in around her, the dots of white paint that so clearly became twinkling lights in the darkness. She left invigorated, and with five new miniature paintings in her jute bag, one for each of the bedrooms. They were all by the same artist, all striking designs in bright colours. There were cheerful beach hut paintings for Rockpool and Canvas, wildflower landscapes for Wilderness and Andalusia, and a sunset for Starcross, the sun a glowing orb hovering above the horizon, a few stars beginning to show in the blue of the gathering dusk.

She realized that, while renovating the guesthouse had been a huge project, and she'd been delighted with how it had looked on opening day, it would never be truly finished. Like everything, it would evolve over time, needing frequent changes to keep it fresh and interesting. It was something she had learned working with Neve on Once in a Blue Moon Days: the things that had once been fashionable and exclusive soon became commonplace, and searching out new and thrilling experiences was a constant challenge. *Once in a Blue Moon Days*, Neve had said, *is more than a great name: it's how we have to approach our work. We have to imagine that we're reaching for the moon every time, and we don't want to fall short.*

Robin missed her every day. Not just her calmness, her words of wisdom, but those huge dark eyes always full of the brightness of life. Neve had been a whirlwind of enthusiasm and positivity, and some of it had rubbed off on Robin. She had felt invincible when she was working with her, but it was like the glow-in-the-dark stars on her bedroom ceiling: they absorbed and held on to light for only so long, emitting their own glow. After a while, they needed another charge, another burst of light. Neve was no longer here to provide that, and Robin sometimes felt that, without her, she was dull and uninspired.

But the Campion Bay Guesthouse was helping her recapture her sparkle. She could be creative for her guests, she could continue to improve the rooms, try new recipes and new ways of adding the luxury that she hoped her business would be known for.

And now she had a side project too, one that didn't take up much time but had, so far, been unsuccessful. The first hamper she had left for Will hadn't been touched, and she had collected it the following day, feeling deflated. He had to take Darcy out for walks, and so he couldn't have failed to notice it. But she wasn't going to give up so easily, and so she had redone it, replacing the packet biscuits with some of her home-baked cookies, and adding some dog treats for Darcy.

This one, too, had been left on the doorstep, though a grin had spread across her face when, putting it back on the kitchen table, she noticed the dog treats had gone. Perhaps Will felt that, because Darcy wasn't cross with her, she could take advantage of Robin's hospitality. It had given her a surge of hope and she had repackaged it again, adding new luxuries, placing it calmly back on the doorstep of number four. Will might not be staying in Starcross any longer, but that didn't mean she couldn't still pamper him like one of her guests.

She had said goodbye to Charles and Elisabeth, to Katy and Dean and, as it was Saturday, would be welcoming new guests into most of her rooms. As lunchtime approached, she got the familiar tightening of nerves in her stomach, wondering if the strangers she'd be greeting would like their rooms, what they would be like, if she'd get anything wrong or encounter any trouble.

The woman who rang the doorbell shortly after three seemed like the exact opposite of trouble. She was whippet thin, with long straight hair that was almost black, pale skin and dark-blue eyes. She was wearing a leather jacket that nipped in at the waist and Doc Marten boots, and held a small canvas bag in one hand and a guitar case in the other.

'Hello?' Robin asked, smiling. 'Are you Lorna?'

The woman's eyes widened momentarily, and then she nodded. 'Yes. I'm in Rockpool, I think. For a week.'

'That's right. Welcome to the Campion Bay Guesthouse. Let me check you in.' Robin invited her in and took her bag.

Once the GuestSmart software was happy, she led Lorna up to her room. 'Can I offer you afternoon tea? I've got English Breakfast, Earl Grey, Lapsang Souchong and Assam, and some fruit and herbal teas. There's also a selection of fresh cakes, and you can have something here in your room, or downstairs in Sea Shanty. I'm around this afternoon, and you're very welcome to join me.'

'Thank you,' Lorna said, her voice so soft that Robin had to strain to hear. 'But I'm fine. I'm going to take some time to settle in. Do you play the piano? I saw one, downstairs.'

Robin smiled sheepishly. 'I used to, when I was little. I've got ambitions to brush up on my skills, but I never seem to find the time.' *Or I forget everything else and burn my dinner*, she added silently, picturing Will standing in the doorway of the smoky kitchen, and what had happened afterwards – his bare torso as he tried to sneak up to his room in only his boxer shorts. 'You play the guitar?' she asked, gesturing towards the case Lorna had rested against the wall.

'I do. Though . . . I've had a break from it, too. I'm hoping that being somewhere new, with a bit more time on my hands, will help me get back into it. If, uhm . . .' She paused, her blue eyes wary. 'Is it OK if I play in the room?'

'Absolutely,' Robin said. 'If it had been a violin or a drum kit, then I'd have to think about it, but I can't imagine you'll disturb the other guests. You don't have a powerful amp hidden in your bag, do you?' She grinned, but Lorna shook her head, her face serious.

'No, it's not electric.'

'You can even play downstairs, if you want to. The acoustics might be better in Sea Shanty. But it's up to you – you don't have to do anything you don't want,' Robin added quickly, when Lorna's flat expression turned momentarily to horror.

'That's kind.' Lorna's voice was a whisper. Robin could see that she was agitated, pressing her hands under her armpits. She was timid and uncertain, but there was something about her, a suppressed energy, the way her large eyes were constantly flitting about, that reminded her of Neve.

'We could do a duet,' she said, trying to help the girl relax, 'as long as you can play "Chopsticks" on the guitar, and have a lot of patience.' She laughed gently, and Lorna smiled.

'I remember learning that, and "Frère Jacques" on the recorder. I drove my mum and dad mad, playing those tunes over and over. I think they regretted buying the piano for a while. At least I could play the recorder in my bedroom.'

'My go-to tune on the recorder was "Greensleeves".' Robin started humming it, trying to add a strangled, squeaky edge to it, mimicking the sound the recorder made when it was blown too hard.

Lorna laughed, her eyes lighting up. 'That takes me back.' She sat on the edge of the bed and smoothed her hair over her shoulder. 'Practice makes perfect, but sometimes practice is torturous.'

'Even so,' Robin said, grinning, 'you're very welcome to play – here or downstairs. I'd love to hear you, though I know how daunting it can be, playing in front of other people, especially if you don't know them.'

'Thank you. I love playing for people. I haven't done it for a while, though.' A flicker of a frown passed over Lorna's face, before being replaced by her gentle smile. 'I can already tell that coming here is going to do me good. Sea air, new horizons and all that!'

'It works wonders,' Robin agreed. 'I'll leave you to it. Please let me know if you need anything – anything at all.' She closed the door behind her and hurried down the stairs, feeling an instant warmth for the young woman, and wondering what had happened to make her so nervous, when it was obvious that there was a bright, excitable personality bubbling below the surface, desperate to get out.

A misty drizzle had begun to fall by the time Robin had checked her final guests, Len and Kim, into Andalusia. They were a married couple in their fifties, with East End accents and polished, pearly grins. They had quizzed Robin on the best pubs in the area, and Kim had squeezed Eclipse tightly when he'd come to investigate the new visitors. The kitten – who was growing bigger and more stealthy every day – had put up with it for several minutes, before wriggling free and stalking off down the corridor.

'I have two Ragdoll cats,' Kim explained. 'Annie and Oliver. They're total darlings, the perfect lap cats.'

'Got no nous about them, though,' Len added. 'No pouncing, no fighting instinct. Like the name, they're a pair of dolls. Floppy. Weird creatures.'

'He loves them,' Kim said, giving Robin a heavily mascaraed wink. 'Falls asleep in front of *Match of the Day* with the two of them snoozing like furry medals on his chest. He's a proper softie.'

'Not as soft as them cats,' Len said. 'That's impossible.'

'Does Campion Bay have any gin bars?' Kim asked, turning away from her husband. 'Looks like I'll need one if he's going to keep this up all weekend.' She winked again, and Robin returned with the local *Eating Out* guide, berating her lack of knowledge about the bars of Campion Bay and with a pang of longing for Will's dry humour, the way he'd teased her at the golf course. Feeling subdued, she left Len and Kim to plan their evening, and went to seek out a hug from Eclipse.

As well as Will, she was missing Darcy. Eclipse was more affectionate than a lot of cats, but he wasn't as soft-centred as the adorable Cavapoo. It had been almost a week since she'd spent the day with Will and Darcy, convinced their relationship was taking a new, wonderful turn – until she'd managed to ruin it all. She had turned her mind to the guesthouse, but she hadn't forgotten about him, and spent more time than she could spare getting her hampers for him just right. The memory of the golf course tormented her. She wanted to hold on to it, to replay it, but it always ran on to what had happened afterwards, the way Will's voice and expression had changed as he'd read out Molly's text.

Robin stared out of the window as the rain got heavier, Eclipse's buzzy purring in her ear, his dry nose against her cheek. Headlights lit up the gloom, and Robin watched as a black Audi pulled up to the kerb, and Tim got out. He was wearing a navy suit and pale-green tie, and hurried past her front door with his suit jacket held above his head. Her heart sank as she watched him bounce up the stairs of Tabitha's house, his blond curls disappearing inside as the front door opened. Had Tim got wind of everything that had happened between her and Will, or had Will invited him to the house? Either way, it couldn't be good. Robin looked at the table where, until a couple of days ago, Tim's extravagant bouquet of flowers had sat.

The plan to keep Tim away from number four Goldcrest Road – which, Robin now knew to her cost, had never been a plan at all – was backfiring spectacularly, and it was all her fault.

Robin was looking forward to spending Saturday evening catching up on *New Girl* and writing a post for her Facebook page about the first few weeks of running the guesthouse. There was no television in Sea Shanty, so she was on her bed, wearing a thin fleece top over tartan pyjama bottoms, her laptop on the duvet next to a bowl of popcorn. It was close to the end of May, but the weather was more like early April. She had watched three episodes of the sitcom and written one and a half sentences of her blog post when the doorbell rang.

She scooted off the bed, wondering if one of the guests had forgotten their key, and found Tim standing in front of her. The top button of his shirt was undone, the green tie at a wonky angle. The air smelled of sea and damp pavements, though it had stopped raining, for the moment at least. Tim grinned at her and blinked.

'Tim?'

'Hey, Robs. How are you? Long time no see.'

'You sent me flowers,' she said, as if this was the equivalent of spending time with him. 'Are you *drunk*?'

Tim gave her an elaborate shrug and stepped into the hall.

Sighing, Robin closed the front door and followed him into Sea Shanty.

'It looks great in here,' he said. 'Really great.'

'It's no different to the last time you saw it. Your flowers have not long faded. Why did you send them to me, by the way?'

'Because I missed you, Robs. I still do. I miss you.' He sat heavily on one of the sofas, his elbows on his knees, and looked up at her.

'This isn't the best time to have this conversation,' she said slowly, sitting on the other sofa, keeping a good distance between them. 'Why are you here?'

'I spent the evening with your neighbour, William Nightingale.' He rolled the words around in his mouth, as if the name was distasteful. 'Took him to the Artichoke, because it seemed like he needed a drink. Turns out he did. God, Robs! What did you do to him? What happens when you stay under this roof?'

Robin sat back, wary. 'Why, what did he tell you?'

'Not a lot,' Tim admitted. 'He got more sullen the more he had to drink, but he's not a happy bunny. Not. At. All. And, when I mentioned you, he grimaced and clammed up. Ergo' – Tim swept his arm wide – 'you are the cause. I want *all* the details.'

'You can have precisely none.' She breathed a sigh of relief that Will hadn't confided in Tim. She wasn't sure how he would have used that information, but she knew he'd find some way to exploit it. 'What are you doing here?'

'Did you two have a thing? Is that what happened? Blurring

the boundary between business and pleasure?' He tutted at her. 'Bad idea, Robs. Schoolgirl error.'

Robin gritted her teeth. Drunk, smug Tim was not someone she was enjoying spending time with. 'Know that from experience, do you?'

Tim pulled out his phone. 'Can I get a taxi to pick me up from here? I can't drive back: too much whisky.' He rubbed his forehead.

'Why couldn't you have got it to pick you up from next door?'

'I wanted to see you. Hello, can I order a taxi, please?' He spoke into his phone, and Robin went to the kitchen and made him an instant coffee. She hoped the taxi would be quick. When she returned to Sea Shanty, Eclipse had taken advantage of the unexpected warm lap and Tim, in his drunken state, hadn't ejected him. They looked quite sweet, sitting together on the sofa, she thought, and then berated herself. Tim did not belong on her sofa, making friends with her cat. She handed him the mug of coffee.

'Here you go.'

'Thanks.'

'Did you have a nice evening, then, with Will?'

'Yeah, he's a good bloke. Solid.'

'As opposed to what, being made of cotton wool?'

Tim grinned at her. 'You're brilliant, Robs. You know that? Smart and funny and sexy and sassy.' His blue eyes flashed at her, and she realized she'd sat next to him, unintentionally closing the gap between them.

'Give me a break.' Robin rolled her eyes. 'Did you . . . chat about the house at all? Tabitha's house?'

'Yup. As you know, I've got lots of knowledge and experience, and Will was very keen to hear my views.'

She swore under her breath. 'He was?'

'He's a good bloke,' Tim said again. 'He'd be a sound guy to hang out with, if he was sticking around.'

Robin stared at him, wondering if he was being manipulative, if the drunkenness was partly an act, or if Will had made plans with Tim, made a deal even, and was already arranging to leave Campion Bay. 'He's not sticking around?'

Tim frowned at her. 'He isn't?'

'You said he'd be good to hang out with, *if* he was sticking around. Does that mean he's not?'

'He doesn't live here, does he? This is temporary. Campion Bay, his aunt's house, all the . . . stuff. It's not an easy decision.'

'Why isn't it easy? What decision? What is he going to do with the house?' Robin forced herself to keep calm, fighting the urge to grab Tim and shake him into talking sense, or make him recount every last detail of his evening in the pub with Will. She had begun to think that it would be a very easy decision for Will, now that he couldn't trust her. He could finish going through his aunt's possessions, and then return to his old life – or some semblance of it. But maybe the charms of Campion Bay had begun to work on him after all.

'Ah.' Tim tapped the side of his nose. 'Can't talk about that. Client confidentiality.'

Robin nodded. 'We'll find out soon enough anyway, if you – if Will's made a decision.'

'There you go, then.' Tim stroked Eclipse, who was purring loudly and looking up at him with adoration. 'You don't need me to tell you.'

Robin's shoulders sagged. Tim's discretion was clearly going to remain intact despite too much whisky, which, she considered, was admirable, even if it wasn't helping her at that moment.

'Are you OK, Robs? I know I turned up unannounced, but – hey.' He stopped stroking Eclipse and took her hand. 'I haven't asked how you're getting on. I'm sorry.' He put on an exaggerated, drunken-solemn expression, his blue eyes cartoon wide.

She laughed.

'What's so funny?' he asked.

'You. I haven't seen you like this.'

'Like what?' He frowned.

'Drunk. I can't remember if we ever . . . I mean, we must have got drunk together, but you're always so in control, so on top of everything.'

'I am in control,' he said calmly. He took a sip of his coffee, then bent forward and put the mug on the floor.

'You're three sheets to the wind.'

He gave a gentle chuckle. 'One sheet, maybe.'

He met her gaze, and suddenly he didn't seem drunk at all. He was proving a point, she knew, showing her that he was in full possession of his senses. Robin felt a flutter of the old attraction, despite herself. Even drunk, even calculating and ruthless, he had a charm that she found hard to ignore.

'Tim.' She said it loudly, wanting to put a barrier between them.

'Robs,' he whispered, leaning towards her.

She was frozen. Part of her believed that he wasn't about to do this, but part of her was too curious to stop him. His face was inches from hers. He smelled of whisky and coffee, sweet and bitter both at once.

'Neither of us wants this,' she said. 'This shouldn't be happening.'

'So stop it, then.' Tim put his hand on the back of her head, his fingers in her hair, and brought her face gently towards his.

Robin's heart was thumping, her eyes focused on his mouth, and then a vision of Will's face close to hers, his lips pressing against hers as the rain started to fall, flashed into her head and she pulled back, slipping out of Tim's grip, scooting as far back on the sofa as she could.

'I'm not doing this.'

Tim sat up straight, giving her his usual grin, but not before Robin had seen the look of annoyance, as fleeting as a flash of lightning. 'Not yet.'

'Not ever, Tim. We can't go back.'

'That's not a rule. Not one I'm planning on sticking to.'

'It's not entirely up to you, though, is it?' She stood, annoyed with herself, and took his empty mug to the kitchen. Her pulse was slowly returning to normal, and the deliriousness that had overtaken her for a second was replaced with cold, hard anger: at Tim for coming round, for drunkenly trying his chances, but mostly with herself for letting him get so close. Things were difficult with Will, stalling before they'd got started, so she had considered going back to what was easy and familiar, even though she knew it wasn't what she wanted. It was lazy and cowardly, and she was in danger of proving Will right. She *wasn't* playing them off against each other, but if she let Tim get this close, then how could she blame him for thinking that? She needed to fight for Will; she couldn't jump at the first offer of intimacy, just because she was feeling hopeless.

'Taxi's here,' Tim called, one hand on the front door. He opened it, his eyes narrowing as he peered out through a fresh rain shower. 'Thanks for letting me take refuge. We must do this again, catch up properly.'

255

'As opposed to you using me as a taxi shelter, you mean?'
She leaned against the wall and folded her arms. 'And there
are some aspects of this visit that we won't be repeating.'

Tim grinned, entirely unruffled. He didn't kiss her cheek
this time, but squeezed her arm instead. 'See you soon,
Robs.'

She watched him slide into the back seat of the taxi, and
then it pulled away and Goldcrest Road was quiet once more.
She thought of Will in the house next door. Did he get into
a sleeping bag every night, or was one of the bedrooms now
clean enough to sleep in? And what about Darcy? Where
did she sleep? She felt a pang of guilt at what had almost
happened with Tim, even though she and Will were as far
from being reconciled as it was possible to be.

She wondered if he was as drunk as Tim had been, whether
he'd been drowning his sorrows because of her. She went
back to the kitchen, to the hamper that stood on the table,
and packed it with homemade chocolate cookies, dog treats,
a couple of bananas, a packet of fresh coffee and some Alka-
Seltzer. She slipped the whole thing inside a large plastic bag
to shelter it from the rain.

Pondering what Tim had meant when he'd said it wasn't
an easy decision, and that he'd like to get to know Will *if* he
was hanging around, she padded quietly down the front
steps. She breathed in the damp night-time air and, closing
her eyes for a moment and angling her face up, felt the rain-
drops against her skin. She left the hamper on the doorstep
in the usual place, and as she turned away, she thought she
saw a flicker of movement at the edge of the curtain.

She made her way back to her room, to *New Girl* and her
blog post, her head now full of Will and Tim and the decisions they'd been making in her absence, of how kissing Will

had made her feel, of Tim's ability to break down her barriers after all this time. She had no idea what to write.

All the progress she'd made in the last few weeks with the guesthouse, all her achievements, somehow seemed insignificant compared with the mess she was making of her personal life. Was she destined to be a great businesswoman, running a successful, admired seaside guesthouse, but an eternal spinster, terrible at relationships, leaving parcels in the desperate hope she could win back the hearts that she'd damaged? Somehow, that didn't seem like a good trade-off.

'Thanks a bloody lot, Tim,' she whispered, and pressed PLAY on the remote.

Chapter 15

The next morning Robin woke with an unsettling feeling, but for a few moments was unable to place the cause. And then she remembered Tim's breath on her face, his blue eyes looking into hers, and felt awash with guilt. Nothing had happened – she had come to her senses early enough – but how could she claim to be pining for Will when she was letting her old boyfriend get so close? It was because she was upset about Will, she decided. She was feeling untethered, unsure of herself.

She had to do something about it. Cookies and coffee on the doorstep weren't going to be enough.

With determination firing through her, and with a host of breakfasts to cook, she jumped out of bed and straight into the shower. Her guests were all on good form, and Paige was adding to the atmosphere, breaking into a loud and somewhat startling rendition of 'Cry Me a River' while she flipped the pancakes. Len and Kim, the couple in Andalusia, and Nina and Ben who were staying in Wilderness, had asked for her new Sunday special, and Paige had declared that making pancakes was one of her favourite things. Lorna, sitting alone at the Rockpool table, had come out of her shell a little and was chatting and joking with the other guests as she dug into pancakes, blueberries and maple syrup, minus the bacon. Robin was buoyed by everyone's good mood, and even the weather felt like it was taking a turn for the better.

She spent the morning kneading and proving a walnut cob and a sourdough bloomer, trying to expel all her nervous energy. She had the radio on in the background, the local station starting to wheel out summer classics at the first sign of late-May sunshine. 'Boys of Summer' by Don Henley, 'Summertime' by Will Smith, 'Summer of 69' by Bryan Adams. She felt like she was stuck in a time warp, singing along to the music she had loved as a teenager, and that reminded her of what had happened with Tim the night before.

She had made the right decision.

Robin didn't tend to wear a lot of make-up, but she found herself applying mascara and trying to negotiate her curls, which she had tied back while she was working in the kitchen, into something approaching organized. She was giving herself a final appraisal in the rectangular mirror next to the front door when she heard light footfalls on the stairs. Lorna appeared, carrying her guitar case.

'Hi,' she said, a smile breaking out. 'Which way is the town centre? I had a quick look on Google Maps, but I don't want to start out in the wrong direction.'

'Turn left as you walk out of the door, and it's about ten minutes along the promenade before you head inland. There's a sign to Seagull Street, and once you're on that you can't go wrong. Got any particular plans?' Robin was intrigued as to why she had her guitar case if she was exploring Campion Bay. She had sudden visions of the case hiding a machine gun, ready to accompany the young woman to a bank, or fifty-pound notes wadded together, the payment in some unsavoury deal. She gave Lorna what she hoped was her most encouraging smile.

'Not really,' Lorna said. 'I want to see what the lay of the land is, do a bit of exploring, that's all.'

'We have a lovely arts centre close to Sainsbury's. They do open-mic nights and a few gigs. They're mostly local talent – we can't attract the likes of Frank Turner or One Direction.' She felt like an old woman, trying to guess the musical tastes of someone younger. She wanted to add that she wouldn't go and watch One Direction even if they *did* decide to perform in Campion Bay, and then realized that might not be strictly true.

'Is that close, then? I got here with a long combination of trains and buses and taxis. I don't have a car with me.'

'Sainsbury's is at the end of Seagull Street, so it's within walking distance. But if you do need a car for anything while you're here, I'd be more than happy to drive you. I pop into Bridport a couple of times a week. Where have you come from?'

'Near Luton,' Lorna admitted, but didn't elaborate. 'That's very kind, thank you. I'll definitely check out the arts centre. I love the sound of an open-mic night; I've never performed entirely on my own before, always as part of a band.'

'I guess it's a middle ground,' Robin said, relieved. Surely she wouldn't want to take a machine gun into the arts centre? 'You get the chance to perform on your own, to see what it feels like, but you're not responsible for the whole evening. You're one important part of a much bigger thing.'

Lorna narrowed her eyes. 'You sound like you're speaking from experience.'

Robin laughed. 'I got to do a solo rendition of "Once in

Royal David's City", aged ten, in the school Christmas concert. I'm definitely not an expert, but I remember that I felt less terrified because I was sandwiched between the school band and the reception class doing the Nativity. The band was great and all the parents wanted to see their youngest children being Wise Men or sheep, so the heat was off me a bit.'

'I always wanted to be an angel,' Lorna said. 'It never happened though – I was a carol singer every year.'

'That seems like it's stood you in good stead at least.' She pointed at Lorna's guitar case, and then handed her a leaflet of *Things to Do in Campion Bay*. 'Have a look at this as well. I'm heading out too, so I'll come with you.' She opened the door for Lorna, gave Eclipse a little wave and then followed the younger woman outside.

The air was filled with a strong scent of candyfloss, the wind circulating the smells from the ice cream stall next to Skull Island. Even before eleven, the greens were busy with people taking advantage of the bright, blustery day, the pavements having long since dried from the rain the night before. Robin said goodbye to Lorna and watched her cross the road and walk up the promenade, her guitar case slung across her body, her hand trailing along the railings. She couldn't help but notice that Tim's Audi had already gone from outside, and wondered how early he'd picked it up, and how bad his headache was.

Maggie spotted Robin and gave her a wave, which Robin returned, remembering something from the fateful day she'd taken Will to show him her golfing prowess. When they'd handed in their clubs and gone running and laughing back to the guesthouse, soaked from the rain, Maggie had mouthed to her to be careful. After what had happened next, Robin had believed that Maggie was in on Molly's charm offensive, and that was the reason behind her warning. But now, she realized, that couldn't have been it. Had Maggie simply been looking out for her, as a friend? Had she seen the kiss, and wanted Robin to be wary about falling for someone so quickly? She realized she was still waving idiotically and, giving a little self-conscious laugh, shrugged and hurried down the steps.

She glanced up at number four, and then stopped. The doorstep was empty, the hamper gone. Triumph, and a small glimmer of hope, made her bound up the stairs. She rubbed her palms on her trousers and then, giving a quick glance at the shiny blue plaque, balled her right hand into a fist and knocked on the door.

She couldn't hear any sounds from inside over the pounding of her heart, so when the door was flung open she jumped back, surprised.

Will didn't shut it on her immediately, which she took as a good sign, but maybe that was because he wasn't fully functioning yet. At least she didn't have to put her foot in the door today. He was clean-shaven this time, his clothes weren't covered in grime from the house, but there were dark smudges under his eyes, a slight sallowness to his skin that Robin knew well from the occasions she'd had too much to drink the night before. But despite all that, his green eyes bore into her in a way that, at that moment, made her feel incredibly small.

'Hi,' she said. Her voice was high, her apprehension on show.

'Robin,' Will said, his tone slightly wary. 'What are you doing here?'

'I wanted to talk to you. I know that before you said—'

'No,' he cut in. 'Not now.'

'But I need to explain. I need you to see where I was

coming from. I thought that now, after a few days, you might be prepared to talk to me.'

He didn't look delighted to see her, but there was still a connection when their eyes met. Robin felt a rush of warmth. She waited, hopefully, while he seemed to ponder something.

'Thank you for what you left,' he said eventually, gesturing towards the step where she had placed the hamper the night before, then running a hand through his hair. 'How did you know?'

She had to work hard not to smile. 'That coffee and Alka-Seltzer might be your preferred breakfast?'

He nodded. 'Did you see me coming back from the pub?'

'I had a visitor last night. It was a bit of a shock to see Tim Lewis, master of all that he surveys, a little worse for wear.'

Will stared at her, his eyes suddenly hard. 'He talked to you – about what we'd discussed?'

Robin shook her head quickly. 'No. One thing Tim won't do is betray a professional confidence. And it's none of my business,' she added quietly. 'I know that.'

'But he came to see you?'

Robin chewed the inside of her cheek, remembering again the smell of whisky and coffee on Tim's breath as he'd leaned in to kiss her. 'He was drunk – as you know – and I gave him a cup of coffee. He called a taxi as soon as he arrived, and ten minutes later he was gone. I can't control who turns up on my doorstep, Will.'

He didn't reply, but instead crouched as Darcy appeared, and ruffled her fur with both hands. Robin stared at the top of his head, wondering what would come next, feeling more confused than ever. He hadn't rejected her, he had thanked her, but she could see he wasn't happy that Tim had visited

263

her, though his silence suggested that he knew he wasn't in a position to question it. He still seemed weary and out of sorts, so unlike the Will she had been getting to know.

'It doesn't just have to be hampers of goodies, you know,' she said softly. 'You could come back to Starcross – I wouldn't even try to talk to you. I could be your faceless guesthouse landlady.'

'That wouldn't work though, would it?' He didn't look up at her, his attention focused on Darcy.

'You can't be comfortable, staying here. How are you supposed to do a full day working through Tabitha's things when you're having sleepless nights? Come back with me, let me fix you a proper breakfast – an even better hangover cure than coffee or pills.'

'Not today, Robin. It isn't a good time.'

She swallowed. 'Why not?'

He slowly pulled himself up to standing, and she could see the tension in his broad shoulders.

'I have to go to work,' he said.

'*Work?* Where are you working? Why? What – what about the house?'

'You knew I'd have to do this,' he said. 'Even without paying for my sleeping arrangements – and believe me, I wouldn't pay a fiver for the conditions here – I can't survive forever.'

So come back to me then, Robin said to herself. *Don't stay here and suffer. Come back to Starcross.* 'Where are you working?' she asked.

'Eldridge House,' he said. 'As a tour guide.'

'Oh.' Robin knew Eldridge House. It was a small, fifteenth-century manor house not too far from Campion Bay that was open to the public. Her parents had dragged

264

her round it when she was small, and more recently, when she'd been visiting from London, she'd gone there to get inspiration for a Once in a Blue Moon Days customer who wanted the full *Downton Abbey* experience. It hadn't clicked until that moment that Will wasn't dressed in his usual scruffy T-shirt. He wore a smart, dark pair of jeans and a slate-grey, short-sleeved shirt. 'Well, that's great. You'll be brilliant, obviously.'

'Thanks. Not feeling at my brightest, as you can imagine. Despite your thoughtful gift.' He caught her eye, glanced away again. 'Thank you for leaving it for me, but I need to get going.'

'Can I – can I come and see you later?'

'No. Not right now, Robin. Let me get on with things here. I've got a lot to sort through.'

'Please, I want a chance to explain.' She held her hands out in front of her, pleading. 'I need you to know that Tim and I – we're just friends. Not even that. He doesn't mean anything to me any more.'

His jaw muscles worked. 'I have to go. I don't want to be late on my first day.' He took a step back and moved to close the door.

'Please, Will. You have to know that everything I did, all my intentions – I really like you. I never meant to hurt you or lie to you.'

He paused in the doorway, and when she saw the look in his eyes she realized that things weren't quite as hopeful as she'd first thought. 'But you did,' he said quietly, and closed the door.

Paige and Adam were leaning on the promenade railings eating Mr Whippy ice creams when Robin pulled up to the kerb after a largely fruitless trip into Bridport. She had stocked up on breakfast and afternoon tea ingredients, but had caught herself wandering aimlessly down the pet-food aisle, staring at a packet of dry dog food with a photo of a Darcy-like dog on the side, thinking of Will's last words to her, and the disappointment in his eyes. She'd bought a fresh packet of dog treats anyway, telling herself that there would be more canine visitors to the Campion Bay Guesthouse, while secretly hoping she would have the opportunity to treat Darcy again in the not too distant future.

She waved at the young lovebirds and hauled her bags out of the boot, and in a moment Paige and Adam had crossed the road to greet her. Adam finished his cone in record time and took the bags from her, and Robin grinned, thinking how lucky Paige was to have found such a caring, polite boyfriend at her age, and then realized the thought alone made her feel old.

'Let me help,' Adam said.

'And I can unpack,' Paige added. 'I know my way around the kitchen pretty well.'

Robin closed the boot, locked her car and narrowed her eyes. 'That's very kind, thank you.'

She led the way into the house, Adam and Paige following her to the kitchen. She put the kettle on, then checked the telephone and the inbox for messages while half-listening to the young couple chatting. When she looked up from the computer screen, Paige was standing in front of her, her hands clasped together like a choirgirl.

Robin frowned. 'Are you OK?'

Paige nodded. 'I have something I wanted to ask you.'

'Shoot.'

Paige exhaled, and gave Robin a nervous smile. She had

her long blonde hair tied up in a plait that circled her head, her simple grey top and skinny jeans somehow making her look effortlessly stylish. 'Do you think . . .' she started.

Robin waited.

'Could we – I mean, Adam and I . . . Will's moved out, hasn't he?'

Robin swallowed and nodded, hoping her regret didn't show on her face.

'I'm so sorry, because I know you liked him.'

'Things don't always work out,' Robin said gently, trying not to blush at the thought of Paige seeing her and Will kissing. 'He made the decision and I have to respect that. What were you going to ask me?'

'It means that Starcross is free, right?'

'For the moment,' Robin admitted. 'Though it's back on the market, as it were. It could have new bookings any day now. Why do you ask?'

'I was wondering if . . . if Adam and I could – could stay in it? I've saved up, and I think that—'

'No,' Robin shook her head, cutting in. 'No, Paige. Not unless I have Molly's word that it's OK. From her, not you.'

Paige squeezed her eyes closed, and Robin could tell she was trying hard not to let her disappointment show. 'You know Adam and I love each other,' she said quietly.

Robin wondered if Adam was listening from the kitchen, if Paige had told him to stay there while she asked the question. 'I do,' Robin said softly, trying to be understanding, trying to treat Paige like a grown-up. 'I can see that, and I know that Adam is a great guy, that he cares a lot about you.'

'So what's the problem?'

'The problem is that you're sixteen, and unless I am one hundred per cent sure that your mum is fine with you and

Adam staying in my guesthouse together, I can't agree to it.'
She leaned forward. 'I don't want to sound harsh or unprogressive, but you know your mum would kill me.'

Paige folded her arms. 'You and Tim were my age.'

Robin paused, wondering how Paige knew that. 'We were, and it was probably a mistake, taking that step so young. Our relationship didn't exactly have the best outcome.'

'But that had nothing to do with what happened when you were sixteen! Anyway, I'll be seventeen in a couple of months.'

'I'm sorry, Paige,' she said. 'I can't, not without speaking to Molly first. Do you want me to do that?'

Paige shook her head. 'No.'

Robin nodded, wishing she could find a way to ease the tension. In the end, she didn't have to.

'Oh, I saw Lorna in town. You know, the girl staying in Rockpool? She was busking.'

Robin sat up. 'Busking? Are you sure it was her?'

'Yup. She had her guitar, and she was singing. She sounded amazing, but she wouldn't look at me – at anyone. It was like she was in her own little world.'

'Wow,' Robin said. 'Where was she?'

'Seagull Street, outside that coffee shop – Cool Beans. I waved, but she didn't look like she wanted to talk, so we left her to it. Why would you come on holiday to busk?'

'I have no idea,' Robin said softly, wondering how this fitted in with what little she knew about the young woman who was staying with her, and if she could ask without scaring her off. 'Do you and Adam want to stay for tea? I've got Tunnock's teacakes.'

Paige paused, and Robin could see she was weighing up whether to stay annoyed with her. In the end she relented, and Robin went into the kitchen to reboil the kettle. She felt off-kilter about the whole thing, torn between keeping Paige's confidence, being loyal to a friend and employee who had been unwaveringly trustworthy and sensible, and telling Molly, her closest friend. As she took mugs out of the cupboard, she saw that Adam was sitting at the table, his fingers moving rapidly over his iPhone screen. It didn't escape Robin's notice that he was in the chair closest to the door.

Molly was furious. Sitting across from Robin in the Artichoke, the pub in town that Will and Tim had got drunk in the night before, she clasped her wine glass with both hands and stared into it, as if she wanted to divine the future in the pale liquid. Robin could almost see her anger bubbling under the surface.

'She actually asked you if she could book Starcross? For her and Adam?'

'She did,' Robin said quietly for what must have been the fifth time. She still didn't know if she'd made the right decision, and had been thinking about it since Paige had asked her. She had realized she couldn't win either way, bound to end up with fury and accusations from either mother or daughter, and while she completely understood where Paige was coming from – the desire at that age to have independence, to have self-control and not answer to parents for every single thing – she couldn't keep it from Molly. There were more risks, more potential for disaster for all involved, if she kept quiet.

Seeing how angry Molly was unnerved her further, but then she imagined her friend's fury at Paige if she found out *after* the fact, and decided that she had made the right decision. Besides, she'd had enough of hiding the truth to last her a lifetime, so – as much as she knew Paige wouldn't thank her for it – she'd had to tell her.

'She actually thought she would get away with it?' Molly asked, incredulous.

'Maybe she thought that, as she works for me, I wouldn't betray her confidence. I feel bad about it, but I know she's not old enough yet. Not really.' Robin chewed the inside of her cheek. Was she a hypocrite? If Paige hadn't been her friend's daughter, would she have allowed it? Was she doing it for purely selfish reasons – for the sake of her own friend-ship? She realized that, lately, she'd been questioning a lot of her motivations. She needed to make decisions and be confi-dent with them, otherwise she'd drive herself round the twist with whats and ifs.

'No, she is *not*,' Molly said passionately. 'I don't care how much of a saint Adam is – he's a sixteen-year-old boy, and she's my daughter. God, Robin, thank you for telling me.'

'What are you going to do?'

'I'm going to keep an eye on her. I won't come down like a ton of bricks. I know how it works – I was a master of doing the opposite of what I was told, and if I treat her like a child she'll only rebel. No, best not to say anything, but it's good to know that this is in the front of her mind.'

'She's very grown up,' Robin said. 'They both are.'

'Not for that.' Molly shook her head. 'Anyway, distract me – come on, tell me about your day. The parts that don't involve my errant daughter.'

Robin paused, wondering whether to reveal that she'd been to see Will again. She stared around the pub. It was old-fashioned inside, with dark wood wall panelling and tables, and sage-green soft furnishings that gave it a cosy, if slightly gloomy, atmosphere. A stray set of white fairy lights lay along

270

the back of the bar, and Robin wondered if they had been left there after Christmas, the landlord deciding that a bit of sparkle was needed to lift the space. The lights glinted against the bottles and reflected off the mirror behind them.

She was about to answer her friend, to tell her about her second, confusing visit with Will – *Tell the truth, remember* – when she was distracted by a figure entering the pub with a guitar case slung over her shoulder. Lorna walked purposefully up to the bar, pressing her palms on it and leaning forward to speak to the barman. Robin thought the young woman had a spring in her step that she hadn't seen previously, and when she turned around, taking a sip of her drink, Robin raised a hand and waved at her.

Lorna hesitated for a moment, and then wove through the tables towards them.

'Who's this?' Molly hissed.

'Lorna. She's staying at the guesthouse. Lorna – hi.' Robin took her jacket and handbag off the back of the chair next to her. Lorna lifted her guitar case over her head and leaned it against the table, shrugging off her coat as she sat down.

'Hi,' she said, smiling.

'This is Molly. She runs Groom with a View, two doors from the guesthouse.'

'The one with pink trim,' Lorna said, nodding. 'I noticed it this morning. Hello.' She held her hand out and Molly shook it.

'Nice to meet you. You're a musician?' Molly didn't waste any time.

Lorna nodded, rolled up her sleeves and rested her arms on the table. She was more relaxed than Robin had ever seen her, a gleam of satisfaction in her eyes. 'I've played the guitar since I was six. I'm in a couple of bands.'

'In Campion Bay? Any chart successes?'

Lorna laughed, a light, melodic sound that was perfectly in keeping with the rest of her. 'No, not at all. They're more . . . big bands, community-led, in the village where I live. We rehearse every week and put on a few concerts a year, but unless Gareth Malone decides to pay a visit, I don't think we'll get near the charts. It's a triumph if we get an audience of fifty people.'

'So what brings you to Campion Bay?' Molly wasn't letting up, and Robin smiled at her curiosity.

Now Lorna looked at the table, shrugging slightly.

Robin stepped in. 'Did you find the arts centre OK?'

'It's a lovely building,' Lorna said, 'and I've heard of a couple of the bands that are performing in the next few months.'

'You *have?*' Robin was wide-eyed. 'God, that makes me feel even more out of touch with today's music scene.'

Molly winced. 'The fact that you call it that is bad enough. Honestly, Robin.'

Lorna laughed.

'You've got an advantage – you have a sixteen-year-old daughter!'

'Yeah,' Molly said, nodding sagely. 'I have no idea what rubbish she listens to, but I'd be hard-pushed to call it music. You'll have to tell us which bands to see, Lorna. Take pity on us.'

'You're not old,' Lorna said. 'Music isn't everyone's thing.' She glanced at Robin as she said this, as if acknowledging she wasn't including her in that statement.

'But it's definitely yours,' Robin said. She took a deep breath, wondering if the next question was an intrusion. 'Paige, Molly's daughter, said she saw you busking earlier today. Is that right? Is that what you do?'

Lorna's mouth fell open. She took a quick sip of her drink before replying. 'Not usually, and not for the money. I work in a college as an admissions officer. It's a good job, the music department is brilliant – they care about all the students, regardless of ability – and I get involved where I can. But . . .' She stopped, glancing to Robin and then Molly.

'You don't have to tell us anything. It's just that I like getting to know my guests when I can, and Molly here is—'

'Incredibly nosy,' she said, giving Lorna a cheeky grin. 'Besides, you've willingly come in here for a drink, which means we need to take you under our wings and show you the error of your ways.'

'*You're* in here though,' Lorna said.

'Yeah, but we're hardened Campion Bay residents. It's too late for us.'

Lorna shrugged. 'I've had to get a bit tougher the last few months.' She kept her gaze on the table, and Robin held her breath, waiting. Molly, too, seemed to sense she needed to let it out in her own time.

'Not long after Christmas, I was mugged. I was walking home after rehearsal, and someone – I still don't know who – came up behind me. They pushed me over, stealing my bag and breaking my guitar.'

Robin swallowed. 'God, I'm so sorry. Were you hurt?'

Lorna nodded. 'I landed on my wrist, and broke it. My parents got my guitar fixed, but I wasn't able to pick it up for two months, and when I did, I couldn't play.' Her voice had thickened, her eyes impossibly large, and an image of Neve flashed into Robin's head. For a moment she imagined that this was her best friend, telling a heartbreaking, shocking story, but one that had a happy outcome. It was briefly

273

comforting to imagine that Neve had survived, but Robin had to remind herself it was another lie, even if she was telling it only to herself. She pushed the thought away and focused on what Lorna was saying.

'Your wrist had lasting damage?' she asked softly.

'No, my wrist healed fine. It was my confidence that was gone. I couldn't go back to the band, I couldn't even pick up my guitar and play a tune. It's what I love the most, and I thought it would be therapy for me, that I'd be desperate to get back to it after such a long absence, but when it came to it, I couldn't. I didn't want to be in the spotlight, to draw attention to myself. It reminded me of what had happened that night.'

'What did you do?' Molly asked.

Lorna shrugged. 'I quit the band and focused on my job, spent my evenings at home, not going out, not seeing anyone. It wasn't until Rick – our band leader – came round to my house unannounced, told me that the longer I left things, the harder it would be, that I realized I was giving up.' She sipped her drink, the sound loud as the straw hit the ice cubes at the bottom.

'So you started busking?' Robin couldn't understand the logic of it. She would have thought that was even more terrifying than going back to where she was welcome, where everything was familiar and she was playing with people she knew.

'I couldn't play with the band again, not immediately. I needed somewhere I felt anonymous. Rick said he spent lots of happy holidays in Poole, that Dorset was lovely, and so I went online and started looking. Your guesthouse appealed to me; I liked the idea of Sea Shanty, of Rockpool – of something different, free of chintz. I thought if I could start playing again where nobody knew me, I wouldn't feel the same pressure. I know I said I hadn't performed on my own, and I haven't. I mean, I don't count busking as performing. Just playing.'

'Has it worked?' Molly sat back in her chair, her eyebrows rising.

'It felt good today,' Lorna said, 'though I'm rustier than I thought I'd be. Having an audience again, even if they were only passers-by, gave me back some of my confidence.'

'You think you could play to a proper crowd again?' Robin asked.

Lorna nodded. 'Eventually. I feel like I have a long way to go, but once I'm back home, maybe I can return to the band.'

'Or we could see if there was a band down here that you could play with,' Robin said, drumming her fingers on the table. 'I could check at the arts centre, see what's available.'

'I'm only here for a week.'

'I've got space at the guesthouse, if you fancy staying on longer?'

'What, so she can have two rehearsals with a local community band? That seems a bit pointless.' Molly folded her arms over her chest.

'It would be a good way for Lorna to get her confidence back though,' Robin insisted.

'I'm fine – busking is great, for now.'

'So what about an open-mic night then?' Robin suggested. 'What if we put on an event so that you'd have a chance to perform on your own, away from everyone you know? If we open it up, get other bands and artists to perform, and they bring their friends along, I'm sure we could get a lot of people to come.'

Molly sighed. 'But we'd have to pay thousands of pounds

to hire the arts centre. And there's no way they'd have the space in a week—'

'Fortnight,' Robin butted in.

'And it's . . . it's a ridiculous idea!'

'You don't need to worry about me,' Lorna said. 'Honestly. Shall I get some more drinks in?'

'It doesn't have to be at the arts centre. It's nearly summer, we could do it outdoors, on the seafront.'

'Who's *we*? Robin, what planet are you on?'

Robin stared at her friend, thinking back to Once in a Blue Moon Days, to private performances of opera singers she and Neve had organized, getting a long-time amateur singer a slot as a supporting act at Scala in London, the extravagant parties they'd put on at short notice. 'I'm on planet possibility,' she said defiantly.

'I'm getting another round of drinks.' Lorna stood, and Robin clasped her arm.

'We could do this,' she said. 'Me and Molly, and the other residents of Goldcrest Road. We could put on an open-mic night, on the golf course or the promenade, facing the sea. We'd promote it and host it – advertise it online and at the arts centre – and have you as one of the acts.'

'In less than a *week*?' Molly asked, incredulous.

'Would you like to stay for a fortnight?' she asked Lorna. 'Would you like us to do this, to give you a stage, to help get your confidence back?'

Lorna stared at her, open-mouthed, and then flicked a questioning glance to Molly.

'Don't ask me,' Molly said, holding her hands up. 'I think she's gone nuts.'

'I used to organize events all the time. It was my job.' She didn't want to sound desperate, but the idea was firmly lodged now, as strong as taking over the guesthouse had been. This idea was more outlandish, and they had hardly any time, but she'd misjudged the residents of Campion Bay so much, had underestimated their community spirit, and this would show them all that she believed in it, that she could bring everyone together and put on something the whole community could enjoy.

Lorna hesitated, then put her glass back on the table. 'Are you sure you can do this? In only a couple of weeks?'

'Yes. If you want me to? I know it's a bit more than a solo at a Christmas concert, but isn't it the same sort of thing?'

Lorna's lips twitched into an almost-smile, and she turned to Molly. 'Can she actually do this?'

Molly looked at Robin. 'Absolutely. Robin may have suddenly become batshit crazy, and I can't imagine there isn't some other agenda here, working alongside her desire to help you – getting a local tour guide to act as compère, perhaps? Or has Will got singing talents that you haven't told me about?' She raised an eyebrow and Robin flushed, though the idea hadn't crossed her mind. 'But I have no doubt that she can put on an event like this, with help from the other residents of Goldcrest Road, in only a few days. If I was you, and I wanted an opportunity to build up my confidence before going home, I'd put my trust in her.' Molly smiled at Robin, and Robin felt a surge of gratitude towards her friend.

'Right, then,' Lorna said, slightly dazed. 'Let me think about it. What do you want to drink?'

When she'd gone, Robin reached her hand across the table towards Molly. 'Thank you.'

Molly laughed and shook her head. 'You are completely nuts. You know that, right?'

'Do you think the open-mic night *could* use a compère?

277

I remember him telling me at the taverna that nobody would want to hear him sing.'

'I bloody *knew* it! Robin Brennan, you sneaky cow.'

'You thought of it!' she said, indignant. 'Will hadn't popped into my head for at least twenty minutes before you brought him up.'

'I don't believe that for a second. But I did think of it, and maybe it could work. If you want to show a certain someone that he's valued in this community, then suggesting a Goldcrest Road event can't go ahead without his input might be the way to do it. I don't think you've got anything to lose by asking him.'

Robin nodded, nerves churning in her stomach. 'And the rest of it, do you think we can make it work? Get some food stands organized, turn it into a bit of a celebration? Do you think people will want to come and perform on the seafront?'

Molly put her hand over Robin's. 'A moment ago you were brimming with enthusiasm. Don't let your uncertainty with Will dampen it. There's a lot to figure out, and not a lot of time to do it in, but I have complete faith that we – you – can pull this off. Now, tell me exactly what you're thinking, and let's see if we can come up with a foolproof plan of how to get it done.'

Chapter 16

Robin had a music night to organize. It was exhilarating and terrifying, but she was determined to see it through. As well as helping Lorna to overcome the fear that remained after her attack, she wanted to use the event to bring the residents of Goldcrest Road together. She knew that the rift was only between her and Will, but she had believed them all – Ashley and Roxy, Stefano and Nicolas, Maggie, Molly – capable of cynically befriending him to protect the seafront from property developers. She needed to make it up to them, even if she was the only one who would ever know that was what she was doing.

On Monday morning she went to see Maggie, because without a venue they were stumped. Lorna had agreed to put her faith in Robin the night before, and had booked a second week in the guesthouse. It meant moving to Starcross halfway through her stay, but Robin couldn't think of anyone she'd prefer to have in the room now that Will had vacated it.

'Some people might think that this was all a ruse to get

more money out of me,' Lorna had said, a smile playing on her lips.

Robin had given her a sheepish grin. 'I'm going to give you a twenty-five per cent discount, if you're happy with that. This is all my idea, so if you feel I'm coercing you – if you think I'm a money-grabbing cow – then I'll understand if you want to forget the whole thing.'

Lorna's smile became a laugh. 'I genuinely don't think that. If I did, I would have turned you down. Besides, I've had a bit of money put aside for this break. I got some compensation after the mugging, and I'm happy to put it towards another week in your beautiful guesthouse. I already know it's going to be awful leaving all this comfort and luxury behind, so staying another week is no hardship at all.'

Robin had nodded, struck all over again by how much Lorna reminded her of Neve, the effect multiplied now that she was coming out of her shell. She hoped that her idea – her wild, outlandish idea – would work, and that she could help the young woman shake off the last of her fear, so that she could carry on with her life in a way that Neve hadn't.

Now, she was wearing a businesslike outfit of cropped black trousers and a cream blouse, and hoping that Maggie would take her seriously.

'You want to hold a music night on my golf course?' Maggie asked, folding her arms.

'Not quite *on* your golf course – it would be on the promenade behind, but making use of your equipment, your electricity for the sound system, the lights you have.'

'You want to hold a music night on the periphery of my golf course?'

'Yes, Maggie, I do. Next Friday, the second of June. Can we do it?'

'Who's "we", Bobbin? What's all this about?'

Robin bounced gently on the balls of her feet. 'One of my guests, Lorna, has been through a difficult time. She's a guitarist, and she's come down here to try and get back on her feet, regain her confidence. I thought that if we put on an open-mic night on the promenade, something that could be enjoyed by everyone, then she could be part of it, and it might help her.'

'And she's OK with this? She's on board?'

Robin nodded. 'She's been busking, trying to get back into performing in a place where no one knows her, and I want to make it a bit more impressive.'

'Old habits die hard, eh?' Maggie asked softly, smiling and thanking a couple as they handed their clubs and balls back to her.

'Something like that,' Robin muttered.

'You miss organizing events, working under that kind of pressure?'

'I miss working with Neve. I wouldn't want to go back to it full-time, not now. I love running the guesthouse too much. I'm still finding my feet and, if I'm honest, I've developed a tendency to get more involved with my guests than I should – Lorna being a case in point.'

'But perhaps not the prime example.' Maggie wiggled her eyebrows wickedly, and Robin flushed.

'I didn't mean it like that.'

'But you have to remember that I had a front-row seat for that particular show of overfamiliarity.'

'That was different,' Robin said miserably.

'Oh, Bobbin.' Maggie's smile fell. 'What happened? I wouldn't have teased you if I didn't think things were well there. I can see why you like him – those eyes alone are enough to make anyone weak at the knees. But it didn't work out?'

'I messed up,' Robin admitted. 'It's my fault. You warned me to be careful, and I was the opposite – I was the *least* careful I've ever been, probably.' She thought, for the hundredth time, that if she hadn't asked him to read Molly's text out . . .

'But he's still here?'

'He'll be here forever if the state of Tabitha's house is anything to go by.'

'So you've got a chance to make it up to him. What's his role in this music night going to be? And don't look at me like that – I know how your mind works, because it's exactly what *I* would do.'

'I'm going to ask him to be the compère. He's a tour guide, so he'll be able to get the audience in the palm of his hand, and hopefully warm up all the musicians before they go on stage. I only hope I can get him to say yes. So far, he's refusing to talk to me.'

'Men! They can be so stubborn,' Maggie said, rolling her eyes.

Robin laughed. 'That's a bit of a generalization.'

'Is it true in his case?'

'Maybe. But he has every right to be angry with me. I'm afraid the more I try, the more he'll close the door on me.'

'You need to get him somewhere he can't escape – where there are no doors to be closed, where he's a captive audience and he *has* to listen to you.'

'How am I going to do that?' Robin asked. 'It sounds great, but I only ever see him going into or out of Tabitha's house, and he's either on his way to shut himself up inside or he's going to his new job—' She stopped as the idea hit her,

Maggie's words repeating themselves. 'A captive audience, huh? He's the one who has one of those, but it doesn't mean I can't turn the tables, does it? Maggie, you're a genius!'

'I have no idea what you're talking about, but you're welcome.'

Robin squeezed her hand and turned to leave.

'Erm, Bobbin – didn't you want to know about the music night?'

Robin looked at her blankly, her head full of this new and potentially infallible plan.

'As to whether you can leech off the golf course to power and contain and basically put on your event?'

'Oh God, yes. Yes – so sorry.'

'Of course you can,' the older woman said, giving Robin a warm smile. 'I'm already looking forward to it – especially the compère part.'

'Thank you Maggie,' Robin gushed, clasping her hands together in front of her. 'Thank you so, so much.'

'Now go get him, Bobbin.'

'It doesn't sound quite as animalistic as Tiger,' Robin said, giving her a rueful smile.

Maggie laughed and shook her head, her long, unruly hair blowing around her face. 'You don't need animalistic. From the way he was kissing you, I'm not sure if you're going to need much in the way of persuasion tactics at all.'

When Robin got back to the guesthouse, she saw that Will's car was parked on the street, and realized she would have to wait to put her plan into action. For the next couple of days she concentrated on getting everything else in place, phoning local food vendors, asking Ashley and Roxy if they wanted to stay open that evening, talking to Stefano and Nicolas about providing a mezze menu for the extra custom that would be there on the night. Alongside a traditional burger or hotdog van, having the café and restaurant providing a cosier, sit-down service at either end of Goldcrest Road would widen the appeal, and she wanted her audience to be as diverse – and as large – as possible.

She made sure that it dominated the guesthouse social media pages, checking with Lorna that she was happy with the way it was being promoted:

Welcome the start of summer with an open-mic night on the prom, in association with the Campion Bay Guesthouse. Special guests Crow's Feet and guitarist Lorna Gregory. A selection of tracks to get you in the holiday mood. Food stalls and refreshments available! To sign up to perform, get in touch here.

Lorna was planning to continue with the busking, saying that everything she could do to get her confidence up before the concert would be beneficial, and Robin had heard her playing in her room. She'd offered Sea Shanty as a practice room too, as the high ceiling would provide better acoustics. She knew a few of the tracks; 'Wonderwall' by Oasis, a couple of Ed Sheeran songs and a few of Taylor Swift's more country-style tunes.

Paige had been ecstatic at the idea of a music night, her eyes almost popping out of her head when she heard Robin had managed to sign up local band Crow's Feet, and had immediately offered her and Adam's services, asking Lorna if she could help with the playlist. She was due to come round that evening.

Lorna seemed to be taking all the attention and fuss in

good spirits, which boded well for her performance, and had also been impressed at the calibre of band she would be playing alongside. The lead singer of Crow's Feet was the son of one of Robin's mum's friends. She had got his number and phoned him as soon as they had returned from the Artichoke, knowing she couldn't waste any time, and he had readily agreed to be a part of the event. She had confessed to Lorna that – not knowing him very well – she hadn't realized his band was more than a group of friends getting together in a garage at the weekends.

Robin was also relieved that the tension between her and Paige seemed to have disappeared. Things were slotting into place; now all she needed was someone confident and charismatic, with a talent for engaging an audience, to introduce the performers on the night.

She'd checked the website the evening before and now, on a warm, still Wednesday that held all the promise of summer, she wrote a note on the whiteboard informing her guests she'd be out for a couple of hours, put her phone volume on loud, and climbed into her Fiat.

It had been several years since her last visit to Eldridge House, and she couldn't remember the last time she'd been on a guided tour of anywhere – save for the private introductions she and Neve had been given when setting up one of their Once in a Blue Moon Days. Today, she was putting herself in the hands of one of their newest tour guides.

Ever since Will had told her what he did, Robin had been imagining him in that particular role, though not always in a typical setting. She'd pictured him giving her and Molly a tour of Campion Bay, of the cliffs and the beach and the crazy golf course. She'd imagined him holding their attention as they visited some of her old haunts in

285

London, and there had been a few daydreams that involved only the two of them, a personal tour of her own guesthouse, finishing up beneath the pinprick lights in Starcross. That one always made her heart beat faster, and wasn't good for her composure.

Now, she was about to see the man in action, to find out what a tour led by him was actually like and, hopefully, convince him to be a part of the Goldcrest Road event at the same time. Surely, he would have to see how wanted he was – not just by the other residents who had already proved their generosity to him, but by her. She needed him to know that her feelings for him were genuine, and if that meant disrupting one of his tours, then so be it. Desperate times called for desperate measures.

Eldridge House looked beautiful in the sunshine, with a sand-coloured pebble approach between manicured lawns and squat topiary bushes. The building itself was a creamy stone, with gabled windows and a red tiled roof. It looked luxurious, the perfect place for the wedding of your dreams, the rooms thick with opulence and history, and Robin felt herself checking for the usual things – access and entrance, the size of the windows, perfect backdrops for photos – that she had done when scoping out Once in a Blue Moon Days.

As she walked towards the main door, the pebbles crunching satisfyingly beneath her shoes, the sun glinted off the windows. The heat radiated around her, and a thin trickle of sweat made its way down her spine. She wasn't that far from the coast, but she noticed the change in the air, the loss of her beloved sea breeze that, even on the hottest days, added a freshness, some respite from searing temperatures.

But she knew, as she stepped from the glare of the sun

into the cool of the stone building and approached the small kiosk to buy her ticket, that it wasn't only the heat that had caused perspiration to prickle to the surface. Now that she was here, away from her guesthouse, where she was wholly in charge, her determination began to ebb away. What would he do when he saw her? Would he refuse to let her come on the tour, tell her he wouldn't host it while she was there?

'Excuse me, miss.' A man who looked younger than Adam, with unkempt hair and large framed spectacles, leaned forward inside the kiosk. 'Did you want to buy a ticket?'

'Oh yes, sorry. And I was hoping to go on one of the guided tours,' she said, even though she knew it started in twenty minutes, had triple-checked the website to make sure she wouldn't miss it.

He confirmed it for her. 'It starts from the bureau over there. Here's a free booklet – or you can buy the guidebook for three-fifty.'

'No thanks,' Robin said, collecting her ticket and booklet, and walking further into the room. It had thick wood panelling covering the walls, high, small windows and red brocade chair covers. It could be forty degrees outside, or three feet thick with snow, and nobody would know, it was so closed off from the world. It struck her, as she approached a low sofa that had a *Please do not touch* sign on it, that in many ways this wasn't so different from Tabitha's house. How could Will get any vitamin D when all he was doing was going from there to here? She hoped a large part of the tour took place in the sun-kissed grounds.

She wandered around the room, reading plaques about the history of the house and taking none of it in, glancing every few moments at her watch, the minutes ticking past excruciatingly slowly. She was conscious of a few more people milling in the hall. A couple in their forties, the woman, her dark hair in a short bob, clutching the guidebook; and a group of six older people, including one man with a walking stick and a woman walking alongside him, a thin, wispy scarf in rainbow colours shrugged loosely around her shoulders. The group were intent on one of the paintings hanging high on the wall, already sounding knowledgeable about it.

Robin hid her smile behind her hand, remembering Will's story about the man who had spent a whole tour at Downe Hall correcting him, and wondered how these people would fare if they turned out to know more than he did. And then she remembered that his tour was about to be disrupted by her, and her pulse began to thump in her ears.

A young family walked in: parents and a girl of six or seven, her long hair in two cute plaits either side, looking up with amazement at the high ceiling. Her father crouched down beside her, pointing out a bust of a man on a plinth next to the door, and then lifted her up to give her a closer look.

There was a change in atmosphere, murmurs among the people in the hall as a door closed and loud footsteps sounded on the floor. Robin recognized the footfalls instantly. She inhaled deeply, a shudder working its way down her neck and all the way to her feet.

'Uhm, Will?' It was the young man who had sold her the ticket. 'You have twelve people on your tour this morning.'

'Cheers, Jim,' Will said, and Robin's heart leaped at the sound of his voice. 'At least it's more than two today.'

'Twelve's brilliant!' Jim said enthusiastically. 'Did you still want me to show you the storeroom later? I'm only on tickets until one thirty, and Mrs Howden said that half the house's history is up there, and the more you know the better you'll be.'

'We'd better not disappoint Mrs Howden, then, had we?' Will said in response, and Robin could hear the amusement in his voice. 'That would be great, I'm keen to know all I can. I guess it's too much to hope that the storeroom has large, panoramic windows that let in lots of sunshine?'

Jim laughed, and Robin wondered if he looked up to Will, or if she was reading too much into the conversation. She could imagine that younger men would respect him: he had a kind of unaffected confidence, but no arrogance, no aware-ness of how admired he was – unlike Tim. Robin thought he sounded happy, confident. This was the old Will, the one she had first met, having dinner with her at the taverna, stripping to his boxers in her hallway, rather than the down-cast version he had been a few days ago.

She almost didn't want to turn round, wishing she could stay hidden in the corner of the room, leave him to get on with his job and not dampen his spirits by being there. But she'd come this far, she wanted to fight for Will and show him that she wasn't prepared to let him slip through her fingers. She tried to summon up some of Molly's brazen courage as Will spoke again, this time to the whole room.

'Who's here for the guided tour?' he asked. She could hear people start to move towards him. 'I'm Will, and I'm going to be taking you on your tour today. It will last around an hour, and will hopefully give you a good overview of Eldridge House and its history. If you have any burning questions, then please ask them. I can't claim to know everything, but I'll do my best, and I can always follow up on facts I'm unsure of afterwards. Hi,' he said, greeting the other visitors, 'nice to meet you.'

'I'm coming!' It was the young girl with pigtails.

'You are?' Will asked. 'Then I'm going to make it extra fun, especially for you.'

Robin couldn't hold back any longer. She took a deep breath and approached the group. The woman in her forties was looking at Will with rapt attention, before he'd imparted a single fact. Will turned towards her, his smile freezing on his face as their eyes met.

'Hi,' she said.

She watched as his Adam's apple bobbed. 'Hello. Are you here for the tour?'

He sounded easy and relaxed. She was sure she was the only one who had noticed the telltale note of tension at the edge of his voice.

'I am. If that's OK.' She cursed inwardly. She had come here to make him listen to her, and already she was checking that it was all right for her to be in the same room as he was. She was hopeless.

'Of course. The tour's open to everyone.' His smile was forced, stopping short of reaching his eyes and sprinkling them full of warmth.

'Great. Thanks.'

'Right.' Will addressed the group. 'Thank you all for coming to Eldridge House. I hope we can make your visit as interesting and enjoyable as possible. We'll start downstairs, I'll take you through the rooms here, then move to the upper floors and, finally, I'll show you some of the highlights of the magnificent grounds, which – on a day like today – are definitely worth exploring. Anyone have any questions before I start? Feel free to ask as we go round, though if it's juicy gossip about current members of the Eldridge family, then it's more than my job's worth to give you any details.'

'Are you one of Lord and Lady Eldridge's sons?' the woman with the rainbow scarf asked.

Will laughed gently. 'No.' He flashed his eyes in Robin's direction, as if wanting to share how ridiculous that concept was with someone who knew him. 'No, I'm only a tour guide. I have met the family, but only briefly. Shall we get going?'

'Course, lovey,' the woman said, as if he'd been talking solely to her. 'You look very handsome, as if you could be one of those young lords. I saw a film where the heir to a castle pretended to work there, to see what visitors were saying about them. People do like to talk, don't they?' She looked up at him expectantly, and Robin watched him hesitate.

'As much as that would be a great story, I'm afraid there's nothing like that going on with me. Although,' he said, leaning in close to her, his eyes glinting, 'if I *was* a member of the family, spying on guests as you suggest, I wouldn't want to admit it and blow my cover. What do you think about Jim on the ticket kiosk? Does he look like he has noble blood? I'll leave you to make up your own mind.'

The woman clasped her hands together in glee.

'But there is a murky past here, isn't there? If you go back a few centuries.' This from the older man with the stick. His stance was so straight that Robin thought he might be ex-military.

Will nodded slowly, glancing at the parents of the young girl. 'There are some dark aspects in the history of the house, certainly. We'll work up to that, and if you'll all follow me to the first room, I'll tell you how Eldridge House came to be built here.' He took the time to look at each of his guests, saving Robin until last, and then led them through a low, arched doorway.

The temperature dropped as they walked into a large hall with a stone floor and stained-glass windows. It was much brighter in here, but the windows tinted the sun's light, giving the room a surreal glow. Robin shivered slightly, and looked up to find that Will's gaze was on her. He turned away as she caught his eye.

'Right then!' He clapped his hands together, the sound echoing across the space and making a couple of people jump. 'Our story starts here. If you're listening carefully, then I'll begin.'

As Robin followed the group round the house, she silently congratulated herself on being right. Will was a wonderful tour guide. He revealed the history of the building with precisely the right amount of drama, making each tale sound interesting, engaging his guests in the distant lives of the family's ancestors. He brought them to life without overselling it, or turning it into pantomime. Everyone was rapt. The dark-haired woman had stepped slightly away from her husband, and kept subconsciously tucking her short hair behind her ear. In every room, he found something of interest for the little girl; a painting low on the wall, a strange sculpture that made her giggle, fabric with a shimmering thread running through it. Will was confident, charismatic and unquestioningly believable in his navy, logoed T-shirt, dark jeans and the familiar tan Wrangler boots. She imagined that, had he wanted to, he could lead them all into the lake and they'd follow.

And yet she hadn't summoned the courage to ask him about the music night. She was waiting for the perfect moment, now unsure if it was ever going to come. She had followed him through elaborate living rooms, bathrooms with high-sided bathtubs and sumptuous four-poster bedrooms without uttering a peep.

'This is the master bedroom,' Will said, leading them into a glorious corner room on the second floor, with windows on two sides and pink and gold furnishings, the carved posts of the bed like twisted rope. 'Anyone have a hankering to stay here for the night, enjoying the views?'

'Ooh, yes please,' the dark-haired woman said. 'Though the bedspread looks like it might be scratchy.'

'Have you stayed here?' asked the woman who had fancied Will as one of the family.

'In this room?' Will raised an eyebrow. 'No. I've had the pleasure of staying in a luxurious room recently, one with a canopy of stars on the ceiling rather than fabric, but not here. Besides . . .' He paused, and Robin held her breath, wondering why he'd made such an obvious reference to her guesthouse. 'Would any of you feel comfortable about staying in this room if you knew that a murder took place here?'

There were a couple of gasps, the little girl looked up at him wide-eyed, and Robin watched Will closely, seeing the amusement in his eyes as he dropped in this piece of drama.

'Who was murdered?' someone asked. 'Are we talking recently, or five hundred years ago?'

Will held up a finger, turned away from them and opened one of the drawers of a large dresser, taking out a small book. For a moment, Robin thought he had pictures or illustrations of the murder, but as she watched he crouched down beside the little girl and opened the first page. 'This,' he said, 'is a story about a queen. She lived somewhere close to here, maybe in this very house, looking out at the deer and rabbits in the grounds, ruling over her faithful people.' He waited while she took the book with both hands, her face alive with the excitement of a story solely for her. The girl's parents exchanged a smile, and Robin felt her heart squeeze.

Will stood, took a step forward and lowered his voice. 'The murder was three hundred and fifteen years ago,' he said. 'The son of a visiting family, the Montagues, took a fancy to Bartholomew Eldridge's eldest daughter, Verity. Lord Bart, protective of his daughter and seeing the Montagues as too low-standing to make a suitable match, set a trap for young Henry, luring him to this room on the pretence that Verity would be waiting for him. Instead it was Bartholomew himself, intending only to scare Henry off. But things went terribly wrong, and Henry didn't come out of the altercation alive.'

'Good Lord!' one of the guests murmured. 'How terrible!'

'That sounds a bit far-fetched,' Robin said, her brain connecting to her mouth before she'd had a chance to moderate the words.

Will turned to her, his expression patient. 'Are you suggesting I'm making it up?'

Robin wondered if she should backtrack, but it was too late for that. 'It's a bit of a coincidence that the most impressive room is home to such a scandalous story. Too good to be true, maybe.'

'Are you questioning my integrity?' Will's voice had an edge now, and Robin licked her lips, giving herself time before she replied.

'No, not at all. I know that someone like you would never, *ever* make anything up. Not even to try and make the tours more interesting.' They stared at each other, and it may have been Robin's imagination, but she thought she saw Will's lips flicker upwards. He walked slowly around the other side of the bed, his loud footsteps steady and suddenly menacing.

'Apparently,' he said in a low voice, 'people who *have* stayed in this room have encountered Henry's presence. He lingers here still, unable to move on from such an unjust death, tormenting guests of the family with his moaning. There have been infrequent sightings too, occasional glimmers of a forlorn figure reflected in the mirror or the window.'

'That is a load of poppycock,' the military man said.

Will grinned and folded his arms. 'So you'd be happy to stay in this room, then? For a whole night?'

'Of course I would,' he scoffed. 'Nothing to it!'

The dark-haired woman took a step forward. 'I'd rather stay in the other room you mentioned, the one with the canopy of stars. It sounds so romantic and, if it's ghost-free, then I'm in.' She tucked her hair behind her ear again, gazing at Will with barely disguised admiration. Robin bit back her laugh, seeing irritation cross the husband's face, and realized she felt a glimmer of envy that was entirely ridiculous, not least because she had no claim over Will at all.

'That room's in a guesthouse,' Will replied. 'So it is available to be booked by the public, unlike here. I have no idea if it's haunted, though. It's in a seaside town not far from here called Campion Bay. It's a very special room. *Unique*, you might say.'

Robin stared, speechless. Was he actually promoting her guesthouse, or was there about to be an unpleasant punchline? Was this some roundabout way of showing her he forgave her, or a charitable act because he'd moved out of Starcross at such short notice? She thought she detected an edge of bitterness in his voice, but his expression was unreadable.

'Oh, I've heard of Campion Bay,' one of the older women said. 'Lovely beach, quaintly pretty. One of the nicest seafronts along this part of the coast. No caravan parks or arcades.'

'It's very beautiful,' Robin murmured, and then realized this was her way in. Will was almost *inviting* her to talk about the upcoming event; she wouldn't get another chance like this. As he led them out of the murderous bedroom, Robin took a deep breath and spoke again, raising her voice so that it carried.

'Campion Bay's holding an outdoor music night next week,' she said, hoping she sounded casual. 'On the promenade.'

'What's that dear?' A grey-haired woman turned towards her.

Robin swallowed. 'The seaside town that Will mentioned. Some of the residents are putting on an open-mic night, people performing summer songs on the promenade. There are going to be food stalls, a mobile bar, and music from some talented musicians. It should be a lovely event, and you can't get a better backdrop than the sea.'

She was getting curious looks now, people wondering why she was hijacking the tour with this irrelevant piece of information.

'It sounds lovely, dear.' A woman patted her arm, and she knew she was losing their attention. She wished she was like Will, able to draw people in with only a few words.

'An open-mic night?' Will asked as he led the tour out into the sunshine. He sounded curious, probably in spite of himself.

'Yes.' She took a deep breath. 'It's something I'm doing with a friend, Molly, and one of my guesthouse guests.' They had all stopped in a group on the sandy pebbles. Robin glanced at the visitors, holding everyone's gaze as Will had done. 'The area – Campion Bay – has such a strong sense

296

of community these days. Something that, until very recently, I hadn't fully realized.'

Now Will's expression did change, anger flashing across his face. Robin ran her sweaty palms down her trousers and continued. 'Anyway, I wanted to do something for the community – *with* them – so we're putting on this music night. But we're missing a compère for the evening, someone who can introduce the acts.' She forced herself to look at Will, and he stared back impassively.

'Ooh, you could get that celebrity – what's his name?' The woman with the scarf clicked her fingers. 'Billy Bragg. He likes a bit of music, doesn't he? I'm sure he lives round here somewhere.'

'That's a good idea,' Robin said, nodding. 'Except that we don't have that kind of budget. I was thinking of someone who has a real presence, who's good at speaking in front of people . . .' She let her words trail off, hoping that Will would step in.

There was a moment of quiet while the warm breeze drifted lazily over them, and Robin thought she heard the cry of a peacock far in the distance.

'Oh!' The scarf-clad woman clapped her hands together. 'What about lovely Will here? You'd be ever so good at that sort of thing, my lovey. You've done such a super job of telling us about the house.'

There were murmurs of assent from the other guests, and the woman with the dark bob said quietly, to nobody in particular, 'I'd definitely go if he was going to be there.'

Robin felt a surge of hope as the chatter grew and people started asking questions. 'When is this event?' 'Where's Campion Bay again?' And, from Mr Military to Will, 'So, are you going to do it, then? Help this young girl out with her community-spirit whatsit?' His voice rose above those of the other members of the group and everyone stopped talking, their eyes on Will to see what his answer would be. Robin held her breath, and waited like the rest of them.

Chapter 17

'You railroaded me. I'm never going to see any of those people again. I don't actually have to do it.'

Will and Robin were sitting side by side on the low wall at the edge of the courtyard in front of Eldridge House, the breeze caressing them with thoughts of summer as the sun moved slowly across the sky. Robin was conscious of how close they were, her bare arm inches from his, tanned and with a dusting of light-brown hairs. Arms that had, less than two weeks ago, held her so closely against him.

'I think most of them are coming to the event now,' she said, 'and they'll be disappointed if it turns out you're not introducing it. Do you make fans like that on every tour?'

Will laughed awkwardly. 'I have no idea what you're talking about. But I don't have to be at your music night, so I won't see their disappointment.'

'You'd leave me at their mercy? They're already looking forward to the Will Nightingale show. You can't back out now!'

'I can,' he said. 'You put me in that position. You came here deliberately to make me agree to this.'

Robin glanced at his profile and frowned. She couldn't tell how serious he was being, whether he was genuinely upset with her, or if this was a remnant of the gentle jibes they had shared when things were good between them. Will was sitting very still, gripping the low wall. She had that sense that he was trying hard to control his emotions and she felt a wave of guilt that she was the cause.

'You were the one who mentioned Campion Bay and the guesthouse to begin with,' she said lightly. 'I was struggling to find a way to bring it into the conversation.'

'So I walked right into it. Again.'

Robin sagged. This time she knew it wasn't friendly teasing. 'Will, come on. It was an honest mistake. I misunderstood Molly and I wanted you to feel welcome! Does it matter now?'

'And what about you and Tim, keeping his involvement in Tabitha's house from me? Was that an honest mistake too?'

'There's nothing going on,' she said defiantly, feeling him slipping away from her. 'There hasn't been since I moved down here again.'

He stood up. 'I'll be involved in the open-mic night if you want me to be. I should repay the residents of Goldcrest Road for their kindness, but I don't want to go over this with you, Robin. Not now. I have to get back to work.'

'Please, Will—'

'Text me what you want me to do. I'll be there.'

'It's not as simple as that,' she called, but he kept walking away from her, towards the house. He didn't look back.

'So everything's set, then?' Lorna clapped her hands together, then picked Eclipse up from where he was licking his paws on one of the benches in Sea Shanty, and held him high above her head. Eclipse dangled, unimpressed, but didn't struggle. Robin bit back her laughter, realizing that growing up in a house full of strangers, all with different temperaments, different opinions about animals, was probably the best thing that could have happened to her little cat. He was so tolerant.

She wondered what he'd think of Darcy if he saw her again now. Will's presence had been missing from the guesthouse for two weeks. In normal circumstances, there would be nothing unusual about that – he'd been a guest, not a lodger – but to Robin it felt like her world was incomplete.

'Most things are set,' she replied, turning back to the to-do list on the table in front of her.

Taverna on the Bay was running a special menu, Roxy and Ashley were staying open late and the food vendors and mobile bar had been booked. She and Molly had checked Maggie's sound and lighting system the evening before, working out how to rig up the amplifier and microphone for the performers, and maximize Lorna's reach with a bridge mic inside her acoustic guitar. There had been a flurry of online traffic in response to the posts she'd put on Facebook and Twitter, and she had fifteen different acts signed up to sing or play on the night, including her special guests.

She'd decided to ask for performers before, rather than accept them as impromptu on the night, so she would have better control over the event. She didn't want to run the risk of Lorna and Crow's Feet being her only acts, and unlike at a club, anyone would be able to watch the performances and she had to have an idea of whom she was putting on beforehand, so she wouldn't cause any offence to families in the audience.

She had taken Instagram photos of the huge bundles of

fairy lights she'd bought, and of the promenade where they were hosting the concert, as the sun went prettily down. She'd posted information and pictures of the open-mic acts, and had taken a couple of shots of Lorna who, she had decided, would open the concert and have another slot near the end, before the Crow's Feet set. The warm weekend seemed to have inspired everyone, and Robin had struggled to keep up with the flurry of comments below her posts, answering questions as quickly as she could to get the buzz going and encourage lots of people to attend.

Now it was Monday morning, five days to go until the Goldcrest Road music night, and Robin was worried by how little there was left to do. Lorna's energy had been growing every day, her excitement and nerves playing across her usually passive face. It was as if she was storing it up, working herself into a fever pitch that she would expel slowly as magical music on the night. She was a different person from the timid woman who had appeared on Robin's doorstep with her guitar case and Robin felt a flush of accomplishment that she was, in part, responsible for the transformation.

'It's going to be incredible,' Lorna said now, lowering Eclipse into a hug, patting the cat's back as if he were a baby who needed burping. 'You have no idea how grateful – amazed – I am that you're doing this for me.'

'I'm very happy to do it,' Robin said honestly. 'It's not on my usual list of special offers, but I had the ability – and the friends – to help you, and I couldn't think of a reason not to.'

'It's very spontaneous.' Lorna sat opposite Robin, the sun coming through the open windows dappling the wooden table, the breeze wafting gently around them, whispering at their hair. 'And you've organized everything so quickly.

But the cost of it – the stage, the equipment you've hired – isn't it going to bankrupt you, if you're putting the concert on for free?'

'So many of our neighbours are giving their time and help for nothing. Maggie's letting us use the electricity at the crazy golf course, Molly and Paige have been helping to promote it online and across as much of Campion Bay as possible, and even Crow's Feet reduced their usual appearance fee.'

'But you've still got to pay them something. It must be costing you a lot more than you're getting back from the food vendors.' Lorna raised her eyebrows.

'It's all fine. Please don't worry.' Robin gave her a reassuring smile. The local, well-known band was the biggest outlay, and the stage and other equipment hire weren't cheap, but Robin had committed to doing it. And it would be worth it to help Lorna, to provide the town with some free entertainment and show the residents of Goldcrest Road that she valued being a part of their community.

'Paige has picked some excellent songs,' Lorna said, as if unable to cope with the silence. 'I never would have thought of Ben Howard or James Bay, but the tracks she's suggested are perfect. And finishing my second set with Bon Jovi is a stroke of genius. Everyone will *have* to sing along – they'll be excited about Crow's Feet by then anyway.'

'I can't believe she picked Bon Jovi. I know they're still going, but not like they used to. Which track? Please say it's one of their earlier ones.'

'"Someday I'll be Saturday Night" – my voice isn't suited to something as rocky as "Livin' on a Prayer", but this one, I can do.'

'That's going to be perfect!' Robin closed her eyes and

imagined Lorna's voice lifting above the crowd as everyone joined in, the sea in front of them, dusk falling slowly, bringing out the fairy lights. 'Oh, I've got shivers just thinking about it.'

'I know,' Lorna said, grinning. 'Me too!'

Her giddiness was infectious and Robin felt the tug of it, wondering how she was going to stay calm and composed for the next few days.

'So who's this guy that's introducing the whole event? Molly said he was a professional, and that I'd be over the moon with the choice.'

'Ah.' Robin's excitement subsided. 'It's Will. I don't know if you've seen him. He's staying next door while he clears it out. The house belonged to his aunt and . . . He's a tour guide. So he's professional in the sense that he talks to people for a living. He's very good at it.'

'Oh great.' Lorna took a sip of lemonade. 'And why will I be pleased with him, particularly? Is he into music?'

Robin frowned. 'I don't know what music he likes, actually. But I'm sure he'll do a great job with the crowd. He's very . . . engaging.' She settled on that word, remembering how he had captivated everyone on the tour, and talked about the guest-house with something approaching longing. But since their awkward conversation sitting on the wall of Eldridge House, she'd texted him several times, asking when would be a good time to meet, but he'd always put her off and suggested she should message him the details. He must know that wasn't a plausible way of doing things, but she understood that he was still reluctant to spend time with her.

Her miserable musings were interrupted by the doorbell and she got to her feet, leaving Lorna at the table. She'd said goodbye to some of her guests at the weekend, had moved

Lorna into Starcross as a young couple from near Brighton had booked to stay in Rockpool, but three of the rooms were unoccupied until Wednesday. She wondered if it was someone enquiring about the guesthouse, or wanting to sign up to perform at the open-mic night.

'Hello?' Her smile faltered when she saw it was Tim. He was in his shirtsleeves, his tie the colour of summer sand, making his blond curls seem even more luminous.

'Robin Brennan,' he said, the words coming out as a sigh. His smile was less than brilliant, and she was shocked at the uncertainty in his expression.

'How are you?' she asked. 'Planning any more wild nights at the Artichoke?'

Tim dropped his gaze from hers, and Robin realized that he felt bad about his drunken appearance. He had lowered his guard in her presence and he wasn't happy about it. 'About my . . . visit, the other night. It was stupid.'

'It was amusing.' *Apart from the near-kiss part*, she added silently.

Tim rolled his eyes. 'So glad I could provide you with some entertainment. Can I come in? I have a proposition for you.'

'Sure.' She stood back and let him in, happy to be on the front foot with him feeling embarrassed about their last encounter.

'Hi.' Tim greeted Lorna as Robin led him into Sea Shanty. Eclipse jumped on to the table, butting his head against Tim's hand and forcing him to stroke him. Robin saw pinpoints of colour on Tim's cheeks, and remembered how he'd uncharacteristically let Eclipse sit on his lap. She was glad her cat wasn't going to let him forget it.

'Hello.' Lorna shook Tim's hand and gave a questioning glance to Robin. 'Are you Will?'

'No, I'm Tim Lewis, not Will. Why? Has Robin been talking about him?'

'He's introducing the open-mic night at the end of the week,' Lorna said proudly. 'Apparently he's going to blow everyone away.'

'It's you that will be doing that, Lorna,' Robin cut in. 'Will's going to introduce the evening, that's all. It's a very small part of it.'

'But the way you and Molly have been talking about him—'

'He's not performing like you are,' Robin emphasized. 'He'll be the bookends holding the evening together. People are coming to hear you and the other acts.'

'And I, for one, can't wait,' Tim said, slipping into easy charm mode, his grin competing with the sun's glare. 'That's what I wanted to talk to you about. I've been following your posts these last few days, and it sounds very impressive. It's a long time since there was any kind of public event in Campion Bay.'

'There were the New Year's fireworks,' Robin said, pouring a glass of iced lemonade from the jug and pushing it towards him. 'And there are some in a few weeks, too.'

'OK, but aside from fireworks, the Campion Bay social scene has been seriously lacking. I can't think of anything better than an open-mic night. What you're doing is beyond generous.'

'Everyone's pitching in,' Robin said. 'The residents of Goldcrest Road have kind spirits.'

'The taverna and the teashop will make heavy profits from the event you're working hard to put on. And you can't tell me that all the equipment you're hiring, the stage set-up, the posters – none of that's costing you anything?' He raised an eyebrow, and Robin gave a tiny shrug.

'In the scheme of things, it's not too much to lay out. The toy shop in town has offered to provide free glow sticks, and the Dorset Outdoors shop has ordered in a stock of plastic ponchos in case the weather turns bad.'

'Yeah, Robs, but all that set-up?'

'So what, you're going to sweep in like a knight in shining armour and pay for it all? How do you know I'm not sitting on a pot of money?' She folded her arms and glared at him.

Tim sat on the bench next to Robin and took a sip of lemonade. 'I'm not offering to pay for it outright,' he said, directing his words to both Robin and Lorna. 'But why not let Campion Bay Property sponsor the event? We'd get some good publicity, and I'd love to be associated with your open-mic night. It's the kind of thing Malcolm and I have talked about doing for a while, and this seems like the perfect place to start.'

'*Sponsor* it?' Robin asked, incredulous. 'But there are four days to go. How much publicity do you hope to gain in that short time?'

Tim's grin widened. 'We can start promoting it on our social media pages, send over our logo for the photos you post, get a banner produced to run along the front of the stage. Every little helps – and in exchange, we put some cash into the event to help with what you've already laid out.'

'Wow,' Lorna said, before Robin had a chance to reply. 'That sounds fantastic. You'd do that?'

Tim nodded, looking serious. 'Sure. It makes perfect sense. If an up-and-coming local business can't get involved in something like this, then they're not trying hard enough to make an impact in the community. The way I see it, everyone wins. What's not to love?'

'There is *nothing* not to love,' Lorna said breathlessly, and Robin tried not to roll her eyes. She had to concede that, despite the personal angle, it was a very generous offer. She couldn't see any way she could turn it down, not now that Lorna was gazing at Tim with eyes that wouldn't have looked out of place on an adoring puppy.

'We spend a lot of time having covert conversations in your hallway,' Tim said, as Robin walked him to the front door. She had wondered if Tim's sponsorship offer was the sole reason he'd come round, or if he was combining it with a visit to see Will. The thought was unsettling.

'There's nothing covert about this,' Robin said, leaning against the wall.

'There is about what I have to say,' Tim said. 'Which is . . . sorry.'

A gasp escaped before Robin had a chance to hold it in.

Tim gave her a wry smile. 'You don't have to look *that* shocked.'

'I just . . . What for?'

Tim put his hands in his pockets, glancing away from her and then back. 'For lots of things: for point-scoring when Will was here, for the other night and what I tried to do. I was drunk, Robs. But the feelings, the sentiment, they're there. I haven't been very straightforward since you've been back, but that's because seeing you again caught me off guard.'

'It did?' She narrowed her eyes.

'I'm sorry for making you feel uncomfortable.'

'And for wanting to develop next door?'

She saw the light leave his eyes, but he recovered quickly. 'That's business, and I'm not going to apologize for trying to make a success of my career. I'm not saying I'll walk away, but it's not up to me: it's up to Will. Anyway,' he said, poking her gently in the shoulder – it was an affectionate, unsure gesture that made Robin feel a squeeze of warmth towards him – 'you've changed the subject. I shouldn't have tried to kiss you last time I was here. And, if I hadn't had four double whiskies, I wouldn't have, but that doesn't mean I don't want to. If the circumstances were right—'

'They're not going to be right, Tim.'

'Why not? Why not give it – us – a chance?'

'Because we're in the past,' Robin said, wishing she didn't have to have this conversation now. Not in her hallway, with Lorna in the other room and Will next door, stonewalling her.

'It doesn't have to be like that. Let me take you out, after the open-mic night. I know it'll be a late finish, but there's this great little bar a bit further along the coast that serves food up until midnight. Delicious tapas, you'd love it. A hidden gem.'

'I'm going to be exhausted after it's over.'

'All the more reason to let me spoil you. Let's get away from here, the two of us, have some time to see how we feel about each other. We can't do that here, with snatched conversations and fleeting visits. Just this once, Robs. Let your sponsor take you out to celebrate – as part of the business deal.'

She looked at him, waiting for his smugness to radiate towards her, but she saw that he was nervous, his lips pinched, eyebrows raised slightly in anticipation. It was that, more than anything else, which made the decision for her. She had no reason not to go with him, and besides, it was only one meal, part of the sponsorship deal. Two people who'd known each other for two decades, catching up. It didn't mean anything if she didn't let it.

'I thought this stage was supposed to be like IKEA furniture,' Molly said, panting, her T-shirt sleeves rolled up to her shoulders. 'It's like the bloody *Krypton Factor*.' She held up a sturdy steel brace and a metal clamp and tried fitting one into the other dejectedly.

'I'm sure if we follow the instructions we'll be fine.' Adam, Paige's boyfriend, was crouched on the promenade looking at the flimsy booklet that had accompanied their hired stage. They were between Maggie's crazy golf course and the sea, the spot where they were holding the music night. Robin had checked the regulations with the council, making sure they could get a temporary noise licence in time. The last thing she wanted was for her event to be broken up by the police for being too loud or in the wrong place. But it seemed that everything she wanted to do was possible in Campion Bay, as long as the concert area and food stalls were appropriately cordoned off. However, there wouldn't be an event if they couldn't get the stage built.

'This is how these companies do it,' Paige said, hands on her slender hips as she surveyed the mess they were making. 'They hire out these things for pennies and make their money by charging to erect them for you.'

'It would have been an extra two hundred pounds for them to build it,' Robin said, wiping perspiration from her brow, the curls around her temples turning to frizz in protest at the heat and exertion. 'At the time, it seemed ludicrous to add that much on for putting it up.'

'And now?' Molly asked pointedly. 'Especially with Tim's sponsorship?'

'Obviously, if I'd known what Tim was going to do, that it wasn't going to be a cost I'd have to absorb, I'd have felt differently,' Robin sighed, realizing that Molly was right, that even if she'd had to pay the extra, it would have been worth it. But hindsight was a wonderful thing and they had to deal with the current situation the best they could.

Her arms were aching and her knees, bare in denim cut-offs and pressing into the hard concrete of the promenade, were throbbing. Not to mention that she felt entirely bamboozled by the pieces of metal and hardboard laid out in front of them. It had been dropped off rather haphazardly, she thought, by the company she'd hired it from, and they'd driven away gleefully after giving her the instructions and a basic risk assessment, clearly aware of the hours of torment that were ahead of her because she had chosen to save some money.

She swore under her breath and tried fitting another part of the metal frame together. She couldn't give up. It was Thursday evening, less than twenty-four hours before kick-off, and she was sure that even if she called the company and pleaded with them to come back and do it for her, they wouldn't send anyone until the following morning. And one rule Robin had learned from her Once in a Blue Moon Days was that you never left anything to the last minute – not if you wanted to survive the event without becoming a puddle of stress. She could also, she thought, have stuck to the rule about paying for professionals and doing everything properly, but it was too late for that now.

'There are four of us,' she said, exasperation edging into her voice. 'How can four of us not make this work? We've refurbished a whole bloody guesthouse between us. I mean, seriously.'

'It's very like scaffolding,' Molly said. 'Or Meccano. Who do we know who's good at Meccano? Adam, are you Meccano or Lego?'

Adam rolled his eyes at the age-related jibe. 'I'm sure if we fiddle about a bit, we can make it work.'

'We are *not* fiddling about a bit!' Robin's voice reached fever pitch. 'People will be *standing* on this stage, in front of a large crowd. We can't take any chances, can't risk it falling down and injuring anyone because we thought it would be OK to "fiddle about a bit"!' She stood up, brushing her knees down angrily, and then realized that Molly, Paige and Adam were looking at her with wide-eyed apprehension.

'Jeez, Robin, calm down,' Molly said. 'Everything's going to be fine.'

'I *know*, but I can't risk Lorna, or any of the other performers – or Will – being up here and then it all—' She stopped in mid-flow, replaying Molly's earlier words: *It's very like scaffolding.* She knew one person who had years of experience working on building sites, who – she was sure – would find this as easy as Jenga, but hopefully with a more stable outcome.

'We'll get it right,' Paige said, patting her shoulder reassuringly.

'*We* might not have to.' Robin dusted herself down and headed purposefully in the direction of number four. 'I'll be back in a jiffy.'

She couldn't help her heart rate ratcheting up a notch as she got closer to the tall grey building, the blue plaque glinting in the evening sunshine. Would he be in? Would he be prepared to talk to her, after over a week of staccato text replies, and refusing to meet with her before the concert to discuss his role? Well, they needed him now. This wasn't a ruse cooked up so that he'd be forced to rescue her. She genuinely didn't know what they'd do about the stage without his help.

She climbed the steps quickly and knocked on the door before she had a chance to change her mind.

She heard movement inside, a low voice, and then the door opened and Will stood before her, looking relaxed in grey shorts and a navy cotton T-shirt that clung to his torso, emphasizing his wide shoulders. Robin was caught off guard, his looks and her attraction to them more pronounced after a few days without seeing him. He was holding a bottle of beer, condensation glistening on the outside, and Robin licked her lips, imagining how good the cold, refreshing liquid would taste.

He didn't start at her appearance. Instead, his eyes widened in what looked like concern. 'Robin, are you OK?' He reached his arm out towards her, his fingers hovering inches from her skin, and she realized how much of a state she must look. She glanced down and saw that her vest top was covered in grease marks from the metal poles, and that her knee was slightly grazed. Her face must be red, sweaty and surrounded by a halo of frizz. The contrast between them couldn't have been greater.

'Oh,' she said. 'Yes. Yes, I'm fine.' She felt a physical ache, wanting so badly to hold on to that moment of caring from him, after days of him treating her like an irritating stranger. 'I mean, no. I'm not OK, not really.'

'What is it? Do you want to come inside?' Now his fingers did graze her arm, and she felt it like a spark of electricity. Their eyes held, and she knew he had felt it too.

'No, I can't.' She dragged the words out. She would love to go inside with him, to finally talk, to start to heal the rift

313

between them. 'We've got a problem with the stage for the music night . . . In that we can't build it.'

Will stared at her, his expression incredulous. 'You're building the stage?'

'Yes. We've hired it from one of those companies, and—'

'You asked for the contract that didn't include putting it up and taking it down again?'

'It was so expensive,' Robin sighed.

'Because it's not that straightforward.' She saw amusement dance in his eyes.

'I know that *now*. Can you – I'm sorry to ask, but there are four of us at it and we're still struggling. And I thought, with you having worked on building sites . . .'

'Yes,' he said. 'I can help.'

'You can?' She couldn't help the smile. 'I mean, I know you *can*, but – but *will* you?'

He didn't answer immediately, and she wondered if he'd temporarily forgotten that he was mad with her, and she'd just reminded him and he was going to say no, and close the door, and then she'd be desolate and stressed, with no way of getting their stage up and a hole in her heart as big as the one that was currently where the stage should be.

'Yes, Robin. Of course I'll help. Give me two minutes to get some shoes on, and I'll be with you.' He gave her a gentle, wary smile, as if he was trying it out after not having used it for a while. 'Here, look after this for me.' He handed her his bottle of beer. 'And if it's all gone by the time I get back, I won't complain. You look like you could use it.'

He disappeared into Tabitha's hallway, leaving Robin standing on the doorstep feeling as light as a feather. She took a long, refreshing swig of beer, enjoying the coolness as it slipped down inside her, and then wondered if, right now, alcohol was the best idea. She was feeling giddy already, at his concern, his kind words, the glimmer of warmth she'd seen in his eyes. She waited for him, knowing unequivocally that she'd made the right decision not to pay for the stage to be erected. For once, it looked like being less than completely organized was about to pay off.

Chapter 18

Will tightened the final screw with the electric screwdriver and stood back, wiping his forearm across his brow. 'They shouldn't be allowed to loan these types of structures without putting them up for you,' he said. 'It's not safe.'

His tone was kind, exhausted perhaps, but Robin still felt guilty. She had always prided herself on doing things to a high standard, but on this occasion she'd let her pettiness get in the way, thinking she could do it all on her own to save some money. Not to mention the minuscule timeframe she'd given them all to work with. However, it had led to Will helping them, which was a definite silver lining.

'This whole thing has been such short notice,' she said. 'My options were limited when I was looking for local companies. But it's entirely my fault that we were left with this job to do. I can't thank you enough, Will.'

'You've saved our bacon,' Molly added. 'And I hope you've been practising your introduction.'

Will put the screwdriver back in its box and grinned. 'I'm not sure what I need to say yet, so . . .'

'Why's that, I wonder?' Molly asked lightly. Robin had been keeping her friend up to date with the terseness of the texts that had been passing between the two of them, so she already knew the answer.

He had the grace to look sheepish. 'I take full responsibility for that, so . . .' He shrugged. 'Now's as good a time as any.'

Adam and Paige returned from Molly's house with a six-pack of cold beers and handed them out. Molly watched closely as, once the adults each had a bottle, Paige passed one to Adam, then took one herself. There was a moment of silence, Robin holding her breath as she waited for Molly to explode, but her friend simply raised her eyebrows and extended her arm, pointing at Paige with a slow, sinister finger.

'Just one, because you've earned it. But don't think this is permission for any other day or occasion beyond this one beer, right here, right now. Understood?'

Paige grinned, clinking her bottle with Adam's. 'Understood. You've got to let me grow up sometime, Mum.'

'Baby steps,' Molly said, a warning in her voice. 'Baby. Bloody. Steps. Don't get any ideas.'

Robin sank on to the promenade wall and Will sat beside her with a sigh. He no longer looked immaculate and relaxed: he looked like he'd spent a whole day on a building site.

'Sorry to ruin your evening,' she said.

Will shook his head quickly. 'You didn't. And this is a good reward. The satisfaction of seeing the stage set up for tomorrow night, and having a cold beer with this view.' He swivelled to look out over the sea, which, in the gathering dusk and beneath the promenade lights, was an eerie violet hue. The water was calm, small waves caressing the shore. Robin closed her eyes and breathed it in, imagining it this

317

time tomorrow, bustling with people, the rhythm of the tide masked by chatter and song.

Sometime in the last few minutes, Molly, Paige and Adam had disappeared without saying goodbye. Robin was sure that was Molly's doing. 'It's perfect, isn't it?' she asked softly.

She felt Will stiffen beside her. 'It's a good view,' he said. 'So, what are my instructions for tomorrow? Do you have something prepared?'

Robin shook her head. 'I've got the running order of the acts and how they want to be introduced, but other than that you have *carte blanche*. Just do what you do best, get the audience's attention, hold them in the palm of your hand.'

'That's a big ask,' he said, laughing lightly.

'No, it's not. You know you can do it. I, uhm . . .' She glanced towards Goldcrest Road and the glowing lights of the houses, wishing that, now she'd got him here, she could hold on to him. 'I need to go back. I promised Lorna I'd run through everything with her this evening, help to quash any last-minute nerves. She's got two slots tomorrow – at the beginning and near the end, because she's the one who started this whole thing off. I'm already later than I said I would be. Thank you, again, for your help tonight. And tomorrow. And I don't know if . . .' She scrutinized him, waiting for her pause to force his gaze towards her. His face was in shadow, but she could sense his anticipation, knew that there was less resistance than there had been before.

'If what?' he asked softly.

'If you'd be willing to talk – I mean, to let me talk to you, properly. To explain everything. Maybe after tomorrow, once this is out of the way?'

He pressed his lips together, and she could see the faint

glint of barely there stubble along his jawline. 'Sure,' he said easily. 'Let me know when you're free. I'll be all ears.'

'Ladies and gentlemen,' Will said, the speakers giving a quick, sharp squeak of feedback before settling down again. He grinned, let his eyes take in his audience slowly, building the anticipation. 'Welcome to the first Goldcrest Road music night.' His voice rose at the end, and a cheer went up from the crowd.

Robin looked at the people who had come to her impromptu, whirlwind event. She guessed that there were a couple of hundred of them on the promenade, some entirely focused on the stage, some milling around behind, queuing at the colourful food stands – burgers, Mexican burritos, a chocolate fountain stall and mobile bar – and a few beyond the stage, listening from the beach, even though the speakers were angled away from them.

The warm evening had helped draw the crowds, and Robin could see families with small children, groups of friends who had come to support their performing mates, couples, young and old, holding hands or linking arms. The performers, all of whom she had met briefly, were in various stages of readiness. There was a young man called Ed, who had a foppish haircut that reminded her of an eighties band, and an ensemble of girls dressed in jeans and red tops, huddled together for a last-minute pep talk. Some hovered at the edges of the area with their instruments, glancing at sheets of paper that contained lyrics or music. Paige and Adam had agreed to be in charge of the acts, making sure they had everything they needed, getting them ready to go on stage, so that Robin could float freely, keeping an eye on the bigger picture.

She watched now as a large group of teenagers, some

wearing Crow's Feet T-shirts, moseyed up towards the stage, chatting and laughing as they snapped glow sticks round each other's wrists, their voices dimming as they joined the back of the audience and listened to what Will was saying. Two men, stepping away from the mobile bar, clinked their plastic pint glasses together. The crowds spilled towards and out of the taverna and the teashop, a steady stream of people visiting Goldcrest Road to take advantage of the unexpected, early-summer fun.

There was a general buzz of excitement filling the air. It was a great start, Robin thought, as her eyes followed the movements of coloured glow sticks dotted throughout the audience. She would be able to get a rough estimate of the full reach of her event from how many were left at the end of the night.

Lorna was standing next to the stage clutching her guitar, and Robin gave her a reassuring wave as Will continued with his introduction.

'I think you'll agree that it would be hard to conjure up a better occasion than this.' He strolled from one side of the stage to the other. He was wearing the sea-blue shirt he'd worn for their meal at the taverna, this time with smart black trousers. His eyes shone out under the spotlights, and Robin knew it was more than anticipation of the upcoming performances that was shortening her breath.

'We've got a variety of food stands offering sweet and savoury treats,' Will said, 'as well as a bar serving soft and alcoholic drinks. Not to mention that Taverna on the Bay and the Campion Bay Teashop are running special open-mic night menus for this evening only. And there are free glow sticks. Everyone loves a glow stick, don't they? Whether they remind you of awkward teenage discos, Take That concerts or the cold, smoky air and bonfire crackle of Guy Fawkes

Night. Who doesn't love taking them out of the freezer and snapping the colour back to life? Come on, admit it. Does anyone here not like glow sticks?' He raised an eyebrow and there was laughter from the crowd, people glancing around to see who would be brave enough to own up. One young man raised his hand, and was met with a few gentle jeers from his friends.

'Fair enough.' Will nodded. 'I won't hold it against you. If glow sticks aren't your thing, we've also got this magnificent backdrop.' He turned, pausing to let everyone take it in, and Robin felt a shift in the atmosphere. 'Someone told me recently that this view was perfect,' he said. 'I didn't agree with her at the time; I was holding back. But do you know what? I think she was right.' He took a breath, and Robin could tell, in spite of the emotions swirling inside her at his words, that he also had the attention of everyone in the crowd. 'I can't think of anywhere else I'd rather be. But if the sea air, the stars winking down on us, and the pull of the tide aren't magical enough, then wait until you hear our performances this evening.

'I've rambled on for long enough, so now . . . It's time. We've got the cream of Campion Bay talent here tonight, some established acts, and some who are just starting out and need all your encouragement. We'll be finishing the evening with what is guaranteed to be a stellar performance from Crow's Feet . . .' He paused to allow room for the wolf whistles and cheering. 'But first, we have someone who has come from much further afield to entertain you. All the way from Windlesham near Luton. Please put your hands together and give your warmest welcome to musician Lorna Gregory!' He walked backwards, gesturing towards the side of the stage, and Lorna came on to a hearty round of applause.

She looked beautiful in her skinny jeans and black leather jacket, and a navy silk top that Robin had lent her. She had teamed the outfit with bold silver jewellery, her eye make-up dark and sultry. Robin watched as she tucked her long dark hair behind her ear, and positioned the guitar across her body. She strummed the first few chords of 'Summer Son' by Texas, and then began singing, the lyrics soaring through the warm air. Robin let out a gasp at the full force of Lorna's voice. She'd heard her practising in her room, but it was nothing compared with this, and she'd always talked about her guitar playing first and foremost, suggesting that singing was an incidental extra. That, Robin thought, couldn't be further from the truth.

She felt a surge of satisfaction and accomplishment, so strong it was like a drug. She had done it. She'd had lots of help – there was no way she could have pulled it off without her friends and neighbours – but it had started from one tiny glimmer of an idea. Now it had become this magical evening, with delicious summery foods, plastic cups of wine and beer, and a mesmerized audience listening to music against the backdrop of the calm sea and twinkling fairy lights.

As Lorna finished her set to resounding applause and the next act, Ed with the eighties hair, appeared on stage, Robin's nerves disappeared and she began to enjoy herself. The range of performers meant that there was something for everyone: some acoustic, some rock, an unassuming woman who looked like she was terrified and then belted out Kate Bush covers with a powerful voice. Some were noticeably nervous, performing in front of a large audience for the first time, but Robin was heartened by the kind spirit of the crowd, encouraging them, cheering and clapping, making everyone feel like they belonged on the stage.

She knew Will would be close to the stage, waiting to introduce each new act. His opening had been perfect. He'd brought everyone with him, making them laugh and building their anticipation when they could easily have meandered off, more interested in the food stalls or the bar. She tried not to think too much about his reference to their last conversation, or what it might mean. A pair of arms squeezed around her waist, making her jump.

'You did it,' Molly whispered loudly. 'You bloody did it, you mad thing!'

'*We* did it,' Robin corrected, but secretly she accepted her friend's compliment. It was a success, no doubt about it, a triumph of community spirit, somehow so much more rewarding than any of the Once in a Blue Moon Days because it was for everyone – not just a small group of satisfied faces, but a whole crowd of people aged eight months to eighty years.

'Your man was good,' Molly said, moving round to face Robin.

'He's not my man.'

'But you're making inroads?'

She gave a quick nod. 'Possibly. But tonight, after this, I have to have dinner with Tim. It— I wish I could get out of it, but I can't.'

Molly squeezed her shoulder. 'Mr Nightingale will still be here tomorrow.'

Robin nodded, knowing her friend was right, but still not entirely comfortable. She couldn't let Will slip through her fingers again.

The last lines of Crow's Feet's most popular song faded into the darkness, the audience singing along with gusto, the quarter-moon glowing down on them. The applause went on for a long time, and then Will came back on to the stage.

'I think we can all agree that was a brilliant way to end the evening. Let's hear it again for Crow's Feet, and all our other performers!' He gestured to the side of the stage and waited while all the acts came back on, lining up and staring out at the crowd, a few waving at their friends and family, some gazing up at the members of Crow's Feet, as if not quite believing they were alongside them. Will instigated a fresh round of cheers and then stood aside, waiting while they bowed again and again, before finally walking off the stage.

'Now,' he said, 'before I let you all drift away to get more food and drink, there are a few thank yous to say.' Most of the crowd held their place, murmuring, and Will waited for their attention to be fully on him. 'Firstly, a huge thank you to all the performers, professional and amateur, for putting themselves forward and making tonight such a success. We've seen a lot of talent on this stage tonight. Next, we have to thank Campion Bay Property, Malcolm Percy and Tim Lewis, for their support and sponsorship of this event. Lots of people have worked hard behind the scenes to make this evening go without a hitch. Molly and Paige Westwood, Adam Steed, and of course Maggie Steeple for allowing the concert to be hosted here, alongside the fantastic Skull Island – watch out for the water features when you next come for a round. Tonight wouldn't have been able to happen without any of you.' He paused, waiting for the clapping to die down, a few wolf whistles from the younger and more enthusiastic audience members.

He looked out over the crowd, his green eyes flickering as if he was searching for someone. 'There is one other person I need to mention. Without her creativity and her generosity we wouldn't be standing here today, Campion Bay wouldn't have one of the most desirable, welcoming guesthouses along the south coast – that's the Campion Bay Guesthouse, put a quick reminder in your phones – and Goldcrest Road would be a poorer, duller place. So . . .' Will swallowed, treating the audience to a slightly embarrassed smile, as if worried he'd said too much – 'could you all put your hands together for the organizer of tonight's concert, and one in a million, Robin Brennan!' He started the applause and others joined in. Robin took a step back, hoping nobody would point her out.

She wondered fleetingly if the seagulls roosting close by were traumatized by the noise, the constant stopping and starting of the cheers and clapping. She hoped she could stop her cheeks from going red, so she didn't give the game away, and breathed a sigh of relief when Will closed the event with a warm goodbye and people started to disperse, drifting towards the food stalls or towards town.

He hadn't needed to say those things at the end, and she wondered if someone had put him up to it – Molly or Lorna. One in a million. Did he really think that?

Lorna appeared and enveloped her in a hug, her blue eyes glittering. 'That. Was. Incredible. Wow, I just – I never knew I had it in me, to perform like that, to be part of something so wonderful. Can we do it every year? I could come back – and get Crow's Feet to headline again, they were amazing!'

Robin laughed, delighted that the evening had been a triumph for her. She had been the catalyst, after all. 'Of course – come back whenever you want. We can think of new things to do, make it bigger and better, get the arts centre involved next time.'

'You've put on such a special event.' Lorna glanced around. 'The setting, the lights, the food. The ocean backdrop.'

'That one's not down to me,' Robin said. 'It's just a benefit of living here.'

'I loved every second! Are you coming back to the guest-house to celebrate with us?' She meant the other guests, Robin knew, all of whom had been in the audience. Paige and Molly had kindly agreed to go to the guesthouse after the concert, hosting the informal after-party while she fulfilled her obligation to Tim.

'I'll be there later, but I have to go and meet someone now.' She squeezed Lorna's shoulder. 'You were brilliant – I knew you would be. Do you think you'll go back to the band when you get home?'

'Will I ever!' Lorna said. 'I'm going to ask Rick for more solo parts.'

Robin laughed and watched the young woman walk towards the guesthouse, a spring in her step. She turned slowly, wondering if she had time to find Will before her meal with Tim. She had so much she wanted to say to him. She was encouraged by his apparent thawing over the last couple of days, and his words on the stage tonight. She saw a flash of toffee-coloured hair beneath the fairy lights and took a deep breath as he approached.

His grin was wide, his shoulders relaxed. She couldn't help but notice that the top two buttons of his shirt were open. 'So, Robin Brennan, that went pretty well. It turns out you're not bad at organizing last-minute events.'

She tried to suppress the happiness bubbling up inside her. 'You weren't too bad yourself. You're a natural-born showman. Are you sure you don't have hidden singing talents? Acting? Are you secretly a world-class dancer?'

Will laughed. 'No, "compère" will do me fine. I enjoyed it, though. I felt . . . a part of something, here. Goldcrest Road.'

He gestured towards the departing crowd, the scene around them, and Robin knew she had to act quickly.

'I've agreed to meet someone now, for a work thing,' she said hurriedly, 'but do you want to get together tomorrow morning, to catch up?'

He nodded. 'Sure. Tomorrow's great, I just thought ...' He turned away, glancing at the beach and the quarter-moon suspended over the sea. He shook his head quickly and turned back to her. 'Who are you meeting?'

Suddenly Tim was at her side, looking as groomed as ever in a black shirt.

He gave Will a quick, triumphant smile before turning to Robin. 'I am the luckiest guy in the world right now. You're the toast of Campion Bay, and I'm the one who gets to take you out.'

Robin felt her cheeks burn. She risked glancing at Will, saw his smile fall, hurt and confusion sparking in his eyes as Tim took hold of her bare arm and began to lead her away. 'I'll come and see you—' she called, but Will had already moved away from her, walking in the opposite direction, dissolving into the darkness.

The bar was cosy with low, subtle lighting and midnight-blue walls, the simple wooden furniture elegant and understated, the leather seats luxurious. Robin sank into one, hoping it would somehow absorb her nerves and her discomfort, soaking them up like spilled wine, while Tim went to the bar. He came back with a bottle of champagne and two glasses.

'I've ordered tapas,' he said. 'I got a bit of everything, so you can try it all. It's a great place, and I wanted us to get away, to have some time alone together.'

'Tim,' Robin said. She was desperate to end this. She couldn't bear the effort he'd gone to, taking her away from Campion Bay to an intimate setting, buying champagne. His usual, arrogant swagger was tempered slightly, despite his wolfish grin.

'Have some bubbles.' He poured two glasses and thrust one into her hand. 'To you, Robs. For putting on such a barnstorming event with very little time or resources. For letting everyone see what you're capable of. Why have you been hiding it for so long?'

Robin froze. 'What? I haven't been hiding anything.'

'I think you have,' he said. 'Don't get me wrong – running the guesthouse, what you've done to the place, is incredible. It's beautiful, it's fresh, and I know that there are always things to do, that it's a constant treadmill.'

'Exactly. It's a tough job, tough to get right. I mean, you can get by, you can make things work, but I don't want to settle for that. I want my guesthouse to be exceptional.'

'Oh, it is,' Tim said smoothly. 'From what little I've seen of it, from the buzz in the town, you're making waves.'

'So what are you saying, then?'

'A guesthouse doesn't make as big a wave as a bold, vibrant event like tonight. With the guesthouse you get to wow a few people, but tonight . . .' He shook his head.

'Why does it have to be about numbers?' she asked, trying not to get flustered. 'Why can't I please a small number of people with the guesthouse? Why is a large crowd more worthwhile?'

Tim took a sip of champagne. 'I'm not explaining myself clearly. I've seen something new in you over the last couple of weeks, a determination that I thought you'd lost after your time in London. After Neve.'

Robin took a deep breath before she spoke. 'I have put *everything* into my guesthouse. I haven't held back, Tim. I know it's different to Once in a Blue Moon Days, but that doesn't make it any less valuable or impressive.'

'Come on, Robs.' He held his hand out towards her. 'I'm not having a go. You seem like you have a fire inside you now, like you're so much more alive. You inspire me, and I want to get to know you again. I realize we can't go back, but that doesn't mean that we can't try again, looking forward, starting afresh.'

Robin took in his handsome face and blond curls, his easy smile. He was a catch, no doubt about it. Determined and successful, charming when he wanted to be. But some of what he'd said niggled at her, and not because she was having doubts about whether to try again with him. That was the one thing she was clear about. It wasn't because he'd implied that the guesthouse was somehow a lesser achievement either, that she'd been treading water until the idea of the music night took hold. It was something else. She chewed her lip.

'Say something, Robs. I'm laying my heart on the line here.'

'I'm trying to think,' Robin said.

Tim chuckled uncomfortably. 'If you have to think, then—'

'I can't, Tim. You must know that.'

His smile faltered and he turned away, thanking the barman as he placed plates of delicious-smelling tapas on the table in front of them. Olives, chorizo pastries, calamari, mini pulled-pork tacos. Robin realized she was famished, but she couldn't eat until she'd said what she needed to, until she'd been straight with him.

'Why not?' he asked, once the barman had left them to it. 'What's standing in the way of us trying again? I've changed, Robs. I'm much more mature now.'

'But you're still you. You still cheated on me, even though it was years ago. And it's not only that. So much has happened to me – to you, surely – to shape and change our lives. We're close again, we're in the same sphere because I'm back in Campion Bay, but I've moved on. We may both be single and both here, but that doesn't mean we should pick up where we left off. I can't do it.'

'You're not attracted to me?' He gave her a lopsided smile and popped an olive in his mouth, but she could see that her words had upset him.

Robin smiled sadly. 'You're sexy as hell, Tim. You know that. But not for me, not now.'

'I could give you more time. We've only been reacquainted for a few months, only since January, and it's not like we've seen a lot of each other. Not like this.'

Robin traced an invisible pattern on the tablecloth. She hated this, hated hurting him, despite what had happened in the past, even though she knew without question that he would survive it, move on, dust himself off. 'It's not going to happen.'

'Why not? Come on, give me one good reason – one. Not that we're in the past or we have a history or you've moved on, because if we're two people who are attracted to each other, then why not at least try? Come on, Robs, what have you got to lose?' He spread his hands wide, his sparkling grin lighting up his face.

She smiled back, knowing that he wouldn't give up unless she was completely honest with him. 'Will,' she said, simply. 'I've got Will to lose, and that's something I can't risk.'

They didn't finish the champagne or the tapas, and Robin was relieved when Tim, now stony-faced, said he'd drive her back to the guesthouse.

'I'm sorry,' she said as she slipped into the passenger seat of his Audi, feeling like she should apologize even though she'd done nothing wrong.

'I should have known,' Tim said impassively. 'That first night I met him. With the cupcakes. I noticed the way you looked at each other. But you're not – together, right now?'

Robin shook her head, thinking of Will's expression as Tim had appeared at her side, ready to whisk her off for what had, surely, looked like a date. 'It's complicated. He's angry with me, for good reason. I didn't tell him about your plans for Tabitha's house. I hoped I could get him to stay here, to—' She sighed. 'It doesn't matter what's happened, what I've done. But I need him to forgive me. If Will decides to sell the house and leave Campion Bay for good, before I've told him how I really feel, I couldn't bear it. And I can't think about anyone else, not when I feel this way about him.'

Tim nodded, his eyes fixed on the road. They passed the rest of the journey in silence, and Robin couldn't remember the last time she'd been so happy to see the guesthouse. Tim pulled up to the kerb. The promenade was quiet now, everything tidied away except the fairy lights and the stage, which would be dismantled by the hire company in the morning, after Robin had agreed to pay their fee. She couldn't ask Will to take it down as well.

'OK then,' she said, turning towards Tim. 'I'm sorry that tonight – that it didn't go as planned. Thank you so much for sponsoring our event.'

Tim nodded, but he wouldn't meet her gaze. 'Take care, Robs. I'm sure I'll see you around.'

'Sure,' she said, a lump coming unexpectedly to her throat. 'Goodnight, Tim.'

She stepped out into the cool air, the Audi pulling away from the kerb as Robin stood on the pavement. She could see the lights blazing in Sea Shanty and wondered who was still in there, celebrating the event's success. She should be there. Not because she was worried about what was happening, but because she was the hostess, the organizer, the landlady.

Instead, she crossed the road and walked around the edge of the golf course, across the promenade and down on to the beach. The light from the quarter-moon was strong in a cloudless sky, shimmering on the water like a picture post-card, stars twinkling down on her as she slipped off her shoes and flinched at the coldness of the damp sand.

Tim had been right. She did have a new determination, a new light inside her. She loved running the guesthouse, meeting her guests and making their stay as special as possible. She loved baking bread and cookies, devising special breakfasts, buying new paintings and decorations for the rooms. And she had loved putting on the music night, engaging her mind with a different type of challenge – even though it had reminded her of the past.

She was fired up; she felt happy and purposeful in her new life in an old town. But Tim had also said that she seemed much more alive, and there was only one reason for that, one person who was keeping her flame burning, who had made the event seem so important, who she wanted to please and impress and inspire. And what had he said, up there on the stage? *She's one in a million*.

Turning away from the sea, she looked up at the houses along Goldcrest Road, the lights glowing, beckoning to her in the dark. There was a first-floor light on inside Tabitha's house, the thick curtains drawn but with a crack of telltale brightness down the middle. Was he up there, watching TV or lying in his sleeping bag? Had he cleared the room, creating a snug space for himself, or was he surrounded by clutter, Tabitha's past crowding in on him, still to sort through? Was Darcy snoozing at his side? She longed to know, to be handed a snapshot of what Will Nightingale was doing right now.

It was gone eleven, too late – after such an exhausting day – to start such an important conversation, to see if her heartfelt apology would be enough. Earlier that day she had felt confident, had seen signs that he was warming towards her again. But after Tim had interrupted them earlier that evening, she wasn't so sure.

Had all the progress she'd made, trying to rebuild the bridge between them – the hampers on his doorstep, visiting him at Eldridge House, his help putting the stage up before the concert – been demolished in those few moments? She pictured again the hurt on his face when Tim had taken hold of her arm. Did he think she'd been lying when she'd said nothing was going on between them? How else could it have looked to him?

Robin made her way slowly towards home, towards the celebration inside. She wondered fleetingly if, by the end of tomorrow, the Campion Bay Guesthouse would be buzzing and bright with another familiar voice, familiar footfalls: Will and Darcy back in Sea Shanty, where, she felt, they belonged. She couldn't realistically see it happening.

She'd spoken the truth aloud now, had forced it out into the air, to the last person she had imagined confiding in. Tim knew how she felt, and now it was Will's turn. He had come to the Campion Bay Guesthouse looking for shelter, a bed for a few nights, and with that culmination of events – her first day as landlady, staying up late to celebrate with

Molly, a leak at Tabitha's house and her initial reluctance to let out Starcross – he had stepped into her guesthouse and into her life, and she couldn't now imagine carrying on either of them without him. Their time apart had only served to help her see it more clearly, her feelings for him growing rather than fading.

She turned quickly, looking back across the sea, at the moon and the stars shining down. It would soon be summer, the guesthouse would be full, Tabitha's house would be empty and everything would change again, beneath the glow of the strawberry moon. Robin couldn't waste any more time; she knew it wasn't going to be easy to get him to believe her, to convince him that he was the only one she cared about, the only one she saw when she closed her eyes, but nothing worth fighting for was easy. She had to tell Will the truth.

The Once in a Blue Moon Guesthouse

WISH YOU WERE HERE

Chapter 19

Robin was facing away from the sea, the warm June breeze whispering at her back. She could hear the waves marking time with their rhythmic ebb and flow, and thought how peaceful it could have been, before nine o'clock on a Saturday morning, with the sun already shining down on the seaside town of Campion Bay.

But it wasn't peaceful, because Darren and Fred, two men in scruffy shorts and navy vests, were taking down the temporary stage on the promenade with as much noise as it was possible to make. Robin winced as another metal pole clattered to the ground, and picked up her takeaway coffee cup, blowing on the hot liquid through the tiny hole in the lid before taking a sip.

'Who put this up, then?' Darren asked, flicking a look in Robin's direction. He was short and squat with bulging muscles, a sheen of sweat on his large forehead.

'It was a friend of mine, mainly. Though a few of us helped.'

'Done a good job,' Darren said, nodding appreciatively. 'It's solid.'

'I should hope so,' Robin replied, laughing nervously. She didn't want to think about what the structure would have been like had it been left to her, Molly, Adam and Paige, trying to read the instructions as if putting together a Lego model. A lot of people had stood on that stage.

As Darren and Fred started flinging the braces into the back of a van with wilful abandon, the sound echoing around her, Robin looked up at number four. The curtains were open, but beyond that she could see no signs of life inside. She longed for the workmen to finish so she could go and speak to Will. She had to tell him why Tim didn't matter to her. She had to lay her heart on the line.

She sipped her coffee in an attempt to calm her nerves, waiting for the moment when the van would drive away and she could cross the road and give it one final, heartfelt shot.

Robin closed her eyes. She heard a door slam further up the street, and the sound of a loud, powerful engine approach and then die. When she looked up, she saw that the car was a black Audi, and it was parking outside the guesthouse. She jolted, almost spilling her coffee. A familiar figure climbed out. He had blond hair and a faded red shirt that struck the right balance between casual and sophisticated, but Tim's usually relaxed face was scowling. Robin felt her chest tighten as she watched him lock the car and bound up the front stairs of Tabitha's house.

'No no no,' she said to herself. 'This can't be happening. I've just got to nip over the road and do something,' she called to Darren and Fred.

'We'll only be another five minutes, love, and we need you to sign off the paperwork.'

'But I need to—'

'What is the *meaning* of this?' asked an angry voice, and

Robin spun to find Coral Harris, landlady of the Seaview Hotel, standing in front of her. The old woman was wearing an overly frilly lavender dressing gown pulled tightly around her slender frame and matching fluffy slippers. Her narrow face was pinched and angry and the effect, along with the soft fabrics and the pastel colouring, was disconcerting.

'The meaning of what?' Robin asked, her eyes drifting back to the houses. Tim was no longer standing on the doorstep. Bile churned in her stomach.

'All this *banging*. So early in the morning. So early!' she repeated, directing her words towards Darren and Fred this time.

Fred shrugged, but Darren had the grace to look contrite. 'Sorry lady,' he said, 'but it's not easy to be quiet when you're working with steel.'

'I'm sure it could be quieter than *this*. I enjoyed your entertainment, Robin, but this has tainted it for me. What about my guests? What about *yours*?'

'I know,' Robin said sincerely, touched that Mrs Harris had taken the time to compliment her on the event, even if it was in the middle of a complaint. 'And I am sorry. But we needed to get the stage off the promenade as soon as possible, and this seemed a better time than late last night.' She shrugged, her mind full of what Tim might be discussing with Will at that very moment.

She remembered saying to him last night: *If Will decides to sell the house and leave Campion Bay for good, before I've told him how I really feel, I couldn't bear it*. She had hoped that once Tim had got over the initial hurt, they could clear the air and focus on being friends. But Tim was also a property developer, and if she'd been thinking clearly then she would have realized that it was an unwise thing to say to a calculating, business-minded man she'd rejected only moments before.

'I do think something else could have been arranged,' Mrs Harris continued, oblivious to Robin's wandering thoughts. 'As guesthouse owners, we should be thinking of our clients before anything else, and this is surely not the best way for them to start their weekend.'

Robin swallowed. 'I completely understand. But it's only one day, and hopefully most of them got to enjoy the free entertainment.'

'It's not right.' Mrs Harris shook her head. 'Not right at all.'

'We're almost done,' Darren said. 'We'll be out of your hair in a jiffy.' He gave her a wide, cheerful grin and Robin watched as Mrs Harris softened.

'I suppose if it's nearly over, then I have no more grounds for complaint. But you do any more of these,' she said, waggling a schoolmistress-style finger at Robin, 'then you need to think about logistics. Didn't you run an events management company before all this?'

'I did,' Robin admitted. 'But the timescales were so short this time. Lorna was only here for a fortnight.'

'Hmmm. Next time.' She patted Robin's shoulder and strode off down the promenade in her lavender night wear.

Robin shook her head, bewildered by the encounter. She wiped her palms down her shorts and looked for any glimmers of movement in the windows of number four. She imagined Tim and Will in Tabitha's large kitchen, free from the dust and grime it had been covered in the last time she had seen it, their postures stiff over cups of instant coffee.

'Did you say you were nearly done?' she asked Darren with forced brightness.

'We're on the last bit . . .' He worked at a joint with the electric screwdriver, and Robin glanced up to see Ashley and Roxy waving at her. She sighed, hoping they were just passing, and waved back.

'Robin!' Ashley gave her a brief hug, bending his tall frame towards her. 'What a brilliant night.'

'Your teashop was heaving from start to finish,' Robin said. 'I heard so many compliments.'

'I can't remember being as busy as that,' Roxy added, her dark eyes wide. 'I'm glad we hired extra staff for the evening.'

'But sadly couldn't extend the teashop's square footage,' Ashley said, laughing. 'If the pavement was wider, we'd invest in some more outdoor chairs and tables.'

'Are you going to do any more events?' Roxy asked. 'It was such a good night, and not just for business. There was so much talent on that stage – the sound carried in to the teashop – and Lorna was wonderful, a real star.'

'I know,' Robin said. 'She's checking out later today and I'm going to miss her. To start with, I barely knew she was in the guesthouse she was so quiet, but the last ten days she's brought so much laughter and fun – not to mention music – that it's going to feel strange without her.'

'Some people are like that, aren't they?' Ashley said.

Robin nodded. 'And it seems to be the guests who stay in Starcross, for some reason. Though there have only been two so far.'

'Maybe there's something magical about that room?' Roxy clapped her hands together, but her husband rolled his eyes.

'Or they're the two people who have stayed the longest, so they've made more of an impression. Will's back at his aunt's now, isn't he? Do you know if he's planning on staying in Campion Bay?'

The couple looked slightly anxious, and Robin wondered how worried they were about the rumours of what Tim would do if he bought the property. She knew, now, that their kindness towards Will, bringing him cupcakes and helping him bag up rubbish on his first day in his aunt's house, had been sincere, but that didn't mean that they weren't also concerned about the seafront changing. Things moved on – of course they did – but Goldcrest Road didn't need an upgrade. It was picture perfect.

'I don't know,' Robin said quietly.

She felt guilty. If Tim was in there, making a deal with Will at that very moment, then she would be responsible. Not in a practical way, but for helping to shape the personal feelings of the two men, which might then impact on their professional decisions. First, hurting Will by holding back the truth, and then angering Tim by rejecting him. If Campion Bay Property made a successful bid then, despite organizing the open-mic night, Robin's hopes of being a valued member of the Campion Bay community would be in tatters.

'Fair enough,' Ashley nodded. 'Guess we'll have to wait and see. Will's a good guy, it would be nice if he decided to stick around.'

Robin didn't voice how much she agreed with him.

They said their goodbyes, and Darren thrust a piece of slightly crumpled paper and a Biro into her hand. 'Sign here please, love, to say it's all been done proper and correct. I've confirmed that the stage was passed back to us in good condition.' He pointed at his own, scribbled name.

'Thank you.' Robin put the paper on the low wall and signed a scratchy signature. She was relieved the stage was gone, the last remnants of the event removed so the prom-enade, and Skull Island crazy golf, could get back to normal.

It should also have meant she could go and see Will, but she realized she'd have to wait until Tim had left. She couldn't say everything she needed to in front of him.

She'd taken two steps across the road when the front door of Tabitha's house opened and Tim came out. She gave a sigh of relief, which was quickly overtaken by anxiety when Will followed him. He was wearing his usual dark jeans and Wrangler boots, and a green T-shirt with a silhouette of the New York skyline on the front. Robin snuck back on to the opposite pavement and watched them walk to the Audi. Will climbed into the passenger seat without noticing her, but Tim glanced towards the sea, and their eyes met. The smirk he gave her was devoid of warmth, his eyes glittering with triumph.

He pulled away from the kerb, and it was then that Will's head turned in her direction. She only saw his expression for a moment, but he didn't look happy.

'What has that bastard done?' Molly was pacing, wearing away the floorboards in Sea Shanty.

'I don't know, but I can take a pretty good guess. He's told Will something about me, something unkind or made-up – or both – and tried to persuade him to sell. I had thought that, after last night, we'd be able to move on from this strange nostalgic dance and be friends.'

'How long did you go out with Tim for?' Molly's blue eyes sparkled with anger, but Robin knew it wasn't aimed at her. 'Have you still not realized that Tim is only out for himself, that all he cares about is getting what *he* wants?'

'I thought that . . .'

'You put faith in him. You're getting soppy in your old age. So now they've gone off together, in Tim's car?'

Robin sank on to one of the sofas and Eclipse climbed on to her lap. 'He looked so righteous, as if now that I won't have him, he can go after the things that matter to me. He's going after Will, and he's doing that by swooping in on Tabitha's house.'

Molly crouched in front of her, her short blonde hair moving in the breeze drifting through the open window. 'Yes, but Will has to agree to it. He has to formally accept Tim's offer, and I don't think he's ready to do that. I saw you sitting next to each other on the sea wall on Thursday and I heard what he said last night. Tim will need some pretty strong leverage to get him to make a decision right now. He's not even finished going through Tabitha's things.'

'And what if he's been inventing stories about me, to try and turn Will against me? I told Tim that I wouldn't try again with him because of Will – though of course that's not the only reason – but he knows how strong my feelings are.'

Molly shrugged. 'So add it to the list of things to talk to Will about. He's seen for himself that Tim can be ruthless. He's not stupid, and he'll have to listen to your side of the story.'

'And if he's already decided to sell the house?'

Molly held her gaze. 'Then it was never meant to be. But I don't think it will come to that.'

'You and Will are together?'

They both turned to find Lorna standing in the doorway, her bag and guitar case over her shoulders. Her eyes were glistening.

Robin stood and went to hug her. 'No, we're not. It's complicated. What's wrong?'

Lorna sniffed and wiped her cheek. 'I'm gutted to be leaving, that's all. My taxi should be here any minute.'

'I could have driven you to the station,' Robin said.

'You've done more than enough for me, I don't know if you'll ever realize how much. Thank you for being so amazing.'

Robin laughed. '*You* were the amazing one. Did you hear yourself up there last night?'

Lorna did a little shimmy, and her face broke out into a huge grin. 'It was the most fun I've ever had. I've caught the performing bug – I'm going to be unbearable when I get home.'

'You deserve to go so far,' Molly said, waiting her turn and then pulling the younger woman into an embrace.

'Thank you,' she said. 'It doesn't matter how far I go, a little piece of me will always be here, on that stage, looking out at the crowd with the moon shining down on us. I've got about twenty glow sticks in my bag – I hope that's OK?'

'Of course it is! Better that than they end up in the bin.'

'Will seemed to be quite fond of them,' she said, giving Robin a careful look.

Robin smiled, replaying Will's introduction in her head. 'Yes. I didn't know about that little quirk.'

'He'd be lucky to have you,' Lorna said. 'I wish I could stay longer – I'd move down here in a heartbeat and have that view every day of my life. Luton feels like it's in a dark hole compared to the light and air you get here. But I – I'd like to be friends. To catch up, to go back to the Artichoke.' She smiled nervously.

'We *are* friends,' Robin said. 'And you're welcome here any time. I've loved having you.' She hugged her again and carried her guitar out to the taxi.

'Thank you, Robin. Thank you for helping me get my life back on track. I'll never forget it. Email me, I want to hear all your news.'

Lorna waved out of the open taxi window, then the car disappeared into the distance and Robin was left standing on the doorstep with Molly and Eclipse.

'Starcross empty again now?' Molly asked. 'I wonder who'll be next.'

'Me too,' Robin said. She chewed her lip, glanced at next door and then rolled her eyes. She couldn't sit here waiting for Will to come back; she'd drive herself mad. Her friend seemed to sense her restlessness.

'Come on. I'll help you with the changeovers, and then you can get out of here for a bit before your new guests arrive. You've been working non-stop on this place and the open-mic night, and don't think I can't see those dark circles under your eyes. If you won't book in for a facial, then this'll have to do. We'll get it done in record time, and you can supply the wine and the takeaway when I come over later. Deal?' She held out her hand.

Robin smiled, wondering what she'd do without Molly to talk sense to her. 'Deal,' she agreed.

The water was calm and smooth even on Campion Bay's wild beach, as if it was a shimmering, turquoise lake instead of a vast sea. Robin walked with her bare feet pressing into the soft sand, warmed by the early June sun overhead. Everything was bright, sparkling, alive. She was alone on the beach save for a couple of seagulls and a rogue pigeon waddling alongside them, looking for all the world like it belonged.

Molly had been true to her word and had helped get the guesthouse ready for the new arrivals. Robin had discovered a recipe for lavender cookies after being inspired by Mrs Harris's amazing ensemble that morning and planned on baking a batch later that day, then putting them in the jars on all the landings, for guests to help themselves to at any time of the day or night.

But, for now, she had a few minutes to herself. She walked away from the water, peering into one of the largest caves that were carved into the cliffs like bite marks. It was gloomy, stretching back into darkness so dense it was like a black hole, and smelt of damp and cigarette smoke.

There were wide ledges at waist and shoulder height, and crisp wrappers and empty beer cans that had got snagged in crevices and not been washed out with the tide. It could have been a treasure-trove, a place of intrigue and history, but instead it made her feel sad. Who would want to spend time in a place like this? She thought of Paige's story about Adam and his friends taking a boat to purposefully explore the caves that were further along the coast, unreachable from any beach. It couldn't be safe doing it on a whim like that. She moved on, peering up at the sandy cliffs towering above her, a few wispy clouds beyond in a sky of paint box blue.

She had a lot to be thankful for. She had to remind herself that she had pulled off a successful event in Campion Bay at very short notice, attended by more people than the New Year fireworks. It would soon be time for the summer festivities, the fireworks and funfair that came to Campion Bay every year, and as Robin perched on a large, flat rock beneath the cliffs, brushing the loose sand off with her palm, she couldn't help but wonder where Will would be by the time the fair rolled into town.

Would he still be here, spending his time in Tabitha's house, working at Eldridge House, still with things to do? Or would he have sold the house to Tim and gone back to Kent or London? Would the seafront be blotted by heavy scaffolding and plastic sheeting, while they butchered the beautiful building where, the plaque announced, Jane Austen had once stayed? The thought left a lump at the back of her throat.

But there was one other option, and that was that Will would have finished sorting through Tabitha's house and was living there, making a life for himself in Campion Bay. Was that a possibility? Could she dare to hope for so much happiness in her future, despite what she'd witnessed this morning? Will could be back by now, from wherever Tim had taken him. She could head home and find him, say all the things that had been building up inside her for so long. But Molly, wise as ever, had been right to suggest she escape for a while. This was her thinking place.

She pulled her legs up beneath her, the rock wide enough for her to sit cross-legged, and pulled out her phone. She scrolled through her photo stream, looking back at the photos she had taken of the rooms when they were first finished. Andalusia, Wilderness, Canvas, Rockpool and, of course, Starcross. Neve would have loved the guesthouse, she was sure. Especially Starcross, with its celestial theme, its nod towards astrology. And Eclipse would have been the perfect Once in a Blue Moon Days mascot. Robin had thought of those rooms, and then created them with the help of friends and family, and with Neve's influence hovering over her like the glowing strawberry moon.

In just over a month, already Robin had experienced more moments of pride and accomplishment than she could have hoped for. Starcross was her tribute to Neve, to their time together, but now it had other meanings for her. Every time she pictured it she saw Will in there, filling the space with his toffee-coloured hair and wide, relaxed smile, Darcy standing patiently beside the bed. She didn't want to lose the connection with Neve, but she couldn't deny that she had begun, finally, to move forwards.

An idea prickled in her mind, firing up her senses like tiny electric shocks, but, as it started to develop, her thoughts were disrupted by barking. It was distant at first but constant, a dog that was either elated or distressed. She looked up, following the shoreline and stilled when she saw the small, brown dog in the waves. She was heading towards her, her tail wagging madly, her movements more like a dance as her paws pounded in and out of the shallows.

And then Robin's gaze moved beyond the familiar dog, the dog that she already loved so much, and found him. His short hair blew in the breeze, his Wrangler boots were in his hands, his jeans rolled up above the ankles. He gave her a brief wave, but was too far away for her to see his expression.

Robin sat up straight, letting her ribcage fill again and again, gulping in the sea air as if it would give her strength. Finally, she had her chance. She would be able to tell Will everything. She only hoped that, despite his time with Tim, despite all that had happened between them, he would understand.

Chapter 20

'Hello.' His voice was soft and unsure, his eyes squinting slightly against the sun as he looked down at her.

'Hi, Will.' Robin slipped her legs out from beneath her as he approached and slid over to the side of the rock. Will sat beside her, nodding thanks at her for making room for him. They didn't speak for a moment, but instead watched Darcy dancing joyously in the waves. She got hold of a long piece of seaweed and tugged at it, loosening it from the sand, her front paws getting tangled in its fronds.

Robin laughed and Will shook his head. 'Ridiculous dog,' he said quietly.

'I've missed her,' Robin admitted. 'I've missed both of you. The guesthouse doesn't feel the same.'

'My current sleeping arrangements aren't anything like Starcross, if it makes you feel any better.'

'It doesn't,' Robin said. 'Are you on the floor, or in Tabitha's old bed?'

'A bed, but not Tabitha's. Her room was the most damaged when the roof leaked, so the bed will need to go. I've got a whole heap of furniture in the middle of the dining room, ready to be disposed of. It looks like I'm about to start a *Wicker-Man*-style fire – it's quite impressive.'

'Don't do anything too rash. You know I'm here, I can still help you.'

'I know that,' he said. 'But things haven't exactly been . . . straightforward.'

'Will, I—' She turned towards him. 'I need to be completely honest with you. About everything; about Tim, what happened last night.'

He didn't look at her, but kept his gaze on the sea. The sun was sparkling on the water like shards of glass. 'I saw him earlier. He came to the house. He told me a few things.'

Despite the warm day, Robin felt a chill run through her. 'What things?'

'Lots of things. Lies, possibly. I don't know.'

'So ask me.'

Will exhaled and leant forward, his elbows on his knees. 'He said that you had suffered a major trauma, before you came back to Campion Bay. That it had affected you deeply, that you were . . . struggling.'

Robin swallowed. It was a moment before she could speak. 'Struggling? Was that the word he used?'

'No. But are you – did something terrible happen, in London?' He turned to face her, his green eyes piercing through the wall that had immediately come up. It wasn't Will's fault, but how dare Tim use what had happened to Neve against her?

'What did he actually say?'

Will winced. 'He said you didn't know what you wanted, that you were behaving irrationally. I haven't thought that for a moment, you've never seemed irrational to me. But he said that you were blowing hot and cold. He gave the impression that you'd rekindled your relationship, given in to old passions, but that you were still unsure. He thought it was only a matter of time before you were back together. I'm sorry, I know this is personal, but he admitted it to me, and—'

'None of that's true,' Robin said. She surprised herself at how calm she sounded. Her stomach churned with a mix of anger and sadness at Tim's fabrications. She didn't know if this was more of his manipulation, or if he still believed, despite what she'd told him last night, that there was a chance for them. But exaggerating her grief at Neve's death was a low blow.

He hadn't been there those first, desperate months when she'd come back to Campion Bay; he hadn't seen her at her lowest. When she spoke again, her voice was icy calm.

'He tried to kiss me that night, after you had been to the pub with him, but I stopped it. I'm not irrational. My feelings for Tim, when I first saw him again . . .' She shook her head. 'We have a past, it had been years since we'd seen each other. I admit that it was confusing at first, but nothing happened between us. He's making it out to be so much more than it was.'

Will nodded, his gaze holding hers. It was open, accepting, and she had to resist the urge to wrap him in a grateful hug. 'But something happened to you in London?' he asked, almost a whisper. 'That bit was true?'

Her heart was clattering now. The peaceful tableau in front of them seemed like a dream; the golden sand, the glittering water, Darcy playing in the waves. That night was creeping back in, swapping places with reality. She had to tell him. She had been planning to anyway, but Tim had given her no choice and, now that the moment was here, it felt like an impossible task.

'My friend, Neve,' she started.

'The one who's into astrology, the flower moon?'

'You remembered?'

'Of course I did,' Will said.

The tenderness in his voice brought her tears closer to the surface. 'She was my best friend. We met at university and then started up our company together, Once in a Blue Moon Days.'

'The events business?'

Robin nodded. 'Special occasions, bespoke experiences. We were good at it; we worked so well as a team and lived together in a tiny flat. It was hard work, but so rewarding when we helped people realize their dreams, gave them the best anniversary or birthday they'd ever had. Neve was the driving force; she was so full of energy, so alive with the possibility of it all. A problem was a challenge, a lesson to be learnt from.' A heavy, familiar weight settled inside her as she felt again the full impact of her friend's loss.

When she paused, Will filled the space, as if he realized it wasn't easy for her to say. He encouraged her, teasing the story from her like thread unravelling from a piece of fabric.

'You're one of the brightest – sparkling – people I know,' he said. 'I can't imagine that you were lethargic by comparison.'

'You never met Neve, though,' she whispered. 'She would bounce out of bed, as if there was a trampoline under the mattress. She had these huge, dark eyes that were always glinting with new ideas; she never ran out of steam or enthusiasm. But then she . . . something terrible happened.' Robin swallowed, she glanced at Will, and then away. 'She died.'

She heard his intake of breath. 'God. I'm so sorry, Robin.' He put his hand on her upper arm. The touch of his fingers on her skin was warm, thrilling and comforting all at once. She focused on the feel of it, the bliss of being so close to him, to help her get through reliving that night. 'What happened?' he asked after a moment.

Robin shuddered involuntarily, and despite Will slipping his arm around her shoulders, increasing the pressure of his touch, she knew this would be one of the hardest things she'd ever done. Her London friends had been there that night, witnessing the horror first-hand, and telling her mum and dad, right after it had happened, was something she could barely remember. They'd done the rest for her; speaking to Molly and anyone else who needed to know, while she tried to pack her emotions away and get on with running the business.

She hadn't let it sink in until she'd come back to Campion Bay, Once in a Blue Moon Days in tatters, impossible without her best friend. When she'd told Tim back in January, she hadn't given him the details, had stayed as distant from it as possible. But now she had to revisit that night, to tell Will, without falling apart.

'It was Neve's birthday. We'd arranged a meal out with some of our friends at a Thai restaurant. We were working to a deadline for one of our commissions, so I told her to go and meet everyone for drinks, that I'd follow on later, in time for the meal. I'd got these helium balloons, star-shaped, one that said happy birthday in gold and red.' She swallowed. 'I finished what I needed to do, and then stayed in the office to pump them up. I was only an hour behind her by the time I left. I'd bought her a necklace for her birthday, an archer for Sagittarius, and a spa day voucher.

'I took the tube; it was only three stops, but it was quicker than walking. People in the carriage had laughed at the balloons and I couldn't wait to see her, to give them to her. I heard the sirens as I got close to the restaurant, but thought nothing of it. Then I turned the corner, and I couldn't see anything except a whirr of blue flashing lights, the screech as more vehicles arrived. People were crying and screaming and I didn't know what was going on.' She closed her eyes, remembering it all so vividly, the dead ache that had settled across her, as if trying to ward off the shock that was to come. 'But then one of our friends, Kyle, saw me, and came over to me. I don't remember what he said; I don't remember anything much after that, about that night, except arriving back at our flat and being unable to process that she wouldn't be coming through the door, that if I waited for her, I'd be waiting for ever.'

Robin dropped her head, pushing at her cheeks, angry with herself for letting the tears fall.

'I'm so sorry,' Will said again. He pulled her gently towards him and Robin didn't resist, letting the warmth of his body rush through her. She inhaled, licked her lips before telling the final part. She was nearly there.

'They said that she'd been looking at her phone, that she'd stepped off the pavement, distracted, and that the woman behind the wheel didn't have time to slow down. Neve was always so excitable and energetic, always doing so many things at once. This time, though . . .' She shook her head, leaned in to Will and stared at the sea, trying to close off the memories again. 'I told you that Neve helped me with the guesthouse, because she inspired so much of it. Starcross – the astrology – and Andalusia is based on what she had told me about her home country, though I never had the chance to go with her.'

'It's not just a boutique hotel, then,' Will murmured. 'It always seemed like it had more heart than that; the attention to detail, the warmth and kindness you put into running it. It's an extension of Neve, of what you did together. I can see that.'

Robin swallowed down a resurgence of tears. 'You can?'

'Now I know the story,' Will said quietly. 'I shouldn't have asked you to go through it again. But after what Tim told me this morning . . .' His hand drifted up, gently stroking her hair, tugging at the strands, twisting them round his fingers. He didn't realize he was doing it, she thought, or understand the effect it was having on her. Fireworks were going off inside her, her breaths shortening. She wanted to stop talking about Tim, about her heartbreak at losing Neve. She didn't want to do anything now but kiss him.

'I'm not irrational,' Robin said firmly, finding a reserve of strength, pulling herself back from the distraction. 'Whatever he thinks. I've been grieving. It's been a year and a half. I tried to carry on with Once in a Blue Moon Days afterwards, but I couldn't do it by myself.'

'It doesn't sound like a one-person operation, even before you take Neve's death into account.'

'Part of me felt that I was running away, coming back here with my tail between my legs. But the guesthouse has been a fresh start. A chance to prove to myself that I can do this, still have ideas, still live. Neve will always be a part of who I am, but I had to do it for me, too.' She took a deep breath. 'But I'd forgotten so much about Campion Bay; it was so different to when I'd left it as a teenager. I hadn't realized how strong the community is now. I'm so sorry, Will. For not telling you about Tim's plans, for getting so confused about things.'

She looked up at him, and he dropped his hand, giving her hair a final, brief tug. He wasn't smiling, but his gaze found hers and didn't let go. 'You've explained it all,' he said softly. 'I was shocked, hurt at first – but I know it was a misunderstanding.'

Robin nodded slowly, relief mingling with confusion. 'So then why . . .?'

Will sighed. 'Why have I kept a distance between us? Because I wasn't sure of your feelings. I thought I was that Sunday, on the golf course. But then after reading Molly's text, all I could think about was that you hadn't told me about Tim, about what he wanted to do with Tabitha's house. Then there were the flowers, his frequent visits to your guest-house; it was obvious how he felt about you. And I didn't know if you still cared about him. I felt like I was stepping into a complicated situation, and with everything that's going on – moving down here, sorting through my aunt's things, finding out the truth about her and my dad – it seemed safer, easier to stay away.' His lips flickered in a half-smile. 'Though it hasn't turned out to be easier.'

'It hasn't?' she asked.

He shook his head, his smile growing, his fingers reaching up to brush her cheek, and then Darcy yelped, bounding out of the waves towards them, soaked and happy. She ran straight to Robin, putting damp paws on her knees and shaking herself, so that Robin squealed and Will shot off the rock, away from them.

'Darcy,' Robin laughed, trying to shield herself from the impromptu shower, even though it was too late. 'Is that because you were mad with me too?'

'It's because she's missed you,' Will said. 'And for that, I'm very glad. If she hadn't been eager to see you, I might have got the full force of her greeting.' He sat back down warily, keeping his eyes on Darcy, who seemed content to settle at their feet and dry in the sunshine.

'I've missed you too,' Robin murmured. She glanced at Will, at his golden-flecked hair, his long neck, his tanned arms. 'I'm sorry for not telling you about Tim,' she said. 'But I only did that so you wouldn't jump at the possibility of a quick sale when going through Tabitha's things seemed like such a challenge. I wanted to get to know you before you disappeared again. It was selfish. I don't want Tim developing Tabitha's house into flats – I don't think he'd even be allowed to, if that Jane Austen plaque is real – but not telling you to begin with was so I'd have more time with you before that became a possibility. Though when you arrived, I didn't know that it wasn't Tim or his boss Malcolm that had prompted your visit to Campion Bay in the first place.'

Will shook his head. 'My relationship with Annie at Downe Hall had ended, and knowing Tabitha's house was down here on the coast, untouched, had been niggling at me for a while. It's coincidence that I turned up when Tim started to get interested.'

'That makes sense,' Robin murmured. 'But you need to know that Tim and I – we're so far in the past, now. And even if there were flickers of attraction between us when I saw him again, they've been obliterated by – by you. From the moment you stepped into Starcross, I didn't want you to go. We've only known each other a short time, but already you've changed my life, Will.' There. She'd said it. She chewed her lip, forcing herself to stay quiet while he absorbed the words.

He didn't reply immediately and she could see the tension in his broad shoulders. He was frowning, his eyes scanning her face. She wanted to reach up and touch his lips with her finger, wished he'd put his hand back in her hair.

'Robin,' he started.

'You don't have to say anything,' she rushed, suddenly afraid of what was coming, of him rejecting her, finally and completely.

He winced, pressing his lips together before he spoke. 'Tim's made an offer on the house.'

Robin felt an unpleasant tingling in her toes, and the butterflies in her tummy started flapping frantically. 'OK,' she said slowly. 'He's given you a concrete figure?'

Will nodded. 'And it's . . . ridiculous. The amount he's willing to pay.'

'So you're going to take it?' It came out as a whisper.

Will closed his eyes, ran his hands over Darcy's ears. 'No. I mean, not yet. I haven't finished sorting out Tabitha's things, and I've told Tim that I won't even consider it until that's done. I'm not accepting his offer of help, either. It's something I need to do alone, for my aunt's sake. But he showed me the plans; he's already done a lot of the groundwork. He's a very confident guy.' She heard the bitterness in his voice at these last words, her shoulders sagging at the inevitability of it all.

'So once you're done, then you're going to sell?'

He stared at the sea for so long, she thought he hadn't heard. When he turned towards her, his eyes were on fire, as if they'd absorbed the sun's heat. 'I don't know,' he murmured. His gaze held hers and then travelled down to her lips, to her hands resting in her lap, then back up. 'I haven't been here long, and I – I'm not sure if I can make this my home. Some of it's been so hard, challenging, and some of it,' his brows lowered in a flicker of a frown. 'Some of it has felt too good to be true.'

'It doesn't have to be,' she said quietly. 'It can be your reality. Life is good here.'

'I'm not talking about this,' he said, indicating the glittering water.

Robin held her breath, but Will didn't elaborate. She could sense his conflict, knew that he was holding back, despite the charge between them, so overwhelming she could hardly think straight. She clasped her hands on her knees and tried her best to sound nonchalant. 'You don't have your own home now, since moving out of Downe Hall, do you?'

He shook his head, his eyes still on her.

'But you do here. That house belongs to you. I know it may not feel like it now, but – hey – I do a good line in refurbishments.' She grinned, trying to break the spell, and he laughed gently.

She had felt drained, relieved that she'd told him about Neve and hadn't crumbled completely, but now she was fizzing with energy. Will wasn't being cold to her any more – in fact his gaze was close to setting her alight.

But despite that, she knew he wasn't ready to go back to where they had been before Molly's text message. She couldn't blame him for wondering about her and Tim, for wanting to keep his distance and not get tangled up in something that had appeared to be more than it was. But she knew that he cared about her. It was in the weight of his stare, the way he had pulled her towards him and slipped his fingers through her hair. She felt that, given time, they could rebuild their relationship. But now it seemed as if they might not have that chance.

'How long do you think it'll take to finish going through Tabitha's house?'

'A few more weeks, maybe. I need to hire a skip, work out

what I want to keep and what I want to get rid of, and then . . .' Will rubbed the back of his neck. 'Come up with a plan, I suppose.'

'Do you want to move back into Starcross while you do it? It's vacant again, from today.'

He gave her a half smile, closed his eyes briefly. 'That's so tempting, but I don't think I can justify it now I've got the bedrooms vaguely clear. Besides,' he added, reaching up to clear a wisp of hair away from her face, the wind conspiring with him to set her senses on fire again, injecting her with a fresh surge of hope, 'if I stayed in Starcross again I might never leave.'

That's the point, thought Robin, her heart pounding uncontrollably, but she didn't say it.

'I cannot believe Tim said that you were unstable,' Molly fumed, squeezing a big dollop of tomato ketchup on to her plate. 'What a fucking asshole. And he implied that you'd slept together, and were on the verge of getting back together?' She shook her head.

'He could still believe that,' Robin said. 'Despite what I told him, his arrogance could mean that he thinks it's only a matter of time before I fall into his arms again.'

'Or it was convenient for Will to think that,' Molly replied, 'so Tim dropped a few hints and let Will's imagination do the rest. I mean, he's got to be a sociopath, right? Possibly even a serial killer.'

'Molly, steady on.' Robin laughed. 'But yes, he did say – or suggest – all those things to Will. Luckily Will didn't believe him straight off. He gave me the chance to tell my side of it, and while I'm shocked, at least Tim's pinned his true colours to the mast. I'm going to stay as far away from him as possible. We all should.'

'Which isn't going to be easy if he's project managing a development on the house between ours.'

Robin picked up a chip with her fingers and chewed it slowly. 'No.'

They were sitting at the large table in Sea Shanty, fish and chips and a bottle of wine between them. The new guests were all safely checked in, though after her conversation with Will, Robin's mind hadn't been fully on the task, and if Molly asked her at that moment to recount all their names, she would fail.

The evening sky was awash with pink and amber, the sea resplendent in its sunset cloak, everything with the heat and tint of summer. It was Robin's first summer back in Campion Bay and she was determined to enjoy it, to help her guests make the most of it and ensure her guesthouse flourished, even with the prospect of Will leaving.

'He hasn't made up his mind, though,' she said to Molly. 'That has to be encouraging, if Tim's offered him a fortune and he's not agreed to it already. It means he's not certain.'

'He can't go back to the place he was before, right?' Molly lifted Eclipse off the table and put him back on the floor for what must have been the tenth time. The cat made a plaintive meow that suggested he might die if he wasn't allowed some cod.

'His ex is at the house – she's part of the family that owns it, so it's messy.'

'Ouch,' Molly winced. 'Though of course good for you.'

'I don't know about that,' Robin said. 'I can see us being friends again, but I'm not sure he's willing to risk anything more. He said he felt like he was stepping into a complicated situation and it was easier to stay away. And even though I've assured him that Tim and I are over, there have been things that have, understandably, given him the wrong impression. The flowers, late night visits, meals out. Not telling him what Tim was planning for Tabitha's house.' She didn't mention the way he had looked at her on the beach, the crackle of electricity between them that had contradicted his cautious words.

Molly sighed. 'I'm so sorry, Robin. If I hadn't sent the text message—'

'How many times do you get other people to read out your texts before you've seen them? *I* was the one who did this. I kept things from him, I assumed things, I messed up. And now I have to live with the consequences. God, Molly, when he said he might never leave Starcross if he came back here, I wanted to get some of those fluffy handcuffs we'd talked about and chain him to the headboard.'

'Robin Brennan, you saucy minx! And *when* did we talk about fluffy handcuffs?'

Robin's cheeks started to burn. 'Not you and me; me and Will.'

Molly's eyes widened.

'No, it wasn't like that, it was – never mind.'

'Never *mind*? You can't mention fluffy handcuffs and then tell me to forget about it. Spill the beans, and I mean *all* of them.'

They moved to the sofas after food, and Robin switched the main lights off and the fairy lights on. She could hear laughter above her, the sound of the television going on before the volume was turned down. They were directly beneath Rockpool, which was currently occupied by a couple from Ross-on-Wye who had brought their King Charles Spaniel with them. That was one thing Robin could remember about that afternoon; Percy the King Charles Spaniel. He was well-behaved, a bit skittish around new people, but with round, melancholy eyes that had made her heart squeeze.

Molly topped up their wine glasses and let out a sigh.

'What is it?' Robin asked.

'Nothing,' her friend said, and then shook her head. 'Well, there is something. I've been thinking a lot about Paige. About what she asked you, and about letting her have a beer the night before your event. When she got back on Friday night she seemed giddy – drunk – though she denied it, and I couldn't smell alcohol on her breath. I'm wondering if I did the wrong thing, letting her have that drink. Have I opened the floodgates?'

Robin sat forward. 'Paige is so sensible for a sixteen-year-old.'

'Seventeen next month.'

'Even so. She's well-behaved, she works wonders for me here, she's bright and bubbly and she could do worse than having Adam for a boyfriend.'

'Yeah, I know. But I feel like we're on the brink of something, that I'm going to have to start letting her do . . . things, make her own mind up – make her own mistakes. I'm not ready.'

'Oh Mol, you're an amazing mum! You're kind and fair; you put your foot down when you need to. Things are going to change, of course they are, but you'll make the right decisions and Paige will love you for it, even while she's pretending to hate you.'

Molly laughed. 'Thanks, Robin. You're wise.'

'Hardly! But I can see this particular problem from the outside, and you and Paige will be fine. Seriously.'

'Let's cheers to that before I tie myself in worry knots.'

They clinked glasses and watched the darkness fall softly over Campion Bay.

'I've been thinking,' Robin said, into the silence.

'Always dangerous.'

'I'd like to change the name of the guesthouse. I've refurbished it, but I didn't even think about altering the name.'

'What would you change it to?' Molly asked, sitting up. 'You'd have to rebrand everything. The website, all your brochures, welcome packs, social media.'

'I know. It would be a big job, but I – I think it would be worth it.'

'What to, Robin?' Molly asked softly.

She took a deep breath, wondering again if it was a ridiculous idea. 'The Once in a Blue Moon Guesthouse.' She looked at her friend, nervous now she'd spoken the name aloud for the first time. 'So much of this place is inspired by Neve, and in some ways it's similar to what we did together, giving people a luxury experience, a holiday they'll remember, and I—'

'You don't have to justify it,' Molly said. 'I think it's a wonderful idea. It's much more memorable than the Campion Bay Guesthouse. The Once in a Blue Moon Guesthouse makes it sound like what it is – special. Unique.'

The word reminded Robin of fluffy handcuffs again, but she pushed the thought away. She didn't feel ready to tell Molly that she wanted to name the guesthouse as a tribute to Neve because Starcross had, since Will had stayed in it, taken on another significance for her; one that, she still held an inkling of hope, would be about her future rather than her past. She hoped Neve didn't mind being usurped. She could hardly argue with having the whole guesthouse dedicated to her, rather than a single room.

'I'm so glad you like it,' Robin said. 'Do you think my mum and dad will?'

'Robin, you changed the guesthouse completely, and they were stoked. They're not going to be annoyed that you want to change the name. Now all you have to decide is how, and when, you want to make the swap.'

'I'm going to make enquiries with a couple of local sign writers on Monday, and see how long it'll take. I'll be guided by them, and once I know when the sign will be ready, I can plan the changeover. Hopefully in time for August, though I appreciate doing it mid-summer is perhaps not the best idea. Maybe I should wait for the autumn and have one high season as the Campion Bay Guesthouse.'

'I think as long as you plan it properly, you can do it whenever you want.' Molly rapped her nails lightly against the side of her wine glass. 'Was it hard, telling Will about Neve?'

Robin sat back and closed her eyes. 'I'm glad I did it, but I wasn't as calm as I could have been. It's been so long since I properly relived that night, and I must have seemed like—'

'Like someone who lost their best friend in a tragic accident?' Molly cut in. 'Did he look at you in horror, make his excuses and leave, or did he listen?'

'He listened,' Robin admitted, remembering how he had twirled his fingers through her hair in a gesture that was so much more than comforting. 'He was wonderful. Patient, kind . . .'

'Like a *decent* man,' Molly said, scowling and shaking her head. 'I still can't get over Tim Lewis's cheek. Next time I see him, I'm going to give him a piece of my mind, I can tell you!'

'Join the queue,' Robin said. 'And it looks like he's going to get to turn next door into soulless apartments.'

'You haven't made enough profit from the guesthouse to buy it off Will?'

Robin laughed. 'I've been open for nearly six weeks, so not quite yet. And I haven't had a chance to look into the origin of the plaque, either. Besides, it sounds like Tim's gone all out, offered Will a whole heap of money. It's obvious he's stepped up his game, trying to close off the deal.'

'That's because he's lost you, so there's no reason to tiptoe around it,' Molly said. 'He's trying to turn Will into a millionaire and put him out of your reach to spite you. That's the kind of thing he'd do, and what happens when you have more money than sense. I'm so glad you didn't go back to him. Can you imagine? If you ever had kids, they'd be half-human, half-snake.'

Robin screwed her nose up, trying to picture it. 'I don't want snake babies.'

'Who does, Robin?' Molly asked seriously. 'Who in hell's name does?'

Chapter 21

Summer fell over Campion Bay like a soft, welcome blanket. The light had a clarity to it that Robin couldn't get enough of, and she rose earlier and earlier, throwing open the curtains in her bedroom and Sea Shanty to let it flood into the guesthouse. With the months ahead showing the promise of sunshine and warmth, the guesthouse bookings were up and Robin was flung into running it, barely finding time to take a breather amongst the check-ins and check-outs, changeovers, breakfasts, tea and cake, excursion route-planning and social media updates. Not to mention that she had chosen to change the name of the guesthouse at the same time. She sometimes wondered if Molly's visits in the evenings were simply so she could shake her head despairingly.

'You're going to start growing into the walls at this rate,' she said one evening, as they sat in Sea Shanty with cups of hot chocolate. 'When was the last time you even left the guesthouse?'

'I went to the supermarket yesterday afternoon,' Robin

protested. 'And I go for a walk on the beach every morning. I saw a crab yesterday. It was huge.'

'It was probably wondering what you were doing up so early! Isn't sleep a more productive use of your time at five in the morning?'

Robin shook her head. 'I need the fresh air. It calms me down, gets me ready for the day ahead. And there's nobody about at that time — I feel like I have the whole world to myself.'

'Obviously!' Molly laughed. 'Anything I can do, Robin, give me a shout. And I'm sure Paige would be happy with extra work once college breaks up for the summer.'

'I'll ask her, thanks. How's it going?'

Molly wiggled her hand in front of her. 'So-so. She's the same as ever, mostly. Talking a lot about her seventeenth birthday. She wants a new camera, so she can take photos to inspire her jewellery, and to help with her project work.'

'That's a lovely idea. And no more rebellions?'

Molly sighed. 'I'm not sure there ever was one to begin with. I'm in paranoid-mum phase, that's all.'

'It's understandable. I'd be a complete wreck in your shoes.'

'You wait, Robin. You'll be there one day. How are things with Will?'

'Who?' Robin laughed lightly, and changed the subject.

After their talk on the beach, Robin and Will had slipped into an easy friendship, chatting on their doorsteps when they passed each other, Robin sparing five minutes to say hello to Darcy whenever she could. Their gazes still lingered, she still felt the crackle of attraction between them, but with the summer guesthouse trade and Will's commitment to finishing Tabitha's house, their exchanges were brief and infrequent.

They had cleared the air, but despite Robin's longing, and her certainty that Will still felt some semblance of the feelings that had led to their kiss, they hadn't delved any further than amiable small talk. Robin often tried to convince herself that was for the best. The thought that they might only see each other for a few more weeks before Will was gone from Campion Bay for good was one Robin chose not to dwell on. But they were working side by side, sometimes only a few feet away from each other, and so in her less rational moments, their emotional distance felt maddening.

Robin had fallen for Will quickly and completely, and those feelings weren't going to go away any time soon. Every time she saw him, whether it was through the window on his way back from a swim, or lugging a bag of junk out to his Alfa Romeo, his T-shirt mucky and his arm muscles straining, her heart gave a leap, as if reminding her that *he* was the one thing missing in her life. Her head knew it, her heart knew it, and her body missed his touch, even though she'd only felt it on a few occasions. They were friendly, but for Robin friendly wasn't enough.

In the evenings, while her guests came in and out, laughing and chatting as they passed through the hall, her house happy and content with the sounds of being lived in, Robin played the piano. She had been inspired by Lorna's determination and the strength in her performance. Robin was by no means as talented as Lorna, she had only ever tinkered with the keys, but if the young woman could gather the courage to play so brilliantly after such a violent event, then what was Robin's excuse?

She played with the lights low in Sea Shanty, the windows open so the sounds of the seafront acted as a backing track; friends enjoying Skull Island, which stayed open later in the summer, couples strolling to Taverna on the Bay or towards town, and the late cry of the seagulls. She practised the tunes she already knew, that were stored somehow in her fingers, and she learnt new ones. She bought a popular piano tunes book from a secondhand shop and went through it methodically, but always returned to an arrangement of 'Where the Sky Is' by Ward Thomas. In the Seagull Street Gallery she found a miniature painting of a cat sitting on a piano stool, its black and white fur matching the monochrome keys. It didn't look quite like Eclipse, but it made her smile, and she bought it and hung it above the piano for encouragement.

'How's the sign coming along?' Paige asked, pushing herself up on to the kitchen counter one Sunday at the end of June.

It had been a frantic morning. The guesthouse was full, and a rather difficult couple in their fifties were staying in Andalusia. Robin had had to change their sheets because the existing set wasn't soft enough – though as she had only one type of linen she wasn't sure how a new set would be an improvement. Then they'd asked to sit at a different table in Honeysuckle so they weren't directly in the sun, causing a switch-around that was more complicated than it needed to be, and lastly, they'd requested egg-white omelettes for breakfast. Robin had accommodated them, but she'd never made an egg-white omelette before, and it had put a strain on Paige to get the other breakfasts finished.

Now they were both exhausted, drinking cold juice in the kitchen, and Robin could feel sweat trickling down her spine. Even Paige, usually immaculate, was dishevelled and red-cheeked.

'It's going well, I think,' Robin said. 'I spoke to the sign writer yesterday, and I can go and have a look at it tomorrow.'

'Oooh,' Paige clapped her hands together. 'That's so exciting. I'm going to take photos of the front of the building once it's up. It'll look so pretty.'

'Fingers crossed.' Robin chewed her lip. She hoped her ideas for the sign would look good in the realization; she wanted it to be fitting for her guesthouse, and for Neve. 'Are you looking forward to your birthday?'

'Yup. I think Adam's going to do something special for it. He's being super secretive, and won't tell me what he's planning. I can't believe I'll be seventeen. It feels so old.'

Robin laughed. 'Wait until you get to thirty-two, then see how you feel.'

Paige wrinkled her nose up. 'You're not over the hill though, are you?'

'Thanks very much!' She flicked a tea towel at Paige's legs.

'I mean, you've redone this whole guesthouse, and then there's Will . . . In some ways it's like you're starting out. You've had a few false starts and stuff, but this is it. The real thing.'

Robin nodded and sipped her juice, realizing how right Paige was. Will wasn't a part of her life – not in the way she wanted him to be – but she was starting again. The guesthouse had given her a new lease of life, a new home, a new community. She felt grounded, settled, the world opening up in front of her from her enviable position on the Campion Bay seafront.

Paige sighed elaborately, cutting into her thoughts. 'I wonder what Adam's going to do. I hope it's the most romantic thing *ever*. I bet you organized loads of romantic surprises when you ran your company.'

'I did,' Robin said.

'What was the most romantic?'

'Oh God, there were so many. One guy proposed to his

boyfriend at the top of Scafell Pike in the Lake District. We couldn't get up there to do much – it's entirely at the mercy of the weather – but we organized the hotel and engagement meal for when they got back. There was a couple in their eighties who wanted to relive the night they met, so we did up a boat on the Thames to recreate this Forties party, dressed all their family and friends – that was a lot of fun, and very emotional. There were musical performances, either setting up a venue so one partner could perform for the other, or hiring a band or musician to play for them both.' She tapped her fingers against her lips, thinking. 'I don't know if I can single out one as the most romantic. It was wonderful working on each of them. To know that we were helping to create moments that would last forever in their memories.'

Paige picked up one of the white chocolate and raspberry cookies that Robin had made that morning as the sun rose, and bit into it thoughtfully. 'That's what you should do for Will.'

Robin was so stunned she didn't reprimand her for taking a biscuit. 'Sorry?'

'For Will. I know you two aren't together, but it's so obvious that you should be. That's what you should do – something romantic, to show him how you feel. You must have loads of ideas, so come up with the perfect one for Will.'

'Paige, I don't think I can—'

'Why not? You want to be with him, don't you? And if it's all become too complicated, then show him what he's missing. Do something bold and crazily romantic that he won't be able to resist.'

'Is that what you did with Adam?' Robin asked, trying to deflect attention away from her and Will. *Could* she do that? Would it work?

'Nope,' Paige said. 'He was besotted with me from the first day of college. I pretended I didn't like him for a while, but there was no point. I fancied him too, so we started going out.' She shrugged and jumped off the counter. 'I have to go home and have another shower. I'm so hot!'

'Thanks for all you've done today. Hopefully it'll be a bit easier tomorrow.'

'No worries!' she called from the hall. 'See you tomorrow, Mrs B!'

'Please don't call me that – it makes me feel old!'

Paige's suggestion played constantly on her mind over the next few days. Is that what would do it? A grand, romantic gesture? Will didn't necessarily seem the type to fall for one of those – he was practical, dependable and logical – and yet, he'd fallen in love with Starcross and the pinprick lights, he'd remembered their talk about the moon names that night at the tavern, and if they were passing each other like ships in the night, too busy to spend any real time together, then wasn't this an option? Robin knew that she might not have much time, with Will working hard on Tabitha's house and Tim's gargantuan offer looming over them. If she was going to do it, she would have to move quickly.

As the last week of June saw a spike in the temperature, Robin's plans began to formulate. Her idea wasn't exotic or elaborate – she didn't have a budget set aside for wooing men – but she thought it would be her best shot, the most personal, special thing that would appeal to Will's heart. Because surely romance was about showing someone how much you cared for them by demonstrating how well you knew them, and the things that mattered between the two of you.

As she stepped out of the music shop on Seagull Street,

tucking her phone into her bag, a familiar figure emerged from the charity shop opposite. Robin's pulse began to race, but she took a deep breath and caught up with him.

'Will? Will, hi.'

He turned at the sound of her voice, and gave her a warm smile. 'Hi, Robin.'

'Getting rid of more of Tabitha's things?' She fell into step alongside him.

'It's never ending. I've been meaning to talk to you, actually. I've got to do something with all her sheep, and I know you were fond of them. There are other things of hers that I'd rather hold on to, but did you want to come and see if there are any you want?'

Robin's heart squeezed. 'Thank you. There are a few that I'd love to have, but maybe we should agree now that you won't let me take any more than five, otherwise I'll transport the whole lot next door and my guesthouse will suffer.'

'The most luxurious guesthouse on the south coast,' Will said, moving his hand in front of him as if imagining the headline of an article, 'run by crazy sheep lady, Robin Brennan.' He flashed her a grin.

'Yeah, it wouldn't work. But I could have a few in my room.'

'They could help you get to sleep, like the stars on the ceiling.'

Will's voice was soft, no longer teasing, but Robin winced, both at the fact that he had spotted her childish decorations and at the memory of the last time he'd been in that room, what was said and revealed. 'I didn't have enough budget for pinprick lights in my room too.'

'That's a shame,' Will said. 'No, actually, I like the glow-in-the-dark stars. They're comforting.'

'But the pinprick lights,' Robin sighed. 'They're the star turn in the whole guesthouse. If I meet my projections and have some money to play with next year, I'm going to put them in every bedroom.'

'*Star turn*, Robin?' Will shook his head slowly.

'Oh, I hadn't realized! That was painful.'

'Pitiful,' he agreed.

They walked in an easy silence that did nothing to calm Robin's nerves. This man was meant to be here. Will Nightingale belonged in Campion Bay. Everyone could see it – she could, and so could Molly, Ashley and Roxy, Maggie, Stefano and Nicolas. She was sure if she asked Coral Harris at the Seaview Hotel, the old woman – who Robin now couldn't picture in anything other than lavender lace – would admit that she found Will pleasing, and would want him to stay on the street. If nothing else, he would be invaluable in a DIY crisis.

A tantalizing toffee smell assaulted her senses, and Robin noticed they were passing the ice cream parlour, a counter open on to the pavement for takeaway cones and cups. She opened her mouth, but Will spoke first.

'We could get an ice cream, then go back to my place so you can look at the sheep. If you have time now?'

'Yes,' Robin said quietly. 'I've got about an hour before I need to be back.' Her mouth was suddenly dry. Not because he was inviting her to look at Tabitha's sheep collection – a strange sounding date if ever there was one – but because of how he'd said it. *My place.*

'Which flavour? I'll stretch to a double cone as it's so warm.'

'Uhm, salted caramel and banana.'

'OK,' he said slowly, turning to her, his frown initially

comical as if he disagreed entirely with her flavour combination. But then his features softened, and the warmth in his expression stilled her. She couldn't look away. Had he noticed her reaction to the way he'd described number four? Had he realized he'd said it?

'If you're sure?' he added eventually, turning back to the counter.

'Yup,' she said brightly, trying to recover her composure. 'Best combination ever.'

He shook his head, but ordered her ice cream, and a pistachio and chocolate cone for him, and then they strolled back along Goldcrest Road, focusing on their ice creams, trying to eat them before they dripped on to their clothes.

When they stepped inside the hall of number four, Robin hardly recognized it. For one thing, it was almost bare; the telephone and table were gone, the mirror on the wall was polished, and there wasn't a thin layer of dust sitting on top of everything. Darcy came instantly to greet them and Robin crouched to embrace her. The dog put her paws on Robin's knees and licked ice cream off her fingers.

'She was asleep when I left,' Will said. 'When it's this hot, I prefer to take her out early or late, when it's cooler.'

'This fur must be hard to bear at this time of year,' she said, stroking Darcy's head, and taking in the change in front of her. 'You've done so much.'

'It's been like wading through treacle,' Will admitted. 'But it's finally begun to pay off.'

Robin stood and walked into the living room. The heavy curtains were pulled back, and while the green sofas, the coffee table and large items of furniture were still there, the small, personal things were gone; the runners along the backs of the sofas, vases and knickknacks and pictures from the walls. A box in the corner was full of neatly stacked paper-work. All that was left was the furniture and the sheep.

Robin laughed as she examined them, picking each one up and turning it over; a sheep with its front hooves on a fence, one with a daisy sticking out of its mouth, a larger ornament with a sheep and two lambs huddled close against it. How would she ever decide?

'I'll leave you to it,' Will said softly, his fingers brushing her arm. 'Let me know if you need anything.'

She listened to his footsteps retreat, and allowed herself a few minutes with her memories of Tabitha, of playing games and naming the sheep, the wonderful stories she had told. She hadn't known, then, how much sadness she had lived with; not only losing her beloved husband early, but the hate and accusations, and then coldness from her brother. It comforted Robin to know that once she'd left for university, Will had started visiting, that Tabitha hadn't been entirely on her own. But she hadn't considered, until now, that what Will was doing, that stripping bare the old woman's house, would feel strange for her too, as if a piece of her childhood was falling away.

She chose her five sheep and put them safely in her handbag, then found Will in the kitchen. It was dated, with beige cupboards and flowered wallpaper, but was clean and dust free. The aroma of coffee made her stomach growl, despite the recent ice cream.

'All done?' he asked.

Robin nodded.

'Do I have to check your bag to make sure you've not over-sheeped?'

Robin laughed and thrust her handbag forward. 'Go ahead.'

'I'm kidding!' Will's smile grew, his gaze intensifying, and the space between them seemed to shrink, even though she hadn't taken another step. Robin held her breath, but then his eyelids flickered and he turned back to the counter. 'Coffee?' he asked.

'Sure.'

'It feels good being able to offer you a drink in here, after all your hospitality.'

'You're not running a hotel. I never expected you to return the favour.' She went to the back door and looked out at Tabitha's courtyard garden, the paving slabs awash with yellow dandelions, buttercups, and a few orange poppies creeping up through the cracks. A small, pink flower caught her eye. 'Oh look,' she said. 'Campion.'

'What's that?' He came to stand beside her, his arm pressing against hers.

'That pink flower is Campion. It's what the bay is named after. You can find it all over the cliff tops – it grows even if the soil isn't good – but I didn't realize it loved patios as well.'

'Maybe Tabitha left it to grow,' Will said quietly. 'I honestly haven't given much thought to the garden, yet.'

'You don't say? I thought this was intentional. Wildflower chic.'

He squeezed her hand. 'Come and have your coffee.'

They leant on the kitchen counter sipping their drinks, refreshing despite the heat, and slowly worked their way through a packet of dark chocolate digestive biscuits.

'You look like you're nearly done,' Robin said tentatively, scared of where this conversation would take them, of what Will might admit to.

'Nearly,' he agreed. 'I've still got to decide about the larger pieces of furniture. There's a small back bedroom to go through, too, and that one is *full* of junk and papers. So,' he said, his eyes not quite meeting hers. 'Not quite.'

'I had no idea how strange I'd feel, seeing it like this. Picking out my favourite sheep. It's so final.'

'I'm sorry,' Will said. 'I know this must be difficult for you too. You knew Tabitha well, and probably spent more time here than I did. It does feel like packing away memories, taking some to the tip and the charity shop. It's not got the same sense of achievement as having a clear-out at home. Did changing the guesthouse feel like that? You grew up there, didn't you?'

Robin nodded. 'But Mum and Dad helped me before they left, so although they were moving out, it didn't feel so sad. Also, I was clearing it out to refurbish it, and I was excited about that. I took things out, but then put new stuff straight back in. This feels a bit like . . .'

'An empty shell?'

'A bit. I'm sorry it's been so hard.'

'It would have been a lot harder without you,' he said, his voice suddenly rough.

She looked up at him, her breath catching at the way his eyes burned into her, contradicting the uncertainty in his tone.

'You've helped me here,' he continued, 'but also at the guesthouse, the way you made me feel . . . You made those early days easier, because you were there, smiling at me in the mornings, welcoming me back every evening. I've missed spending time with you. When we . . . when it fell apart, I wished I'd never knocked on your door, because I didn't want to have known you, to have felt like that, only to discover it had all been a lie.'

She parted her lips, but his openness made her stutter. 'Will, I—'

'But then,' he continued, 'you told me it wasn't, that it had never been a lie, and that's somehow made it harder. I haven't wanted to spend time with you, to allow myself that happiness, when I know that all this is coming to an end.' He looked away, ran his hand over his face, as if trying to wipe something off – his feelings, those last words?

'I've missed spending time with you too,' she said, aware of how lame it sounded. She could barely think straight, wondering how best to respond to his admission. She couldn't force his hand; he had to make the decision. *Knowing all this is coming to an end*. Was that it? Had he made up his mind? She swallowed, gripped her coffee cup tightly.

'Well, now there's less to do,' he said quietly, as if he was embarrassed by his outburst. 'We can have coffee breaks and ice creams together. It's slowing down, getting easier.' He dropped his head, his eyes studying the floor. 'I can see the end in sight.'

Yes, Robin thought, *but what happens at the end?* She didn't want to ask him outright, for fear that he'd tell her he'd found somewhere else to live in London, or he was moving back to Downe Hall, that he'd already accepted Tim's offer.

'It doesn't have to be the end.' She said the words in a whisper.

He looked at her, his handsome face suddenly pained, and Robin didn't want to hear whatever he was going to say next.

'I have to get back,' she rushed. 'Thanks so much for the ice cream and the coffee. And the biscuits. God, I thought hot weather was supposed to quash your appetite.' Her laugh was unconvincing.

381

He didn't reply, but walked her to the door, Darcy following patiently behind. 'Thanks for the sheep,' she said. She turned to face him, and found him so close that she could feel his breath on her cheek, his green eyes covering every inch of her face like searchlights.

He reached up to tuck her hair behind her ear, and Robin shivered from head to foot.

'Will?' she prompted.

He nodded suddenly, dropped his hand, his finger grazing her cheek as he did. 'Sure,' he said. 'She would have wanted you to have them. You know you can come round whenever you need a break? I'll be here.'

'Thank you,' she murmured, 'I will.'

As she turned away from him, feeling the warmth of his body behind her, her gaze snagged on the blue plaque, gleaming in the sunshine. What would happen to that when Will was gone, and she was the only one left to defend the memory of Jane Austen's time in Campion Bay? It was another loss that Robin wasn't sure she was prepared to deal with, and after what had just happened between her and Will, she was even more convinced she could do something to try and prevent it.

'Maggie, can I use your crazy golf course again?' Robin gave her her most sparkling smile, and the older woman rolled her eyes.

'What are you up to now, Bobbin?'

'Oh come on, you have to admit that the open-mic night was a success.'

Maggie narrowed her eyes, and then sighed. 'Yes. It was brilliant. So?'

'So, I want to do something else here, but something smaller, more private.'

'Private?'

'For Will. I want to, ah . . . Can I put a grand piano on your golf course?'

'What on *earth*? What are you cooking up this time?'

'I've not worked it all out yet, but I'd like to borrow a grand piano from somewhere and have it delivered here, and then – then play something for Will, on the piano, at night. Under the moon. I mean, if it's not cloudy of course – I can't control that part. Obviously.'

'Have you finally flipped?'

'Possibly. Yes. Yes, I have, but that's what Will has done to me, and I want to show him how much he's made me flip – in the best possible way – by doing something incredibly romantic.'

'And why is my crazy golf course the best place for all these things to happen?'

Robin shrugged. 'Because you have the power supply to put up fairy lights. And you're so lovely, and so willing, and nobody else would consider humouring me or my ridiculous plans.'

'Flattery, Bobbin, will get you everywhere.'

'Does that mean it's a yes?'

'It's a yes. Come and meet me later and we can sort out logistics. A grand piano is likely to go right through one of the greens, but there are other areas surrounding the course you can use. Are you using Stefano's grand piano?'

Robin's eyes widened. 'I didn't know he had one.'

'I think it got relegated to make way for more tables, so it's only wheeled out on special occasions. But ask them –

I'm sure they'd let you borrow it, and would help to get it over here too.'

'Maggie you are *wonderful*.' She leaned in and kissed her on the cheek, and then raced back to her guesthouse, leaving the older woman looking more surprised than she'd ever seen her.

It was all coming together. Paige had been right; she needed to show Will how much he meant to her, how much she wanted him to stay and make a life here in Campion Bay, with her.

She had thought that he was planning on leaving, taking Tim's unbeatable offer and setting himself up somewhere else far away, with a brand new, comfortable life, but after his admission in the kitchen, she was more certain than ever that he still had feelings for her. Maybe he was refusing to give in to them because he still thought it was too complicated, but she knew she had a shot at bringing them to the surface. And if she embarrassed herself, if she tried and got it wrong, then she would be losing him anyway.

The sign was almost ready, Maggie was on board and the other residents of Campion Bay knew about her plans, some of them having their own part to play.

She had decided to take Will on a goodbye tour of Campion Bay. It would involve cupcakes from Ashley and Roxy, a drink at the taverna, and a short, entirely false history of Skull Island crazy golf, including an assertion that one of the plastic pirates was responsible for the death of the skeleton on hole fifteen, because he wasn't good enough for the pirate's daughter. She wanted to remind Will of his time here, admit to him where she'd got things wrong, and then finish with her rendition of 'Where the Sky Is' on the grand piano under the stars.

She wanted it to be funny, tongue in cheek, but – above all – romantic. Of course, Robin didn't know what Will's plans were, if it would be enough to make a difference to how he saw his future, but she was going to pull out all the stops. At the very least, it would be a memorable way for Will to end his time in Campion Bay.

Robin scooped Eclipse into her arms as she went to her computer, to check that everything was in place for the name-change on her website and social media accounts.

Things were always changing in Campion Bay. Paige would soon be seventeen, moving closer to womanhood, taking steps that Molly wasn't ready for. Tim was developing more properties, changing the face of Campion Bay, perhaps even the seafront in the coming months. Robin had thought that, once her guesthouse was up and running, then it would continue in the same vein for years, that she would only tinker with the rooms and perfect her existing routine. But already she was changing the name, revitalizing it, taking the next step. There were expectations to surpass and dreams to aim for, and – like the constantly moving tide – nothing ever stayed the same.

Robin looked down at her kitten, at his black, sleek body and the crescent moon of white at his throat. He was growing fast. She wondered how much she had changed since she'd come back here, and whether – if Neve or Tabitha suddenly appeared – they would recognize her as their friend. She knew she couldn't hold on to things, that people moved away, grew up, died, that she couldn't control the desires or fate of other people. But she wanted to hold on to Will Nightingale. There were so many things against him staying – Tim's attentions to her over the past few months, his offer on Tabitha's house, the fact that the seafront property was dated, too large for a single person – but that didn't lessen her conviction, or her determination. Robin Brennan was going to resurrect her business, put on another Once in a Blue Moon Day for old times' sake. And this time, it was going to be for her.

Chapter 22

It was Saturday morning, and everything was in place for the following day. The early July sun beat down on Goldcrest Road, making the sea glitter like a field full of diamonds, the aquamarine beneath deep and inviting, almost as if they were on some exotic island instead of the south coast of England. Tomorrow would be the full buck moon, also known as the thunder moon, but she hoped that a summer thunderstorm wouldn't show itself. The forecast, for the moment at least, was reassuring Robin that extreme weather wouldn't get in the way of her plans.

She stood looking out of the window, drumming her fingers on the sill until Eclipse started to paw at them, thinking it was a new game thought up just for him. She pulled him into a hug and he gave a catty chirrup of pleasure.

'If this works,' she said to the cat, 'then you and Darcy will have to make peace. I know you can do that, you're very grown up now.' She rolled her eyes at her own words, and even Eclipse seemed to give her a condescending stare.

'Uh, excuse me?' Robin turned to find Billy, one of her

guests, standing in the doorway. He was in his early twenties, and was staying in Wilderness for a few days with his girlfriend, Sarah. Sarah's parents were in her Spanish-themed room Andalusia, and Mrs Winters, Sarah's mother, had spent a good twenty minutes the day before when they checked in explaining to Robin why they'd picked her guesthouse rather than gone for self-catering. *This way we get our own space*, she had said at the end of her speech, *and it's our first holiday with Billy here.* She had looked at him adoringly and for an awful moment Robin had thought she was going to ruffle the young man's reddish hair. She had a lot of respect for Billy, aware that this must be a daunting holiday, to say the least.

'Come in, Billy. What can I do for you?'

He stepped into Sea Shanty and crossed his arms tightly over his chest. 'Do you do bottles of champers?' he asked. 'Only, I want to treat Sarah tonight. Her mum and dad are going to a choral concert in Poole this evening, so I thought we could have a night in.'

'I can get one for you,' Robin said. 'Let me know what you'd like and when you'd like it brought up to the room.'

'Great, thanks. Could I pay separately, rather than it appearing on the bill?'

'Of course.'

'And, uhm, some chocolates. A nice box. Thorntons or something?'

Robin nodded. 'No problem at all, Billy. I'll get it all prepared for later.'

'Cheers. That's very kind.' He shuffled out of the room, his arms still folded, and Robin smiled to herself as she turned back to the view beyond the window. He was only a few years older than Adam, and while Tim had never behaved in that way – he was always outwardly confident and sure of everything – she remembered the urgency of young love, the eagerness to please, to get things right and make an effort. She would pick up a bouquet of roses, display them in Sea Shanty but put a single flower in a vase when she took up Billy's champagne. Or maybe the rest could decorate the top of her grand piano.

As Maggie had suggested, Stefano had one hidden away in the back room. It was well kept and beautifully tuned, and free of dust, despite not being in the main restaurant. When Robin asked if she could borrow it, Stefano had almost cried with happiness, stroking its polished wood softly, as if it was a son or daughter about to fulfil their potential. He hadn't minded about it being put outside and had told her that he and Nicolas and other members of their family would happily be in charge of getting it there and back again safely.

Robin was delighted – and relieved; she didn't think that if she, Molly and several of the guests tried to haul her mum and dad's old upright piano out of Sea Shanty and over the road to Skull Island, either the piano or their spines would come out of it well. But Stefano knew what he was doing and had taken on one of the trickiest jobs – offering to organize the heavy lifting – before she'd even asked him. Besides, an upright piano wouldn't have the same effect as a moonlit grand piano. She patted her trusty upright, wondering if her practicing had been enough.

A flicker of movement outside caught her eye and her breath stalled as Will hurried down the front steps of next door. Or, as he'd referred to it, *my place*. She had thought a lot about that since their encounter a week before. The sheep stood proudly on her dressing table, reminding her of that afternoon, the way he had come close to admitting the strength of his feelings for her before backing gently away, starting a countdown clock against his time left in Campion Bay. She watched him now as he unlocked his car, looking ready for summer in charcoal shorts and a royal blue T-shirt, and noticed that he was holding what looked like an overnight bag. Darcy was waiting to jump into the back seat.

'No,' she said quietly. 'No no no.'

Molly appeared and quickly intercepted him, their voices friendly, the open window allowing their words to drift in to reach her.

'You're not escaping without saying goodbye, are you, Will Nightingale?'

He laughed, and Robin was instantly warmed. It was a sound that always lifted her spirits, however frequently or infrequently she heard it.

'No,' he said. 'I've got a couple of errands to run. I've been putting them off to try and get this place finished, but I can't wait any longer.'

'You'll be back later today?' Molly kept her voice casual, but Robin knew she was *asking for a friend.*

Will's gaze flickered towards the sea, then back to Molly. 'I'm not sure. Maybe not today, but I won't be gone long. Don't worry Molly, I'm not leaving it like this.' He indicated the house, and Molly frowned.

'There's nothing wrong with the exterior that a good clean wouldn't fix.'

Will grinned at her. 'Noted. See you soon.'

Molly nodded dumbly as he put his bag in the boot, let Darcy jump into the back seat and then opened the driver's door. He glanced up at the guesthouse and Robin moved quickly to the side, unsure whether he'd seen her. But then she heard the car door shut, and the Alfa Romeo puttered away from the kerb.

As soon as he was gone, Molly looked straight at Robin and flung her arms in the air. Feeling slightly nauseous, Robin went to open the door.

'So,' Molly said, walking straight past her and into the kitchen, putting on the kettle without asking. 'You've organized this wonderful, romantic tour to show Will what he means to you, got everyone on Goldcrest Road involved, borrowed a *grand piano* from Stefano to play him a song in the moonlight, and you didn't think it was important to check that Will was actually going to *be* here for it?'

Robin sank into a chair. 'I didn't know he was going away.'

'But did you ask him? Did you subtly investigate, to be on the safe side? Surely you thought of a way to ensure that, at least for this weekend, he wasn't going anywhere else?'

Robin shook her head. 'I thought about it. But all my ideas to try and keep him here seemed so obvious, so unlikely, that I knew he'd see through them and everything would be ruined.'

'Not as ruined as they'll be if he's not here! God, Robin. Even if you'd kept him in Campion Bay by chaining him to a radiator with those fluffy handcuffs you seem so keen on, it would have been better than this. Mildly alarming for Will for those few hours he thought you'd kidnapped him, granted, but then you'd take him on the tour and all would be revealed.' She made two swift cups of tea, oblivious to the mess she was making as she deposited the used teabags in the compost caddy, and put one in front of Robin as she joined her at the kitchen table.

'He could easily be back by tomorrow,' Robin said.

'Or he could come back on Tuesday and you'll be stuffed. I'm guessing Stefano's going to quite a lot of trouble to get your grand piano in place?'

'He is,' she admitted. 'And it won't be the full moon by Tuesday, either.'

Molly sat back. 'Do you need to check that he's a werewolf before you commit? I don't get it.'

'It seems important, OK? When we went to the taverna, it was the flower moon. He remembered, he . . . I don't know. He loves those pinprick lights in Starcross, too. So there has to be moonlight, a *full* moon.'

Molly leaned forward, her elbows on the table. 'Can you text him? Create some kind of crisis that will force him back here?'

Robin shook her head. 'No. I'm not starting this off with a lie. I'm going to carry on with it all as normal – and he'll turn up. I know it.'

'So that's your plan? Hope?'

'I like to think of it more as confidence. It's meant to be, so that's what will happen.'

Molly shook her head and grinned at her. 'You're nuts.'

Robin smiled back. 'I think you might have told me that before.'

The doorbell rang and her stomach tightened, because it was likely to be the delivery she'd been waiting for, the reason she'd been staring out of the window in the first place.

Her new guesthouse sign was here.

A young man and slightly older woman introduced themselves as Stuart and Danni and explained that they would remove the old sign first and then get the new one out of its wrapping. Molly and Robin had an agonizing wait, Robin busying herself with making tea for Stuart and Danni, while they took down the sign that had been on the front of the house for close to thirty years. Her palms were sweaty, her confidence that this was the right decision suddenly wavering.

Once they were done, Robin took a photo of the naked front of the guesthouse, and wrote a quick post for her social media feeds to accompany the picture.

'Do you want to keep the old one?' Stuart asked.

Robin shook her head. 'I don't know where I'd put it.' There were enough memories and history, people who had stayed in the Campion Bay Guesthouse, without having to hold on to it. She had discussed it with her mum and dad, who seemed almost horizontally relaxed after only a few months in Montpellier, and they had fully supported her decision. Sylvie had even sounded slightly teary when Robin had told her the reasons behind the new name.

Stuart and Danni opened the back of their shiny black van and slowly negotiated the new sign out of it. It was covered in bubble wrap so thick that Robin couldn't see anything to begin with.

'We'll lay it out on the pavement,' Danni said, 'make sure you're happy with it, and then put it up.'

Robin nodded and Molly jiggled beside her. Nobody else had seen it yet. Robin had visited the sign writer several times, checking on progress, and had seen it close to completion, but it wasn't the same as it being here; adorning the front of her guesthouse. It felt like the final piece of the puzzle, making it fully her venture, her business. Her future.

'Holy shit,' Molly said, once the bubble wrap had been carefully removed. 'That is stunning, Robin.'

'It is, isn't it?' Robin smiled, all doubts disappearing in a flash.

The background was pale grey, *The Once in a Blue Moon Guesthouse* written in deep, velvety navy, the font bold and slightly italicized, the navy also running as a border around the edge of the sign. Silver accents gave the letters depth, and at the right-hand side was an illustration of a blue moon, its surface pitted with craters. Finally, the grey background was dotted with metallic silver stars that, Robin could see, would catch the sun's light as it rose and then fell; a hint of shimmer that added a magical touch.

This time they didn't go inside, but stayed on the pavement as Danni and Stuart secured it to the front of the building, their teamwork and efficiency demonstrating that they had done this many times before. Robin leaned against her Fiat, feeling the sharp press of tears as they gave the sign a final wipe with a cloth, and then put their ladders back in the van.

'All right, then,' Stuart said. 'You settled up with the boss last week, so we're all done.'

'Thank you, you've done such a wonderful job.' Robin shook their hands, and gave them a tip and a discount voucher for the guesthouse, feeling a surge of pride at the new name printed along the top. It felt right that Danni and Stuart should be the first people to see the newly branded marketing. She waved as they drove away.

'Bloody hell,' Molly said, as they stared up at the sign, at the moon and the stars, the new, fitting name for the guesthouse that, in its short life, had made Robin feel fulfilled again. 'Good call, Robin. It definitely works. Have you got the new brochures and welcome packs ready?'

'Yes,' Robin said. 'I'll go and replace them all in a moment. If I can ever stop looking at it.' She felt Molly's hand on her shoulder.

'Neve would have loved this, you know. She would have said it was the first step towards world domination. The events company, then the guesthouse.'

Robin laughed, grateful to Molly for helping to dry her tears.

'One little guesthouse on the south coast doesn't feel much like world domination,' she said. 'But it's enough for me.'

'We should have had some kind of launch, drunk some champagne and then smashed the bottle against the wall.'

'That's not how it works, you're meant to smash a full bottle against it. And isn't that for boats, anyway?'

'I don't know,' Molly said, 'but I won't be a part of something that involves wasting champagne.'

'Tomorrow, maybe. Once . . .'

'Once Will's seen it?'

'Once I know for sure. I'll be able to get on with my life, then. No more wondering.' She pressed her hands under her armpits, feeling the jitters begin. She wouldn't get rid of them until it had played out, Will either turning up or causing her to fall at the first hurdle. And if he did turn up, would he be swept off his feet or bemused and nonplussed by her unique, romantic gesture?

'Don't sound so negative,' Molly said. 'You might be getting on with your life *with* Will. I have a full afternoon of clients, and I'm catching up with Beardy Jim at the Artichoke this evening, but I'll come and see you in the morning, OK? You're very welcome to come to the pub with us. Kerry will be there too, and you've not seen them since the refurbishment.'

'I'd love to,' Robin said, 'but I'm not sure I'd be the best company. I have to settle the new guests in, and then I want to go over everything for tomorrow.'

'Check it all for the umpteenth time?'

Robin nodded.

'Don't go round the twist, Robin. Give yourself some breathing space.' Robin watched her friend head back to Groom with a View and then found her eyes returning to her new sign, as if they were magnets attracted to each other.

She took several photos and uploaded them to Twitter and Instagram as she leaned against her car, the warm summer breeze whispering gently around her.

In reality, she hoped this would be the final destination on her tour, after the grand piano. She wanted to show Will the new name, the stars with their silver metallic paint winking at the real stars in the night sky. She hoped he would come back with her, so that they could start again. Starcross wasn't free that night, but it was only a one-night booking, the room unoccupied after the Sunday morning check-out. She could picture it all perfectly, and as much as she knew perfection was a hard thing to live up to – she couldn't help it. She had to aim for the stars, or what was the point?

'Who's this lovely thing?' she asked, crouching down to stroke the black-and-white dog that had accompanied Mr and Mrs Khanom into Sea Shanty to check in. In fact, the dog looked more like a pompom than an animal, and Robin was slightly concerned that it was about to challenge Darcy in the cuteness stakes.

Mrs Khanom laughed, a rich sound that filled the whole room. 'He's called Dexter. He's our daughter's Pomeranian. She's on a French exchange, so we thought we'd have a break too. Your rooms are pet friendly, so here we are.'

'He's lovely,' Robin said. 'Hello, Dexter.' The dog looked up at her, made a noise that could have been a sneeze, and then nuzzled her hand. She forced herself to stand and give her human guests more attention than their four-legged companion. 'If you could add your car registration – if you have one – and then sign here, I'll get your key and show you to your room.'

'Sounds great,' Mr Khanom said. 'I'm guessing we can't

take Dexter on the beach?' He glanced out of the window, and Robin followed his gaze. The sand was busy, covered with colourful windbreakers, lots of bare flesh on show as people braved the sea for a swim, or sunbathed on oversized beach towels.

'Not here,' Robin said. 'But about half a mile down the coast it's fine, and there are also some good paths along the cliff tops if you head in that direction.'

'We'd love some information about walks in the area, if you have any?' Mrs Khanom added.

Robin rifled through a drawer and handed her a glossy leaflet, and then took the couple up to their room.

It was close to six before the doorbell sounded the arrival of her last guests, meaning all the rooms were now taken; Billy and Sarah were in Wilderness, Mr and Mrs Winters in Andalusia – though they had already left for their concert in Poole – Mr and Mrs Khanom in Rockpool, and a man in his fifties, Jamie Percival, in Canvas. He had told Robin he was here for work, but that he couldn't stand the soulless travel lodges and always looked for something more inter-esting when he travelled to meet clients, even if it was further to get to the meetings. Robin thought it must be a lonely existence, but her offer of afternoon tea had been turned down, so maybe Jamie had got used to being alone on his work trips.

She left her book face down on the sofa, although her head was so full of worries about tomorrow that she hadn't taken any of it in, and went to answer the door. She flung it open, her smile faltering.

Adam and Paige stood on her doorstep, looking at her expectantly.

'Hi, guys,' she said. 'What can I do for you?'

Adam stood up straighter, his chest puffed out. 'We've come to check in. To Starcross.'

Robin didn't reply immediately. She blinked, trying to force her brain to catch up with his words. 'Sorry?'

'We've booked it for tonight,' Adam said. 'For Paige's birthday. It's a legitimate booking, so you can't stop us.'

Robin stepped back, her mouth moving but no words coming out. 'But Paige's birthday isn't until next week,' she said lamely.

'I know, but it had to be Starcross, and it was free tonight.'

Paige was glancing between her boyfriend and Robin, her eyes wide with anticipation, expectation – maybe even fear.

'No,' Robin said slowly. 'No, I have a-a – it's Andy and Penelope . . .' Her words drifted away. 'You booked it under false names. Online.' She sighed, thinking of the one-night booking that had made her hopeful for Will's return to Starcross on Sunday, and then cursed under her breath. 'Come inside, so I can explain why I'm not going to let you book into Starcross tonight.'

'It's a legitimate booking,' Adam said again.

'Yes, but you're too young.'

'Where does it say that on your website?' Adam asked. 'I couldn't find it.'

'Come in, please, the pair of you. I'll get you a drink, we can discuss this.'

'Please, Robin,' Paige said, her voice on the edge of whining. 'I had no idea Adam was doing this, but don't you think it's the most romantic thing ever? He knew exactly what I wanted, and he's sorted it all out. You can't deny that.'

'No, I can't,' Robin agreed. 'It is wonderfully romantic – Adam, you're incredibly thoughtful, but it doesn't change the facts. I am not letting you two stay here unless I have full consent from Molly. Please come in off the doorstep.'

Paige shook her head. 'Not until you agree. It's only one night. And Mum's at the pub, so you can't ask her.'

Robin waggled her mobile phone. 'I can, and it may be one night, but it's a night that – I don't need to spell it out for you. You're both smart, and you're great together, but it doesn't change the facts.'

'Mum doesn't even need to know,' Paige said in a stage whisper.

'I am not lying to your mum,' Robin said. 'And we shouldn't be doing this here. Come in, please.' She stepped back, but the young couple didn't budge.

'No. If we come in, then we're staying in Starcross. We've *booked* it – how can you stop us?'

'Very easily, Paige.' Robin held up her phone again. 'But I don't want to do that, I want to talk to you. Let me fix you both a hot chocolate.'

'Oh my God!' Paige spat. 'Stop treating us like we're *kids*! We're ready for this, and we wanted to come here. You should be flattered, Robin, not turning us away!'

'Paige, come on. You know where I stand on this. It's not for me to let you, and I'm not going to be complicit in you going behind your mum's back. You're not a child, I know that. God knows you help me out enough and you're incredibly grown up, but that doesn't mean that I can let this happen.'

Paige shook her head, her blue eyes flashing with an anger Robin had never seen. 'You're so patronizing. And such a hypocrite! You're planning this special thing for Will, I *bet* you're hoping you end up sleeping together—'

'Paige—'

'And yet when Adam does something like that for me you shut it down. It's cruel and it's heartless. I thought you believed in love, in romance. I thought you cared about me!'

'I do! I care about both of you, which is why I can't agree to this. Come in for a few minutes, that's all.'

'What? So you can call my mum and get her to drag me home by the ear? No fucking chance!'

'Please calm down.' Robin reached out to take her arm, bare in a short, navy dress that wouldn't look out of place at a cocktail party, but Paige flung it away.

'Fuck off, Robin! We're going. Come on Adam. If you won't have us, I'm sure someone else will!'

'Don't do this Paige. Please—' They turned away from her and walked down the steps. Adam had a rucksack slung over one shoulder, Paige with a large red handbag, big enough for one night's worth of clothes and make-up. 'Paige! Adam!'

They ignored her.

Cursing, Robin ran into the kitchen to find her shoes, then headed out of the front door. The young couple had disappeared. Feeling a huge rush of relief, she realized they must have gone back into Molly's house. She hurried down the steps and up to the pink front door of Groom with a View. She knocked, rang the doorbell, peered through the front windows, but the house remained steadfastly quiet.

'Shit.' She turned and looked at Goldcrest Road from her elevated position at the top of Molly's steps. Although it was early evening, the July warmth ensured the beach was still busy, people still in the water. There was a queue at the ice cream stand and Skull Island was doing a good trade, and as Robin scanned the tableau in front of her it felt like the hardest *Where's Wally* competition. She couldn't pick out Paige's blonde hair, navy dress or even her bold red bag. And

Adam had dark hair, and had been wearing a black shirt and jeans. Besides which, they could be inside Molly's and ignoring her, perhaps changing their plans now that Robin had denied them a night in Starcross. Her stomach churned uneasily.

She tried Paige's phone but it rang and rang and then went to voicemail. She rang it again and pressed her ear against Molly's front door, listening for the sound of the dance-track ringtone, but she couldn't hear it. Walking slowly back to the guesthouse, her eyes scanning the beach and promenade, she tried Molly's number this time. That, too, went to voicemail. She left her a message, asking her friend to call her as soon as possible.

Robin closed her front door and leant against it, opening her texts and firing one off to Molly as a backup: *Paige and Adam booked Starcross under false names. I turned them away – worried they'll do something stupid. Call me ASAP. R xx*

All thoughts of Will and her plan for tomorrow pushed aside, Robin returned to her book, but was even more distracted now. When the landline rang she felt a surge of hope – it would be Paige apologizing, or Molly telling her she'd spoken to her daughter, or was about to. Either way, it would be a relief.

'Hello?' she asked breathlessly.

'Uhm, hi. It's Billy. In Wilderness. Have you got those things I asked for?' He whispered the words, and Robin could picture Sarah sitting on the bed, giving him a curious smile, excited and nervous on their first holiday together.

'Of course,' she said, 'give me five minutes and I'll bring them up.' As she went into the kitchen to get the champagne out of the fridge and untangle a single bud from the bouquet of roses, she knew that she had made the right decision about Paige and Adam. She couldn't let it happen under her roof, not without Molly's say-so. She couldn't stop them going elsewhere, but even though Paige had been angry, she knew that she was essentially sensible and, perhaps more importantly, romantic.

She would want her first time with Adam to be special, she wouldn't do anything reckless – and surely Paige would realize that she didn't actually want her mum's best friend knowing all the details, the when and where of it, so Robin was sure she had done them a favour in the long run. Feeling slightly reassured at her own pep talk, she put the bottle of champagne, the chocolates and a single red rose on a tray.

Robin's phone beeped as she was drifting off to sleep. She blearily picked it up to look at the message. It was from Molly:

Ta for info re P. You did right thing! Sure all fine, will talk to her in the morn. Molly xxx

A relieved smile played on her lips and she put her phone on the bedside table, soon drifting back towards sleep, visions of Will under a full moon slipping happily through her thoughts, along with images of the grand piano on the beach, even though that was something Stefano had told her would have been impossible, the instrument too heavy for the soft sand.

She was startled out of her slumber by someone knocking on the door. It seemed like she'd been asleep for moments, but the sun was streaming through her thin curtains and her alarm clock read 5.45 a.m.

'What the hell?' She got hurriedly out of bed, wanting to stop the persistent banging before it woke her guests. Pulling on her thin, star-covered dressing gown she went to the front door, Eclipse blinking and stretching as he padded down the hallway, as intrigued as she was.

'Do you really have to—' she started to say as she flung the door open. 'Shit. Molly? What is it, what's wrong?'

'It's Paige,' Molly sobbed, stepping forward and putting her arms round Robin.

Robin went cold. 'Tell me what's happened,' she whispered, though she wasn't sure she wanted to know the answer.

Chapter 23

Eclipse was on Molly's lap the second she sat down. Robin stood for a moment, wondering whether to make coffee, and then realized she needed to know first, before anything else happened.

'Her bed hasn't been slept in,' Molly said, rubbing her face with her palm. 'I've phoned and phoned, left countless messages, but she hasn't got back to me. She's not at Adam's – I've spoken to his parents. I tried not to alarm them, but I don't know if it worked.'

'It's still early,' Robin whispered, but knew that wouldn't make a difference to the way Molly was feeling. 'She and Adam weren't there when you got back last night?'

Molly shook her head. 'I – I don't think so. It was late, I'd had a few drinks . . . I knocked on her bedroom door to say goodnight, and I thought I heard a grunt. I didn't think I needed to wake her up, that it would be overkill if I went storming in there.'

Robin swallowed. 'But you saw my text?'

'I thought she'd be angry, and then Adam would help

her cool down and it would all be OK. I'm the *worst* mother. I just assumed, I didn't check up on her.' She looked up at Robin, the distress plain on her face. 'What exactly happened between you? I mean – how bad was it?'

'She got very angry,' Robin said, wincing as she recalled the conversation. 'She called me patronizing, swore at me. I tried to follow her and Adam when they left, but I thought they'd gone back to yours.'

'This isn't your fault, Robin. You did the right thing, but I – I don't know where to start. I can call her college friends in a couple of hours, but – she's never done anything like this before.' Molly stared at her, her hands pressed against her cheeks, looking like Munch's *The Scream*.

Robin kneeled on the floor and put her hands on Molly's knees. 'We will find her and it will all be fine. Paige is sensible. I've pissed her off, she's a teenager, and she thinks that I – perhaps both of us – are holding her back. She'll be furious for a few hours – she's probably gone to a friend's, or maybe another hotel or guesthouse. She'll want to defy us, she'll appear later and be pleased she's given you a scare, and then she'll feel awful.'

Molly nodded, but she didn't look remotely reassured.

'I'll go and get us some coffee, and we can work out who we need to call.'

'Isn't she meant to be helping you with breakfasts this morning?'

Robin's heart leapt. 'Exactly,' she said, clapping her hands together so loudly that even Eclipse jumped. 'She wouldn't let me down, she's too conscientious. Give it a couple of hours, and everything will be right as rain.'

But as the clock struck eight o'clock and Mr and Mrs

Khanom came down for breakfast, there was no sign of her. Robin's heart sank, and Molly's pallor increased.

'I have to do this,' Robin said quietly. 'But the moment I'm finished, we'll look for her. OK?'

Molly nodded and, moving as if she was sleep walking, started taking cutlery out to the courtyard.

'Molly, come on,' Robin said. 'You don't have to help.'

'But you're on your own.'

'And I can cope by myself. Seriously. Go and phone Paige's friends. You can use my room if you don't want to be disturbed.'

'I need to get my address book from home.'

'Sure.' Robin forced a smile, trying to keep her spirits up for the sake of her friend.

That breakfast service was the longest and hardest of Robin's short time as guesthouse owner. Molly returned with her address book and went into Sea Shanty, and Robin was kept hectically busy, doing the breakfasts for seven guests and all the serving and carrying on her own, when her mind was entirely distracted. She felt horrendously guilty, knowing that it was her fight with Adam and Paige that had led to this. She went over and over it in her head, wondering how she could have approached it differently, what she could have said or done, perhaps inviting them into the house before she'd turned them down. Had she been condescending? Her thoughts were so muddled she couldn't be sure.

'That's soy sauce, love,' Mrs Winters said, when Robin took the condiments out for her fry-up. 'Do you have any ketchup?'

'Oh God, I'm so sorry.'

'Not to worry,' Mrs Winters laughed. 'Soy sauce is delicious on mushrooms.'

'I'll have to try that,' Robin murmured, going back to the kitchen for the right bottle.

When the last guests had returned to their rooms Robin raced into Sea Shanty, ignoring the fact that the kitchen looked like an angry ghost had emptied all her cupboards, and looked expectantly at Molly.

Molly shook her head, her face stricken. 'Nobody's heard from her,' she said. Her voice was barely more than a whisper and Robin had to strain to hear her. 'I've tried all of her friends, everyone that I can think of.'

Robin swallowed down the panic that was threatening to take over. 'Right then,' she said. She stared around the room, then at the blissfully glorious day that was mocking them from beyond the panes of glass. 'So we start looking.'

'Round here?'

Robin nodded. 'We'll start with Mrs Harris, because she runs a guesthouse, and we have to accept that as a possibility. And if she doesn't know anything, then we knock on doors, see if anyone saw Paige or Adam yesterday evening, ring round the other hotels in the area. We'll find them, Molly.'

Molly nodded and stared at the floor. She took a moment to compose herself, and then sprang off the sofa, clutching her address book to her chest. 'OK,' she said. 'Coral Harris. Let's go.' She managed a smile that Robin thought must have taken all her resolve, and followed Robin to the front door.

'No, I haven't. When do you suppose I would have seen her, exactly? She hasn't booked in here, for goodness sake!' Mrs Harris, it turned out, wasn't in a very understanding mood. Wearing a simple white blouse, grey skirt and green apron – no lavender frills in sight – she scowled as if they'd asked her whether she was harbouring a wanted criminal inside her guesthouse.

Robin closed her eyes, wondering why Mrs Harris couldn't see that tact was required. She could feel Molly quivering beside her and had to resist the urge to shout at the older woman. She remembered her appraising the newly decorated guesthouse without an ounce of interest or compassion, being accusing rather than complimentary when Robin had been overcome with nerves.

'Well,' Robin said, keeping her voice as calm as she could, 'if you do see her or Adam, could you please call Molly or me as soon as possible? It's very urgent.'

'No time for tearaways,' she muttered, her hands on her hips, and Robin gripped Molly's arm tightly.

'Come on,' she said as they retreated down the stairs of the Seaview Hotel, 'let's talk to Ashley and Roxy. They might have seen them, and at the very least they'll be more willing to help.'

Molly only nodded. Robin hated seeing her friend so downcast. All the determination and spark that she had for solving other people's problems was gone, now that her daughter was missing. Paige had never done something like this before, and of course she'd been angry, but Robin was sure that they would find the lovebirds in another guesthouse along the coast, or with a friend Molly didn't know about. Or – even more likely – they would come creeping back sometime later that day of their own accord, their tails between their legs.

Though it was still early, the tantalizing smells of chocolate and dough wafted around Roxy when she opened the door.

'Hello!' Roxy beamed at them. 'The cupcakes are *in the*

oven, Robin! We're all set to be a part of your romantic day. How exciting!' She clasped her hands together and then took in their expressions, her smile dying in an instant. 'What's happened?'

Molly swivelled to face Robin, her mouth agape. 'Will,' she managed. 'Your tour for Will. That's today. Oh sh—'

'Don't even think about it,' Robin said. 'In the scheme of things, it isn't remotely important. We have to find Paige.'

'What?' Roxy asked, glancing between them. 'What's happened to Paige? What's going on?'

As Molly explained, Robin stood patiently on the doorstep. Of course her Once in a Blue Moon Day for Will didn't matter now. But in the maelstrom of thoughts about Paige and how she could have handled that situation differently, there were other worries building up inside her like a tornado. Stefano, Nicolas and Maggie had given up some of their Sunday to get the grand piano set up while Robin was leading Will round Campion Bay, and Roxy and Ashley had gone to a lot of trouble to help her put some of the smaller touches in place. But Will wasn't here anyway. Even without Paige and Adam's disappearance, she had called on their generosity for nothing.

Today, Robin decided, as Roxy expressed her horror at the situation and said she would get in touch the moment she spotted Paige's lovely blonde hair, was not one of her favourite days. It had held so much promise, but now everything was unravelling, slowly but surely. She wondered if she should have checked her horoscope for the weekend before planning anything, and then pictured Neve's face, her dark eyes alive with possibility.

Neve would have told her to stop moping and get on with it. There was still a chance it would all work out. Paige would be found safe and sound, Will would return, the tour could still go ahead. All she had to do was believe.

'Let's go and ask Maggie.' Robin took hold of Molly's hand and waved goodbye to Roxy. 'From her position in that hut she's got more intelligence than MI6. She will have seen where they went last night.'

'God, you're right,' Molly said, sounding hopeful again. She almost ran across the road.

Belief, thought Robin, as she gave a silent thanks to Neve, was all it took. The sun shone down on them as they made their way to Skull Island, certain that this particular drama would soon be behind them.

But Maggie hadn't seen them, and neither had Stefano or Nicolas, or the owners of the ice cream hut. As the sun rose high in the sky and then began its descent, Molly tried Paige and Adam's phones for what must have been the hundredth time. They were running out of ideas. Will hadn't returned either, and despite the fact that her grand romantic tour was quickly becoming an impossibility, Robin wanted him there. He was so logical and dependable, so calm. He would know in a heartbeat what to do, how to reassure Molly. She missed him like an ache in her chest, which only made her sadder that she wasn't going to get her chance to show him how she felt; not in the way she'd planned.

By late afternoon, the whole of Goldcrest Road, it seemed, had adapted their Sunday ventures to help with the search. Stefano and Nicolas were scouring the town in between their lunch and evening service, checking the cafés, pubs and arts centre. Ashley and Maggie, from their various vantage points, were showing photos of the young couple to all who entered the teashop or crazy golf course. Robin had decided against returning to the Seaview Hotel to ask Mrs Harris for assistance, and while she had suggested Molly should stay at home and wait for Paige's return, and was grateful that Roxy had agreed to stay with her, she couldn't sit still herself.

The guesthouse was ticking over by itself, her guests enjoying the warm evening, and she had no rooms to change since her one-night booking for Starcross had turned out to be Adam and Paige. She walked along the beach, her head scanning constantly, looking at the figures soaking up the last rays of sun, peering at those paddling or swimming in the sea, all the while trying not to let panic get the better of her.

Surely if Paige was only making a point, she would have returned by now. Soon it would be twenty-four hours since Robin had turned them away, and that felt like a long time for a young couple if they had nowhere to go. She held on to the thought that the most likely place was a friend's house, someone Paige had met at college that Molly didn't know about. She tripped over the corner of a beach towel, apologized to the man lying on it, and carried on.

Anything? a new text from Molly asked.

Still looking, was her quick reply.

As she walked, the crowds began to thin out. The beach stretched away from the amenities – the car park, the ice cream shop and the public toilets – and the bright windbreakers became less frequent. Robin felt a sudden tightening in her chest. The sand was unspoiled here, an empty paradise of beach and surf, cliffs and caves. This was where she came to think, to be alone. Had Adam and Paige done the same thing, escaping the lectures of know-it-all adults to be by themselves? She picked up her pace, running further along the beach.

The tide was coming in, slinking closer to the sharp, looming cliff face, threatening the dark recesses of the caves where ledges provided a false sense of shelter. She was breathing hard now, her trainers pounding the sand. The buck moon was already visible in the evening sky, where turquoise rose up to an inky blue as twilight made its first move. Soon it would be dark, the moonlight the only illumination at this end of the beach.

Her phone rang in her pocket and she pulled up, hoping her instincts were wrong, that this was a call from Molly to say her daughter and Adam had returned.

'H-hello?' she panted.

'Robin, it's Will. Can I see you? I knocked on the door, but there's no answer.'

'You're back?'

'Yes, I – what's wrong, Robin? Where are you?' His tone changed, she could hear the concern in his voice, but there had been an urgency there to begin with, she was sure of it. Had Stefano still found time to set the piano up? Had Will discovered it?

'Wild – wild beach,' she said. 'Paige and Adam are missing, and I think that – that they might be here, somewhere. Tide's coming in.'

'Right. Hang on.' He hung up abruptly, and, with no other course of action, Robin started moving again.

In front of her, as she left the comfort of Goldcrest Road behind, the cliffs jutted further down the beach, so that while there was a wide strip of sand where she was, ahead she could see the waves already lapping at the bottom of the rocks. 'Crap,' she murmured, running on.

This part of the beach was empty. Away from the street-lights of the promenade, with only natural light as a guide, it made sense that people came here infrequently, especially when the tide was rising and darkness had started to fall. Robin chucked her phone on to the sand, not knowing how deep in the water she would have to go, and aware that it wouldn't survive a soaking.

She kept going, swallowing down her panic as she splashed into the shallows, the water cold on her ankles, the sand in front of her disappearing beneath the waves. They were still lapping, still gentle, but she knew that in hardly any time they would be higher, pounding relentlessly against the cliffs, using anything in the water as an accessory to their assault.

She reached the first dark cave mouth, but this one was tiny, not big enough for a single person to squeeze inside, and already close to being submerged. She pressed on, shouting for Paige and Adam, all the time wondering if she was wrong, if this was a ridiculous mission and she was putting herself in danger for nothing. She heard barking behind her and turned to see Darcy, her ears flat back, running at full pelt towards her.

'Darcy!' she called. Behind her, also racing across the sand, was Will. She didn't think she had ever been so pleased to see someone. 'Will!' He raised his arm in acknowledgement and she waved back, and then turned again towards her task. Soon, Darcy was ahead of her, splashing through the waves. And then the little dog was swimming, keeping her head above the water, following the line of the cliffs, Robin staying close behind.

'Paige?' she called. 'Adam, are you here?' She fell silent, straining to hear voices above the sound of the waves, but there was nothing. The water was up to her thighs now, the cliffs looming above her, her pulse pounding in her ears.

'Hey,' Will was suddenly alongside her, breathing hard. 'You think they're here?'

'I don't know, I – I have this feeling. The caves . . .' She looked at him, at his green eyes creased with concern, his chest rising and falling.

He nodded. 'OK.'

'But we can only go so far; the tide's coming in. We'll have to get the coastguard.'

Will glanced behind him, back to where the cliffs receded and the sand was waiting. 'Sure. But for now—'

'For now we go forward.' They stayed together, wading through the rising water, clutching each other's arms for balance whenever a larger swell reached them. Robin knew the further along they went, the harder it would be to get back. They were running out of time.

And then Darcy barked. It was a high, strangled sound, her neck straining to keep her head above the water.

Robin's heart skipped a beat.

'Paige! Adam!' they shouted and then fell silent, listening for a reply. Robin shook her head at Will, exasperated, and then they heard it.

'Here! Help!'

'God.' Robin pushed forward, Will at her side. They reached the largest cave, the one Robin had pointed out to Will on that first, fateful tour. It looked so eerie now twilight was upon them, the moon casting its bold, too-white light, the cave mouth a gaping hole of darkness. With Darcy ahead of her and Will just behind, Robin stepped into the cave.

The sea pressed up against the walls, its usual rhythm distorted, the swell churning irregularly, sound echoing around her. 'Paige?'

'We're here,' said a high, terrified voice, only feet away. 'We can't get out.' Robin looked up, peering through the gloom, and saw them on the highest, narrow ledge. The moonlight struggled to reach inside, its light reflecting off the water, making everything shimmer and shift disconcertingly.

'We were leaving but then Paige hurt her ankle,' Adam rushed, his words tumbling out. 'I tried to carry her, but the tide was coming in and I know how dangerous it is.'

'Don't worry about what happened,' Will said. 'But we need to get you out quickly. Here.' He held his arms out. 'Can you slide down? I'll catch you.'

Paige nodded, pulled her legs over the side of the ledge and slid forward, hesitating at the very edge.

'I'm right here,' Will said. His voice was soft but urgent. Coaxing her.

Paige edged forward and Will caught her round the waist as she dropped, then lifted her higher, one arm around her back, one under her knees.

'We need to get going,' he said to Robin.

Robin held her hand out, and Adam took it and jumped down, soaking them both. The water was up to her waist now, and as they emerged out of the cave mouth, following closely behind Will and Paige, the sea was a churning dark mass all around them. Robin was gripped by an immobilizing fear; they were in the middle of the ocean, the cliffs high and unscalable at their backs, with no means of escape. She turned back and saw Darcy's head bobbing out of the cave towards her, legs below the surface paddling hard, and realized if Will's dog had the courage to keep going, then so did she.

To her right, Will was surging ahead, keeping close to the cliff face, Paige in his arms. He glanced behind him every few seconds to check they were following. 'Robin? You OK? We have to go.'

It was Adam who, still holding her hand, pulled her after them, not letting her succumb to her fear. It was much harder going on the way back, the water deeper, the swell forcing them towards the cliffs on their right. But it was a calm evening with hardly any wind, and for that Robin was immeasurably thankful. It didn't stop her picturing them being smashed against a rock, or a riptide dragging one of them under the waves in a second. She was comforted by Adam's hand in hers, and that they were all together, Darcy swimming alongside. She thought fleetingly that the dog must be exhausted, but then her panic returned as a large swell surged against them, much higher than the rest, urging them all towards the unyielding cliff face before breaking against it, filling her mouth with salty water. She heard Paige squeal, and coughed harshly, blinking water out of her eyes.

'OK, Robin?' Will called, looking back at her.

'F-fine,' she gasped, and Adam squeezed her hand.

They kept going. It seemed endless, a nightmare, but then suddenly the steep rock face was no longer against her shoulder, as the higher ground receded away from the coast, and now to her right there was the pale glimmer of beach that years of coastal erosion had created.

They were still submerged up to their waists, but they had escaped the cliffs. Will turned sharply, wading through the water towards that hallowed strip of sand, grey rather than golden in the dusk. Adam and Robin followed, Darcy paddling ahead, until her short legs found purchase and she splashed out of the water and stood, shaking herself vigorously, her fur straggly and unkempt.

Will reached the sand, kept going until they were beyond the tideline, then lowered Paige gently on to it and sat next to her, his elbows on his knees. Adam and Robin dropped on to the sand in front of them, nobody able to speak while their pulses settled and their breathing steadied.

Darcy ran to each of them in turn, thrusting her face towards theirs, licking cheeks and hands. Robin ruffled her fur and Darcy yelped, her tail wagging, but she didn't stay with Robin for long before going to Will, putting her front paws on her master's arms. Will pulled the dog to him and held her close, and the sight made Robin laugh with happiness and relief, a lump forming in her throat.

They were safe – all of them. They'd found Paige and Adam, and it had been hairy, and dangerous, and probably reckless, but it was done.

'Are you OK?' Will asked, turning to the teenagers.

They both nodded, Paige hiding her face in her hands. They were shivering. Robin realized they all were.

'How's your leg?' she asked.

'It's my ankle. I think I've sprained it.' She wouldn't meet her eye.

'I need to call Molly,' Robin said. 'And then an ambulance.'

Paige's head shot up. 'We don't need an ambulance. We'll be fine.'

'Robin's right.' Will dug in the pocket of his shorts and pulled out his phone, shaking water out of it. 'You've had a shock, you've hurt your ankle and that water isn't warm, despite today's sun. You should get checked out. But does anyone have a working phone? Mine's finished.'

'Ours both ran out of battery a long time ago,' Adam admitted sheepishly. 'Before they got drenched.'

Robin remembered throwing hers on to the sand before she reached the cliffs. She cast about for it, eventually spotting its bright green case not too far from where they were sitting. She hauled herself up on legs that felt like lead, and went to retrieve it, dialling the number before she'd returned to the small, cold group.

'Molly? It's me. I've found them.'

'Oh God, oh God, oh God. Is she – are they . . .?'

'They're OK, Molly,' Robin said, slumping back on to the sand. 'They were in one of the caves. Paige has hurt her ankle, so I'm going to get them an ambulance to be on the safe side, but they're fine. Here.'

She handed her phone to Paige, and watched as she listened wide-eyed, and then let out a sob. 'Mum, I'm so sorry.' She turned away from them all, the phone clutched to her ear, and Robin tried tactfully not to hear what she was saying.

Will was still clutching Darcy to him, his breathing beginning to return to normal after the exertion of carrying Paige back through the waves. She caught his eye and he gave her a weary smile. Night had almost fallen, only a thin wash of paler blue tinged with gold above the sea line, showing that the sun was hovering, for a few more moments, below the horizon. Further down the beach, the lights of Skull Island, the promenade lamps and the glowing windows on Goldcrest Road looked cosy and inviting, but down here, on Campion Bay's wild beach, they had only the pale light of the buck moon to guide them.

The moon and the sea had shown what they were capable of. Robin had always known they were to be revered, respected, but she hadn't felt their full force until tonight, until she'd been at their mercy.

Paige lowered the phone and handed it back to Robin. 'Mum said not to call an ambulance, that she'll take us to hospital. I don't think I need one, and she wanted to come and get me first. I promise I'll get checked over, though.' She wrinkled her nose, perhaps at the prospect of what Molly would say to her once she'd finished hugging her tightly and rejoicing in her safe return.

'What happened?' Robin asked. 'How did you get trapped in there? Have you been there since last night?'

Paige shook her head, looking down at the sand. 'No, we found another bed and breakfast last night, on the other side of town. But then, this morning, I – I didn't want to go home. I wanted to show Mum – and you . . .' She grimaced. 'I didn't want to make it easy for you. Adam knew about the caves, and so we came up here.'

'We weren't planning on staying this long, Robin,' Adam added, his expression contrite. 'But then we saw the tide was coming in, and when Paige tried to jump off the ledge she – she hurt her ankle.'

'You didn't think it would be best to hobble out of there anyway?' Will's voice was calm, curious rather than accusing. 'You could have supported her. The caves aren't safe. Well, I don't need to tell you that now.'

Paige shook her head. 'I got scared. The water had begun to come in, my ankle hurt and I – I panicked, I was worried we'd get stuck in the water. Both our phones had run out of battery and I thought we could sit it out, so Adam pulled me back up on the ledge, and we–we stayed there. Then it started to get dark, and the water was getting higher. I was so scared. We both were.'

'Thank you for coming to get us,' Adam said.

'How did you know where we were?' Paige asked, accepting another flurry of affection from Darcy.

'I didn't,' Robin said, the potential consequences of that fact beginning to hit her. 'We'd looked everywhere else, and I had this feeling. But if I hadn't, if I'd left the beach . . .'

'Don't think about that,' Will said, his voice close, making

419

Robin jump. 'Everyone's safe, that's the important thing.' His fingers wrapped around her arm, squeezing gently and, despite her exhaustion, and the cold and the fear that were only just beginning to recede, Robin felt giddy with happiness. Paige and Adam were safe, and Will was here. At that moment, nothing else mattered.

Chapter 24

The round of hugs that Molly gave them all when she'd reached the beach, along with Ashley and Roxy, seemed to go on for hours, though of course she saved her first and longest for Paige.

'You muppet,' she said, pushing a chunk of straggly blonde hair off her daughter's face. 'You could have *died*. Both of you. And you could have taken my best friend and Will with you too. What were you thinking?'

'We didn't! We were . . .' Paige shook her head, her sigh becoming another sob. 'Mum!'

'OK, OK, don't worry. Let's get you seen by a doctor. My car's at the edge of the beach, parked very illegally, so it's not that far to hop.'

'Let me,' Will said, stepping forward.

'Absolutely not. You and Robin have done enough. Ashley and I can get Paige to the car, and I'll drop you two and Darcy at home on the way.'

Robin inhaled, and shook her head. 'Thanks Molly, but I want to walk, if that's OK?'

Molly stared at her, incredulous. 'But you're soaked and your teeth are chattering. I reckon the two of you could do with a checkup as well, after rushing in to rescue my daughter like that.'

'I'm fine,' Robin said.

Will nodded. 'We'll be good, Molly. Thanks, though.'

'I'll come and see you first thing.' Molly pulled Robin into another hug. 'I can't ever repay you for this, you know,' she whispered in her ear, so that only Robin could hear.

'Let me know how Paige is?'

'Sure thing,' Molly said. She stepped back and grinned, her face lighting up, competing with the moon. 'Superstars. All three of you – Darcy included.'

Robin and Will stood on the beach and watched Molly and Ashley support Paige up to the car, Adam and Roxy walking behind. The velvet blue of night was complete, the sea shimmering beneath the full moon. Robin turned to Will.

'You didn't have to walk back with me.'

'I wasn't going to leave you alone, in the dark.' They faced each other. 'That was a brave thing you did. Brave but, if I'm honest, fairly reckless.' There was a hint of a smile on his lips. His T-shirt was sodden, clinging to him, and Robin had to use all her willpower to stop herself from jumping on him and holding him tightly against her.

'I know,' she said. 'But I had to check. If they'd still been there . . .' They both turned towards the sea. The tide had reached its highest point, the sliver of beach they were standing on greatly reduced, the cliffs being pummelled by the waves. If they were in the water now, Robin knew, it would be above head height, even pressed up against the cliff face. She wasn't sure if the cave Adam and Paige had been in was ever completely submerged, or if on that ledge they'd retain a small space above the waves. Even so, she couldn't imagine the terror of being in there at high tide, not to mention in total darkness. 'We did the right thing.'

'*You* did,' Will stressed. 'You saved them.'

'But you—' she started, then realized she didn't have the energy to argue.

They walked slowly in the direction of the promenade and the lights, leaving the wild beach behind them. Robin's trainers squelched, her sodden cut-off jeans rubbing uncomfortably against her skin, but her top was already beginning to dry in the warm evening breeze. She watched as the lights of Skull Island dimmed, and knew that the course was closing for the night. It was almost ten o'clock, almost time for her performance. She had no idea if the piano was even there, or whether Maggie and Stefano, knowing the situation with Paige, had decided not to move it from the taverna. She laughed quietly, thinking how much her day had veered off the course she had set for it.

'What is it?' Will asked.

'This isn't how I'd expected today to turn out,' she said.

'No. Me either.'

They exchanged quick smiles and Will slipped his arm through hers, pulling her gently towards him. Robin closed her eyes, her tired, cold body tingling at his touch. And then she remembered something.

'You called me – before you knew about Paige. You said you wanted to see me.'

'I did. I have some news.'

Robin inhaled, her insides freezing as if she was taking in pure ice. Was this it? The moment he told her he'd accepted Tim's offer?

'What is it?' he asked. 'Why have you stopped?'

'Are you . . . is this—' She stopped. 'Sorry. Sorry, just tell me. I won't interrupt.'

'OK.' Will nodded, and they started walking again. He didn't take her arm again, but they were close, their forearms brushing, and she could feel the heat of his skin. 'I went to see my dad yesterday,' he said. 'I thought you'd want to know. I took the letters and told him what I'd discovered.'

'God. You did? How did he take it?'

Will gave a humourless laugh. 'Not that well. He's no less stubborn than he was, but I think, I *hope* I made him see what his behaviour, his decisions, did to Tabitha; all the pain he caused. And how it's affected the whole family. He didn't offer up any forgiveness or regret, but then I did spring it on him.'

'He didn't seem sorry for how much he'd hurt Tabitha?' Robin whispered.

'He didn't dial down his anger. And he wasn't happy that I've been at her house, but he did say, as I was leaving – he said I should come back soon. And there was something in his eyes, some thawing. I don't know – maybe it's wishful thinking. I hope that he'll begin to realize how wrong he was to turn her away, and how strong Tabitha was for choosing love, for not giving up on it; for never backing down, despite what it cost her.'

'I'm so sorry, Will. I'm sorry it wasn't easy, but I think you were right to confront him about it – and brave, from what little I know of him.'

'It was never going to be easy, but I had to stand up for Tabitha. Now I'm coming to the end of it all, of all her possessions. It was the least I could do.' His fingers brushed against hers and he squeezed them briefly, without looking up.

There were pebbles beneath their feet now, mingling with the sand. The ice cream kiosk was closed, the lights from the houses on Goldcrest Road bright with safety and warmth. Robin looked up at the guesthouse, wondering how her guests had fared with her being absent for so much of the day. But they all had her mobile number, and apart from the texts and calls from Molly and then Will, it had stayed resolutely quiet.

'Back home?' Will asked. He touched her waist gently, trying to steer her away from the beach and towards the houses. 'There's something else I wanted to talk to you about.'

'Hang on a second,' she murmured, peering towards the crazy golf course, the position she and Maggie had decided on for the piano. She knew everything had been taken out of her hands, and she didn't think she'd have the energy to lift a single finger now, let alone play a whole song, but she had to check. Her heart sank when she saw that the course was empty, no grand piano waiting patiently for her in the moonlight. Maggie and Stefano had done the right thing – of course they had – but it felt like with the piano gone, so was her hope.

And then her phone vibrated with a text. She looked at the screen, and then glanced up at number two Goldcrest Road, where Maggie lived. Was she watching them? *Hole thirteen*, the text read. *Don't worry, the water feature's turned off. Go get him, Bobbin. And lock up when you're done – key in the pyramid.*

Grinning, she took Will's hand. 'Come with me.'

'What? Where are we going? Don't you want to go and get dry? There's something I have to tell you, Robin.'

'I'm a lot dryer than I was. Humour me for a minute.'

He sighed good-naturedly and let her lead him to the entrance of the crazy golf course. She took off her soaked shoes and waited while he did the same, leaving both pairs in a quickly forming puddle. Then she pushed the gate open and let them both in.

'What are we doing here? Are we breaking in?'

'It's unlocked. Hold your horses.' Her heart was beating faster now, wondering what Maggie had done. She wove through the course she knew so well, finding the right green amongst the skeletons and pirates.

When Will saw where they were he stopped, dragging Robin back. 'I'm wet enough as it is, thanks.' But there was something new in his expression, his weariness replaced with an anticipation that made Robin shudder.

'The water feature's turned off,' Robin said, pulling him forwards. When she saw what was in the centre of the green she stopped dead, all words momentarily escaping her.

'What's this?' Will whispered. Darcy padded up to the small display and sniffed it, but Robin could see that she, too, had used up all her energy.

'It's for us,' she said simply. There was a bottle of champagne and two glasses, a bouquet of red and white roses, similar to the ones currently in a vase in Sea Shanty, and a cardboard box in the brown and blue of the Campion Bay Teashop logo.

'Cupcakes?' Will asked. 'Flowers and champagne? Robin, what's going on?'

She turned to face him, dropping his hand, and let herself drink in the sight of him. He was dishevelled and exhausted, he had sand stuck to his legs and his shorts, and his T-shirt was ragged, drying in uneven patches. But the spark in his eyes, the way he was looking at her, gave her a fragment of hope. This might be the last time she looked at him before he told her his news, what he'd decided about his future, and that fragment was shattered into nothing.

426

'Today,' she said, 'before Paige and Adam went missing, I had a plan.' She sighed, laughed at how ridiculous it would all sound, how trite it would seem now that she was having to tell him rather than act it out. 'It was a plan for me to show you how much I care about you.'

A flicker of confusion passed over his features, but he didn't say anything, just waited for her to go on.

She tried not to be unnerved by his silence. 'I was going to take you on another tour of Campion Bay, one that involved cupcakes, a visit to the taverna, a historical tour of Skull Island with entirely made-up facts.' She gestured around her. 'I was going to finish by playing you a song on a grand piano, beneath the full moon. It's the buck moon, by the way. July is the buck moon.' She nodded, clinging on to the one bit of her explanation that was undeniably the truth, and didn't sound wholly absurd.

'The buck moon?' he repeated, raising an eyebrow, looking down at her with such intensity that she struggled to find her next words.

'May is flower, June is strawberry, July is buck. But then . . .' She shook her head, 'Paige and Adam went missing, and so the day got taken up with searching for them, and you'd picked this weekend to disappear, and so it was point-less anyway. Maggie and Stefano must have decided not to move the grand piano, knowing it wasn't going to happen, and she's done this instead. Champagne and cupcakes and . . . well, classic romance. Which seems wrong now, because I haven't had the chance to give you the tour, to remind you of some happy moments, to show you that, even though we've only known each other a short time, you've made a huge difference to my life.'

She swallowed, her emotions bubbling to the surface,

forcing her to take a deep breath and compose herself before continuing. 'You've turned it upside down, you've made me laugh and hope and – and feel so deeply, something I was scared to do after losing Neve. But the way I feel about you, those emotions, they're such happy ones. When I'm with you, when I think about you . . .' she faltered. Will didn't look exhausted any more, and he didn't look confused. She didn't have time to process his expression, or the way it was affecting her already weak legs, so she kept going. 'During the course of this tour, I was going to tell you all that, but in a much better, more coherent way.'

'You'd arranged to do all that?' Will asked, taking a step towards her.

Robin nodded. 'I had. I was going to pull out all the stops, even put my dignity on the line – I'm not a natural tour guide, like you are. I wanted to – to show you how much you matter to me. Because you do matter to me, Will. More than I think you realize.' She held her breath, pressed her lips together, barely dared to look at him.

'Oh I realize,' he whispered, pushing her straggly hair behind her ear with his thumb. 'I definitely realize.'

She shivered at his touch, as soft and tender as his voice. She looked up, meeting his green eyes, watching as his lips curved into a tentative smile.

'And?' she managed.

'And I've got the upper hand,' he said. 'Because I know how much I matter to you, but you clearly don't know how much you matter to me, Robin Brennan.'

She shook her head minutely, her body alive with anticipation as his hand, still in her hair, slipped to the back of her neck, and he lowered his face to meet hers. 'This much,' he murmured, his lips brushing over hers as he spoke.

His kiss was gentle, searching, taking his time to explore her, but his arms around her were purposeful, his embrace locking her so tightly to him that she could barely breathe for pleasure, happiness coursing through her veins. She let herself get lost in him, her exhaustion fading to nothing.

She could have stayed like that forever, but eventually he pulled back, until their noses were inches apart and she could see the flecks of brown and gold in his irises, the brush of faint freckles beneath his eyes. She knew that she would get to know this face, to know him, so much better. Every smile, strand of hair, every laugh and sigh.

'You care about me?' she asked giddily, one hand squeezing his waist, the other in the damp hair at the nape of his neck.

'I care about you, Robin. From that very first night, when you offered me your unique room, when you showed me into Starcross, I knew that I was in trouble. I didn't realize then how much, or that it was irreversible.' He stroked her cheek. 'There was a time I tried to not care, to put you out of my mind, but your kindness and your drive for life, the way you do everything with warmth and humour, had already got to me. You're brave and generous and beautiful, and I was always fighting a losing battle, trying to stop caring about you.'

Her heart leapt. She pulled him closer, their bodies fitting together, only thin layers of fabric between them. 'I'm glad you lost,' she whispered. 'I'm glad it was too strong for you.'

'*You* were too strong for me, Robin. How could I ignore you?'

She smiled up at him, wondering how it was possible to go from uncertainty to pure, bursting happiness in such a short space of time.

'But do you think we could take these inside?' he pointed

at the hamper Maggie had left them. 'I could do with drying off properly.'

'Getting out of your damp clothes?' Robin asked.

Will nodded.

'I think we've been here before.'

'Do you know what?' he said. 'I think you might be right.'

Will picked up the hamper and Robin found the key in the pyramid. They locked up the crazy golf course, picked up their shoes and crossed the road, making their way towards the guesthouse. Will stopped suddenly, and Robin had to pull him out of the path of a car as it drove slowly towards them, headlights blazing.

'The sign,' he said. 'You've changed it.'

Robin nodded, unable to stop grinning. In the moonlight, the metallic silver paint highlighting the title and the stars shimmered as she'd hoped it would. 'It's the final step towards making the guesthouse mine, to remembering Neve and keeping her in my memories in the right way, without fear or grief.'

'It's beautiful,' Will said simply.

The July evening wasn't a patch on the warmth inside the guesthouse. The large windows had absorbed heat throughout the day, and it engulfed them like a blanket as they stepped in-to the hall. Robin felt a fresh wave of exhaustion as she checked Sea Shanty and the kitchen for notes, or signs that the guests had needed anything. She came back, shaking her head.

'All quiet,' she said. 'Though considering how late it is, I'm not surprised.'

Darcy yelped, and Eclipse appeared in the kitchen doorway and gave Robin such a plaintive meow that she couldn't help laughing. 'He hasn't had any dinner.'

'He's probably at death's door,' Will said.

'Oh, definitely. Does Darcy want some food?'

'I don't think she'll turn it down. She must have worked up an appetite swimming round the cliffs.'

Robin went quickly and quietly into the kitchen, Darcy and Eclipse following her and waiting, remarkably patiently, for her to fill bowls with food and fresh water, and put them on the floor.

When she returned to the hall Will was standing upright, being careful not to lean against the wall in his ruined clothes, the hamper at his feet. He was swaying slightly, and only opened his eyes at her approach. They stood, facing each other, a sudden, nervous silence stretching out between them.

It reminded Robin of the first time they'd met, the awkwardness over the room and the way that, already, Will's green eyes and his warm, easy nature had been working their way into her heart. She stepped towards him and reached her hands up behind his neck, pulling him forward into another kiss that, despite her having instigated it, took her breath away all over again. He responded, his breathing elevated, the desire sparking like fireworks between them.

'Starcross is empty,' she murmured between kisses, as Will ran his hands through her hair. 'We could go up there.'

'No,' he said, 'not Starcross. If I get to have you, I want all of you, and I've been thinking a lot about those glow-in-the-dark stars, the lights around your headboard.'

'You have?' She pulled back.

'It's a great room.'

'OK, then,' she said, laughing and breathless as she found the key to her bedroom door, unlocked it and pushed it open, sensing Will behind her. She switched on the fairy lights, the bedside lamp and then, without even casting her eyes over the state of the room, turned towards him.

Robin's nerves were tingling, her heart swelling as he locked her in his gaze and stepped closer, cupping her chin in his palm, his lips finding hers, his touch electric. Spellbound didn't even come close, she thought, as she dissolved into the kiss. Spellbound was a fragment of what she felt for Will Nightingale.

A beep sounded from the hallway and Robin recognized the tone of a text message.

Will hesitated for a second, a smile flickering on his lips. 'Not this time,' he said. 'I'm not reading out your messages any more. I've got much better things to do.'

Robin's cheeks flushed briefly, but the embarrassment was obliterated by Will's touch and she laughed into his shoulder. 'I wouldn't dream of it,' she said, and pulled him down on to the bed.

As the sun peeped through the curtains and Robin's alarm clock displayed 6.15 a.m., they sat in bed drinking coffee and eating cupcakes. The previous day felt like a dream; the race through the water to find Adam and Paige, the swell of the tide bearing down on her as she'd stepped out of the cave, and then the golf course, the gifts Maggie had left, Will admitting his true feelings to her, him in her bed. Only coffee and happiness would get her through today, after so little sleep on top of her existing weariness.

'The text was from Molly,' she said now, wiping cake crumbs off her summer dressing gown. 'Paige and Adam are both fine physically, except that Paige's ankle has a bad sprain. They are apparently the most regretful pair of teenagers in the world.' She read the rest of the message, then put her phone down and lay against Will's chest.

'That's a relief,' he said, stroking her hair. 'Do you think they'll still be fine after Molly's finished with them?'

Robin laughed. 'I don't think she's going to go full psycho-mum. It really shook her up, Paige disappearing like that, and I think she's begun to realize that her daughter is growing up fast – despite the very infrequent bad decision-making. Molly's a great mum.'

'I can see that,' Will said. 'And you're a great friend, for doing what you did yesterday.'

'I wasn't on my own. I'm not sure I would have been able to go through with it, get Paige back safely, if you hadn't been there.'

'You would have, but I was glad you didn't have to do it alone.'

'I had you and Darcy,' she said quietly. 'Do you know, Eclipse and Darcy were sleeping next to each other on the rug when I went to get the coffee? I think they've mellowed.'

'Maybe they've realized that they're going to have to get along,' Will said. 'That staying apart isn't going to be an option.'

Robin smiled into Will's bare chest, kissing it lightly. 'And why's that?'

'Because,' Will said, sitting up slightly, 'I'm hoping that my visits to the newly-branded Once in a Blue Moon Guesthouse will be a lot more frequent, now that I know what I'm doing.'

Robin's smile faded. In all the emotion of the previous day, thoughts of Will's limited time in Campion Bay had escaped her. When they'd been kissing, undressing each other in her room, she had been lost in him, not thinking that it might only be short-term, beautiful but brief. Had he accepted Tim's offer? Dread crept over her as she remembered that he'd wanted to tell her something else last night on the beach, but she'd been too caught up in what Maggie had left for them to listen to him.

'What are you doing?' she whispered, squeezing her eyes closed.

He sighed, rubbed her arm, and moved slightly away from her so she was forced to sit up. 'Look at me.'

His expression gave nothing away. How regular did he want his visits to be? How far would he be travelling from every time – as far away as London? She couldn't imagine having a long-distance relationship with Will, spending long days and weeks without seeing him. She held her breath.

'I'm not taking Tim's offer,' he said quietly.

She blinked, replayed the words in her head, and breathed in deeply. 'W-what?'

'I'm not taking it,' he said again. 'I know it's generous – unbeatable, apparently – but Tabitha's house has come to mean so much more to me than money. And Campion Bay is . . .' He gave her a lopsided smile. '. . . It's starting to feel like home.'

He took her hand but she barely felt it, the words swirling inside her head while she tried to grab hold of them and make sense of what he was saying.

'I have nowhere else to be,' he continued. 'And even if I did, it wouldn't matter. The house is too large for me, but it's mine, and I have time to think how best to use the space. And I know this – us – is very new, only a few hours old, in fact, but I'd like to see if it could get older, become long-term.' He frowned, rubbed his face. 'That doesn't sound appealing, but you know what I mean.'

'Yes,' Robin said, laughing. 'Yes, I do, and I would like that very much. To become older and long-term with you too.' She felt dizzy, overwhelmed. Will was staying in Campion Bay, to be with her. She couldn't quite grasp hold of it, or the fact that she would have to cook breakfast for her guests in less than two hours' time. She leaned in to kiss him, but he put his finger on her lips.

'There's one last thing,' he said.

'What?' Robin asked, wondering how much longer she could stand the rollercoaster of emotions, of hope and uncertainty, nervousness and elation.

'Don't look so worried,' Will said, smiling. 'It's a good thing. It means Tim's offer might not have stood, even if I had wanted to accept it. When I was at Downe Hall we used a local historian, Jeremy, to research the facts about the house, any historical inaccuracies or gaps, and I arranged to meet up with him when I went back to see Dad. I found some papers in Tabitha's house, in the very last room, of course.' He slipped out of the bed and found his shorts, unbuttoned one of the pockets and pulled out a bundle of folded paper.

He climbed back under the duvet and tried to peel the sheets apart. They were stuck together, still damp in places, ripping even though Will was careful. Robin saw that the ink had run, all that had been on them becoming illegible after their dip in the sea.

'Shit,' he murmured.

'Is that it?' Robin asked.

He shook his head. 'These are copies of copies, thank God. But it's the provenance of the plaque, Robin. Documents that prove its authenticity. They're copies of letters between the owner of this house and a friend at the time Jane Austen stayed here – and then years later, after *Persuasion* was published. They were in a folder, along with confirmation from a historical society that the facts in the letters tie in with what's already known about Jane Austen's visits to the area, that the timings fit, and that there would have been no reason for the owner to make it up, not back then. My aunt must have kept it all together and then misplaced it amongst all the other things in that room.'

'Tabitha didn't have the original letters?' Robin asked, peering at the crumpled sheets.

Will shook his head. 'From the date of the society's letter, it looks like the plaque was put up before Tabitha moved to Campion Bay. The previous owner must have passed the whole folder on to her, as part of the house deeds and documentation. The historical society probably has the original letters – they're over two hundred years old, can you imagine? I took the folder to Jeremy and he double-checked all the details.'

'What did they say, about her visit?' Robin had given up trying to read the copies, too ruined by seawater to be legible.

'That she visited with her parents, that she stayed in one of the bedrooms on the second floor, and that she had been taking notes, though it isn't revealed what about. But the society's letter, and Jeremy, confirmed that the details match with her documented trips to Lyme Regis, when she researched and wrote *Persuasion*. So,' Will said, putting the papers on the bedside table, 'Jane Austen definitely stayed in Campion Bay on one of those visits, in Tabitha's house. It means that, even if I had been intending to sell, there might be restrictions on any developments. Jeremy's looking into that now, to see whether the building's listed or protected in any way.'

Robin leaned back against the pillows, giving Will a sideways glance. 'Your house has a habit of holding on to bundles of revealing letters, doesn't it?'

He gave her a wry smile. 'It does.'

'Wow. After all that speculation, all those disbelievers, Jane Austen genuinely stayed there.'

'I think you're going to have a few I-told-you-so moments.'

She grinned at him. 'I am, aren't I? Real life Jane Austen, in *your* house, Will Nightingale. Because it's yours now, yours and Tabitha's. I am so glad she was my next-door neighbour.'

'Why?' he asked, scrutinizing her, his eyes slightly narrowed. 'Because otherwise you'd be without your ceramic sheep?'

'I do like them, but that's not it.'

'Because if Molly was next door you'd have knocked a hole in the wall by now and neither of you would ever get any work done?'

'Cheeky!'

'Because if it—' Robin stopped him, pressing her finger against his lips this time.

'Because Tabitha brought you to me,' she said simply. 'And I wouldn't have wanted things to turn out any other way.'

He held her gaze, the smile reaching his eyes. 'Neither would I, Robin Brennan. Let's raise a toast, to Aunt Tabitha and her leaky roof.' He held up his coffee mug, and Robin did the same.

As the sun rose higher in the sky, and the first seagulls squawked their morning greeting outside the window, Robin rested her head on Will's chest. She knew she had a lot to be thankful for; for her beautiful, burgeoning new guest-house, the memories and inspiration of old friends and the love and kinship of current ones, the sea and the sky, ever changing outside her window. And now, Will Nightingale.

She didn't know if it was fate, if it had been written in the stars, but she couldn't imagine feeling as happy and complete as she did with this man, who was nothing like Bear Grylls, who was good at crazy golf and swam in the icy, early morning sea, and loved the adorable dog that had been thrust unexpectedly upon him. But Robin didn't need an astrology book or Tarot cards to tell her that they belonged together; she had known it, deep down, from the moment she saw him. And now he was here, beside her. She had found her special moment, her Once in a Blue Moon Day, except it looked like it was destined to last much longer than twenty-four hours.

She took Will's coffee cup from him and placed it on the bedside table. He gave her a questioning look and Robin answered it with a kiss, running her hands through his hair, her actions leaving no room for doubt. There was still an hour until she had to start on the guests' breakfasts. Even if this happiness was going to last forever – and she truly hoped it was – she was still going to make the most of it. She was going to make every minute count.

Chapter 25

The fireworks shimmied and sparkled, lighting up the velvet black of the night sky. Robin stood on the doorstep and turned up the collar of her coat, smiling as Will wrapped his arm around her and pulled her close.

'Happy New Year, Robin,' he said.

'Happy New Year, stud muffin.' They clinked glasses, and Will laughed.

'Stud muffin? That's a new one.'

'I know. I just felt like saying it, wanted to see how it sounded.'

He nodded, his face pensive, considering for a moment. 'It sounds ridiculous, but I'm not going to stop you.'

'Good.' She kissed him, feeling the tingle go through her, the flush of happiness and desire warming her better than any wool garment could. 'Better than sugarplum?'

Will rolled his eyes. 'Yes. Much better. Remind me not to get a bad habit ever again.'

Robin chuckled. She had started to call him sugarplum every time she saw, heard or smelt him sucking one of his

439

rhubarb-and-custard sweets. He had been trying to wean himself off them and she thought the irritating nickname might have helped, though she wasn't sure it was entirely responsible for him finally giving them up. Maybe the Bridget Jones method really was the most effective.

'Have I missed them all?' Molly asked, rushing outside.

'Not yet,' Robin said, turning to her friend. 'All OK?'

'Yeah. Sure. Fine.' Molly nodded, smoothing down her blonde hair which now fell to her shoulders.

'You've not left any grenades in Starcross, have you? Hidden any spy cameras?'

'Will Nightingale!' Molly shrieked. 'Do you think I want to *watch* it? Or obliterate my daughter and her boyfriend while they're . . . they're . . . Shit, I can't even say it.'

'In the throes of passion?' Will suggested, and Robin gasped.

Molly glared at him and kicked his shin.

Will's eyes danced with amusement. 'I'm just intrigued as to why you wanted to check the room out before they go up there? What were you looking for?'

Molly shrugged, and Robin could see the telltale spots of colour on her cheeks. She knew how hard it was for her friend to relinquish that hold on her daughter, to let her be a grown-up.

'Have you left a strategically placed packet of condoms somewhere?' Robin asked softly.

Molly held her gaze, but her blush deepened.

'You haven't?' Will said, incredulous. 'You *have*? Bloody hell, Molly!'

'You don't have kids yet so you don't know what it's like. I did what I had to – now, can we please stop talking about it and drink some more champagne?'

Robin slipped out of Will's embrace and hugged her friend, then went inside to get a fresh bottle.

The guesthouse was full; it was mostly full, these days, and even as her first autumn as owner had approached and Robin's nerves had increased, the bookings kept coming. The new name had gone down well, the brand was popular and stood out, and she'd had lots of comments about it.

Tonight, Emily and Jonathan Hannigan, who had first come to the guesthouse in May for their wedding anniversary, had returned, staying in Andalusia this time. The twice-married couple were enjoying the fireworks from the promenade, along with her other guests and lots of the Campion Bay residents. Adam and Paige were there too, and would then be heading up to Starcross to spend the night in her most coveted room. She had even spotted a tall head of blonde curls in the crowd, a long-legged brunette on his arm.

Once Tim had found out about the provenance of the plaque, his attention had left number four Goldcrest Road and he'd set his sights on other properties. Robin hadn't spoken to him properly since their awkward dinner after the open-mic night, but she had no regrets about that. She didn't even feel a twinge of sadness that they were no longer friends. She had much more important things to focus on now, including her perfect, permanent next-door neighbour.

She checked on Eclipse and Darcy, who were shut in Sea Shanty because of the fireworks. They didn't seem at all bothered by the loud bangs and were sleeping side by side, their furry bodies stretched out, taking up a whole sofa. After their first, less than happy encounter, the two of them now got on well, although Eclipse wasn't beyond exerting his authority if Darcy ever got too complacent. The cat was helping her to become more playful, which meant that Will often had to deal with the aftermath of Darcy's mad half-hours, when things inevitably got knocked over and broken in his house.

His house. She smiled as she took the fresh bottle of fizz outside, and topped up their glasses.

'What are you smirking about?' Will asked. 'Have you been helping yourself to our midnight snack?'

'No no,' Robin said. 'That's all still safely tucked away in the kitchen, ready to be put together and cooked. Though I don't know how excited the guests will be about having cheese on toast and garlic mayonnaise as their first meal of the New Year.'

'That's because they haven't tasted yours yet.'

'Isn't it Hellmann's mayo?' Molly asked.

Robin laughed, but Will shook his head sadly. 'Don't spoil the magic, Molly.'

'God, your boy-next-door is irritating sometimes,' Molly said, elbowing Will in the ribs.

Robin thought for a moment. 'I know. But I love him anyway. And I was thinking about next door, about what colours we could use to decorate the living room.'

'I thought we were going for neutral,' Will said. 'Grey and white. Why? What did you have in mind?' He narrowed his eyes, and Robin felt happiness bubble inside her. Not only did she have the most wonderful boyfriend, now estate manager of Eldridge House, but he was very receptive when it came to updating and redecorating his seafront house. He had even decided that, with so much space and only he and Darcy to accommodate, he would rent one of the first-floor rooms out. With its large windows capturing the light, it was ideal for Paige's first studio, a place to develop her jewellery designs, and she'd been over the moon when he'd suggested the idea, offering it to her at minimal rent from the moment it was ready. If everything went to plan, she'd be able to start moving her equipment in by February.

'Well,' Robin said, flashing a knowing glance in Molly's direction, 'I wonder if we should have another think, to see if we should match it to the colours in this.' She held out her hand, and Will took it, his face crumpling in bemusement.

Molly grinned at them. 'I'm going to go and find Paige, give her a final pep talk.'

'She'll love that, I'm sure,' Will called, as Robin led him inside. 'What's going on, Robin?'

'I got you something. Kind of a late house-warming present.' She led him into Sea Shanty and then pulled out her gift from behind one of the sofas. It was large and thin and wrapped heavily in bubble wrap. She slid it round in front of the window. 'Open it.'

'OK.' Will put his glass down and crouched in front of it, slowly pulling off the bubble wrap to reveal the Arthur Durrant nightscape that she had shown him in the Seagull Street Gallery all those months ago. For a few moments he just stared at it and then he looked at her, his eyes wide with shock.

'What is it?' she asked, her confidence wavering. 'Don't you like it?'

'I love it,' he said. 'Truly. But you – you bought it for me?'

She nodded. 'I did.'

'But – how? It was there – we saw it – back in the spring. Before . . .' He shook his head.

'I bought it for you as soon as you told me you were staying. The house is so big, there's so much space on the walls, and I knew it had to be in there, in your house. I asked them to hold it at the gallery for me, until you were in a position to start thinking about paintings. But if you don't want it . . .'

'I do, Robin. More than anything.' He stood and pulled her into his arms, squeezing tightly. 'Thank you.' He murmured the words into her hair, and Robin was touched by how overwhelmed he was at her gift.

She pressed her nose into his neck, feeling that familiar pull, the desire to be alone with him. She didn't mind whether it was in her room, under the greenish glow of her plastic stars, or under the pinprick lights that had been installed in his bedroom on the second floor of number four the month before. Or even under the real stars, glinting down at them from the silky sky as they lay on the sand of Campion Bay's wild beach, although tonight might be a bit too cold for that. She didn't mind where, she just wanted him to herself.

They broke apart as chatter filled the hallway, the guests returning now the fireworks were over, pink-cheeked and rubbing their hands together. Robin went to greet them.

'Come and have some champagne,' she said, ushering them all into Sea Shanty. 'Please, help yourselves. There are glasses and bottles on the table.' They filtered in, Emily stopping to give her a hug. Robin had come to realize that, despite the fleetingness of her relationships with her guests, some of them could become friends, after all.

A woman with a short, dark bob was the last in, closing the door behind her.

'Great fireworks,' she said breathlessly.

'They're not too shabby, are they?' Robin asked, giving Lorna's arm a squeeze. 'You all ready for the New Year's Day concert? Has the arts centre given you everything you need?'

'It's all sorted!' She gave Robin the thumbs up. 'I'm so

444

excited to be back here – thank you for helping to organize it.'

'It's my pleasure,' Robin said. 'We can't wait to hear you.'

'You *and* Will?' she asked, her eyes darting towards where he was examining his painting again, before carefully wrapping it back up.

Robin laughed. 'All of us. But me and Will especially.'

Grinning, Lorna went to get a drink, and Robin stayed in the doorway, watching her guests collect generous glasses from Molly, who had put herself in charge of the makeshift bar. Darcy and Eclipse had been woken by the commotion and were blinking sleepily, heads raised, deciding whether the excitement was worth leaving their cosy spot on the sofa for. She caught Will's eye, and he gave her a knowing smile.

'Will you help me carry this next door before the party gets going? I don't want to risk it getting damaged.' He kissed her, his cheeks still cold from the winter's night.

'Of course. Then you can help with the cheese on toast.'

'It's a deal.'

The door flung open and Paige and Adam came rushing in, laughing, and headed straight for the stairs.

'Do you two want a drink?' Robin asked. 'I'm sure Molly will let you have a small glass of champagne.'

Paige shook her head and came up to Robin, flinging her arms around her. 'No thanks – we're good. And thank you so much for letting us stay in Starcross tonight. I've always said it's your most romantic room.'

'You're welcome,' Robin said. 'But it's down to your mum, you know that. I hope you, uhm, enjoy it.'

Paige gave her a perfect, pearly grin. 'I'm sure we will,' she said. 'I've been looking forward to staying in your beautiful room for ages. Though it's not all going to be as . . . uncharted as Mum thinks it is. But please don't say anything to her,' she rushed, when Robin's eyes widened. 'Happy New Year, Mrs B! Happy New Year, Landlord!' Paige kissed her, and then Will, on the cheek, Adam gave them both a quick wave and then they disappeared up the stairs.

Robin turned to Will, speechless, but he was grinning.

'Did you doubt that?' he whispered.

'I . . . I didn't realize.' She shook her head. 'What about Molly?'

'I bet Molly knows,' Will said. 'Don't worry.' He tucked her hair behind her ear and kissed her softly on the side of the mouth.

'OK,' she murmured, letting his touch wash her concerns away. 'Landlord, huh? How does that feel?'

'It feels pretty good,' Will said. 'It'll stop me rattling around in there quite so much. Now, are you going to help me carry this incredible painting out of harm's way, before your guests and our pets turn the Once in a Blue Moon Guesthouse into Campion Bay's most dangerous New Year's Eve nightspot?'

Robin laughed. 'You sound nervous.'

'Do I?' He flashed her a grin. 'I can assure you that I'm not. I'm perfectly steadfast and confident and brave and . . .'

'And just like Bear Grylls?' Robin raised her eyebrows.

'*Exactly* like him. I'm sure some of his most daring missions have been inside seaside hotels.'

'They have?'

'Where else?'

Robin lifted up one side of the painting. 'I'll have to take your word for it.'

They manoeuvred the framed, bubble-wrapped canvas to

446

the door, Will walking backwards, her forwards, and stepped out on to the porch.

Now the fireworks were gone, the night was quieter, the moon and stars looking down on them from above a cold, calm sea. The moon was a glowing orb, one thin segment sliced off it, stopping it being perfectly round. They were two days away from the first full moon of the New Year; the wolf moon.

Robin let her gaze drop back to Will and the painting, making sure she put her feet in the right place, walking slowly down the front stairs of her guesthouse and then up to number four. Will paused, rearranging his grip on the frame and opening the front door, his look silently asking her if she was OK. She nodded in response, glancing up at the Once in a Blue Moon Guesthouse sign, the silver paint reflecting the moon's glow back at it, shimmering in a way that always reminded her of Neve.

She walked steadily forwards, past the blue plaque on the wall and over the threshold into Will Nightingale's house, leaving the waves and the moon and the quiet, night-time Campion Bay seafront behind, but only for a moment. Her guesthouse, full of guests and friends and pets, brimming with good cheer and laughter, would be waiting for her when she returned, Will's hand in hers, ready to start a new year at the helm of the Once in a Blue Moon Guesthouse.

Robin's Lavender Cookies

Robin is inspired to make lavender cookies after seeing Mrs Harris in her amazing lavender night wear ensemble. They're very simple to make and a hint of lavender gives them a refreshing, flowery taste.

Ingredients

- 225g butter, at room temperature
- 110g caster sugar
- 275g plain flour
- 2 tablespoons fresh lavender flowers

Method

- Preheat your oven to 160°C / gas mark 3, and line a baking tray with baking parchment.
- In a bowl, cream together the butter and sugar, then mix in the lavender flowers and the flour until the mixture has a smooth consistency.
- On a lightly floured surface, roll out the mixture until it's about 5mm thick, and use biscuit cutters to make your desired cookie shape – Robin has a moon-shaped cutter as she puts them in jars labelled 'midnight cookies' on each floor of the guesthouse.
- Put your cookies onto the baking tray, allowing room in between each one as they expand slightly, and cook them for 15 to 20 minutes.
- Leave them to cool, sprinkle with decorative sugar or extra lavender flowers and then tuck in!

Roxy and Ashley's Cupcakes

Roxy and Ashley's homemade cupcakes play an important role in Robin's story. A favourite sweet treat, you can flavour the icing with pretty much anything you fancy!

Ingredients – Cupcakes

- 150g butter
- 150g sugar
- 3 eggs, beaten
- 150g sifted self-raising flour
- 1 teaspoon vanilla extract
- 1 tablespoon milk

Ingredients – Icing

- 75g butter
- 150g icing sugar
- 1 tablespoon milk
- Vanilla essence / lemon juice or zest / dark chocolate to flavour
- Your favourite food colouring

Method

- Preheat your oven to 180°C / gas 4.
- Cream the butter and sugar together until they're light and fluffy.
- Gradually mix in the eggs, the vanilla essence and milk.
- Gently fold in the flour, and when you've made sure it's mixed well, place the mixture in cupcake cases on a baking tray.
- Bake for 15 to 20 minutes and allow to cool before adding the icing.
- To make the icing, beat the icing sugar and butter in a large bowl, then add your extra flavouring and food colouring until the mixture is smooth.
- Beat in the milk, and continue to beat the whole mixture until it's light and fluffy. Add to the top of cooled cupcakes – pipe it on in swirls if you're especially crafty – and decorate with hundreds and thousands or crystallised flowers.

Robin's Pancake, Bacon and Maple Syrup Breakfast

Robin is often coming up with new breakfast ideas for her guests, and this is one of my favourites – though it doesn't score many healthy points! It combines sweet and salty flavours perfectly and is very easy to make.

Ingredients

- 60g plain flour
- 1 medium egg
- 175ml milk
- A pinch of salt
- Oil for frying

Method

- Place the flour in a large bowl and stir in the salt.
- In a separate bowl, lightly beat together the egg and milk.
- Pour this over the flour a little at a time, whisking it to make a smooth batter.
- Leave the mixture to rest for 30 minutes, and while it's resting, grill several rashers of streaky bacon.
- When the mixture is ready, lightly oil a non-stick pan and pour in the desired amount of mixture.
- Cook each pancake for 1 minute on each side or until golden. You can warm the cooked pancakes in a low oven until you're ready to serve.
- Place one pancake on your plate followed by a couple of rashers of bacon, layer another pancake on top followed by more bacon, and repeat the process until you've used everything up. Finally, drizzle your stack with a generous serving of pure maple syrup. It's enough to set anyone up for a whole morning of sightseeing, or even running a busy, seaside guesthouse!

Also by
Cressida McLaughlin

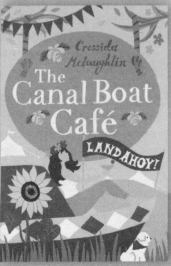

The Canal Boat Café

Available to buy as **serialized ebooks**, or in **full paperback** format.

Discover the
Primrose Terrace series

Wellies and Westies — PART 1
Cressida McLaughlin

Raincoats and Retrievers — PART 3
Cressida McLaughlin

Sunshine and Spaniels — PART 2
Cressida Mclaughlin

Tinsel and Terriers — PART 4
Cressida McLaughlin

Also available as **ebooks**
and **full paperback** format.